Shades of Artemis

A Novel of Ancient Greece and the Spartan Brasidas

Jon Edward Martin

PublishAmerica

Baltimore

First printing

ISBN: 1-4137-4582-2
PUBLISHED BY PUBLISHAMERICA, LLLP
www.publishamerica.com
Baltimore

Printed in the United States of America

For Kevin, Peter, Erin, and Eric

Acknowledgments

I would like to thank Dr. Nicholas Sekunda of the University of Torun for his patience in fielding my many questions about ancient Sparta. His expertise on the subject proved invaluable. Thanks, too, goes to my daughter Erin, who helped in the final assembly of the manuscript. Her keen eyes and writing skills contributed greatly.

Historical Note:

In 480 BC, the city-states of Greece, led by Athens and Sparta, turned back the massive invasion of the Persian Empire, saving Western civilization from extinction. With this great victory, Athens had become the undisputed naval power in the region, while Sparta continued to field the finest land army in all of Greece. Eventually these two allies, without the immediate threat of Persia to unite them, rekindled the natural rivalry that existed amongst all Greek city-states. Less than twenty years after the invasion, three men were born who would figure prominently in the coming war: Brasidas, one of Sparta's least known but most unorthodox and successful generals; the Athenian demagogue Cleon, whose political fortunes depended upon the conflict; the general Thucydides, opponent of Brasidas and chronicler of this great war.

"The allies complained, saying that since they contributed far more men than the Spartans, their generals should rightfully be in command, so Agesilaos instructed all the allies to sit down together, and the Spartans separate from them. Next he asked the potters to stand up, and when they had done so, then the smiths, then in turn the carpenters, the builders, and workers in every other craft. Thus all the allies stood but not one of the Spartans. So Agesilaos laughed and said: 'Do you see how many more soldiers we send out than you?'"

Plutarch

Principle Characters

Alkidas - member of Thrasymidas' boua in the Agoge.

Archidamos - one of the two kings of Sparta at the start of the Peloponnesian War.

Argileonis - mother to Brasidas.

Artemis - goddess of the hunt and protector of youth in the Agoge.

Brasidas - Spartan commander during the first phase of the Peloponnesian War.

Damatria - wife to Brasidas.

Epitadas - best friend to Brasidas, commander of Spartan forces on Sphacteria.

Eukles - Athenian general, friend to Thukydides.

Hylas - Athenian boy rescued by Brasidas during the Spartan invasion of Attica.

Kleandridas - mentor to Brasidas and father of Gyllipos.

Kleon - Athenian politician and rival to Thukydides.

Knemos - older brother to Thrasymidas.

Kratesikles - father of Knemos and Thrasymidas, and ally to King Archidamos.

Lichas (Turtle) - friend to Brasidas and companion in the Agoge.

Lykophron - friend to Brasidas.

Perikles - leading Athenian strategos at the beginning of the Peloponnesian War.

Pleistoanax - one of the two kings of Sparta at the start of the Peloponnesian War.

Polyakas - older youth in Brasidas' company in the Agoge.

Xenias - Helot working on the farm of Kratesikles.

Styphon - older friend to Brasidas, commander of his troop in the Agoge.

Tellis - father to Brasidas.

Temo - Helot farm girl and Brasidas' first love.

Thrasymidas - rival of Brasidas.

Thukydides - Athenian general and historian of the Peloponnesian War.

Sparta
One
ΣΠΑΡΤΗ

Quickly he drew his knees up and sprang from the dust, then with a swipe, cleared the blood from his chin. "To your feet!"

The widespread arms of Defeat began to tighten his embrace, but Brasidas scoffed at him. He launched himself at Alkidas, captain of the rival team, driving a bruised shoulder into his opponent, folding him in two. Disconnected from the earth, Alkidas flew directly into the moat. A chorus of cheers and hoots resonated from the crowd of onlookers, while some pressed forward to the edge of the moat, pumping their fists in the air, inciting encouragement or derision. Brasidas paused, deaf to them, attuned only to the enemy line. With his legs burning from exhaustion he staggered forward, waving for comrades to advance. The opposing boua, or troop of youths, doubled his in numbers, but still they moved warily, hesitating to come to grips. Compelled by caution and fatigue, his surviving teammates eased forward, moving shoulder to shoulder, slowly coalescing to formation.

"What next?" asked Epitadas, smearing away the mixture of sweat and dust that blackened his face. He sucked both phlegm and dirt from his throat then spat it contemptuously.

Brasidas paused for a moment, taken aback by the question for he was but one of many and not in command. His eyes darted about for his captain; Styphon sat, drenched and crestfallen, upon the far embankment of the moat that surrounded the game field of the Plantanista. He had lasted an hour in a contest that most times was decided in minutes. No one had contended with the champions this long.

"What do we do?" pleaded Epitadas.

Now, as though a god spoke through him, Brasidas issued his commands. Only six remained of the entire company while eleven of their adversaries stood across the riven field. After nodding that the order was understood, a pair scurried off to the right, stalking the far flank of the wavering line of opposition. Brasidas winked. Without hesitation Epitadas and the two others slunk to the left.

Only Thrasymidas of the eleven rivals stood tall, surveying the field with sureness; the other ten crouched, measuring Brasidas' troop with uncertainty. "Keep to formation," he bellowed. His warriors edged closer, compacting the group into a tight but undulating line.

A high-pitched whistle sliced through the steamy morning air, sending Lykophron and Turtle stampeding into the two outermost of the enemy line, tumbling to their hands and knees, clutching, grabbing, and flailing.

"Toss that pair into the moat," shouted Thrasymidas, his impatience growing at the hesitancy of his flankers. Turtle wrapped each thick arm around an adversary's leg, anchoring two. Lykophron intertwined his gangly limbs about a single opponent and hung on with both hands, confounding and embarrassing the boy. Soon more of the enemy combined to attack the pair, but they could do little to move them or free their comrades.

The enemy line, which had appeared so cohesive and unassailable, began to dissolve. Seeing this, Brasidas waved to Epitadas and the others, sending them into a headlong sprint toward the remaining flank, and just as they crashed into the braced bodies of their adversaries, Brasidas barreled forward.

"Thrasymidas!" he cried out, striking him hard with his flexed forearm. Both youths crashed to the dust. Oil and sand, which had been rubbed most carefully onto each competitor prior to the contest, mixed with sweat to produce a second skin that thwarted any grip. Brasidas scrambled to his knees then lunged for Thrasymidas, but his fingers, gouging flesh for purchase, slipped free.

Thrasymidas faltered a bit, but nimbly palmed the ground to stay up, and at the same time squeezed a fist full of dust that he deftly tossed into Brasidas' face, then began to pound him with one fist while clenching his hair with the other.

Instinctively Brasidas fought to pull free, lurching rearward, desperate to clear his eyes and gain a brief respite, a moment to think, to gather. Thrasymidas, being almost a half a head taller, was wearing him down, for with every desperate jerk toward escape, his enemy countered with a savage punch and tug.

Suddenly Brasidas' neck curled back, froze motionless, then whipped forward into Thrasymidas' mouth; the youth staggered, gripping his shattered face while blood pulsed from between his fingers. Brasidas wavered, then shook his head as a wet dog might to dry himself, clearing his vision. He refocused. His adversary stood hunched over and slowly raised his eyes—eyes which burned like the red-hot rivets of a shield in the forge. "I will kill you." His words bubbled through the blood. Rage propelled him forward. Easily Brasidas stepped to the side, grabbing Thrasymidas as he passed, accelerating him into the dust; momentarily stunned, he knelt, red spittle hanging in gobs from his hollow mouth. Brasidas bent over too, his lungs convulsing for air, not seeing the three that closed on him from behind. They struck at once and together, not one of them courageous enough to attack alone, and grappled him to the earth. His limbs, now devoid of strength, offered no resistance, but defiantly he clamped his teeth into the soft flesh of a neck and bit till his mouth tasted the salt-iron of blood. A blow struck. He bit all the harder. Now fist upon fist hammered his ribs until he surrendered his grip. He could feel his arms and legs being pulled tight, drawn away from his body like a hide on a tanning board. One final hateful fist seemed to plunge through his stomach to the dirt beneath, then he felt his body leaving the ground, floating and bouncing, powerless in the grip of his enemies. Silence. Then like a thunderclap from Zeus, water crashed around him. He heard cheers. Then his own name shot at him from the crowd. He rolled to his knees and wiped his eyes clear. Senses regained, he sprang to the embankment, skidding up its slope on all fours, where the long shaft of a walking staff plunged into the earth, intercepting him. He gripped it, ready to sweep it aside.

"Stop!" bellowed the figure towering over him. The man moved slightly to the side, unleashing a bright shower of sunlight, which he had until then eclipsed. "It is over."

Brasidas sat. His chest heaved, from fury to be sure, for his spirit was roused and now could find no satisfaction, but fatigue also compelled him to draw deep breaths. The hulking figure moved out of the halo of sunlight; Archidamos crystallized into view. Although a king, Brasidas saw him as an adversary first, as great a menace as Thrasymidas, but one he could never contend with, so he drew this hatred deep into himself, beneath a mask of feigned respect.

Thrasymidas and his cronies stood atop the Plane Tree Ground, victors in the Battle of Bridges, as it is called. The night prior each company of boys had, as tradition required, selected by chance one of the two bridges that crossed the moat—bridges that were named for Herakles or Lykourgos—sacrificed a black puppy to Enyalios, god of war, then watched as two picked wild boars fought, one representing each team; the victor forecast the outcome of the impending contest. Alkidas' and Thrasymidas' boar had won, ensuring victory for them, or so they surmised.

From the depth of the moat, Brasidas spied his father, Tellis, and his mother, Argileonis. Behind them he caught sight of his sponsor, Kleandridas. The three, in a most discreet manner, smiled at him when he looked their way.

Like a pack of wolves protecting their kill, Thrasymidas and his boua huddled about the bridge of Herakles, hardly satisfied with their hard-won victory. The cost was more than he was willing to pay. Thrasymidas spit, tongued his bleeding, empty gums, spit again, then began to pace restively, waiting for Brasidas and his company to yield their bridge. "I meant it," he growled as he passed Brasidas. "I will kill you." Brasidas heard nothing and continued along with his troop to collect himself before exiting the Plantanista, his gait and manner hardly one of the defeated. They had accomplished what no other troop had done before them; they pushed Alkidas and his boua to the edge of defeat.

The victorious troop strode out ahead of them to quiet accolades and polite congratulations from the pressing crowd of spectators. With back straight and eyes ahead, Brasidas marched out, followed by his mates. This same crowd began a muffled chanting, but soon the single word they repeated over and over rang clear. "Courage!" "Courage!"

Both troops approached the stone benches reserved for the two kings, five ephors, and the paidonomos, or headmaster of the Agoge. Brasidas grinned a bit as he marched by his parents, searching out then acknowledging each face that tossed his name his way. Kleandridas, reticent as always, offered a polite smile to each of the boys, exhibiting nothing more or nothing less to his protege. The most raucous cheers issued from the Paides; the youngest enrolled in the Agoge—the seven- to twelve-year-olds that blanketed the near slope of a knoll directly behind the seats of honor. Over and over they shouted, "Brasidas!"

As captain, Alkidas stepped up to accept the trophy wreath of laurel. Still the Paides chanted the name of Brasidas. Alkidas did his best to ignore them, accepting the crown graciously, touched his brow, then led his boua away. Epitadas, however, exhibited all his hate as he scowled at the boys on the knoll.

Styphon, Brasidas, and the rest turned to face the pathway that led north, back to their barracks at the terminus of Hyakinthia Way and commenced their march. Epitadas began to belt out the paian, and although no flutes played, the troop instinctively broke into the quick-step pace of the Embaterion march, sixty pairs of bare feet slapping the hard limestone road in unison.

Brasidas drew a deep, savory breath and grinned beyond what was acceptable deportment for a youth in Sparta. The day was perfection: sky bright as Apollo's eyes, the sun warmed him, and Artemis had answered his prayer, his solicitation of courage. He dare not petition Victory. That goddess delivers her gift only to the worthy.

Upon approaching the barracks tent Saleuthos, their drill-master, barked out his commands. "Smear and scrape," he shouted, "then assemble here quick as you can."

No one wished to pair up with Turtle for the cleaning. Oh, he would rub and scrape his partner with dexterity and thoroughness, but, as his name implies, no one wanted to work the stlengis on him, its small scraping blade and his huge back poorly matched for the task. Delay was painful; each and every one of them was anxious to assemble and march to the theatron for the bout of sphairomachia—battle-ball—that the young men from the villages of Pitane and Limnai would engage in this afternoon. Now they would cheer for Saleuthos in his competition of the Gymnopaidia festival.

Brasidas, stripped as were the rest, hunched over, smearing oil upon his calves, working in even strokes, rubbing the dirt from his bruised legs.

"Give me that," said Epitadas, his voice ringing with condescension.

Brasidas passed him the aryballos flask with one hand while working the grime from his knees with the other. Unexpectedly he felt the cool oil drizzle upon his back.

"Do not presume this every day," chided Epitadas as he worked the oil. He ground the heels of his hands into his friend's back, reminding him to derive no pleasure from this, but only expect to be a bit cleaner after the experience.

"If it's a gentler touch you crave, then steal away to your Helot darling."

Brasidas' heart drummed at his friend's remark. "What Helot?" he answered, trying to exhibit his manufactured composure

"That little epaikla that I saw you with yesterday morning." He referred to the prized dessert cake that everyone cherished, and many nicknamed their young loves. "When you tire of her, I think I will keep her company." Epitadas chuckled, then smacked Brasidas hard upon his back, grabbed the stlengis and commenced to scrape the oil from him, being sure to impart more than a few well-remembered strokes. Muscles twinged, eliciting a laugh from Epitadas.

17

"Your turn," said Brasidas. With a firm grip he secured his friend from escape, then twisted him 'round, releasing the thick and fragrant fluid from the aryballos upon the dark skin of Epitadas. His partner cringed. Brasidas turned laughing, and caught the eyes of Polyakas locked upon him.

* * *

"That is Thrasymidas' brother," shouted Epitadas over the roar of the spectators. Two teams of sphaereis—ball-players—competed within the huge box marked out on the groomed earth of the theatron. Epitadas pointed to the tallest and seemingly most powerful of the Limnain team. Certainly it was Thrasymidas' brother, for he wore his same dark look, a beard that grew so thick and black it appeared painted on his scowling face and his twin eyebrows thick and joined above his nose. "Do you see why they call him Pan?" added Epitadas with an evil grin.

This game of battle-ball was by far a more brutal contest than their water-bounded wrestling match of the morning. Very simply, one team had to advance the ball across the mid-line, cross the interval of their opponents marked ground, and exit the far side of the rectangle. An economy of rules. There are no others. It was war without weapons, simulating much encountered in phalanx combat except death, although young men did at rare times perish in this arena.

Two hands clamped down upon Brasidas' shoulders, gently but with undeniable firmness, imparting a strength and power that he knew belonged to Kleandridas.

"He is very good, isn't he?" asked his mentor. "Knemos, brother of your rival."

Brasidas turned slowly, wrinkled his brow, then answered. "Sir, I know by your tone you do not want me to agree with you. But I must admit reluctantly that he is more than good. He is exceptional. His team also has never been defeated. And no opponent has ever snatched the ball from him, once in his hand. Why, even your team have yet to lure Nike from him."

"He wins because there are rules. Few I admit, but the contest is governed by them." Now Kleandridas slid down from the higher seats to sit beside his pupil. "Why do you think he is dubbed Ametaklitos?"

"Because it means steadfast, as his performance in battle-ball demonstrates?" Brasidas knew the meaning of this nickname, or so he thought.

"There is a second meaning to this name, my boy—inflexible. A trait that could prove disastrous in war." Kleandridas leaned closer to Brasidas. "Guard against this most Spartan of aspects, unless of course you mean only to fight exclusively with other Spartans." He smiled, pushing himself up from his seat with a hand upon the crest of Brasidas' shoulder.

"Do not forget your lessons. I will expect you this evening after the aiklon meal.

"You would study even during the festival?" asked Epitadas, quite taken aback.

Brasidas shrugged his shoulders. "Kleandridas says learning should take no holiday."

* * *

"Tonight we will suspend our discussions of taktike, the movements of battle, and speak of a distinctly un-Spartan discipline." Kleandridas tossed the wax tablet with the scrawls of phalanx rank and file upon it, leaned back in his chair and drew a breath.

Brasidas waited in silence until, by the length of his instructor's pause, he was expected to respond. "What discipline is that?"

"Brasidas, you know that long ago Lykourgus deemed it proper for our people to begin our education from an early age, for it is well-known that while other children in Hellas commence their journey of life late and in a haphazard fashion, we in Sparta have marked the route clearly and follow it precisely—lessons not only in the mechanics of war, but also the comity of a nation of brothers." He lifted the half-empty kothon from the table, sipped a bit of wine, then lowered it deliberately to its place. "What we learn here in Sparta, it is sad to say, is appropriate only in Sparta."

These last words evoked a look of puzzlement from Brasidas.

"Today, when all seemed lost in your mock battle, was it Spartan discipline that sustained you?" He stared at the youth intently, awaiting a response.

"Yes—I mean, no. Not entirely, I mean," stammered Brasidas in a fit of diffidence.

"Well, my boy, you are correct," said Kleandridas with an understanding smile. "On all accounts you are right."

Brasidas paused in rumination. Now he reached for his cup of cut wine and doused his parched throat, wrung dry from the uncertainty of the discourse.

"How did you endure, or should I more appropriately ask, how did your boua endure?" Again his look urged thoughtfulness. "Was it tried and true methods that pushed a far superior foe to the edge of defeat?"

Brasidas swallowed hard. "Our actions, from our adversaries' vantage, were confusing. But within our company, our expected duties were not." He smiled. "Still, we did not win."

"Good. And what do you think Thrasymidas and his pack expected?"

"Why, I would say he expected us to do as we had been taught. To close ranks, tighten our formation, and wait for his greater force to attack."

"And do you think your instructions of polemachia flawed somehow?"

The boy clamped his mouth shut, preventing any thoughtless word from slipping past his lips. Rarely flummoxed, even by Kleandridas, he now fought to sort out the confusion whirling in his mind. War-drill, which his mentor referred to, became the foremost education of the Paidiskoi, the age grades of thirteen to seventeen years. Sparta would hardly squander five years of the Agoge on superfluous tasks.

"You think on this tonight. An adequate commander prepares his men for battle. A great commander prepares the enemy."

Brasidas felt a certain relief at his dismissal. He must take these words and digest them, understand them as though they were his very own. Only then would Kleandridas be satisfied.

Kleandridas remained in his seat sipping wine, hardly acknowledging his protege's exit. "Beware the vanquished," he warned, looking over the rim of his cup.

He thought this a strange apothegm, for he was the vanquished, and paused a moment as he slipped through the portal, but continued on, offering no words. Darkness had settled over Lakedaimon and he was late to his post in the agora. His company, as contenders at the Plane Tree Ground, received no pardon from their duties as sentries in the market place. He picked up his determined walk to a jog, wanting not to be reprimanded for tardiness by Saleuthos.

The trot along the lane was pleasant enough for this late summer's evening. The breeze sweeping down from the Taygetos Mountains carried the scent of pine and myrtle, while the advancing night stirred crickets to a ubiquitous chorus. Before him the dark form of the Skias loomed over the road, the building stealing the moonlight as he passed. Suddenly a tall figure slunk from its darkened columns.

"Brasidas," hissed the faceless figure, still hidden in the inky shadows. "We would speak with you."

Three others emerged from the Skias, moving 'round him as wolves would surround their quarry. When one stepped further out into the road, the moonlight struck his face, revealing the toothless snarl of Thrasymidas.

"A rematch!" stated Brasidas with cool certainty.

* * *

Turtle and Epitadas hustled along the dark street, toting the slumped form of their friend between them. With every misstep, partial stumble, and sway Brasidas winced, but exhibiting typical Spartan durity, he uttered no cry or groan. He had never felt pain as excruciating as this before; no beating or punishing exercise of the field of polemachia produced comparable injuries, nor did the Theft of the Cheeses. Even the aches and discomfort of the Battle of Bridges seemed distant and trivial to him.

"Do not do this," he said in a gasp.

Both comrades scooted along, ignoring his pleas. He sensed them turning off the road and down a narrow path, the sound of the low scrub and grass scraping them. Hardly as quiet as they were trained to be, their urgent footfalls sparked movement within the house. The head of a balding, thin man bobbed out from the doorway.

"We must see Kleandridas," announced Epitadas to the servant as he jerkily repositioned his grip under the armpits of his friend. Turtle easily carried the weight of both legs with one arm wrapped around them. The man flung open the door, dousing the trio in flickering lamplight. He bent over the injured boy, studying him with concern.

"What is going on here?" snapped Kleandridas as he moved into the portal, temporarily eclipsing the light.

"It is Master Brasidas," answered the servant Ateokles.

"In with him." Now he turned to the pair. "How did you know I was not in my barracks?" Neither answered as the old man pressed backwards, holding the door open.

"Over here," said Kleandridas as he moved beside a sleeping pallet not far from the door, the one used by Ateokles when he kept watch over the entrance to the house. Others approached from the inner courtyard. A door creaked open and into the room hurried Kleandridas' mother Eurymache, trailed by his sister. The little girl shuffled along while rubbing her eyes, still clinging to sleep.

"The iskai," said Eurymache. The servant sped off across the courtyard, returning in moments with a pitcher of water, linen, and a bowl of brown granules. She gently swabbed clean his face, peering at each cut and bruise. Blood refilled a long gash beneath his left eye as soon as she wiped. She opened her palm, then wriggled her fingers impatiently. The servant pinched some of the powder, transferring it quickly to the lady's beckoning hand. Punctilious but gentle in manner, she crumbled the iskai into the cut, wrapped a scrap of linen about her fingertip, then daubed it dry. Within moments it had stanched the bleeding.

"Sorcery!" said Epitadas in amazement.

"Hardly," answered Eurymache, still scanning Brasidas for other wounds. "It is a cautery."

"You two best return to your posts," commanded Kleandridas. "We will tend to him now."

Epitadas stood tall and faced his host. "Thank you, sir." He curled his index finger, signaling Turtle to depart.

"This was Thrasymidas' doing," Kleandridas said, looking over the shoulder of his mother as she worked on the boy. She offered no words, but gently smoothed back the close-cropped hair from Brasidas' forehead, blotting away the streaks of blood. His face began to swell beyond recognition. A purpled lump across his chin seemed to grow as she watched, while his left eye retreated behind a thick and fleshy lid. His nose had been flattened.

"Son, you too should go, or they will miss you at the barracks. He will be fine."

"I will be gone soon enough, mother."

While she continued to clean and dress the gashes upon his face, Kleandridas ran his hands gently up the boy's sides, then over his chest, searching out hidden fractures or pooling blood. He repeated the same upon his legs.

"Broken ribs, for sure," he stated matter-of-factly as he straightened up. "Ateokles, run to the house of the iatros Menekles. Tell him I will double his fee if he hurries."

Without hesitation the servant snatched a cloak from the hanging peg beside the door and sped off. In less than an hour, he returned with the physician. Eurymache had left little for the iatros. She had salved each wound, bound his chest, and snuggled him in fleece.

"At least I can administer an anodyne." Menekles reached into the reed basket that hung from his shoulder and lifted out an orange vial. From this he carefully withdrew a loaded measuring stick. Ateokles handed him a kothon of cut wine, into which he tapped the compound, finally stirring it all with a finger.

"Have him drink this. It will bring on sleep." He plopped his wine-wet finger into his mouth and smiled.

It took much urging and almost a quarter hour's time, but Brasidas finally drained the kothon of elixir. Ateokles sat beside the pallet, keeping watch over the boy and the entrance, while Kleandridas swept up his drowsy sister from a cloak that had been spread upon the floor near the hearth. He followed his mother out of the room and into the courtyard, and as he began to climb the narrow stairway, he noticed the brightening sky of Eos scattering Night as the goddess prepared the way for Helios and the coming day.

Sparta
Two
ΣΠΑΡΤΗ

The cook led the procession of food into the tent of the phidition—the Spartan name for the messes of fifteen warriors that shared every evening meal together. Mess cook for the Spartan army, like the priesthood in other cities, was a hereditary post and Amythaon and his line had fed Spartiate warriors for six generations. He directed the arranging of each relish platter, the large bowl of steaming black broth, and to everyone's delight, a basket heavy with wheat bread.

Kratesikles, senior of the phidition, eased himself into a chair, initiating an ordered seating by the remainder of the men. "Kleandridas, may I be the first to congratulate you on Brasidas' play at the Plantanistas yesterday," he said courteously, while rending a fist-sized hunk of bread from a loaf. He nodded, at the same time dipping and swirling his bread in the black broth, then scooped the hunk deftly into his mouth; with the back of his hand, he swiped the drips from his beard.

"And honor to your son for his victory," responded Kleandridas, with the barest tone of sincerity. "By the way, to whom do we owe this treat?" He pointed with a tip of his kothon mug, indicating the mound of loaves centered on the table.

"Our senior has provided the additional fare this evening," offered Megathon as he looked to Kratesikles.

"Is this in celebration of the Gymnopaidia?" Kleandridas slid his mug upon the table. Now he snapped a glance at Amythaon, who immediately dispatched a servant with the relish platter. One olive, three fingers of cheese and two figs—that is all he plucked from the orange-and-black-painted serving dish. With a backward wave of his hand, Kleandridas sent the man on.

"Of a sorts," Kratesikles answered. "Celebration of Knemos' victory in battle-ball yesterday."

Now several others offered their congratulations to him, which only caused him to lift his chin higher than usual. Kratesikles always looked down his nose at anyone he addressed, even men who stood over him, both in stature and rank.

"Tell me, Kleandridas. Word about is that your protege has taken the worst in a brawl. Is this so?"

Kleandridas methodically sponged the last bit of broth from his bowl, dropped the morsel of bread into his mouth, then raised his finger, indicating he would answer in a moment. Kratesikles grew impatient; he knew full well Brasidas' condition, for it was his youngest Thrasymidas who had boasted of it.

"No brawl. I surmise a pack of runaway Helots attacked him." Kleandridas snatched his kothon and sipped from it slowly, all the while keeping sight of Kratesikles above the rim.

"And why would you think a Helot guilty? Surely a Spartan boy such as Brasidas would have nothing to fear from a Helot." Kratesikles' anxious hand hovered over his bowl, awaiting a response, before snatching more food.

"Most certainly Helots. No band of Spartans would lurk in the shadows like thieves."

"Well, it was an entire band you say?" Kratesikles said almost mockingly. "Is this what the boy says?"

"Why, no. Brasidas has said nothing of it. The others who witnessed it told me of the numbers." Kleandridas smiled behind his cup.

"There are witnesses?"

"Several, and all of noble families."

"Then why do not they come forward to our friend Megathon, the paidonomos?" Kratesikles fired his words quick and sharp now. His gaze was fixed and unblinking upon Kleandridas.

"Megathon? Now why would they go to the master of the Agoge with charges against Helots, unless of course we are speaking of Spartan youth? But how would you know that?"

Kratesikles shot an audible breath while shaking his head, slammed his kothon upon the table, then stood. "Seems my appetite has fled." He pushed his chair away, turned from the table, and headed for the exit. "Good evening to you all," he said as he pushed his way through the flap and out into the still, warm night.

Kleandridas proved wary of goading Kratesikles, for he did not want the submerged feud brewing between the two most prominent families of Sparta to manifest itself openly. Kratesikles and his clan owed allegiance to Archidamos and the Eurypontids; Kleandridas stood by King Pleistoanax and his family of Agiads. Supporters of each maneuvered for advantage. For the good of the polis, he would bury his hatred of Kratesikles, but like an old, unhealing wound, it would throb with recollection, rarely abating; He would hardly prove complaisant.

* * *

For two hours he stood, training shield upon his shoulder, in the heat of this extraordinarily bright day. "Focus," he repeated over and over. He could feel himself sway. The grove of trees seemingly danced before him. He shook his head, trying to keep things clear.

Saleuthos, his drill-master, was not without compassion, but the punishment was immutable. Brasidas had abandoned his post and now he must stand with shield. A simple task for a moment or two. Much longer and even the most robust warrior in other armies would be compelled by fatigue to drop it to the earth for relief.

"Enough," bellowed the paidonomos Megathon as he strode up beside Saleuthos.

Brasidas slid the wooden bowl of the training shield free of his shoulder cap, fighting to control its weighty descent. The lower rim dug into the soil. He leaned it carefully against his thigh, glad to be free of its fifteen-pound burden.

Megathon turned to Saleuthos. "Your duty is done."

Now he walked around Brasidas, studying the boy from the head to heel— hip to hip. His left eye, purpled and shut, could not return the glance; his right eye he forced to look down, following the sandaled feet of the Spartan Peer.

"Who did this?" Megathon was a large square-shouldered man who loomed over him like the door to a great fortress, dark, heavy, impenetrable.

Brasidas said nothing.

"I will only ask once, then you will be responsible for the consequences." Megathon slipped his staff under the boy's chin, lifting his face to look eye to eye. "Who did this?"

"I did not see them," he stated without emotion.

"And why not? You see better than most in the dark, although right now I would not wager on that," Megathon said with a chuckle.

"They were hiding in the Skias."

"You still have not told me why you did not see them." They all feared Megathon's unrelenting questioning. Again he lifted Brasidas' chin with the staff.

"Sir, there were three of them. They were upon me quickly."

"If you cannot tell me who they were, then surely you knew who brought you to Kleandridas' house?"

Brasidas swallowed hard, as though a fist-sized stone clogged his throat. "I do not recall," he said with a sigh.

Megathon flicked the staff from under the boy's chin.

"Sir," shouted a voice from behind. Brasidas knew to whom it belonged, but he dare not move his eyes from front forward. Saleuthos burst into view, halting before the paidonomos. "Kratesikles wishes to speak with you immediately."

Megathon nodded, then turned to Brasidas. "You are relieved. Your father has summoned you."

Brasidas hefted his shield back upon his shoulder and trotted off to the armory at the rear of the barracks. Tantalos, a seventeen-year-old of his agelai, stood with spear in hand over the entrance to the barred doorway.

"I'll take it," he said, grabbing the aspis. "If you collapse here, then I shall have to run to fetch someone."

Before Tantalos unbolted the door, Brasidas scooted off, heading down the Aphetaid Road. A few older men stood upon the stairs to the sanctuary of Athena as he passed, and he only caught sight of them through a furtive glance, being careful to keep his eyes in the dirt when approaching any Peer. The tomb of the Eurypontid kings punctuated the Aphetaid, whereupon he scampered to the right and onto the main thoroughfare of the precinct of Pitane. With exertion came pain. His ribs ached. The swollen eye throbbed with a painful cadence. He counted every house in passing, knowing his father's to be the eleventh beyond the turn. As he hit the seventh, he looked high above the red-tiled rooftops to see a spur of the Taygetos Mountains chiseled dark with the shadows of dusk. *She would be there tonight,* he thought gazing up.

Barking. His father's two hounds, Atlas and Herakles, sounded their alarm at anyone's approach, a mean excitement filling the yapping until, as though they finally recognized the stranger's footfalls, the two dogs whined restively. As always the gate creaked in its familiar and comforting way. Brasidas had forgotten the pleasant aroma of the kitchen garden and the mingling scent of thyme and tansy that summer evenings coaxed from it. He smiled, stopped at the door, then tapped firmly yet with deference.

"Enter."

The latch clattered free. With a groan the door swept open and in he stepped, eyes downcast. The two Kastorian hounds, heads high as his waist, whirled around him, each tail flaying from side to side with such enthusiasm that their haunches lifted off the floor.

"Look up, lad," commanded Tellis.

Brasidas reluctantly lifted his chin, revealing his face to his father.

"By the Holy Twins," he bellowed, "that is a prize winner." He moved toward him, clutching a small earthenware lamp that was slick and soggy with oil. With wrinkled brow he bent low, studying his son's face while flashing the lamp side to side. "That will heal in time, although I cannot say the same for Thrasymidas' mouth." Tellis, still grinning, smacked Brasidas hard upon the back. "Sit, my boy."

No sooner had he settled into the low-backed chair near the hearth than the servant Deinokara slid a ribbed kothon of wine before him; then she sprinkled a bit of goat cheese and a few pearls of barley into the mug, bringing a grin of delight to Brasidas. He sipped it, savoring the mixture while watching his father. Atlas and Herakles snuggled contentedly beneath his chair.

"I understand it took three of them."

Brasidas merely nodded, keeping his lips hidden in the rim of the cup.

"You cannot let this pass," said his father intently. "Or respect will be forfeit. But you must choose the proper time."

"Did you think I would resort to prowling the dark streets with a pack of my comrades to set this right."

"Of course not. But remember, there will be opportunities. Like on the Plantanistas. I have no doubt that in any contest, you will best him." Tellis was truly proud of his son, but also feared that his impatience would rule him. "Beat him with your skill, not your rage."

Brasidas sat swirling wine in his mouth, pondering the words of advice he received this past day: Turtle and Epitadas had volunteered their services in revenge; his father, still clinging to the old ways, pointed to the ancient method of redemption by calling out your adversary in contests of skill and athletics; Saleuthos, in blank-faced earnestness, suggested beating out the remainder of Thrasymidas' teeth. Kleandridas' words were more chilling; only one of two paths did he suggest taking, the first so very brutal and the other almost laughably impotent—kill or befriend him. With Thrasymidas there could be no alternatives.

"What will you do?" quizzed Tellis.

"Prevail."

His father stood slowly, arched his back in a stretch, then moved toward the door where he snatched his triboun cloak from its peg. "I must be off to the phidition. Stay and eat. Deinokara has prepared some epaikla, your favorite."

In silence the old serving woman shuffled to the far side of the hearth and brushed two sweet cakes from the warming pan with her quivering hand. She then grabbed a bowl filled with strips of goat meat and slid it upon the table before him.

"Have you seen her?" whispered Brasidas.

"Who be that?" she answered, moving off to close the cupboard door.

"Temo," he said with a tinge of impatience.

The old woman wobbled slowly around to face him, exhibiting a tight-lipped grin. "I see'd her today, in the olive groves."

"And is she well?"

"Better than you be," she answered with a cackle.

"Will she be there?"

"I told of the place—and the time. Be up to her now."

He scoffed the meat and doused his still-full mouth with wine, grabbed the two cakes, then sped off. "Thank you," he shouted back through the open doorway.

He could spare little more than an hour, for even at his father's summons, he would not be relieved from sentinel watch in the agora this night. He vaulted over the low fence in the yard then sprinted for the cover of the grove of oaks behind the out buildings on his father's property. In playful leaps, the two hounds chased after him, halting when he did at the edge of the woods. "Shhh," he scolded. The twin dogs dropped their heads in obeisance, puling.

The trail upslope proved taxing, especially upon his tightly wrapped ribs, which reminded him with each breath of Thrasymidas. Suddenly the hounds took off, tails wagging, into a cleft in the hillside. He trotted after them, pushing through the snarls of underbrush that spanned the narrow opening. He stopped. Framed by two white birch stood a hooded figure, in the dark of late evening not more than a shadow. The dogs twirled about, bobbing and prancing. He stepped forward, while the world fell away from his thoughts, his only desire to hold her. They embraced, no words exchanged for long moments, until her hands ran over the strips of linen wrapped about his chest.

"What has happened?" she asked, her voice almost breaking. She smoothed back his cropped blonde hair, wincing at each gash she uncovered.

"Nothing," he responded quickly, looking into her worried eyes, all the time smiling.

"Your eye."

"Please, Temo. I have been through all this with my father." Again he pulled her tight to him, savoring the caress.

"Brasidas, I think we can meet here no longer," she said. "I saw two Hebontes stalking this slope last evening. I am sure they were Krypteia." She spoke of young men the ages of eighteen and nineteen, recently out of the Agoge. They hid by day watching Helots and other slaves like her, reporting any unseemly or brazen behavior, and on occasion and by orders of the ephors, dispatching unruly ones in the dark of night. He felt her tremble now at this talk. These surreptitious bands kept order by instilling fear.

"They may not be, Krypteia. The Phouaxir has begun for the older boys. They could merely be hunting."

"They did not look like hunters to me. No hounds, or snares. No spears either," she added. "A sword and a xuele knife. That is all."

She did indeed describe agents of the Krypteia, for the boys training in the Phouaxir—Fox Time—would always be solo, never in pairs. Only the Krypteia worked in tandem.

She buried her face in his chest, seeking comfort, but he felt only the burning in his loins and thought of nothing but quenching it. Awkwardly he fumbled with the knot in the shoulder of her chiton and tugged it free, moving it down her pulsing body until it spilled loose upon the ground. Her flesh felt warm and smooth upon his, its sweet scent intoxicating. He pressed into her, his fingers searching, shallow breaths racing faster. She returned nothing, but he did not care. With his arms clenched around her, he lowered them both to the earth, bodies entangled, one demanding, the other succumbing. Without resistance she opened her thighs. Without tenderness he filled them. His passion, worse than rage, passed quickly. He fell limp in her listless embrace. Lifeless until now, she began to quake in sobbing.

"What is it?" He slid from atop her.

"You are one of them." She curled up, facing away and pulled the cloak to cover her. "Soon they will give you a knife and send you hunting for me."

"I am what I am, but I do not apologize for it. We are all not so bloodthirsty." He rubbed her shoulder, but she pulled the cloak all the tighter.

"You will grow and forfeit your heart. And your mind. Sparta demands both." Her sobs reduced to a sniffle. She swallowed hard. "You are more a slave than I." A cold breeze filtered through the trees, stirring a whisper of leaves. Temo shivered, her fingertips and face the only flesh outside the protection of the cloak.

"Only animals are truly free, and then only some. My master is the Law. An oath between heaven and earth."

"You take another oath. You all do. Why do you declare war upon us every year?" Her body shook again with a succession of sobs. "Your oath of murder."

"I shall protect you and any loyal Helot." He tugged on her shoulder to look into her eyes. "This I swear before Artemis, Apollo, and all the gods." She said nothing, but turned to him, lifting the cloak. He slid against her. They held each other, drifting near sleep, until duty, like the cold hand of a drill-master, shook him awake. "I must go," he whispered. "We guard the agora tonight." He slid his hands down the length of her, then gently pushed away. Not but two steps into his departure he turned, patting away the wrinkles in his crimson chiton. "Will I see you soon?" She smiled silently. He tugged a small linen bundle from his belt, peeled it open, revealing the two sweet cakes, and placed them upon the cloak next to her.

* * *

"He saw her," said Styphon, grinning a most threatening grin. "I know it. Even with his swollen lip, I can see him smiling. See if his stick is still wet."

"No talking!" snapped Saleuthos.

All heads shot forward toward their bowls of barley gruel. They all knew the rules: silence when they ate; silence when they stood guard; silence when in formation; amongst citizens silence always unless questioned. Only when they attended the mess halls of full Peers, the phiditia, would they be allowed discourse while eating. For now they learned by attentive listening.

Saleuthos stood. Without hesitation the one hundred and fifty other boys rose up from their cross-legged postures on the hard ground and began to file out of the courtyard by age grade and in line behind their drill-master.

"I hate this," whispered Turtle to Brasidas. Without a word he nodded in agreement.

The troop marched along the Aphetaid Road until they came to the Ephorion. This is where inspections took place. The line stretched over half a stade, its right terminus directly at the base of the stairs of the building. The twin doors swung open and out strode the five most powerful Spartiates of the city, each newly elected for a one-year term; in this year they would hold sway over the Senate and the Assembly of citizens.

Kratesikles, first from the Ephorion, stepped solemnly down the stairs, ever looking down at all around him. Following him were Damonidas, Leontiadas, Charilaos, and Aketos. Each man represented a precinct of Sparta; Brasidas knew Damonidas to be from his village of Pitane and a good friend to his father, Tellis.

Kratesikles glared at Polyakas, the first youth in line of the seventeen-year olds, whose ruddy complexion disguised his oft-triggered rage. They were the oldest in the Agoge and privileged to endure the inspection first.

"Good," he said approvingly as he admired Polyakas' trim but muscular physique.

Now he passed by the next few nodding his head, leading the other four ephors down the line, passing without incident the other age grades until he came to the thirteen-year-olds and Turtle.

"You are a bit thick in the middle," he observed with disdain. He spun around, his eyes searching. "Saleuthos, cut his ration."

As he passed by Styphon, the youth sighed with relief then stared wide-eyed, hoping that his loud exhale went unnoticed. Thankfully Kratesikles strode on. He poked at one whose stomach seemed less than taut, cautioning Saleuthos about paring back his rations also, then moved down the remaining line swiftly. Abruptly he halted before Brasidas, sending the boy's heart into a frenzied drumming. The ephor stared at him over the tip of his nose, then shook his head and walked off. Damonidas passed by next, smiling with a furtive wink.

The five men ringed Saleuthos, each talking in turn while the bouagos dipped his head several times in affirmation. Once dismissed, he scooted down the line in reverse order of the inspection, instigating their march as he passed Polyakas.

"What a stare he gave you," Epitadas said to his friend under his breath.

Brasidas failed to answer, but gazed empty-eyed at the road before him while pondering his future under the new ephors. So distant were his thoughts that he failed to notice the direction of march; they moved not back toward their barracks but east, passing the offices of the Magistrates of Games, further still beyond the Persian Stoa—built from spoils of the war with the Great King—toward the River Eurotas and the Babyx Bridge that spanned it. The stonework of the bridge, where bared of soil, scorched their feet, for it had been under the fiery gaze of Helios all day long. After a quarter hour or so, they halted before the meadow called the Field of Silence. Saleuthos issued no order, nor was one required. The company dispersed into five troops, each comprised of thirty boys. Saleuthos lifted his right arm high overhead. Every boy did the same. They would now begin the Anapale, or pantomime of war.

Led by their drill-master and in perfect synchronization, each slid his right foot rearwards till it lined up toe to heel with the front, keeping the right arm high. Slowly up swung the left arm, bent sharply at the elbow as though it hefted a double grip infantry shield. Now, imitating battle, the right arm cocked back, grasping a phantom spear. The back foot slid forward, then the front and then every right arm pumped with unhesitating precision. No one faltered. For three-quarters of an hour, the company echoed in perfection the deliberate movements of Saleuthos; each dip, thrust, heave, and step performed as though one mind fired every muscle and tendon of the group. A Spartan would be taught to command his own body before he would command others.

Finally, and only when Saleuthos discerned a noticeable quivering in the younger boy's limbs, did he relent. "The river!" he shouted, ending the exercise.

These two words initiated a full-tilt sprint back along the road to the Eurotas, shoulders and elbows swinging in earnest to clear the way for the stronger. At about a hundred meters, the company began to stretch: the faster few at the front; in the middle the bulk of the youths; at the rear dragged the youngest. Only a single Rhobidas broke forward from his group.

Brasidas, urged on by Nike, shoved his way from the middle, passing boys that the filter of exertion had separated by age grades. At the outset he had bested the other thirteen- and fourteen-year-olds, and now found himself in the midst of the fifteen-year-olds. Ahead and increasing the interval were the Propaides of sixteen, mixed in with the oldest boys.

"Look at him," yelled Polyakas to Styphon, who strode beside him. The two quickened their pace, anxious to separate themselves from any competitors. When the distance they had put between them and the rest seemed insurmountable, both turned to catch sight of their pursuer.

"He's gone!" shouted Styphon.

Sure enough Brasidas had disappeared from the pack immediately trailing them. So large was their advantage that Polyakas slowed to a jog, then halted completely, searching out the crowd of boys for Brasidas.

"By the Twins, I don't see him." Polyakas spun back around and then broke into a sprint, urged on by the sight of the last hillock separating them from the river. Only Styphon managed to stay with him. They would be first into the cold currents of the Eurotas—first as age had rightly dictated.

Polyakas skidded to a stop on the crest of the rise, grabbing Styphon to halt with him. Flummoxed, the two stared into the river. A single bather frolicked; he dipped below the surface, then exploded skyward, tossing his head from side to side.

"How—?" Polyakas said, shrugging his shoulders.

Again Brasidas plunged into the racing waters, then popped up quickly, slicking back his short hair that glistened golden under the late-day sun. He waved to his friends.

Polyakas looked to Styphon. Styphon returned the glance with a smile. Both launched headlong down the slope, crashing into the river, heaving through the ever-deepening water until they reached him. Not stopping, they trampled him under, laughing all the while. The scene to all the world appeared to be a fierce contest—to the three only play.

At long last, and after Styphon and Polyakas had exacted a bit of vengeance for their defeat, they allowed Brasidas to stand unmolested. His chest heaved for want of air, but in laughter also. The gods had bestowed a most perfect smile on him, which he displayed often. His humor, in victory or defeat, never left him. Even the bruises on his face seemed to shrink away under the spell cast by his good nature.

"Do you ever lose?" asked Styphon as he swiped the water from his eyes with the back of his hand.

Brasidas' grin left him. "Only in the past," he answered gravely.

Fully refreshed, the trio swam the width of the river, striding through the shallows before they climbed out onto the reed-choked bank. Brasidas stumbled.

"Lost your land legs?" quipped Polyakas. He looked down at Brasidas. "By Zeus and Apollo!" he exclaimed. "When did you do that?"

Brasidas sat amongst the reeds clutching a purpled and swollen ankle. "Ambushed by a log," he said, shaking his head.

Win the race to the river he did, but the route he took proved far more treacherous though shorter. Yes, a log had caught his foot. But then a rabbit burrow, followed by a teetering stone. On the third stumble, he heard the rip of tendon.

"Come on," commanded Styphon. "Get beside him so we can lift him."

He motioned for Polyakas to go 'round to Brasidas' right side.

"No! I will walk."

"You will shut up," bellowed Styphon.

The two heaved him onto their shoulders and strode up the embankment, wobbling a bit with each step until they reached level ground.

"What is the matter with him?" asked Saleuthos as he surveyed the boys emerging from the Eurotas.

"Nothing," said Styphon matter-of-factly. "Turtle, get me a sprig of ivy for a garland. We honor today's victor."

The two strode off along the main road, shouldering their friend, Turtle chasing after them, twisting a strand of ivy into a makeshift crown.

Athens
Three
AΘHNA

"Master Thukydides, don't you ever smile?" asked his servant Ataskos while fumbling with the boy's satchel.

"Hurry, will you. Taureas will not take kindly to tardiness."

The pair pushed their way through the crowded and narrow street, jumping over the foul-smelling gutter that sliced down the middle of it. Ahead lay the Dromos boulevard and the corner of Athens' Agora. Thukydides halted at the intersection.

"Quite a sight," he muttered as he stared up, fascinated at the High City and the new temple that grew upon it. He studied it for a while until he had seen enough. Abruptly he heaved forward into the swirl of people that clogged the Dromos, riding its current past the inner Kerameikos and through the Dipylon gate. Once outside the walls the traffic thinned, allowing a quicker pace—a pace that poor Ataskos dreaded. His knees ached, as did his back, but now that they walked along the portion of the road flanked by the graveyards, his legs regained a bit of their former spring. Here and there he spotted a magnificent sculpted stele nestled in the grassy slopes, although most of the graves were marked by stumpy columns of painted marble. Higher up on a knoll, heavy slabs of plain stone covered the earth in a grove of olives. This was the home of the dead, and he hardly felt welcome here.

Within the quarter hour they arrived at the gymnasion. Ataskos hobbled after his young master, fumbling into the hide satchel. "Here it is," he announced, grinning. "Your sponge."

Thukydides ducked his head under the fountain spout, then slowly turned around, backing into the water. Ataskos stroked him clean with the sponge, toweled him dry, then plucked the alabastron flask from the sack. Carefully he drizzled the oil upon the boy's back, rubbed it thoroughly over his body, then scooped the fine sand from the black-glazed bowl that sat atop the bench outside the changing rooms, filtering it carefully through his fingers to cover the boy.

"Watch his left hand," warned Ataskos.

In the center of the gymnasion, a half dozen or so of the youngest boys, mostly twelve-year-olds, spaded the sandy floor of the arena, softening the ground as they always did before a match. Taureas shooed them away when satisfied with their work.

"I see you managed to get here on time today." He wore an even sterner look than Thukydides as he glared at the youth. "Eukles. Step forward."

Thukydides stared across the bright exercise ground, straining to catch sight of his adversary as he emerged from the shadowed colonnade. At a fast step a tall, broad-shouldered youth moved toward him, wearing a completely unreadable look. No grin, no smirk, no smile—his face was blank as unquarried stone. Warily the two approached each other, bowed their heads, then reached out with their arms, anticipating the word. Eukles winked at him, then flashed a broad grin, thoroughly breaking Thukydides' concentration.

"Now!" barked Taureas as he lowered the wooden staff that separated the two.

Thukydides stepped forward, then recalling Ataskos' warning, slid to his left, watching Eukles' clawing left hand. Thukydides retreated from a feigned lunge while reaching out to grab his opponent's neck. Eukles bobbed his head then dived straight for the knees.

"Keep your legs moving," shouted Taureas. "Offer no target." He scampered free, but stumbled a bit, his equilibrium momentarily lost. "Balance! Balance!"

"I know," mumbled Thukydides. "If only my feet would listen."

Eukles slapped Thukydides' right arm away, closing quickly to grapple him with both hands. He flinched a bit as Thukydides dipped to the left but guessed this defense and swung an arm around his neck. In response, Thukydides defiantly spread his feet, bracing against any attempt to break his footing. Two pairs of feet churned the ground while kicking up the powdery sand in this frantic dance of contention. For a moment neither boy moved, limbs locked and legs anchored, muscles trembling with strain while their chests heaved for air. Then another explosion of scuffles.

Thukydides gagged. His throat closed, snugged by the vise of Eukles' arm. He watched the tossing legs of his adversary fly by, then the colonnade. The last he saw was a streak of blue sky....

* * *

37

At first he heard the soft spilling sounds of water upon stone. It soothed him. Then a grating voice interrupted this pleasantness.

"Master. Can you hear me?"

Reluctantly he peered through heavy eyelids to see the sun-red face of Ataskos looming over him; his breath reeked of onion.

"How are you feeling?" He lifted his head off the cold marble of the fountain's base. "I preferred it when I was asleep," he said, rubbing his eyes.

Eukles laughed. So did Taureas, which was a rarity. Ataskos hoisted his master to his feet, staying beside him as he wobbled over to the shade of the colonnade and an empty bench of carved Pentelic marble. Eukles followed. "You must challenge another," he suggested.

"Why? You are the finest wrestler in Athens. If I outdo you then the others become—superfluous."

"My, my, such a large word for such a small boy." Eukles smiled, then rubbed Thukydides' head. "Maybe someday, my friend."

"You Little Ones," said Taureas, as he would always call the boys between twelve and fifteen like Thukydides and Eukles, "sit and observe the Big Boys wrestle."

Now six pairs of boys—hardly boys but almost men—proceeded from the columned perimeter into the center of the exercise grounds. The flute player struck up a tune, and at Taureas' signal, the multiple bout began.

Thukydides stared at the spectacle. These boys carried on past a quarter hour before a single victor emerged. Another quarter hour and still three pairs kept at it. Finally Taureas had to step in to end it all with the last pair, for he was sure he had heard at least one bone crackle.

Several of them hobbled away grimacing, holding an injured arm or favoring a game leg. Taureas turned around to face Eukles, Thukydides, and the rest of the Little Ones.

"Remember. This is but a gentle contest when compared to war."

* * *

The two sped along the road, quickly through the outer Kerameikos, the double-gate, and into the walled precincts of Athens.

"The curfew, Master Thukydides," warned his pedagogos Ataskos. "The sun is setting."

There was indeed a curfew on youth in the city. Needless to say young girls, even women, rarely traveled the alleyways and streets, day or night. Boys, until they became epheboi at eighteen, could only move about during daylight hours, and then only when accompanied by their pedagogos. Thukydides knew full well the punishment his father, Olorus, would exact. He broke into a jog, dragging the shuffling Ataskos in his wake.

"Where are you running to?"

Thukydides skidded to a stop. A pair of figures slid from the doorway of a perfume shop into his path.

"Afraid of the dark?"

"Mindful of the law, Kleon," answered Thukydides in a lecturer's tone.

Kleon, a tall, reed-thin youth strode closer, paused, then began to circle both Ataskos and his young charge. "At the gymnasion again?" he snapped while prying open the hide satchel to steal a look inside. "Wish I had time to squander like that."

"Let me pass." Thukydides could feel the fire rise in his face.

Kleon sensed it too. He sealed off any advance with a defiant stance, straddling the gutter that split the road in two.

"Clear your own way." He shoved Thukydides back.

Ataskos squeezed in between the pair, but Kleon's companion Menander pulled him away. "Stay out of it, old man."

"If it's a beating you want, come to the palaestra. Otherwise stand aside, for I'll not fight in the gutters with the likes of you." Thukydides wrapped his right leg behind Kleon's, while driving the palm of his hand hard upon his shoulder. Kleon flew backwards, landing hard on his haunches. Thukydides bolted by, not halting to savor this unexpected victory.

"Master," puffed Ataskos as he shuffled to catch up to the youth. "I have never seen you employ that move in a bout."

The two kept up their pace, weaving through the traffic of Agora. The temples on the High City stood black against the dimming sky, sparsely dotted by the flicker of lamplight revealed from within. The sun slipped below the low rooftops now. He would be home just in time. Upon reaching the doorway to the small courtyard, Thukydides slowed, carefully unlatched the door, quietly sliding into his town house. Holding his index finger before his lips as a warning, he whispered to Ataskos. "Go quietly to the kitchen. I will slip by to the stable. Remember, we have been here for some time."

Ataskos moved with the stealth of a thief, disturbing not a pebble as he moved across the courtyard. Thukydides removed his sandals, then stalked his way in the deep blue shadows of the columns toward the stable. Suddenly a bright shaft of yellow cut the darkness.

"In here. Now!"

Filling the open doorway to the andron, his father, Olorus, barked the command.

This he feared far more than the thug Kleon and his lackey Menander. His father's wrath never abated before a full measure of punishment was exacted—many times two full measures.

"Ataskos!" yelled Olorus.

The old man hobbled submissively from kitchen doorway toting a smoldering brazier, primed and ready for cooking. In the heat of summer no cooking could be attempted indoors. The slave deposited the glowing iron basket, then wiped his hands on the front of his chiton, stepping toward father and son.

"It is your responsibility to observe the curfew. I'll not have him spoken of as unruly and ill-mannered." Olorus swung the broom handle which he snatched conveniently from its roost beside the door and whacked the slave across his shoulder. He pulled back, readying to swing again when Thukydides stepped forward to take the blow.

"It is no fault of his," offered the boy. "My doing and mine alone." Thukydides loomed like a shield over the slave.

Olorus' face burned redder than his russet beard. "You will spend all your days learning the Poet's lines. Gymnasion is a privilege now forfeit." He flung the now useless weapon across the courtyard, then swung around, his figure overwhelmed by the brightly lit andron as he stormed in.

Later that night and opposed to Thukydides' wishes, Ataskos informed Olorus of the encounter with Kleon. "No breeding. A merchant's son," he muttered. "but the punishment stands."

* * *

His father's harsh reprimands had stolen his light-heartedness by the time he was eight. Now at fourteen humor rarely afflicted him. This pleased his instructors, especially Antiphon, for the boy always took his lessons in grammar most seriously. Thukydides hunched over his wax tablet, which he propped across his knees, pressing and flicking at its surface with the pointed end of the stylus.

"Incorrect. That is the modern wording," snapped Antiphon.

Thukydides spun the stylus to bring the blunted end forward. He pressed

40

clear the misspelling then tried again.

"Now it is correct. Complete the others."

The boy merely nodded. Methodically he commenced to duplicate the Poet's verse, eight lines in all. He worked so hard to get the ancient words correct that he hardly comprehended the story being told. Antiphon moved off to view another student's work. Thukydides paused over the lines, rereading them for understanding.

"Stop," commanded Antiphon. "Pack up. We will be going on a short walk."

From the back wall lined with benches, each student's pedagogos rose. Ataskos spread open the hide satchel for his young master to fill with a wax tablet, two writing styli, and his tightly rolled copy of the *Iliad*. He stared for a moment, wishing the contents to be transformed somehow to sponge, stlengis, and his other accessories of the gymnasion. It had been a month since this new ban had been imposed.

"It is at the Agora that we will continue today's lesson. We shall listen to a speaker. A man who has written an inquiry into the war with Persia."

Antiphon led his flock of students through the alleyway and out onto the Dromos. From here they could see the crowd gathering about a man standing in the cargo bed of a freight wagon. Thukydides worked his way forward, insinuating his body into the tightening crowd, squeezing toward the wagon.

"Good people, my name is Herodotos of Halikarnassos. Today I will entertain you with a selection from my work on the great war with Persia, with a lesson to be summed up by a Persian no less."

The crowd condensed forward in silence. The boys of Antiphon's class looked up tight-lipped and wide-eyed.

"This Persian, a man of royal blood, said to his countrymen before their defeat, 'There is nothing more frustrating in a man's life than knowing exactly what to do, but having not the authority to do it.'" He paused with a knowing smile. The same smile spread across the faces of his listeners.

Eukles, at ten the youngest in Antiphon's school and Thukydides' only friend, leaned to him. "He is good. I heard him yesterday."

"Did he talk of The War?"

"No. More interesting things. Of giant ants that dig for gold in far-off India. The flying snakes of Arabia that guard the nutmeg."

"Then he speaks of fables," said Thukydides disdainfully.

"No he speaks of what he or others have seen. He also ends each reading by saying, 'I have given you the facts. Now you judge the truth.'"

Thukydides listened. He listened intently. This story of The War had always been told to him in Athenian words, and as seen through Athenian eyes. He enjoyed this shift in perspective. The others, it was clear, marveled at *what* tales were told; he pondered over *how* they were told. By mid-afternoon Herodotos finished this portion of his books, ending with the Spartans, Athenians, and their allies marching down from Kithairon Pass toward the road to Thebes and the waiting army of the Persians. Thukydides knew without doubt that he would return for the next installment.

Antiphon led his troop of students away from the center of the Agora, past the old council building and on towards the stoa of Zeus. He gathered them all beneath the shady branches of the largest plane tree in front of the stoa. His students circled around him. He lowered himself to a seat upon the sparse grass while waving them all to do the same.

"So what do you think of his inquiry?" Antiphon rarely asked his students their opinion. Stunned to silence, no one spoke. He studied a scroll in his lap. "Thukydides. What is your assessment of it?"

Maintaining his deadly serious manner, the youth offered, "Why do men blame their misfortune on the gods?"

Now Antiphon snapped his head up, nonplused by the boy's question. Finally, after gathering his thoughts he spoke. "Explain your question."

"Well, at every misfortunate event Herodotos blames the gods."

"And do you not think the gods capable of such action," Antiphon asked.

"Of course. But why? Men need no assistance to summon ill fortune. Their bad judgment is enough."

"And how would you tell such a tale?"

"With the words and deeds of men only. I cannot presume to understand the gods. Can he?"

"Today's lesson is over." Antiphon admired the youth's answers, but hardly had the energy to explain them tactfully to the others. After they dispersed, each accompanied by their pedagogos, Antiphon walked home wearing a pleased grin.

Thukydides sped the distance to his house, taxing old Ataskos, mindful that his early arrival might earn him some hot bread from the kitchen-servant Bublo; she would always sneak him a loaf before his father came home, then admonish him on looking a bit heavy, "fat in the face," as she would say.

The activity within surprised him. As soon as he entered the courtyard, he had to contend with a half dozen slaves, superintended by the steward Alexon that toiled at grooming and tidying the garden, fountain, and inner walls.

42

"What is all this?" Thukydides continued on toward the steward while Ataskos toted his satchel up the staircase and into his young master's room.

"Your father will entertain tonight."

"His club again? They dined here but a few nights ago."

"General Kimon attends this evening."

Even though a relative, Thukydides knew the importance of such a man. The greatness of his victories was only surpassed by his generosity. This was indeed a signal occasion.

"Master Thukydides. New clothes have been bought for you. Your father instructed me to see that you wear them tonight."

"Why new clothes?"

"You will attend. Your father has ordered it so."

He had hoped to spend the evening in peace with his lines, to learn them thoroughly by tomorrow and keep to Antiphon's good temper. With a certain resignation he spun away from Alexon and dashed through the open door to the kitchen beyond. Not a word was required. Bublo turned from the hearth, clutching a steamy loaf of flatbread.

Thukydides smiled broadly. "Thank you, Bublo." He kissed her on the forehead, snatched the loaf, then ran out and up the staircase. Inside his room Ataskos hunched over an open chest, carefully emptying his satchel item by item into it.

Upon the sleeping pallet sprawled a bright chiton of saffron, bordered in waves of sea-purple embroidery. Beside it lie a pair of red-dyed sandals with silver gryphon clasps; a fresh garland wreath leaned upon them. Tonight must indeed be important.

* * *

Thukydides stayed only for the meal. When the platters of boar-fish, octopus, and wheat bread were empty; when the bowls of figs, dishes of olives, and goat cheese yawned vacantly, hinting of their former contents only by a pit, bone, or souring scent, were they finally removed by the servants. Only then did the wine servants and musicians enter. Being not yet of age, convention bade him to depart, but he lingered awhile in the courtyard near the open door.

"Befriending Sparta has already cost you dearly, Kimon," lectured Olorus.

"But this friendship has delivered our city. Granted, the Spartans fought us at Tanagra, but the invitation to that battle was issued by us." Kimon paused. No one responded. "They are content to be masters of the land and relinquish the sea to us. Remember, when the Medes invaded it was only with Spartan help did we secure victory. If the barbarians return, only Spartans—side by side with Athenians—can repeat that victory."

"People's memories are short. For all of your victories, the demos has pushed you aside, preferring the agreeable over the honest and the brave."

Ataskos exited the hall, startled by Thukydides squatting by the door. "Master, you must leave before they find you out."

He cocked his head for one long moment, but caught nothing but a verse being passed from diner to diner, so he rose quietly, following Ataskos and his lamp. Undetected he slid into his room, where he carefully unclasped his new sandals, then slipped free of his chiton, collapsing naked onto the sleeping pallet.

Ataskos moved about in the flickering lamplight, casting monstrous shadows on the bare crimson walls. Thukydides watched the floating images in silence. He ached to talk with the slave, to have his symposion, but it was beyond them both. Ataskos worked his old bones into the pile of fleece and rags at the foot of the pallet. Within moments he snored, released from his burdens.

Thukydides lay awake, listening to the slurred choruses in the andron. Only the distant bark of a dog pulled his mind from the singing. Soon his thoughts drifted from the revelry to the man Herodotos and his inquiry. He had never heard such tales. Oh, he had often been read to about the deathless gods and their meddling in human affairs. But these had always been ancient stories—un-testable ones. This man recorded the events of two generations. Because he has written this down, his words will always be his. Unchanged for all time.

Sparta
Four
ΣΠΑΡΤΗ

He blew into his hands while rubbing them, trying to work away the stiffness that the cold morning had cast upon him. Vapor squeezed through his fingers, dissolving quickly into the shafts of early morning sunlight that filtered through the trees. A hare would do just fine. Now he wished he had one of his dogs, either Atlas or Herakles, with him. His feet were the last to leave the shelter of pine bough and oak leaves; these he kept warm as long as possible by immersing them in the trough of foliage much as a bather might dangle his feet while sitting at a fountain's edge. He prayed to Artemis to aid him in his hunt and to offer one of her creatures to him as a meal.

Finally, with dredged-up energy, he rose to his feet and began stalking breakfast. First he checked the several snares he had strung across likely runs, places where he had snagged a hare before; these were untouched. In the summer he could easily catch a lizard or snake still lethargic from the night's chill sunning itself. Not so in winter. The easy game slept through this season. For a time he scoured the bleak ridge in his hunt. *Today I will steal*, he thought to himself at the growl of his belly.

The Phouaxir—Fox Time— was well through half its course. With the coming of summer and the festival of the Hyakinthia, Brasidas would again join the civilized world, the world of his polis Sparta. But for now, as every nineteen-year-old was compelled to do, he prowled the edges of it, surviving by his wits, a single himation cloak, a water flask, and a xuele knife his only possessions.

For a quarter hour or so he squatted in a puddle of sunlight that warmed a boulder near his shelter, pondering where his meal would come from.

"Ah, Kratesikles' farm," he mumbled into his cupped hands.

He sprang to his feet and scrambled up the slope to the crest of the ridge, following the spine of the hill as his own private path. His belly groaned. It twisted, cramping in pain, reminding him of its wants. As soon as he spotted

45

the kleros, he began his descent, keeping under cover of the near-naked trees until he came to the boundary stones marking the property.

Two Helots were in the yard sowing feed amongst a swirl of clacking, head-bobbing hens. No, it would be more than a chicken today. He stared at the largest of the out-buildings, not the stable but the barn. The door creaked open. A Helot emerged from it toting a pitching fork and spade. A woman yelled. The three left their chores and headed to the smaller of the two mud-brick dwellings. Now was the time.

Like a shadow, he glided over the interval of open fields, making sure to stay low in his scamper from tree, to bush, to the stubby rock fence that ringed the yard. He slipped through the partially open doorway, pausing just inside; light leaked through the weathered and patched door. His sight adjusted quickly to the dark. Inside he saw several goats tethered for milking. His eyes passed over them quickly. Still in his crouch, xuele dagger drawn and pointing forward, he stalked further. A deep, guttural snort froze him mid-stride. He smiled and moved toward the noise.

In the far corner of the barn lay a brown spotted hog; at every teat she suckled a piglet, all still pink, eyes squeezed shut in their infant blindness. The sow raised her head at his approach while snorting again. The piglets nursed blissfully. Brasidas knelt at arm's length from the litter, staring.

"Now, mother be good and be quiet," he whispered assuredly. No doubt the Helots had handled her litter before. With patience he should be able to snatch the prize without alarming her, so in a soothing and deliberate manner, he began to stroke her side. The sow shook her head, then settled back, blinking her eyes in contentment. He surveyed the brood, settling on the largest of them. Slowly he moved his hand down her flank, all the while continuing to murmur assuringly. He slipped his fingers over the piglet's snout and pried it from his mother's belly.

"Thief!" A figure loomed in the bright rectangle of the open doorway.

Brasidas sprang to his feet. Not thinking, his hand had slipped free of the piglet's mouth; the animal squealed in terror. Now the sow wrenched from side to side, releasing a succession of snorts, until she gained her feet. The Helot in his path shouted to his fellows. He did not move from the single exit, knowing he need only keep his captive within until help arrived. Quickly he scanned the building's interior searching for his options: two shuttered windows, a ladder to a narrow loft above, and the guarded doorway. With one hand wrapped around his prize, he bounded up the ladder, making it to the loft with three expanded strides. From up here he could see the shaft of light from the door, with the shadow of the Helot outlined upon the muddied floor. He crawled ahead, toward the front of the barn and directly over the doorway and the now unseen sentinel.

Suddenly two Helots blew through the doorway into the center of the barn, one wielding a pitching fork and the other a spade; both wore tight-fitting dog-skin caps. The taller of the pair craned his neck, searching the loft.

"He's up there, I tell you," yelled the one in the doorway.

The tall one, pitching fork in hand, began his ascent. Two rungs from the top and Brasidas lunged from the shadows and kicked the ladder free, sending it arcing rearward. The Helot's eyes opened wide and white. His chin dropped. The top of the ladder slammed into the far wall; it snapped mid-way, dropping the man on his back, leaving him clutching the top half as it crashed to the ground.

"I'll kill that Spartan bastard," he snarled as he rolled to his knees. The one with the spade helped him to his feet.

Brasidas sliced his xuele dagger through the thatching on the roof, cutting the strands of grass rope that bound it to the cross-staves. Sunlight slipped through the creases, encouraging him to continue. Soon he had torn away a hole large enough for him to squeeze through.

"Get the other ladder!" commanded the Helot with the fork. The guard left his post, running. Soon Brasidas heard the growl of wood being dragged across the cold, hard soil of the yard.

Two of them worked the ladder through the doorway and propped it at the far end of the loft. He could just see the pair of them, spade and fork in hand, gripping the chest-high rung of the ladder. The third came into view, cradling something in his left arm. This one reached to his left, into a basket and plucked out a fist-sized rock.

"If he sticks his head out, hit him," bellowed the tall one as he planted his right foot on the bottom rung. When he got mid-way, the second one heaved up onto the ladder, toting his spade.

A stone rattled off the mud-brick wall, skipping by his head. Brasidas remained motionless.

Now the tall Helot cleared the final rung. "I see him," he hissed through a yellow-toothed grin. Slowly he crawled towards him. The second approached the edge of the loft.

Brasidas maintained his cower, pressed into the corner of the two walls and the roof, muffling the piglet all the while.

"He's scared. Probably shit himself," bellowed the Helot to his friend behind him as he closed in to within a few feet.

Suddenly Brasidas exploded up through the hole, leaving the Helot grabbing at air. He fell from the roof, tumbling to his side in front of the door to the barn. Quickly he swung the rickety door on its hinge pin, crashing it into the warped frame and lintel, then dropped the wooden bolt-peg into the frame.

With his plan complete, he whirled around to his escape, but found his route blocked. In his path stood a youth of his own age wearing a dog-skin cap like the others, but somehow familiar. His face was not distinctive, but his eyes—he stared into the boy's eyes, but it seemed he looked at his very own, reflected in a pool, polished marbled, or a burnished shield. He shuddered, not from fear but from something just as deep. For a long moment they studied each other, then Brasidas stepped around him and found himself at a full sprint, flying across the ploughed fields. In moments he was amongst the trees, dissolving into the forest beyond.

* * *

He checked the breeze again to be certain he was downwind from the nearest kleros. With a few sharp strikes of his xuele against a small stone, he had sparked the tufts of dried moss and pine shavings into a web of embers. Carefully he breathed onto it, coaxing small licks of flames, while feeding it with dry twigs he had snapped into the perfect size for his stripling fire to digest.

He had already drunk the blood. The piglet lay upon the ground next to him like a bundle of pink rags, hardly resembling anything that had ever been living. With an expert tug, he opened the gut, worked his fingers to grab the small slippery entrails, then yanked them free of the tiny carcass. The minuscule heart and liver he plucked free of the viscera, placing them upon a flat stone near his hearth. The remainder he tossed into a shallow hole, for he knew the smell would soon bring the wolves. He must eat quickly.

The meat he did not cook, but merely warmed, singeing the outside black. With the flesh gone along with the heart and liver, he worked on the bones, sucking out the scant marrow. This was his finest meal in months.

"My compliments to you, Kratesikles," he said quietly.

As the warming sun slipped low in the sky, the forest turned to a place of cold blue shadows; individual trees blended into dark snarls of naked limbs while the winter wind raked through, stirring up the carpet of leaves that smothered the unseen earth. His modest fire cowered under the icy breeze. He hunkered over it, soaking up what warmth it threw, protecting the waning flames. Soon only smoke lifted from the spent wood.

Solemnly he mumbled a prayer of thanksgiving to Artemis for his meal, fastidiously entombed the remains of the piglet, erased all traces of his fire then trotted off, up to the crest of the ridge and the trail back to his shelter.

The eyes burned in his mind; they worked on his memory and this troubled him. For sure he had never been to Kratesikles' kleros before, and certainly this Helot was not one he had seen in Sparta proper. The night proved a restless one for Brasidas as he nestled into his bed of leaves and pine boughs.

* * *

He slept much less, but lingered awhile in his forest bed, the frigid morning air stealing his ambition. But his belly was full and he knew without a fire the only way to keep warm was activity. He would sneak a visit to Temo.

The trek from the outskirts of Sellasia south into the plain north of Pitane took longer than he recalled. The road certainly would carry him quicker, but he must not be seen, especially by the Eirenes in the Krypteia, the only ones who monitored the young men during the Phouaxir. The thought fired the image of Thrasymidas in his mind. It would suit him to confront Brasidas. There would be no witnesses. Nor would it be the first time a participant in the Phouaxir failed to return to the city.

A little past midday he rested, sitting upon a knoll, wrapped in his himation cloak and flanked by two thick-trunked oaks, watching a mora of five hundred bronze-clad Spartan warriors chug along the road south toward the city. He strained to make out the individuals in the triple-columned formation, but the uniform dress of crimson chiton and triboun war cloak made discrimination impossible. Only the transverse horsehair crests of the officers betrayed any dissimilarity amongst them. They sang the same paian and pounded their feet to the Embaterion march, as he had so often done while training in the Agoge.

He longed for the companionship of others. Where was Turtle? And Styphon? Lykophron for sure would flourish on his own in the forests. His mind settled on the image of his dear Epitadas; he would best them all. He felt so inadequate, dwelling on the cold and hunger that occupied his thoughts. They would never submit to them as he had done.

Night came—a frigid night. The bitter cold crippled him. He did not kindle a fire. He barely scratched out a sleeping trench, and filled it with little bedding. His lethargy persuaded him to desist in cutting boughs. The scant blanket of leaves he gathered was scoured out of the shallow hole by the wind. He shivered, knees drawn up under his single himation cloak, praying for Eos, goddess of dawn, to appear and deliver him from this life-stealing night.

Even before the first shafts of sunlight pierced the trees, while the sky was till iron gray, he forced himself up and on the move. Within a quarter hour his muscles warmed. His spirit warmed also. At this pace he would be on the fringe of the city by afternoon. By evening he would be with her. With luck he would catch sight of her in the fields, working the soil for the coming planting season. He required no more rest.

As evening approached he could easily scamper across the road unseen and into the woods that would take him on the lower slopes of Taygetos. He would follow the contours of the mountain's lower spur right up to the cliff behind his father's house and the kleros of the polemarch Anaxandros where she lived.

He scrambled up the hill to the perch he always used to spy the farm and waited there, scanning the fields. He grinned at the sight of her, and went skidding down the friable slope. Suddenly he winced as if in pain when the loose stones spilled across a boulder, clattering upon the rocks below. He paused and listened. Satisfied he was not seen, he uncoiled from his crouch to begin his descent.

A strong hand grabbed him. "Where are you going?"

Instinctively he tumbled to the earth, trying to wrest free from the grip. It did no good. The hand stayed clamped on his arm. His attacker pinned him with a knee, while pressing both shoulders into the stony ground.

"Brasidas. Don't you recognize me?"

He peered up at the scruffy-bearded face. It was a lean face, young but chiseled, trim, and ferocious sitting upon an equally slim but muscular body. In the eyes he saw something familiar.

"It's me," he exclaimed while relaxing his grip on Brasidas.

Brasidas lay back, furling his brow as he stared. "Turtle?"

He smiled. "Have I changed so much?"

"By the deathless gods, you have changed." Brasidas grinned beneath his wispy beard. "But why are you here?"

"To save you, my dear friend." Turtle rolled off, then yanked Brasidas to his feet.

"To save me from what?"

"From Thrasymidas." Turtle's great smile fled. "Sit and I will tell you."

"But he is now in the Krypteia, is he not?"

"To be sure, and it is you, my friend, he is determined to find." Turtle paused, popped open his drinking flask and chugged down a few gulps. "He knows about Temo."

"How?" Brasidas heart plummeted. "Thrasymidas could kill her and nothing would be said," he pointed out, adding, "not over the life of a Helot girl."

"That I do not know. But Kleandridas—who found me too easily in my hiding place—made me swear to find you before you came here."

"When did you see him? Kleandridas, I mean."

"Just yesterday. He told me of your visit to Kratesikles' farm."

"How did anyone know I was there?"

"You mean how did Kratesikles know it was you." Turtle snatched a twig, studied it for a moment, then clamped it in his teeth.

Rhamnous
Five
ΡΑΜΝΟΓΣ

Thukydides reveled in the thought of wearing his black ephebos cloak to the theatron this afternoon. He could not help but strut a bit as he walked about wearing it, receiving admiring glances from the young women and respectful ones from the boys. Veterans hardly acknowledged him. Eighteen years old and in his first year of military training, he along with the other first-year epheboi always drew garrison duty on Attika's frontier. The local townsfolk more than accommodated these free-spending young men, always willing to provide any goods or services that might wring an obol from their swollen purses. The people of Rhamnous grew rich on them. Oil, a sought-after commodity for its use in exercise, commanded high prices here. Food vendors at the theatron also charged a premium.

"A few months, at the beginning of Thargelion, and we ride, my friend." Eukles smiled at his announcement. He moved down the alley to the theatron's entrance, caught in the flow of the chattering crowd.

Eukles was right. Two more months and they would begin frontier patrol on horseback. Only the young men from the best of families could afford this prized duty; they must supply their own mounts and Thukydides' family bred the choicest horses in all of Attika.

The theatron was modest by comparison to Athens'. Centered on the floor of the orkestra lay a mound of earth; behind this the skene resembled a barbarian city, steps rising up from the ground to meet the doors of an opulent building, its facade painted with giant, beast-like gods. Suddenly a chanting commenced. The chorus of actors entered, continuing their song to the repeating rhythm of a cymbal clanging two short beats followed by a long one. Each face bore a clay mask resembling men of the East; curled long hair and beards were fashioned upon them and the eyes outlined in black.

The chorus began. "We the old men stay at home while the youth of Persia have gone to Greek soil...."

"Have you seen this before?" asked Eukles.

Thukydides nodded. "Aeschylus' play, isn't it?"

"That it is, but hardly as I have seen it performed," Eukles whispered. The cramped theatron and poorly furnished actors urged comparisons with the city's fare. Eukles went on, but Thukydides politely ignored his friend, keeping his attention on the play.

"You do not wish to listen to the tale of the Battle of Salamis?" Thukydides admonished.

"I have heard it a dozen times, and told in more lavish settings than this."

"It should be heard two dozen times—and more."

From behind a hand dropped to Thukydides' shoulder. "I knew you two would be here."

"Gryllos!" Eukles turned, clasping his friend's arm.

Thukydides rose to greet him.

"Sit, sit, my friend," said Gryllos as he gently pressed Thukydides back to his seat. "I have good news."

Now both spun around to face him, ignoring for the moment the performance below.

"Well?" Eukles urged.

"We three will be assigned the same duty—patrol in Phyle."

"How do you know this?" quizzed Thukydides. Before he finished the question, the answer came to him. Gryllos' father—for this year—was one of the ten strategoi, or generals of the Athenian army.

Gryllos' answer was a smile. The three quietly settled in to watch the play, sharing the loaf of flatbread that Gyllos had smuggled into the theatron. The performance seemed much longer than at Athens. The actors' skills, quite unpolished, mired the pace. Still Thukydides displayed obvious approval at the retelling of the Persian defeat at Salamis. It was a generation and more past, he pondered, since the Spartans and the Athenians stood allied, as yoke-fellows, leading all the Hellenes. Now, after a brief and muddled conflict, a frangible peace had been effected between the two greatest of cities. He prayed for it to endure.

After the play the trio reported back to the barracks at the fort, dined with their company of epheboi, then dispersed to their individual guard posts along the crenellated frontier wall. The evening air cooled quickly. Thukydides ascended the narrow wooden ladder wearing his kranos helmet pushed back atop his head to reveal his face, shield carried tortoise-like upon his back.

Only epheboi and old men drew garrison duty. His guard-partner this evening was Praxis, a veteran of the Great War with Persia. He had fought at Plataia under the command of Aristides the Just. At the time he was barely twenty, but at a mere hint could recount every detail of that battle.

"So, sprout, do you wish to hear of the Great War again?" He moved a bit closer to the crackling fire in the brazier, unfurling his cloak to let in the warmth. "There are a scant few of us left that can tell of it, you know." The shadowy firelight deepened the wrinkles of his well-worn face; his eyes still gleamed with the enthusiasm of youth.

"You apprised me of our Athenians in the battle innumerable times," said Thukydides respectfully. "But what of the others? What of the Spartans?" Listening was a skill Thukydides had honed at an early age, but it was only recently did he learn to fashion the proper questions to induce others to speak.

Praxis rubbed his hands together over the flames. "Do you think your training difficult?"

"More arduous than anything I have done in my life."

"And do you think it burdensome?" Old Praxis grinned as he finished the question.

"Two years is a long time to spend away from home in military drill."

"A long time?"

"Why, yes. We know now how to form up in phalanx order, march to the salpinx, and wield our sword and spear." Thukydides felt the snare tightening, but he continued anyway. "And this we learned in two short months."

"If you were a horse breeder—as I know your father is—would you spend time on fishing?"

"Why, no," he answered quickly.

"If a farmer, would you devout your days to cobbling leather?"

"Of course not," Thukydides replied confidently.

"And why not?"

"My vocation deserves my attention. Only when this has been attended to fully could I indulge in any distractions."

"And what is your vocation, young Thukydides?"

"Like my father, to manage my estate," he said then paused, realizing his greater responsibility. "And to serve my polis."

"And how would you serve your polis?"

"By executing my duties, as I now do. To attend the assemblies. And if I am so fortunate, to serve on the boule as councilman of the city."

"Many duties. But which is primary?" Thukydides did not answer—Praxis would for him. "Your duty to defend the city is paramount, for in failing this,

54

all the other responsibilities and privileges become extinct."

Thukydides thought for awhile on these words. The wind picked up now, squashing the flames in the brazier. He gestured for a slave to stoke the fire.

"To answer your first question—what of the Spartans?"

The young ephebos looked up from the mesmerizing flames, into the glistening eyes of Praxis.

"We fought with courage at Plataia. The Spartans fought with—for lack of a better word—serenity."

Thukydides puzzled look beamed from his face.

"Does this sound strange? Well, to them war is a respite from their training. It soothes their spirit as good wine and hearty food does ours."

"But my father says they are uncouth brutes, hardly able to read and write."

"Because, like the diligent farmer who must tend to his crops full day to insure his livelihood, they too tend to their vocation." The frosty night pushed him closer to the brazier as he spoke. He took a bit of wine. "It has been said that war is what we Hellenes do best," he said, snugging his long cloak with his hands from within. "The Spartans are most certainly the best of us all."

Thukydides plucked several hunks of charcoal that lay unburned beneath the brazier, then tossed them into the fire, reviving the flames.

From the shadows approached another man, old as Praxis, using his spear as a walking staff. "Remember this, youngster. Spartan boys of your age began their training while you were still sleeping in the women's quarters. By the time you became a cadet, they had been in their Agoge eleven years." He continued past, the clicking of the bronze butt-spike of his spear fading into the night.

"Why do we quarrel with them?"

"For the same reason you tangle with Kleon. Two lions cannot share the same den."

Praxis' servant appeared, wicker basket in hand from which he presented two warm loaves of bread, a wrapper of cheese, and a flagon of wine to his master. Thukydides and Praxis sat upon their cross-legged stools, enjoying their snack, while talking away the night of Sparta.

Lakonia

Six

ΛΑΚΩΝΙΚΑ

Getting in was easy. The Helots were at the far stretches of the kleros, weeding the barley. Only the old woman remained in the small hut, tending to relics of breakfast, wiping clean the black-glazed bowls and dipping oily wooden cups clean in a basin. Brasidas crept silent as a shadow.

"Don't cry out," he whispered as he pressed the curved blade of his xuele against her sagging throat. The smell of her age repelled him.

She held her head motionless, straining her eyes wide to their limit, trying to catch a sideways peek of her attacker. "Poor pickings here," she muttered.

He eased up on the blade. She sighed. "I want nothing from you but information."

"And what can I tell a Spartan?"

Keeping the knife close to her throat, he turned her around and calmed the old woman with his own steady gaze.

Looking beyond the first glimpse, she stared, studying him like a painting, a written verse, or intricate sculpture. "You want to know about him," she offered before the question could be posed. "The one with eyes like yours—eyes of iron."

Her answer unsettled him. "Who is he?" he asked through a dry, tight throat.

"His name is Xenias," she replied.

"Is he your son?"

"Mine?" she said, holding back a chuckle. "Why, no. But I did raise him as mine."

"Then who is his mother? And his father?" He lowered his xuele, but not his intent gaze.

"I do not know."

The blade flew up to her neck. "A gift from the gods perhaps?" he snapped.

"A gift from a Spartan. I found him abandoned in the chasm of Apothetai.

56

Forsaken for the want of an eye."

"An eye?"

"Oh, he has two, but only one can see. Too far from perfect to be one of you."

He fell back into the three-legged stool behind him, his mind in a tangle. Voices. He heard two men chattering, the sound of their talk growing louder. In an instant he bounded to the window, crouching low in its frame to peer outside. Not but a few feet from the door stood the Helots who had trapped him in the barn. Dust floated from the door as it smacked hard against the wall, swirling in the shaft of morning sunlight that poured through the open portal. The two entered.

The woman rubbed the bowl with a rag, dunked it again, then placed it on the single shelf near the hearth. "We had a visitor this morning," she announced, while still working the last dish in the basin.

He flew through the field, faster than the fastest of Artemis' deer, faster than he had ever run in any race before, his pounding heart the only sound. Up the slope, over the crest, and into the ravine on the far side, he maintained his sprint until his lungs felt like they would explode. He collapsed to the base of an ancient oak, closed his eyes, and listened to the gasping breaths diminish. Here he hunkered, listening——watching. No men followed his flagrant trail, but still he hunched down in the tangles of brush until stealthy night arrived. Confident in the darkness, he made his way back to his den.

* * *

Morpheos, god of dreams, tormented Brasidas all night long with images of himself. He dreamt it was he who worked the fields of Kratesikles, beaten like a mule at any offense by Thrasymidas and his father. His own father, Tellis, stood by, deaf to his entreaties, deaf as he was to any Helot's cries. Only his mother dared to look upon him, but without fail her heart, a Spartan heart, chased away any affection.

It was an icy night but he awoke hot, body soaked, his single cloak wet and clinging to him. He fumbled for his water flask, took a few sips, then settled back into his leafy trench, staring up. Singly, then in bunches, the stars began to blink out; murky clouds slid across the sky. The trees, silent till now, struck up a loud chorus led by the wind. He heard the crescendo of rain pelting the foliage. Bright flashes ripped the black. Thunder crackled. In the intermittent explosions of light, shadows in the forest reformed, tricking his eyes: a tree trunk—a figure—a tree trunk again.

Another specter hid amongst the trees, but he dismissed it. But this one moved. A tall woman clad in a short white chiton strode toward him. Her hair was long but tied back by a garland, shining golden in the flashes of lightening. She clutched a bow in her left hand. Quickly he gathered his feet under him, crouching, his knife hand thrust out before him.

The woman smiled. "Brasidas," she said with a velvety but potent voice. "Is this how you welcome your protectress?"

He began to shake. Fear was something new to him, and he despised himself for it. "How do you know me?"

"Brasidas. How do you not know me?" She glided over the wind-stirred leaves to the edge of his trench. Her hand reached out to him. "Stand up, my dear."

His will lost, he extended his empty hand, all the while fixing his gaze upon her face. She was extraordinarily beautiful, like no woman he had ever seen before, surpassing even his own mother. He had seen her before. But where? A festival perhaps, for she was certainly not from his village of Pitane.

She kept her knowing grin. "You, of all the Spartans, have honored me best."

The altar. The altar of Artemis Orthia, that is where he had seen her. But the statue hardly did justice to her beauty and strength. He bowed his head and touched his brow. The knife fell from his hand.

"You do remember."

He tried to answer but could not. *This is my chance*, he thought, staring through panic-filled eyes. *A sacred encounter to ask any question, reveal any wish and I cannot. Will I be brave in battle? Is Temo safe? Was he my brother?* Desultory thoughts rattled in his mind.

"My dear Brasidas," said the goddess, her voice mellifluous as honey. "The answer is yes." She extended her slender-fingered hand, lifted his chin, and smiled. The air fled from his lungs. His head spun. He folded to the earth.

With the first gray streaks of dawn he was up, stalking the games runs in silence, checking his snares. Only a small mouse dangled still living from a loop of thin sinew. He reached for the tiny animal. It spun in his hand, twisting its head until it clamped its toothy jaw onto his thumb.

Brasidas smiled. "There is nothing so tiny that it lacks courage." He slipped the sinew from the mouse and let it run free, stamping his bare foot to send it scampering.

* * *

Hints of spring began to tease him: green buds speckled the once colorless trees of winter; he caught a snake sunning itself on a boulder one morning; the ominous cawing of crows was now joined by the chorus of sparrow and lark; grain stalks in the fields reached up like the spears of a triumphant army. For a week or more he maundered at the edges of the Eurotas Valley, moving south towards the city.

He watched her for two days. At night he patrolled the woods, searching in earnest for signs of the Krypteia and Thrasymidas. On the third he descended from his look-out spur at the foot of Taygetos, pulled his long himation cloak up over his head, and walked straight down the road.

Temo hacked away at the weedy soil with a wooden hoe, stopping every so often to smear the sweat from her brow with the back of her hand. The sight of a tall stranger walking the road alone compelled her to pause. She stared at him. Something in his gait was familiar.

Brasidas, determined to carry out his ruse, tightened the cloak about his chin, hiding his face deep within its folded peak. He shrugged his shoulders as he past, as though he fought off a chill. She turned and struck the earth with the hoe.

"Can you help a stranger?"

Startled a bit, she peered back over her shoulder at the figure.

Slowly he peeled back the cloak. Her eyes widened to show every bit of white. Then she smiled, and let the hoe slip.

"I thought you dead," she murmured to him, her face nestled in the curve of his neck as they embraced.

"Dead?" He kissed her. And again. "Who should harm me?" he asked defiantly.

"I saw them—your Krypteia. Two of them came at night to my hut, threatening to kill us then and there. My father and brother still bear the marks of the blades upon their faces." Now she began to sob.

"Did they harm you?" Brasidas, flushed with rage, stood back to look upon her tear-streaked face.

She shook her head then sniffled. "They only wanted to know of you."

Unconvinced he lifted her chin to study her face, all the while looking beyond her beauty, searching for the slightest bruise or scratch. "What did they look like?"

She convulsed with violent breaths until she had no tears left to expend. Without a word she bowed her head, sniffled, then wiped her reddened cheeks with the back of her hand. He daubed the remainder away with the corner of his cloak. "They both looked hungry," she answered. "Hungry, not like men, but like beasts. A ravenous look." She paused and swallowed hard. "The tallest of them was missing his teeth," she added.

He knew this may be the last time he would see her for many months. Thrasymidas would certainly return, and if he found him here would kill them both. He thought of Kleandridas and the two choices offered; he would choose the second.

With the night almost gone, he leaned over her as she slept, gently brushing the chestnut hair from her tanned face, then kissed her forehead. Still caught in a dream, she smiled. In silence he darted through the trees at the edge of the field, turning to look back only when he made the crest of the ridge.

* * *

He had seen the storm of dust appear over an hour ago, the precursor of an army on the march, so he found a convenient hillock to spectate. Now the sound of flutes rolled up the valley, soft at first until the cliffs of Taygetos penned it all in amplification. A squadron of horse broke into view first, only about fifty, followed by the flute players. Next the familiar wave of crimson and bronze swelled through the pass; over five-thousand Spartiate hoplites marched in cadence to the pipers, King Pleistoanax leading them. For almost an hour they passed below him on the road from Sellasia until the engineer and quartermaster train finally rambled into view. The groan and squeal of their wagons drowned out the fading music of march. Wounded men filled several carts.

Where from? he said to himself. *Athens was stirring trouble in the Megarid as always, but after their defeat four years previous at Koronea by the Thebans, they avoided any contest of arms with us. Pleistoanax admired Athens, as did King Archidamos, both because of the tenacity and prowess it displayed in the war against Persia. After the war we had abdicated leadership, preferring to wallow in our concerns in the Peloponnese. Athens swiftly stepped in to take our place. We had fought to stem an invasion, to keep Lakonia free of foreigners, but with Athens it was different. They wanted payment for their part in the war. Liberty for their fellow Greeks was just another transaction, a business arrangement that must be fulfilled, so they began to extort tribute, strangling trade with any competitors and working to cower our allies. My father fought them at Tanagra more than ten years ago. We were gracious in victory, returning their dead and wounded. In thanks, like pirates, they burned our port city of Gytheion. We also had but two choices in our dealings with this city.*

Leipsydrion
Seven
ΛΕΙΠΣΓΔΡΙΟΝ

The six beaters whooped and yelled while slamming their ash poles into the tangled underbrush; Thukydides and Eukles sat atop their horses, tense with focus, hunting spears poised. Suddenly the foliage rippled, like water in the wake of a trireme. The boar exploded into view. Thukydides' mount reared up, avoiding the charge, but spun awkwardly, allowing him no clear shot. Eukles yanked hard on the reins, sending his horse in to a gallop.

"Get him!" Finally Thukydides stifled his mount's estrapades and raced after his friend, yelling encouragement from behind.

Leaves and branches tore by Eukles as he strained to keep his eyes on the prey. The boar's hooves drummed into the hard soil. Eukles heard every grunt and snort the beast made. He reared back his spear and launched it. The animal squealed in pain then spun around wildly, trying to shake free the weapon. As he whirled, the spear-shaft struck the trunk of a bent oak. The boar shot off through the underbrush.

For more than an hour they followed the blood trail, up the ridge that overlooked the fort at Leipsydrion, and down again into a marsh on the far side.

"Shhh," whispered Thukydides. "Can you hear that?"

All stopped. All listened. From a thicket marked by a single tall plane tree, the sound of labored breath could be discerned, faint at first, but growing louder as they cocked their ears. Eukles and Thukydides slid quietly from their mounts, both wielding gleaming-tipped hunting spears in one hand and xiphidion daggers in the other.

Thukydides parted the branches with his spear. In the thick brush lay the boar, his furry coat glistening wet and red; his chest heaved as he fought for every breath; his sad eyes turned toward the hunter.

"He is yours," said Thukydides.

Eukles, without hesitation, plunged the razored spear-point into the boar's chest. It kicked both rear legs in an instinctual sprint while releasing one final, terror-stricken squeal, then went still. After studying its now lifeless eyes for a moment, he lifted its fleshy throat, dragged the xiphidion deftly across it, then rose up to stand triumphantly over the prize. Thukydides found himself staring at the pooling, steamy blood as it blackened the earth.

"Hang it up," Eukles commanded to one of the beaters.

Thukydides reached up onto his horse, snatching a small leather sack. He plucked out a flask, then tossed the sack to his companion. "Some bread for you."

The two sat upon a boulder, trying to keep their feet out of the muck of the swamp while their servants dressed the kill.

"Thirty years!" said Eukles. "Peace for thirty years."

"With Sparta at least." Thukydides swigged the wine.

"Sparta is our only match. No one else dare test us."

"But why did the Spartans leave after they had beaten us?" Thukydides was still puzzled by the unexpected withdrawal of the enemy's army.

"They are an honorable foe. They had proven superior on the field of battle; that was enough for them."

Thukydides turned toward their bagged game. A servant plunged a blade at the boar's tail, carefully slipping it up the groin, belly, and chest, right up to the neck. He worked his bloodied fingers under the hide and began ripping it away from the glistening red sinews; it tore with the sound of wet sailcloth. Within minutes the carcass hung stripped, a lure for flies.

"The Thebans would not be so generous in victory," reminded Thukydides.

"A few more months and our training will be over. The army will have no need for us with thirty years of peace in the offing." Eukles smiled, stuffed a piece of bread into his mouth, then stood. "Time to bring our dinner home."

* * *

The two were the talk of the garrison at Leipsydrion that night. Fresh meat—with the gods' portion of bone and fat withheld of course, which they burned at the altar of Zeus Protector of the City for the truce so recently attained—was thoroughly enjoyed by their comrades.

For the next month, the edgy boredom experienced by the garrison induced by the ever-present specter of Spartan invasion gave way to frivolity. Even the captain of the fort eased his tough demeanor toward the epheboi, no longer meting out punishment for napping in the guard towers, unattended weapons, or the smuggling of whores into the barracks.

By early autumn, during the month of Bodromeion, when day and night are equals, Thukydides' family held a feast in his honor. Having completed his two years of military training, he now stood on the threshold of full citizenship.

"You must have some of this," his father, Olorus, insisted, shoving the servant with the platter of octopus toward his son. "The sauce is delicious."

His son plucked a slice of roasted tentacle from the orange-glazed platter, slurping it into his mouth quickly. His eyes widened with delight. "That is excellent."

"Are you two acquainted?" said Olorus as he motioned to the young man seated upon the divan. The man rose, then nodded politely. "This is Archestratos, son of Lykomedes. He is a year older than you, I think."

"Yes," said the young man. His beard was dark and thick for someone so young. A white scar on his ruddy nose drew Thukydides' attention. "You want to know about this?" he asked as he dragged the tips of his fingers across it.

Thukydides face burned with embarrassment. "Why, no." He was a poor liar.

"From a Spartan sword." Archestratus beamed with pride. "The scar on my helmet is far worse."

"You fought at Eleusis?"

"Was not much of a fight. By mid-morning they had us on the run."

"What was is like—fighting *them*, I mean?"

"Unsettling. They do not shout or yell to summon courage. They march to the pipes without a sound. Not a man among them faltered. Not hatred nor fear did I see in their eyes as they hit us. That statue there had more expression," he said while pointing to a marble Athena. Now his smile left him as he looked away from them all, calling upon his memory. "Strange. We ran, but they did not pursue. They still fight by the old ways, with valor and restraint."

Olorus let loose a belly laugh that turned all heads. "They did not afford the Medes at Plataia so pleasant a retreat. That was a slaughterhouse!"

"Precisely because they were not fighting Hellenes did they abandon the old way. The Persians deserved no such accommodation." Archestratos startled them all with his pedantic tone. Realizing his manners he added, "So says my father, Lykomedes."

The wine steward entered the andron, leading two others, each staggering under weight of an orange glaze pitcher. They spilled them empty into a large bowl. Olorus walked over to instruct them further.

"One part water. No more. Let our guests enjoy the vintage." He clapped his hand three times. A pair of flute-girls scurried forward. "Play."

Olorus started the song. He completed a verse and sent it along to his son to embellish. Thukydides passed it on to Archestratos, a gracious gesture to someone he had just met. Soon the ditty jumped from one couch to another, stretched richer by a verse at each stop.

It took them till long after midnight to empty the wine bowl and by then the game of kattabos became much too difficult, for no one had the aim to toss their last dreg of wine into the empty bowl. The guests said their goodnights to their host and his son. Archestratos lingered.

"Thank you, sir," he said respectfully through glazed eyes to Olorus. "And thank you, Master Thukydides." He turned to leave, but stopped at the threshold. "I forgot. A friend of yours asked me to send his regards."

Thukydides, swaying a bit from the wine, then shook his head to clear his thoughts. "And who was this?"

"His name is Kleon."

* * *

Drunk as he was, he awoke well before dawn, the name of Kleon ringing like a smith's hammer in his head. Now there is someone he would gladly fight—not some unknown and noble Spartan, but a familiar and palpable enemy; a man, in Thukydides' mind, that was more a threat to Athens than any foreign adversary. For two years he had forgotten that name. Kleon was older, a coeval of Archestratos and a man who Thukydides longed to forget. He re-entered his life along with the nausea of last night's wine.

He reached for the chamber pot. Not sure whether to puke or piss, he lay upon his sleeping pallet, aiming his mouth at the clay bowl. A patch of yellow moonlight struck the mocking figure of Dionysos upon the pot, one hand clutching grapes, the other a full kylix of wine; he heaved into it. The door creaked open. Thukydides kept his face to the pot, spitting the stinging vomit from his mouth. Painfully, he glanced to the side, toward the open doorway.

"Master. I have some bark tea," whispered Ataskos. The old man shuffled quietly into the room. He knelt at the pallet, offering up the warm cup. "It will settle your stomach."

Thukydides winced as he sipped. He kicked the chamber-pot under the pallet, while finishing off the potion. "Thank you," he said.

Ataskos had no response. Never had he been thanked by anyone for a service rendered. Thukydides' out-of-place politeness flummoxed him.

"It is more than the wine." Ataskos reached for the empty cup.

"Yes. But how did you know that?"

"Master Thukydides, you talk in your sleep. And never of pleasant things. I heard the name of Kleon many times tonight."

Ataskos slept just outside on the balcony, upon a pile of fleece and old rags. Thukydides, older now, would not have a servant sleeping in his room, no matter what his father said.

"I have not heard that name in many years."

"Neither have I," moaned Thukydides. He fell back upon the pallet.

Sparta
Eight
ΣΠΑΡΤΗ

The five of them ringed the small fire, the aspect of solemnity bordering on fear apparent on each face. From the silence an owl shot out a single, piercing hoot.

"It is Athena," remarked Styphon.

"It is an owl," blurted out Epitadas condescendingly.

"Are you frightened?" said Turtle, looking directly at Brasidas.

"Of what?"

"Of what will happen tonight?" whispered Lykophron.

"What is to be frightened of? We kill a cock, and offer the sacrifice to Artemis." Brasidas felt a certain familiar comfort in invoking the goddess now, a comfort he would never reveal. He looked around at his friends. They were different. The Phouaxir had changed them. It changed him too.

From beyond, footsteps rustled in the pathway. Saleuthos bobbed into the halo of firelight. "Come."

The five rose up and followed through a path in the tall reeds that insulated the perimeter of the sanctuary from prying eyes. Two older Eirenes guarded the entrance. "Wait here," said Saleuthos. He peered past the guards into the sanctuary, waiting for the signal. "Follow me."

Brasidas slipped between the pair of guards and into the clearing in the wood that formed the sanctuary. The brightly colored marble altar and statue of the goddess reflected only the pale orange of the torchlight within. Another Eirene of Saleuthos' age, Isarchidas, stood astride the altar and next to him was a young Helot, clad in white, clutching a rooster. The bird flailed its scaly feet and fluttered its wings, convulsing to free itself from the boy's grip.

"You, Brasidas, son of Tellis, have completed the Upbringing," said Saleuthos almost in a chant. He nodded to the Helot. The boy held out the struggling rooster, offering it to Brasidas.

"This is your final sacrifice to the goddess as a boy." Memories burst like lightening in his brain. The public sacrifices to Artemis he had performed with the other boys, some guarding her altar while the rest tried to snatch packets of cheese from it. They whacked each other with cornel saplings, the only weapons allowed during the ritual. He got his share of cheese and stripes.

Isarchidas, fighting back a grin, spoke. "It is time."

Brasidas looked to both Saleuthos and Isarchidas. "The knife," he said.

"There is no knife. You must dispatch it with your teeth."

The pair grinned upon seeing his face. He felt ashamed he had conveyed any outward sign to them. The bird writhed; Brasidas stared into its soulless, darting eyes, then shoved its flailing neck between his teeth, clamping his jaw down like a vise. Hot blood overwhelmed his mouth, gagging him with the taste of iron and wet feathers. It still wriggled with life. He spit, then ripped its head free of the body. Again he spit, but now more defiantly.

Saleuthos whacked him on the back with typical Spartan affection, almost driving him to his knees. "Well done!" He slapped him again.

The Helot snatched the dead rooster, splattering its blood upon the altar of Artemis Orthia, mingling it with the crimson puddles of a dozen recent victims, then he carried its carcass to a criss-cross of logs where he flung it atop the others.

Saleuthos led him to a stream of the Eurotas where twelve others hacked and spit, some washing, others drinking and spitting again. Eight Helots stood holding torches.

Someone shoved him from behind. "And that teaches us what?"

Brasidas spun around. There was Turtle, wiping a tiny white feather from his black beard; he licked his front teeth with his tongue, wincing. Brasidas winced too. "It teaches us that nothing comes to us easily. It also honors the goddess who protected all of us during the Phouaxir."

Epitadas staggered into the group, gagging. "I would rather eat bull's balls." His chest expanded in a spasm, then his mouth gaped and out roared a stream of vomit. He hacked and spit, swallowed hard, then began it all again until finally a Helot rushed forward to offer him a bowl of water. "Look at him."

From the pathway wobbled Styphon, his face glistening red in the torchlight. He wiped his eyes clear with the back of his hand and grinned with satisfaction. "The taste is unique." He nodded his head slightly. "It needs something. Thyme! A pinch of thyme would do just nicely." Styphon waved at a Helot to bring him a bowl whereupon he doused his head, then shook like a dog to dry himself. "You know, a month ago that bit of neck would have been a feast. I wonder how he did it?"

"Did what?" Brasidas tossed a handful of water onto his face.

"Kill the cock." Styphon grinned. "Thrasymidas, I mean. That gap in his mouth left him weaponless. He must have suffocated the poor bird." Styphon mimed the event, spinning 'round with an imaginary rooster clamped in his mouth, twirling and twirling, until at last he fell to the ground in feigned exhaustion.

Saleuthos, with Isarchidas at his side, pushed through the reeds into view. "Follow us."

The seventeen youths, soon to be men, snaked down the narrow, dark trail, emerging into a shower of firelight. The interleaved pile of wood blazed, sending their sacrifices skyward in twirls of smoke and spark. Brasidas' eyes followed a bright ember as it shot above the trees, flicking out amongst the stars.

"Tomorrow begins the Karneia," announced Isarchidas, "when you all will be initiated to manhood. You will petition for a phidition. You will eat with others of your bloodline in warrior style. Tonight we sing to Artemis Orthia, patroness of you all."

At first only Saleuthos and Isarchidas sang, their voices ramping in volume, until the rest joined in. The chant elevated them in thought, expanding the senses to truly experience the presence of the goddess. Song was holy, Spartan song the holiest.

Shadows danced amongst the trees, given life by the roaring flames in the clearing. Brasidas snapped his head quickly to catch sight of movement flirting with his field of vision. His eyes drilled the darkness. A figure glided through the forest, halting at a tree trunk to look at them, then wafted like a mist to another tree, stopping once more. He smiled. The goddess smiled back.

* * *

He had only been back in his barracks for three days, called down from the mountains prior to the festival of Karneia, ending the Phouaxir. Every one of them sported beards, even Styphon, though barely, for he had remained to him at least, embarrassingly unchanged, hardly grown in height—but his voice boomed like a giant's.

"It's not long enough." Saleuthos laughed at Brasidas as he watched him fumble with his hair.

He reached for a crescent-shaped tortoise shell comb, one with a figure of Herakles carved into its semi-circular grip, then dragged it through his hair. It would be a least another year until he could braid it into the eight locks of a warrior. He remembered the words of Lykourgus: "*Long hair makes handsome men more handsome, and ugly men more fearsome.*" He wished for a bit of both.

They wore wool chitons of scarlet, the military type woven and stitched by their families' women as they marched out of the barracks toward the agora, spilling into the crimson stream of men that crammed the road. Soon they would attain their most prized possession. Soon they would be called warrior of the city.

He spotted his father first, then his mother, both together as expected. Kleandridas was nowhere to be seen. He saw King Archidamos talking leisurely with the polemarchs and other high officers of the army. Absent also was King Pleistoanax.

An army herald, Tolmidas, strode into the center of the agora. All chatter ceased. "We begin with the Staphylodromoi."

A tall man, unrecognizable because of the tatters of fleece draped over him, moved next to the herald. "Runners, come forward," bellowed Tolmidas.

Slipping from the crowd, four naked young men moved aside the herald. One was Saleuthos.

The herald lowered his staff of office as a barrier to the four. "Run!"

The tall man sped off, barreling down the road east towards the river. When he turned out of sight at the far end of the agora, Tolmidas swung his staff. The four sprinters exploded after their quarry.

"I pray Saleuthos gets him," said Epitadas above the cheers of the crowd.

"He is fast," assured Brasidas. Cheers raced with them and soon the only trace of the sprinters was the dissolving pall of yellow dust that hung above the road.

"It will be awhile," said Styphon to Lykophron. "We should retire to our camp."

"And us to ours. Tonight then." Brasidas tugged on Epitadas' arm. Ahead of them both, Turtle was already shouldering his way through the crammed agora. The three were of the phratry of the Dymanes, the bloodline of their ancestors, and would dine in the tents erected for them. Lykophron and Styphon would eat with their clan, the Hylleis. Seven tents for each phratry, the twenty-year-old initiates from each clan, joined by the most important older members—officers, battle-priests, city officials—imitating the field messes of the army on campaign.

Brasidas, tempted by the abundance of food before him, had to fight to summon his manners, but even a year in the wild had not stripped him of these entirely. He ate slowly, returning conversation when engaged, but nimbly turning it away from him and toward the others. It was a subtle skill, practiced effortlessly, but appreciated by those around him far more than he knew.

Dusk, cool and fragrant, beckoned them to the theatron for the nocturnal choruses. This festival of the new year, celebrated at the height of summer, was the last of the three holy festivals of the season. Brasidas knew also that it was this very sacred celebration that kept his countrymen from fighting alongside Athens against the Persians at Marathon and from marching with their own King Leonidas to Thermopylae. He honored the gods also, but thought it absurd that the very festival that celebrates their martial life prevented them from battling their enemies. The Athenians would rationalize away the gods for a time if it suited them, then reinstate them when needed—not so in Sparta. Like most all things here, piety was also immutable.

* * *

The second day of the Karneia, the day Brasidas had yearned for since he could remember anything. He stood in file with the other twenty-year-old, Hebontes, outside the sanctuary of Artemis Orthia, the late summer heat building as Helios rose in the flawlessly blue sky. His modest beard was trimmed to shape, his hair oiled and combed. Now he moved up in the queue as the young men before him slipped into the precincts of the sanctuary. They formed a great circle around the altar. King Archidamos, resplendent in his scarlet chiton and polished bronze breastplate stood at the altar next to the agetes, the priest of the sanctuary. A salpinx trumpet rent the silence, then a parade of Helots silently marched in, carrying stacks of triboun war cloaks. All the Hebontes kept to their inward facing circle as pairs of slaves stopped at each one of them, snapping a cloak to its full length. Brasidas let the mantle embrace him as the slave fitted it to his shoulders.

Now another procession of servants entered the sanctuary clad in white, each solemnly carried a gleaming bronze shield emblazoned with a scarlet lambda—ensign of their polis. Brasidas could feel the pride swell in him, clouding his eyes and pinching his throat as he stared at the shields and their impeccable brilliance. *Perseus' shined no brighter*, he thought. One by one they were called forward by the agetes, presented with a shield and a few words. "Brasidas, son of Tellis," announced the priest.

He strode into the center towards the altar he had sacrificed at the night prior, glanced up at the statue of the goddess, and whispered, "in your honor," before presenting himself to the priest and King Archidamos.

The king nodded, prompting a slave to stretch out the shield to Brasidas. "With this or on it," said Archidamos so very formally, then he winked with a couched grin made known only to the young man. Brasidas instantly knew the full extent of the warning and pledge the king had bestowed on him with that perfectly concise Spartan apothegm: *return from battle victorious with this shield or be carried dead upon it.* These words epitomized his city.

* * *

As long as the festival lasted so did their release from duty. Brasidas, as did his friends, immediately made for home. They would have two nights, then be back to the barracks.

The gate creaked as always; the air redolent with the pleasing aroma of herbs. Strangely the dogs did not bark. He rapped politely twice, and on the third the door swung open. The smile disarmed him for his father rarely displayed it for him.

"Let me see this young warrior," he said approvingly as he stepped back and ran his eyes up and down. With an ever-growing smile upon him, he clutched his son's arms, shaking him affectionately.

Deinokara relieved him of his shield. The servant wore a grave look, and seemed to avoid looking at him directly.

"Where is mother?"

"With your aunt Polyboia. We will dine at the tent of our phratry this evening." Tellis continued to beam, proud of his son, and reminded of what he was once like and the soaring emotions evoked upon this day many years past.

"Where are Atlas and Herakles?"

"Tied up in the stable."

Brasidas opened the door. "I shall be back shortly, Father. Allow me to take them for a run."

"Brasidas." He announced it not like his name but a warning. "She is gone."

"Who is gone?" His heart raced wildly. He must push these feelings deep. Reveal nothing.

"Your Helot plaything."

Brasidas worked up his best look of incredulity. "If you don't want me to run the hounds, say so."

"She has been sent to Gytheion."

"Who has been sent to Gytheion?"

Tellis clutched his son's arms again, but more firmly now, and with no trace of a smile upon his face. "You were seen. I petitioned the ephors to have her resettled. Be thankful they did not kill her."

"Be thankful," he shouted, the rage spilling from him like the torrent from an overwhelmed dam. "Why didn't you throw her in the Apothetai like you did my brother."

Tellis drove an open hand across his son's face, the red of the strike melting quickly into the blush of fury.

"I saw him. There is no doubt. No doubt too that you tossed him away like a broken pot!"

He struck again, but with more anger. Brasidas absorbed the blow, his silent defiance more than Tellis could bear. He shoved Brasidas aside, sweeping past him through the door. The gate screamed on its rusting hinge pins then crashed shut.

Deinokara bent to pick up the chair that had fallen in the fracas. Brasidas moved closer, gently gripping her tanned and wrinkled arm.

"I am sorry," he said apologetically.

"For what, Master Brasidas?"

"For behaving like him."

* * *

He would not attend the evening meal at his clan's tent, but sat propped against the trunk of a plane tree on the edge of the Field of Zeus, tearing grass from between his feet, then letting it flutter from his grip.

"You look lost."

"Epitadas." Brasidas awoke from his trance upon seeing his friend.

"Have you eaten?"

Brasidas did not reply, but continued to pluck at the grass.

"Wait here." Epitadas hurried away, returning within minutes; in his arm he cradled a bundle of linen. He tossed it into his friend's lap, then sat in the grass facing him.

"So?"

Brasidas grinned at him. "So—what?"

"So what has happened?"

Brasidas paused, peeling back the cloth. "It is Temo. She has been sent to Gytheion."

"To work at the docks? Why?"

"He did it." He reached into the basket. Out came a handful of figs. "Called her my Helot plaything."

"Truly, Brasidas, what else could she ever be?"

"But I wanted to end it, in my way." He said the words, but they seemed like they belonged to someone else.

"But—there is more?" Epitadas had the god's gift at peeling away the layers of perception that everyone worked to present.

"I have a brother."

"Why that is wonderful news," said Epitadas buoyantly. "Where is he?"

"As far from us as one could possibly be."

Thrake
Nine
ΘΡΑΚΗ

Olorus, his father, had dispatched him to the Thrakian city of Skapte-Hyle. There he would reacquaint himself with his family's holdings and connections far from Athens. The land here was rich in timber, horses, and vines, but especially gold; far from his city he would make a living as his father had.

They dressed somewhat rudely, excepting the richer merchants, mostly wrapped in coarse wool cloaks or in jerkins of animal hide. The soldiers and the wealthy strode about in boots, the poor, the children, and the slaves in bare feet. Like Athens, the city had familiar and comfortable trappings: an agora for markets and assembly; a temple of Artemis; a shrine to Herakles; a small gymnasion. But the larger portion of the city retained its barbarian nature, with vast crowds braying and baahing unintelligibly like sheep. Their red hair caught his notice, but he fought off staring. More disturbing was their notion of agreement and dissent, for if they nodded their heads they meant no, and if they shook from side to side, the response was affirmation. These Thrakians, kin of his father, were tall folk who carried the smell of their livestock with them. *They would make fine warriors*, he thought.

With his horse finally off-loaded from the freighter, he set off for the family estate. For the first time in many a year, he felt a certain satisfaction, almost a delight. He was truly on his own. His military training complete, he had talked his way out of an early marriage to a proper Athenian girl, saying that until he could discharge his responsibilities in Thrake, he would not abandon a young bride to his wanderings. Only Ataskos accompanied him, and Thukydides had managed to divert his slave to the agora to purchase some provender and wine upon disembarking. His father's holdings were extensive, and he being the only son stood to inherit it all. Now, right now, he must learn to manage them.

The road led him away from the river that it had paralleled for several miles, up into the hills that loomed over the coast. As he cleared the trees and broke into a meadow, the ocean's breath poured coolly over him. He turned to see the silver swells dancing in the harbor and the bright sailcloths of the merchant vessels tied up on the quays. A triple-banker warship, its square sail stitched with an enormous golden owl, sliced through the water, patrolling outside the breakwater. He paused and focused on the piping of the rhythm keeper on board the trireme. Beyond was the island of Thasos, smudged to the color of violet by the haze.

The boundary stones were stacked head high, painted ochre and blue. When he rode between them, the red roof tiles of the house peeked above the swaying tree tops. The gate was tied open. A slave hustled forward to grab the reins of his horse.

"He needs water," instructed Thukydides.

The slave nodded and tugged the animal off to the stables. He watched him for a moment, deciding whether to enter the house or peruse the grounds. The wide hillcrest beckoned. "My very own acropolis," he said as he scanned the vast openness of the place.

Truly it was. He could see the entire harbor and most of the city from here. With his eyes he tried to measure it all, using the memory of Athens as a gauge. The open field that surrounded the house and stables would, without difficulty, swallow the Agora back home and stretch to the base of the Areoupagos Hill. But it was far more green here. Above and behind the cliffs shot up like stony curtains hung by the gods. He sucked the salty breeze and smiled.

"Nephew."

He turned to see a block-shouldered man with a tousled beard calling to him from the shaded porch.

"Uncle Sikanos."

"You can inspect the property later. Come eat." His eyes gleamed joyously above the beard. "We saw your ship in the harbor. Gave me time to set them to cooking." He swung his platter-shaped hat toward the open doorway, inviting his nephew in.

The dampness fell upon him like a cloak as he entered. Even at midday the great hall yawned dark, lit only by a dangling triple-spouted oil lamp that twisted slightly in the breeze that he had admitted inadvertently. Jason, golden fleece in hand, his ship, the *Argo*, behind him filled one wall. Painted upon another wall were two warriors battling before an enormous towered wall. He knew Achilles by his armor, and felt a bit of sadness as he glanced to proud Hektor.

"My favorite wall is Poseidon," said Sikanos, motioning to the green-bearded sea god that flanked the doorway; he looked like a man in a bathing tub, surrounded by toy ships. But the toothy sea beasts with dish-shaped eyes that swam around him belied this first impression.

"I honor Poseidon, for he granted us an uneventful journey." Thukydides rolled onto the divan and stretched out. A servant hurried forward with a tray.

"Thasian wine. The very best."

The servant nervously filled the two cups, bowed then backed out of the hall. Beyond the inner doorway, they heard the echo of footfalls upon the polished marble.

"Father tells me we have five domestics."

"The farrier makes six actually. He is seeing to your horse now." His uncle sipped the wine slowly, attempting not to appear crude to this young Athenian. His beard glistened wet. He waited until the young man turned his attention before wiping it.

"How many horses?"

"Two dozen. Would have been more but a foal died last week. Killed by a lion."

"Did you hunt it?"

"For three days, but to no avail. But the mantis says it will return. The sign of the lion was bright in the sky last night."

* * *

Thukydides, accompanied by his uncle, toured the vineyard, the stables, and then rode off to inspect the mines. The grade proved easy for the first hour of the journey until they came to a fast-flowing stream. Here they paused to watch. Men stretched out portions of fleece, slopping them with thick coats of rancid grease mixed from animal fat. Others carried the prepared hides into the water, pegging them into the stream bed.

"What are they doing?"

"Let us see," said Sikanos in a luring tone.

The pair rode up to the bank to watch a pair of slaves untie a fleece from its pegs in the water, where after fumbling with the slippery knots, they carried it to dry land. As they shuffled up the embankment the sun hit it, setting it to a brilliant shimmer.

"Gold!"

"Yes, Nephew, it is."

"Like the golden fleece of Jason!"

A ring of women surrounded several of these hides, picking the tiny granules from the unctuous traps. Two cloth-lined baskets were already filled; a third would soon be.

"They fill about four baskets on a good day. This would seem a very good day." Sikanos rubbed his horse's neck while whispering to the animal. He reached into a bag slung over his shoulder, scooping out a handful of grain. "For you, sweetness," he said as he slipped his hand beneath the animal's searching mouth. In an instant the grain was nuzzled from his hand. Now he rapped his heels hard into the horse, turning away from the stream and back onto the mountain trail.

For another hour they rode, stopping every so often to spell the horses at Sikanos' insistence. The air grew cool and crisp. The trail tilted ever steeper. Now the murmur of distant voices could be heard mingling with the ping of metal on stone. Dust and smoke drifted above the trees ahead.

It was not like Laurion, the mines he had visited outside of Athens. That operation was vast, honey-combing the Attic hills with one-meter-square shafts. Here they mostly dug in open pits, extracting the ore more easily from the bruised and scarred earth.

"No shafts?"

Sikanos pointed. "Over there."

On the far side of the bowl-like excavation, two square shadows seemed cast upon the hillside. A small boy crawled out of one, dragging a bulging sack half his size. A man grabbed the sack and spilled it empty, then handed it back. No gold, just stone and soil.

"They are carving out a gallery first."

Thukydides counted. Sixty-seven men worked here in the pits. "How many in the tunnels?"

"Twenty, but all boys. They are the only ones who can fit."

The sky was crystal blue, but they looked to it, trying to find the source of rumbling, certain a storm, still unseen was on its way. From one of the shafts scrambled a small boy. "Cave in!"

As he tumbled out, a black cloud followed him, rolling from the shaft, ever expanding in the openness beyond. He collapsed, exhausted and sobbing.

The men ran forward to the beamed opening, anxious for the pall to clear. "There is a space!" one of them shouted.

Thukydides vaulted from his horse. "See to the boy," he commanded as he passed a dumbstruck slave. Soon he was on all fours, crawling into the shaft, eyeing the debris and what remained of the passageway. "Lamps!"

The stony soil ripped his flesh as he clawed at it. The small aperture grew. Another man, a slave, shouldered his way next to Thukydides and began tearing at the rock. He glanced to him for a moment. Thukydides returned the look. "Has this happened before?"

"Every few days. With all the timber around here, they give us little to shore up the tunnels."

Miners on the far walls of the pit barely slowed their excavation; the scrape and ping of tools upon stone echoed unabated until Thukydides screamed at them to help. Only a few moved with urgency. Most approached him dragging their implements across the floor of the pit. Now he turned to his uncle. "Where is the iatros!"

Sikanos rolled his eyes. "We have no physician here."

"Send for one now!"

Thukydides walked amongst the injured, men and boys reduced to a single hue by the gray dust of the mine, the pure crimson of blood the only other color visible as it streaked from their wounds. A man sat, holding the limp form of another in his arms as he rocked and sobbed. He squeezed the corpse tightly to him mumbling, "my brother, my brother." Thukydides paused over him, wanting to speak, to comfort, to reassure, but he could not. The words, even the thought of them, retreated.

Little by little the miners rose up and moved away until only the dying and the dead lay strewn about the opening to the shaft. He lingered there, ordering water to be hauled up, organizing the litter bearers, keeping the uninjured to these and other tasks and did not even consider leaving until the iatros had arrived with his attendants. He waved to Sikanos, who sat upon his horse in the shade of a tall pine, to join him on the road.

They took the trail to the crossing where his slaves filtered gold. There he bathed quickly. The cold water soothed his bruises but reminded him of every open cut and scrap. His uncle sat upon his horse watching in silence. They did not linger here, but continued their descent toward the coast until Sikanos led him to a new trail.

"Where are you taking me?" he said curtly.

"You will see." Sikanos rapped his horse gently.

They could hear their destination long before they could see it. The distinctive snap of ax upon wood resonated all along the slope. The din led them into a clearing filled with men and wagons.

Axes struck in alternation as a trio attacked the thick-trunked pine, chunks of yellow pulpy wood exploding with each strike. Louder by far than any ax strike, a crackle boomed from the trunk, scattering the men. The tree shivered, its foliage dancing in the breezeless afternoon. Another crackle, then the tree-top swayed; the cleft trunk crunched under its own twisting weight, until finally the tall pine swooned with a whoosh. The great tree struck, bounced, then struck again. Like spearshafts the trees grew true and straight, fine timber for shipbuilders.

They stayed and watched for a while as the lumbermen hacked away the branches, leaving a long tapering shaft pocked with sap-oozing scars. The air was pungent with resin. Slaves dragged the discarded limbs to a pit where they fed a smoldering fire.

"Come, nephew," said Sikanos. "We shall ride along with the wagon."

Before they departed Thukydides turned to the foreman. "The subsequent wagonload goes to the mines."

The man looked awkwardly to Sikanos for confirmation.

"What? Don't you understand me?" shouted Thukydides.

Sikanos nodded discretely.

"You care too much for slaves, nephew."

"No more than you do for your horse." He struck off, breaking his horse to a gallop.

"The value of my horse far exceeds that of any slave," he yelled as he set to pursue.

The road proved steep and difficult to negotiate for the fully laden timber wagon. Even roped tight, the load of four trunks groaned and twisted with every bump, turn, and unexpected descent. By late afternoon they had made the harbor, just in time to see a wide-beamed Korinthian trader slip into port.

Thukydides had seen them before, but not often; Korinthians were not welcome in Athens but had on occasion been allowed to dock at the Piraios during squalls, a begrudged courtesy extended in deference to Zeus and Poseidon. The sailors looked the same to him, swearing as much as any Athenian, while they worked the rigging and wrestled with the great square-cloth sail.

"This is our client's vessel," said Sikanos. "Where is your captain?" he shouted to a crewman who knelt nearby working a line dexterously through a ring on the quay.

He snapped his head to the side, pointing with his chin to the stern. There stood a red-faced Korinthian, his skin made darker by his crown of thinning white hair. Beside him stood two men, both about the same age as Thukydides, their hair long in locks, with red cloaks draped about their shoulders.

"Spartans," said Thukydides, mildly amazed. He stared awkwardly at the two until they returned his gaze.

"This your timber?" barked the captain.

"Is yours now if the price is agreeable." His uncle imitated their Dorian accent.

The two Spartans stepped forward, spun their cloaks about their arms for convenience, then disembarked. The first nodded to Sikanos as he passed; the second one smiled.

"Are they our buyers?" he said in a guarded voice to his uncle.

"I assume so. I was told that a Korinthian would put into port for it. Didn't know he was hired out." Sikanos watched them as they walked the timber from end to end. "Spartans do not build ships."

"No, but our friends do," said one, still smiling. "I am Brasidas, and this is my companion Epitadas, both of Pitane." He extended his hand.

Thukydides reached out with his. "I am Thukydides, son of Olorus, from the village of Halimos. This is my uncle, Sikanos."

"An Athenian," bellowed the captain from above as he leaned over the rail. "Long way from home."

"So are we all," added Brasidas.

* * *

Although his uncle did not approve, Thukydides invited the Spartans to the estate on the hill. The groundskeeper netted several lark and a half dozen quail. His guests supplied pomegranates and quince, part of their cargo.

Brasidas sipped from the kylix. "Excellent wine."

"From Thasos," said Sikanos, grinning with satisfaction.

Epitadas slid his still full cup atop a table. He enjoyed the quail, but left most of the wine to his hosts.

"Forgive me, sirs, if I seem impertinent, but I have been told that Spartiates rarely travel. Your presence here confounds that notion." Thukydides' curiosity got the better of his manners.

"Nephew!"

"Oh it is quite all right, sir. The observation is an honest one, and I shall endeavor an explanation." Brasidas lifted the kylix and sipped. "It is true that we travel infrequently. But on the other hand Sparta has many visitors, some who insist on reciprocating our hospitality."

"So you visit guest-friends in Thrake?"

"Not in Thrake, Master Thukydides. In the Chalkidike. We put in here for your timber." Epitadas looked into the cup, frowned, then abandoned it again.

"You do not like your wine?" Thukydides seemed puzzled. "Thasian wine is amongst the very best."

"The wine is very good," said Epitadas politely. "It is the amount I frown upon."

"Should we thin it?" offered Thukydides.

"I would not presume to instruct you as to serving wine, but we drink only to quench our thirst. Anything more is—well, not for Spartans."

"So you sail for the Chalkidike?" quizzed Sikanos, moving them away from the question of wine. "To what port, may I inquire?"

"Skione. Timber for friends." Brasidas felt at ease amongst these foreigners. For a young Spartiate he had seen much outside his native city, listened to foreign speech, and tasted the diverse fare of strange lands.

"For warships?" Thukydides asked.

"For trollers," answered Brasidas.

"And you, Master Thukydides. What are you doing so far from Athens, in such a fine house?"

"My grandfather's family hails from Thrake."

Brasidas stared at him, smiling. "But I do not see a trace of red on that head of yours."

They all laughed, even Thukydides. So unlike a Spartan, Brasidas could disarm with words. He spoke to them respectfully, but with a comforting humor that encouraged trust, evoking an easy manner in them all. Quickly his young host lost his uncommon smile, summoning the stern and grave manner he thought more suitable.

"When do you sail?" Thukydides asked. He studied Brasidas; the young man's long hair seemed an anachronism to him, for this style had long been abandoned in Athens.

"Tomorrow, before the weather turns," answered Brasidas. Late summer ushered in the unpredictable mistrals that would sweep down from the north, increasing the hazard of a sea voyage to the Chalkidike. Even the Great King Xerxes, almost forty years past, had a immense channel cut across the peninsula to avoid rounding it in a chancy sea. The canal he had dug now sat choked with silt. They would sail south on this very route he sought to avoid.

"Then I must learn all I can about Sparta tonight." Thukydides meant this not as a pleasantry of conversation, but in all earnest. Few men he knew had conversed with Spartans. The war had kept them separate. Peace and a fortuitous visit afforded him this chance inquiry.

"And what would you like to know of our city?" Epitadas' eyes gleamed with pride.

"Can you read?"

The answer brought another admonishment from his uncle, and as before Epitadas contained himself graciously.

"Of course I can. Why do you ask such an odd question?"

"Because my teacher once said that Spartans can neither read nor write." Epitadas mused a bit. "And has your teacher ever been to Sparta?"

Thukydides restrained his reply, his silence as good as an answer.

"No other questions?" Epitadas finally lifted his cup to his lips.

"Are you ruled by your women?"

"By the gods, who has been teaching you?" Brasidas' face contorted under his attempt to suppress the laughter that threatened to erupt. "We hear legends that no Athenian can tell the truth. These I dismissed along with the frightening tales of childhood about baby-eating gryphons, satyrs and gorgons."

"But you are different, are you not?"

"Than you Athenians, certainly." Brasidas realized at this moment how Kleandridas felt quizzing him, imbued with an enjoyable yet benevolent power.

"How are we different?" Thukydides leaned forward, anxious for the answer.

"We both follow the law—only we do not change it so easily when it suits an immediate purpose, as you do."

"I did not realize Spartans were also educated in rhetorika and erastics."

"As I understand it, is it not a technique used to win an argument at the expense of the truth?"

Thukydides' sternness became magnified. "In a manner of speaking, yes. I think what you mean is that one skilled in rhetorika can present a persuasive argument, in spite of facts."

Brasidas grinned. "Ah, so many words for so little expressed. So our conception of Athenians is accurate."

Epitadas cleared his throat loudly. "Gentlemen, the war is over. Let us keep it that way."

"Forgive me," apologized Brasidas. "I meant only to engage in conversation as I thought an Athenian would."

Sikanos, smiling with pride, began to boast of his home and a subject they might find less contentious. "There is everything here a man could want. Gold, timber, horses, grain, and of course the very best wine." He drained his kylix in a gulp. "And all secured by our allies in the north and by our colony of Amphipolis, and the River Strymon to the south."

The two Spartans smiled and nodded in agreement. Thukydides artfully added, "Uncle, there is no reason to remind our guests of the abundance here in Thrake and our diligent military that protects it. We are now friends."

"Master Thukydides, I thank you," now Brasidas turned toward Sikanos, "and your uncle for your hospitality, but we must be off. We sail at the turning of the tide, and that is well before dawn."

Thukydides and Sikanos walked out with their guests through the courtyard to the stables where the farrier had gathered the Spartans' horses.

"Torches," ordered Sikanos.

"We have no need of them, sir. Thank you, just the same." Brasidas swung up onto his mount and tugged the reins taunt. "I invite you to my home, sirs, to try some modest Spartan fare." Brasidas nodded good-bye. The pair slipped into the black of night, the clatter of horses' hooves fading with them.

"They are not the monsters that Saleuthos said they were," said Epitadas as they rode the descending trail toward the harbor. "I saw no evil in them."

"Do not say such a thing, my friend, even if it's true."

Epitadas reined to a halt. "Why?"

"Most men, taken one at a time, appear little different than you or me, Thukydides included. But he is from Athens, a city where men are bright, ingenious, and full of energy. But it is also a place where ambition tramples duty. Yes he is an Athenian—a dangerous condition for which there is no cure."

Lakedaimon
Ten
ΛΑΚΕΔΑΙΜΑ

Their freighter dipped under the heavy swells whipped up by the northeast wind, its mast and rigging moaning with dread, its crew hushed. He sighted the harbor, flickering torchlights visible through the smothering spray. His heart lightened. Upon the single bark of a command from the pilot, hollow echoes of oars clattered as the rowers shoved them outboard, preparing to heave the ship to land. Above him the broad sail fluttered in protest as the crew worked the rigging, furling it in. Brasidas stood on the bow like the carved figurehead of a god, staring ahead through the gloom, eyes fixed upon Gytheion. Directly ahead a lone figure stood on the edge of the quay waving a torch.

"This be a rough one," warned the captain. "Sir, I would advise ye to stand amidships till we dock."

Unmoving, Brasidas merely smiled. For sure it was a rough one, the fog, the spray, the shuddering waves all pushed them far beyond the familiar to a realm of uncertainty. He shouldered his courage like a shield, accepting the challenge without hesitation. As they turned broadside to the wind, the vessel rocked violently, whipping the naked mast to and fro, loose freight drumming in the hold. Everything on deck glistened wet; several men careened across the slick deck as they moved to their stations while the captain, braced by the rail, staggered to the bow and commenced to shout orders. Now the rowers dug into the waves as the pilot leaned hard into the steer-board. No one needed encouragement or coercion; the storm set the pace and the pace was frantic indeed. Thankfully, and due to the vigor of their efforts, they slipped into the shadow of land, leaving the wind behind, but the rocking stayed in their legs until they slid alongside the quay.

Brasidas vaulted over the rail, not waiting for the dockman to work the lines. His legs wobbled. He extended an arm, bracing against the convenient sacks of freight and files of amphora that crowded the pier. It took a moment

85

for normal balance to return before he could step without swaying to the rhythm of the sea. "I shall meet you at Poseidon's temple."

Epitadas yelled out, "You won't find her. In ten years you haven't."

He paused only for a moment waiting for his friend's words to catch then pass him, but did not acknowledge or respond. Quickly he put the pier behind him.

The dank morning cast a trance-like spell upon the harbor town, more shadow than substance as it seemingly hung numbingly in the mist. Movement, indistinct at first, drew his eyes to a handful of fishermen, their salt-stained nets slung from shoulder to shoulder and looking like a great lifeless serpent as they trudged by him toward the beach. His attention quickly refocused; a few feet before him a stream of rancid water shot out into the alley followed by a hasty slam of a door. He wacked the door as he passed, instigating a muffled curse from within. Most every ramshackle he passed nudged the alley in brutal starkness, each small window shuttered, every weathered door sealed shut.

His thoughts moved to higher places. Quietly he thanked Poseidon for his safe return and called upon Artemis for a small favor. After a quarter-hour's walk, the alleyway opened up into a wide boulevard, its earth bruised by wheeled carts and the spade-like hooves of sumpter beasts. The torn earth exuded the rank smell of a blend of manure, swill, and mud; without a breeze it pressed against him, moving him even quicker.

Ahead three women stood in the doorway of a fuller's shop, their hands bleached white from cleaning linen. They lowered their gaze in obeisance as he approached. These were new faces, faces that for the past ten years have never had the question put to them.

"Do you know a woman named Temo?"

The three mumbled unintelligibly amongst themselves, then shook their heads.

"Are you sure? She came from the north. From Sparta."

They mumbled. They shook their heads. He walked on.

Coming upon the edge of the agora, he heard the groan of a ripper's cart as it wheeled toward him. Two men led a mule team harnessed to it, the smell of fish hung like an invisible cloud around them.

"You, man!" shouted Brasidas to the older of the two.

They stopped. The cart rocked to a stand-still. "Say again," growled the older one as he bent forward cupping his hand behind an ear.

"Temo, do you know her?"

"A Spartan like yourself?"

"No. A Helot."

The younger one scratched his mangy head, then picked and plucked, grooming it for lice. "'Bout your years, sir?" he offered. "At the armorer's, sir."

"How long ago?"

"Last month, but me can't be sure. Memory, ya know. It comes 'n' goes like the tide."

He pushed by the pair, through the agora and beyond, following the road to the weapons forge where Helots rolled barrows of wood through a door into the orange glow within. The line advanced by a meter or two, then paused, each man straining to balance his load on the single tiny wheel of his barrow. Again they heaved forward a bit. Again they halted. He strode past them all as though he were foreman, owner, and king of the place. Inside several furnaces were fired, two boys working each bellows. Women ducked low, shoving half arm's lengths of wood into each burner.

"Temo?" He tugged a young women away from the wood.

She stared back, eyes white with fear. Again he asked, but received no answer.

In the corner near where they unloaded the barrows, a women stood, who brushed the wood dust from her while glancing his way. By her body she looked to be his mother's age, but by her face much older.

"Taken by a Spartan, not but two days ago."

"Taken to where?"

"Sparta, I reckon."

"Was he young or old? Did he have a name?"

"No name, none at least that I heard talked. The woman was afeared of him as though he were Death himself." Suddenly her eyes widened as she was struck with recollection. "But his mouth was empty and black as night."

* * *

By early evening they rode into Amyklai, then took the Hyakinthia Road north to Sparta. On the outskirts of Therapne, in the shadow of the Menelaion Hill, several riders approached. They slowed, keeping their gaze upon them. Even with their keen eyesight, the two groups of riders virtually reined to a halt, staring through the gloom at each other, searching for recognition.

"Turtle," shouted Brasidas finally. Styphon and Polyakas reined up beside him, flashing smiles, but quickly their manner turned serious. A fourth rider trotted into view. It was his father, Tellis.

"What is it?" Brasidas asked directly of Turtle, not acknowledging his father as he reined up.

Turtle looked to Tellis, deferring the answer to him. "King Pleistoanax has been exiled." Brasidas said nothing. His manner alone beckoned further explanation. His father tugged on the reins to steady his horse. "Archidamos, Kratesikles, and the other Eurypontids drummed up charges of collusion with Athens." Finally his horse settled down. "Kleandridas is gone too."

"Gone where?"

"Tegea perhaps. We do not know. It all happened quickly. No assembly. Just the ephors and the Geruosia ruled. No one to challenge them."

"And who else has been implicated in all of this?" Brasidas clenched his teeth as he spoke. "What of you? And mother? What of my friends?"

"Archidamos must surmise that without Pleistoanax and Kleandridas, we are no threat. Besides, you have allies." Tellis nodded confidently. "Who, by their presence, keep them in check."

"And what was Thrasymidas doing in Gytheion?"

Now his father's face turned dark. "Then you know."

"Yes."

"Brasidas, think before you act. Why did he take her? To provoke you of course. Do not dance to his flute."

"Let us go." He smacked his heels hard, sending the horse to a gallop, his father and his four comrades chasing after. In no time he rode into the agora, where he spotted youngsters posted as guards in the shadowed porticos of the public buildings, their eyes gaping at his appearance. He sped by towards the foothills. The six rumbled up to the fence beside his father's stables, setting the hounds to barking. A door creaked open, spilling a shaft of orange on to the dark blue of the night earth. Two dogs barreled out, tails wagging, jaws yapping.

"Down! Down!" He scolded them instinctively, but in truth savored their affection. The two pups of Atlas cowered at his admonishment, chins rubbing the floor while their rear ends swayed high under whipping tails.

His father led the way into the cottage and quickly latched the door shut, once inside. "Sit."

Brasidas did not answer him. His mother entered, and she also knew not to speak but stayed hovering near the doorway.

"I would think that after ten years, you would have forgotten her." He moved beside his son, looming over him like a storm. "I know how many times you have been down there, looking for her. "'Twasn't easy keeping her from you. And why do you think he takes her now? He is counting on you to come for her. He is counting on you to come to him."

"Why now? Why not last year, or ten years ago?" Brasidas squirmed in the same chair he squirmed in throughout his youth under his father's interrogations.

"Because now you are the last of their impediments."

"I am no child. I know what I am, and painfully I know what she is. I only wanted to see her one last time." Brasidas stood and began pacing in front of the hearth. Now his father took the chair.

"One more time may mean your death. He would easily prove to the ephors that any provocation was yours. That he took your life in defense of his. But now you have other lives to care for besides your own. Next summer you wed. Have you forgotten Gyllipos? Have you forgotten your city?" His father reminded him of responsibilities—his betrothed Damatria, and his protege in the Agoge Gyllipos. Both would need him. Both were Spartans. "But if all this means nothing, then think on this; you have made her prominent—a trait that will prove deadly to any Helot. If you care for her at all, forget her."

"Do not worry, Father. Do you think so little of my judgment? I will act, but when it is to my advantage."

"Son, your daimon compels you to be who you are, for it demands that you place your friends and family above yourself. You put your country above them. But you put honor above it all. The wicked will use this against you." Exhausted by the conversation, he sighed. "For them all I call upon you to take an oath. An oath to forget her. You cannot place her above our city."

It all rang true. He could not summon his anger to shield him from his father's words. He could not call upon his intellect to refute them. Reluctantly he stood before his father and bent his eyes skyward. "With Zeus as my witness, I swear never to see her. From now and forward we are dead to each other."

Tellis rose up and embraced his son as though he had seen him for the first time in many years. He wriggled his fingers at the servants in the doorway. Quickly they scurried in, pulled two plain black-glazed tankards from the chest by the hearth, then filled them from an equally homely pitcher. For a long while, the two sat in front of the hearth, emptying several deep cups in silence.

"What are they up to?" mumbled Tellis into his half-empty cup.

"Who, Father?"

"Archidamos, Kratesikles, and the rest. They charge Pleistoanax of colluding with Athens. Why, coming from Archidamos, the accusation is absurd."

"Why is that, sir?"

"Archidamos is close with Perikles, the Athenian strategos." Manners aside, his father gulped the wine now. "Pleistoanax ended the war with little cost to us and on terms to our benefit. Our allies grumble and we exile a king to placate them. Sadly it was the wrong king."

"But everyone says Athens' aim is to enslave Hellas."

"Athens wants riches, not slaves. We want security." He sipped again, then chuckled in his cup. "It is Thebes I worry about."

"Thebes? They are our ally."

"An ally of convenience. They want neither riches nor security. They are much more dangerous. They want to be noticed."

"Kleandridas never spoke kindly of them, but I thought it was because of the Great War and their alliance with Persia."

"That and other things. Athens is our rival. We contend much as two athletes do—for glory, admiration, and the crown of victory. But it ends there. Thebes does not honor the contest but seeks only the rewards. Truth be told, they would revel in our destruction along with Athens'."

* * *

Later that night, after the conversation had been exhausted, Brasidas reported to his barracks. Sthenelaidas greeted him. "Brasidas," he said curtly. "Your journey?"

"Evening, Commander. Fared well until we put ashore."

Even in the darkness outside the barracks, Sthenelaidas' broad smile shone bright. "Your comrades told you then?"

"Oh yes."

"Patience is what you need now, not action, although I know this course is contrary to your very nature." He wrapped an arm around him, leading him from the doorway. "Although I am their commander, the entire company would follow you. Do not abuse their loyalty. Wait. Opportunity will arrive, then we must both seize it—for our friends and our city."

Brasidas slipped into the barracks hall to his pallet, passing by the pair of

Helots that tended the lamps. One hundred and twenty-seven men snored; he slept little, repeating the words, "From now and forward we are dead to each other."

* * *

"He is made of iron."

Brasidas nodded in agreement with Epitadas while keeping his eyes fixed upon Gylippos. The youth tore across the playing field, leaving the four others in his wake. "His seventh race and he tires not," said Brasidas with a modicum of pride. "Faster than I ever was."

"Modesty?" Epitadas turned to him, smiling. "I never saw you follow anyone, not in a race or in any action. Or was it that we all were so eager to follow you?"

"Modesty is a trait of the vanquished. I merely state fact. His speed and stamina are superior."

"With his father gone, he will look to you all the more." Epitadas pointed. "Look. He challenges another group."

From their vantage point on the knoll, they clearly saw Gylippos waving three others to the starting line; two were older and this pair shook their heads in refusal, but there was a younger boy who took up the challenge confidently.

At the far end of the field, the pair lined up, each in a sprinter's stance, upright but with a slight lean forward. A third youth acted as judge, holding a wavering tree branch in lieu of the typical iron rod used to signal a start. He dropped the branch. The two exploded forward.

Gylippos, tired as he was, struggled to keep his slim lead. The younger boy leaned hard, pumping his arms furiously to quicken his stride. He gained a little, then a little more. His strides seemed to stretch his legs beyond control. Suddenly each step expanded wildly, sending his head lunging forward, until he tumbled. Gylippos glided to the finish, then looked back for his rival. As soon as he saw him sprawled in the dust, he trotted back and offered him a hand. The boy reached up, grasping the victor's arm, then with a tug brought him down. They rolled on the ground in a fit of laughter.

Brasidas smiled at the tussle until he spied the paidonomos enter the field with his squad of whipping boys. He fired a piercing whistle, then yelled out, "Gylippos!"

The youth sprang to his feet, brushed the dirt from him frantically as he jogged up the slope toward the summons. All the way he kept his eyes down, watching his own feet and nothing else.

Brasidas wrapped his arm around the boy's shoulder. "And how many did you beat today?"

"Twenty in all."

"And who was that?" he asked, looking down to the field. "The plucky one who challenged you last?"

"He is Lysandros."

"Do I know his family?"

"Indeed. He is the son of Aristokleitos."

Brasidas knew him. A friend of Saleuthos, his commander in the Agoge. He also knew that if he was like his father, he hung precariously to his citizenship; his modest farm barely produced the minimum required for retention in a military mess. One bad harvest and he would be out. That is why Aristokleitos never shied away from a chance to prove himself. "Cut from the same cloth," he mumbled.

"I will see you at supper?" Epitadas yelled back over his shoulder as he trotted away.

Brasidas nodded. "Would not miss it. You bring the game tonight. Venison, I hear?"

Gylippos looked at him, eyes beaming joy and confidence. Then like an actor changing masks, he became dark-browed.

"Thinking of your father?"

"Yes, sir. You remind me of him."

"You honor me with the comparison." He led the boy toward a copse of plane trees that dominated the hill above. Late afternoon and this favorite haunt of the older Spartiates who would keep watch over the training was now vacant.

"Sit."

Gylippos folded to the earth cross-legged at the command. Brasidas lowered himself to one knee, studying the boy. A cool breeze swept up from the Eurotas; its reed-covered banks seemed to shiver. The boy fell back, stretching out like a hide on a tanner's board.

"He will return soon."

"That is not what the others say. They say King Archidamos will never let them back."

"And who are they?"

"The boys in my troop. And the paidonomos. They say my father and

King Pleistoanax betrayed Sparta."

"You know better, as do I. But we are the enlightened ones," he said, laughing. "Others may take longer to comprehend the obvious."

The boy lay on his back, the cool grass caressing his naked form as he watched the clouds glide overhead. Brasidas continued to study him contentedly, awash with memories of his own youth, reminded of tough but carefree days while in the throes of the Agoge. From the field below a salphinx trumpeted out the call to assemble. "I must go." He bounced to his feet, then launched into a sprint, soon disappearing into the swirl of boys forming at the end of the field. A piper struck up a rhythm-keeping tune while the boys commenced to belt out verses of the paian.

He stayed upon the hill, watching the band of youths tromp off toward their barracks. The sun angled low, stretching shadows and coloring the western sky the scarlet of war-cloaks. In the past this would be an evening to savor. This fleeting pleasantness poured from him like wine from a shattered cup. Like the cup, he felt broken and empty.

* * *

"We play tomorrow," said Epitadas enthusiastically. "Against the Limnain team."

Epitadas, Turtle, and Styphon stared, grinning. Brasidas cleared his throat then spit. He arched his eyebrows in a question, then shrugged his shoulders before he strode off.

"Did you hear me?" Epitadas ran after him.

"Yes. Another game of battle-ball," Brasidas replied apathetically.

"Not just another game. The Limniain team and Thrasymidas!"

He continued to walk away from his three comrades, keeping silent. They caught up, buzzing around him like flies around milk. "This is your chance. Even the score with that empty head," insisted Turtle.

"That is what he would expect. That is what everyone expects." He kept moving.

"Then why disappoint them," whispered Styphon as he tugged at his friend's shoulder.

Abruptly Brasidas turned to face the trio. "I will play, but not for vengeance. I play for victory."

* * *

The morning had been more than hot; this afternoon the very ground shimmered beneath their feet, liquefied by the relentless gaze of Helios. The two teams stood upon the field at the Plantanistas, this being marked out in a rectangle bisected by a shallow trough. The rule of the game is simple—advance the ball across the midline. How to accomplish this was not. Fifteen young men comprised each team, all between the ages of twenty and thirty.

Brasidas, captain of the Pitanate squad, looked across the field, assessing the enemy. He watched to see which ones eagerly moved to the front of their pack as they formed. He took note of the less enthusiastic. A few even held trepidation in their gaze. In front of them all, hands on hips and head cocked sideways, loomed Thrasymidas; he turned toward Brasidas bearing a cavernous grin, then scooped a bit of dust and rubbed it over his forearms to soak up the sweat.

The teams lined up facing each other, a phalanx in miniature, two ranks deep. One of the five bidaioi, or games supervisors, stood outside the rectangle holding a head-size leather ball, wrinkled and malformed like an immense raisin. Each one of them kept an eye on him and an eye on his opponent directly across the line, crouched low and ready for the inevitable collision. The official tossed the ball over the midline, sending both sides crashing.

It remained loose for only a moment, by chance being struck to the Limniain side. There Alkidas snatched it up and surged forward. "Push!" he screamed. "Push them over!"

Unlike their mock battles, the playing field was purposely narrow, leaving no room for maneuver. This was a test of strength and stamina, plain and simple, and the more experienced men from Limniai were inching forward. "On!" shouted Alkidas.

Brasidas drove his legs hard, heaving toward his adversary's screams. He felt a pinch upon his arm; a Limniain had clamped his teeth into his biceps. Brasidas drove the butt of his hand into his forehead, sending him clear. The wound oozed hot-wet.

In the midst of the tangle of bodies, he pushed, glancing back and forth at the ones before him, looking for a misplaced foot or twisted leg, anything that might gain an advantage for him. Unexpectedly their ranks shuddered, driven back by another surge of the Limniains.

"Push!" bellowed Alkidas. "Another foot! Push!"

Brasidas, his feet dug into the earth for purchase, leaned forward, imparting every ounce of his strength and mass to obstruct his opponents' advance. He looked for a weakness, but saw none. His feet began to slide backwards. Turtle dropped to all fours beside him, pushing his knees and hands into the churned soil. Still they slid. Across from him he saw Thrasymidas crumble to his knees, bereft of balance and vulnerable. No one would see him strike now. Suddenly the ball flashed before him, but a foot from his face, cradled in an arm, but otherwise unprotected. Alkidas, in his haste to push it across the midline, exposed the prize.

"No!" Brasidas shot his right fist at the ball; it flew from Alkidas' grip, bouncing wildly to the back-line of the Limniains. Their wall of bodies crumbled like a dam overwhelmed by winter rains. Styphon and Turtle, still on all fours, scrambled forward like dogs. Styphon fell on the ball, then Turtle fell on him, followed by the entire Limniain team. Brasidas stood and bellowed out the cry of victory. The crowd ringing the Plantanistas exploded with cheers.

He heard the sound of groaning at his feet; there lay Thrasymidas, writhing in pain, cradling his arm. A sliver of slick gray erupted through the skin. He tried to lift the arm, but it dangled uselessly from his elbow. A hideous crackle emanated from the wound, followed by spewing blood.

"You!"

Brasidas turned to find Kratesikles barreling toward him, walking staff held overhand like a spear in battle. He struck at him several times, landing sharp blows upon his crossed forearms. Brasidas stood, accepting the beating until Damonidas arrested a swing mid-course. "Enough," he said snarling. "Go to your son."

Kratesikles' face boiled red, veins pulsing at his temples, until his unvented rage finally subsided. He shoved Brasidas aside then knelt to tend to Thrasymidas. No other moved to help him, but left father and son alone in the trampled dust of the Plantanista. Brasidas ignored the pair and the cheers and embraces of his teammates as he pushed his way off the field and onto the road, returning quietly to his barracks where he cleaned and wrapped his wounds before supper. Unsetteld by both Thrasymidas' injury and Kratesikles' accusations, he mulled over the empty triumph, a triumph without honor. Finally his comrades rumbled in, carrying the cheer of Nike with them. He could hardly manage a grin.

"Look at our captain," commanded Epitadas, addressing his buoyant teammates. "By the gods, you would think him defeated."

Brasidas sat upon the edge of his pallet, arms upon his knees, twirling a comb between his fingers.

Polyakas, understanding his friend more than the others, abstained from joking. He lowered himself onto the pallet next to him. "Why don't you celebrate?"

Brasidas, still fingering the comb answered, "There is no glory in defeating other Spartans."

Athens
Eleven
ΑΘΗΝΑ

He had been here a half-dozen times since meeting the Spartans, and each time he landed in Skapte-Hale, he recalled that evening vividly. Now Thukydides was forced to return to Athens; news of the battle between the Korkyreans and their mother city, Korinth, had compelled the recall of all Athenian citizens. Korkyra had petitioned Athens for aid; Korinth was a staunch ally of Sparta. War loomed at the threshold.

Good omens. Dolphins, companions to the god Apollo, raced ahead of their bow since they turned westward at Sounion, guiding them it seemed, toward the harbor at Piraios. As they veered north-west, a southerly filled their sail, pushing them effortlessly; the oars were stowed as the breeze did the work. Through the mid-afternoon haze, he spotted small blossoms of color sprouting on the horizon.

"Warships!" bellowed a crewman who had shinnied up the mast as a lookout. "Fifty. All Athenian," he added through a proud grin.

By early evening they passed the picket of triremes, slicing through the swollen waves that raked the waters off the harbor. Thukydides bent over the rail, spying the quays that swarmed with dock-wallopers, sailors, and merchants, all busy with the typical trade of the port. From the starboard a trireme cut deep and fast, passing them as though they stood at anchor, the rhythm-keepers piping the only sound reaching them over the slap of the waves. Oars plunged and pulled, then rose gleaming from the water, only to slice quickly down once more.

He strained to make out the vessels in each of the three harbors. Zea and Munichia, the circular two facing them now, housed the ship-sheds of the navy. War triremes poked out of these like eels out of their burrows, sleek, black, and baring the polished bronze fangs of battle.

The third harbor, Kantharos, lay beyond the outstretch of land that formed the head of the Piraios. All along the shore, hazy snakes of smoke writhed skyward from the shops, manufactories, and warehouses. Gaggles of boys ran in amongst the rocks, hunting gulls and playing at war. The ship groaned. The rudder bit hard into the swells while the bow swung toward the crenellated walls that traced every bit of coastline. From a tower flanking the open gateway, a signaler waved them through.

Merchantmen filled the slips. They would have to drop anchor off the quays and ride a skiff to shore, until one of the freighters had taken its cargo and departed—a long wait, for the tide would not turn for several hours.

"Come," beckoned Eukles as he vaulted into the tender. A pair of slaves manned an oar each, and they hardly appreciated the awkwardness with which Eukles had arrived. The boat rocked with each step, eliciting mute sneers of disdain from the rowers.

"Sit down. I wish to arrive dry, my friend." Thukydides cautioned him several times, but Eukles would have none of his serious nature; he purposely tromped to and fro, scaring the slaves and dismaying, not humoring Thukydides. Tired of his boisterous march he crumpled to the bench.

"They do not allow children aboard these," admonished Thukydides.

"Nor ancient, humorless men." Eukles smiled disarmingly. His comrade returned only a scowl. "You are a melancholy friend. More so than even your father."

"Because I do not play the fool?"

"No, because you are afraid to play the fool. I think you would die if someone laughed at you."

Eukles knew not to speak further, and took to watching the dockworkers tossing cargo on and off the multitude of swollen traders that jammed the Kantharos.

Thukydides felt the truth in these words strike him. They penetrated the armor that he donned every day, reminding him that he was mortal and a creature of pain. No one shall ever know. As a boy he cultivated few friendships, still fewer as young man. He feared Eukles' tolerance wore thin.

Discarding conversation the pair jumped to the dock. No sooner did their feet hit than they were assaulted by a rag-worn gang of youths, hands fingering the air as they pleaded for a coin.

"Kind sirs, an obol. Food for my sick mother."

"Your sick mother wants food?" quizzed Eukles with a smile.

"Noble sirs, Death is at her door," said a dark-eyed, stick-thin boy.

Thukydides, motivated more by impatience than sympathy, reached for a coin. Eukles placed his hand upon his friend's, stopping him short of the purse.

"How long has it been since she has eaten?" Eukles asked as he knelt, looking eye to eye.

"A week, sir." The boy's face pleaded for compassion.

"I will pay for a feast," announced Eukles.

Thukydides' dark-browed face went white. Eukles clasped his friend's hand, while his look spoke of patience.

"You seem to be an honest lad. And your comrades too." Eukles surveyed the lot of them, smiling. They smiled back, meekly but with satisfaction.

"A feast for your mother, then."

The skinny one flung out an open hand.

"Oh no. I would not give you the money, then have you risk it by dealing with the unscrupulous types in the Piraios who would rob a simple lad like yourself." Eukles grabbed the boy's open hand. "Lead on. I should like to meet her myself."

The boy stood dumb as a post, staring at him. Thukydides, caught off guard at first, began to grin.

"Come, come. We must be off. Lead on."

The boy wrenched his hand free of Eukles, and stumbled backwards. The panicked gang bolted, sending ripples through the crowd as they escaped.

Eukles let out a belly laugh. "Wait!" he yelled mockingly. "Our feast." He and the dock-men around them laughed. In his fit of humor he turned to his friend, catching the remnant of a smile as he pulled it back.

"Ah! You do have teeth."

"Teeth are for eating." Thukydides, tip-lipped, motioned ahead. "I want to see the arsenal."

They followed the main road south that cut across the Piraios toward the military harbors. Soon they would pass before the arsenal of Philon and then take the east road to the city.

It was by far the most imposing of the buildings at the Piraios—over 120 meters long, twice as wide as his house in Athens and capped at each end by massive double bronze doors. These yawned open as they approached, squealing and groaning on their over-burdened hinge pins. Into the arsenal slaves pulled two wheeled carts filled with rigging, stowed sails, anchor stones, and other paraphernalia of warships. Thukydides peered into the building. Shafts of golden light sliced through the dark interior, spilling from square windows high on the walls. Inside huge chests alternated with aisles, forming a criss-cross pattern the entire length of its interior. Into these, slaves folded brilliantly colored sailcloth. Upon the walls hung coils of rope, stacks of hooked gaffs, and polished cedar oars. He fell in behind one of the carts, but with a single exaggerated stride, a youthful guard stepped into his path. "Can't let you pass, sir." He squeezed his spear nervously, but would not relinquish his position. Eukles grabbed his friend by the arm and led him away. "Serious business, I would say."

The walk from the Piraios proved welcome after the day-long cruise on the freighter. It would take them an hour or so depending on how much traffic choked the slender road that cut between the Long Walls, monuments to self-reliance that Themistokles had built after the Persian invasion. He looked up. Tall and majestic, the High City reflected the bronze light of late afternoon. Thukydides strained to spot the great statue of Athena, her golden-tipped spear gripped in her right hand gleamed like a beacon, arresting his sight.

"There is no other city like it."

"For once, you are right," admitted Thukydides.

With the approach of evening, the usually crowded streets began to empty, allowing for quick passage right up to the agora. Before the steps of the Strategion, a large crowd had gathered around a speaker, forgetful of the hour or so, mesmerized by his words, time no longer prodded them. Every so often the crowd growled in agreement, while heads nodded.

"Let's hear what he has to say," urged Eukles.

Like most audiences, the fringes were loosely packed. The two easily slipped nearer to the steps until the congestion bade them stop.

"Look. It is Kleon!"

Thukydides' glance shot up, as though the larum of an enemy attack had been sounded. Indeed it was Kleon, prancing back and forth across the wide top step of the Strategion.

"...and so Perikles says be satisfied with your lot and do not provoke the Spartans. If I were him, I too would be satisfied with mine. A fine estate. A fine inheritance. Wealthy beyond your dreams or mine."

"Why does he upbraid Perikles? Athens prospers under his guidance." Thukydides, not answering, placed a finger before his lips to quiet Eukles.

"I, like you, must work for my bread. I am not satisfied with my lot, are you?"

Again the mass grumbled in assent.

"Tell me, good citizens, how many here have a Spartan king as their guest-friend? Our general Perikles does." He spun around and pointed at the doors of the Strategion where the ten elected generals convened for their deliberations.

Thukydides felt his face grow hot, hotter than the day Kleon had crossed paths with him returning from the palaestra. "Let's go." He pushed his way back out through the milling crowd, drawing cross looks from the few he bumped. Eukles hesitatingly followed.

"You really despise him, don't you?" asked Eukles as he pulled up shoulder to shoulder with him.

Thukydides kept moving, his gait changing from a walk to a determined march, all the while Eukles peppered him with talk, trying to provoke a response. At the edge of the Agora he suddenly stopped. "In days past, Kleon only tormented me. Now his ambition moves him to do the same to Perikles. Who next? He is a man who measures himself not by his accomplishments, but by the failures of others." He recommenced his march toward his house. After several minutes they turned onto his street, catching sight of the white-and-ochre-painted walls of the courtyard, and from within he heard men singing. From the unshuttered windows, bright light and music poured forth.

"A welcome-home celebration?"

"Father does not expect me for several days." He paused at the gateway of the courtyard, listening. "Come, Eukles. I am sure Father can accommodate two more."

Alexon, bent over from his years, appeared like a shade in the columned courtyard wall. "Master Thukydides, should I announce you?"

"I think I will announce myself," he said with a bit of defiance dredged up from his encounter with Kleon.

He strode through the door into the andron, as though he had been at the symposion all along and was returning from nature's call.

"Why it is the young master," announced a curly bearded man who reclined on a couch near Olorus.

He recognized him immediately. "General Perikles, good evening." He scanned the room quickly. Hagnon, a close companion of Perikles, he also recognized. Another he supposed to be Phormio, for he knew where Hagnon went so did he. He walked straight to his father's couch.

"Father, I hope you are well," he said rather stiffly.

"Fine, I am fine. And your voyage?"

"Endurable."

Perikles laughed the loudest at the response. "Don't you like the sea?"

"Not as much as our city," he answered, "and its dry and motionless soil."

Perikles winked in approval. "I would, with your father's permission, entertain you with some introductions." Now Perikles lifted his kylix as a pointer, careful not to spill any wine as he moved it about. "General Hagnon, I think you have met. And General Phormio. And General Proteas, whose son Epikles I believe you also know."

"Gentlemen," he said respectfully as he looked directly at each of them. "This is my good friend Eukles."

"Well, lads, sit and join us. I am sure your time at sea has whetted your appetite for some Athenian delicacies." His father rarely exhibited such sociability, especially in his presence, but the wine had been at work for quite awhile so he excused the odd behavior.

Bublo entered, shuffling along as best she could, anxious to bring Thukydides and Eukles a platter of remnant food. Three onions, a handful of olives, and a small bowl of figs sat upon Bublo's platter. "Master Thukydides, we have soup." He whispered to her to fetch the soup; she returned shortly with two deep bowls. The two sipped quietly as they listened to the talk.

"The Korinthians are fomenting trouble. We should prepare," insisted Proteas over the rim of his cup.

"Prepare for what?" Perikles asked, somewhat distracted by his empty cup and the slowness with which a servant filled it.

"War. Sparta will come to Korinth's aid, as we have done with Korkyra."

"Korkyra is an island. The Spartans may be unrivaled soldiers, but I believe they still cannot march across water." They all laughed at Phormio's words. Thukydides and Eukles did also, but more out of politeness than humor evoked.

"King Archidamos says his country does not desire war," said Perikles over the fading laughter. "Pleistoanax is still in exile and can exert nothing to the contrary." Now he smiled as Bublo filled his kylix. Unexpectedly he looked at Thukydides. "I understand you met a pair of Spartans at Skapte-Hale. Entertained them to dinner, if I am not mistaken." He glanced to Olorus for confirmation.

"Years past. Not what I expected at all."

"Hmmm. And what did you expect?" Perikles dangled the cup beneath his lips, then drank slowly, savoring the wine.

"I cannot say. Someone less—"

"—like us!" broke in Perikles. "King Archidamos told me of the two you met, Epitadas and Brasidas. Both companions to Pleistoanax, and both to be held in check by the more sensible in Sparta."

"In check?" Thukydides blurted out.

"Pleistoanax's friends hope to rescind his exile. A war would expedite their wish."

Thukydides frowned at these words.

"You do not concur?" Phormio said upon noticing his face.

"Oh I do not deem the two I met would hesitate a bit at the invitation to war. But neither do I think they would risk their country for the sake of a single man."

"For a single man, no. But to secure their alliances and at the same time bring him home, I am certain they would. Their advocate, Pleistoanax, authored the last peace only reluctantly. Ironically his enemies at Sparta used this to fashion his exile."

Olorus cleared his throat to gain attention. "We talk of enemies, and you mention Sparta. I see danger closer at hand."

Perikles eyes widened. "Do you?"

"Come now, dear gentlemen," Olorus said. "Which offers more peril, a vast enemy outside our walls, or a single one within? One dangerous man, who craves power, could easily steer the people toward destruction. Smooth talk flows easily through empty heads."

Now the men burst into laughter. Hagnon, the first to quiet down, shook his head. "Do you accuse Perikles here of smooth talk?"

"Of course I do." Suddenly silence struck the andron as they all stared at Olorus. "But his intentions are honorable. Athens is his bride, and he would do nothing to defame her. Others—demagogues—would intoxicate our city with false promises, seduce it, then once satisfied, abandon it like a used whore."

Sparta
Twelve
ΣΠΑΡΤΗ

Brasidas watched as his two sons hurtled through the yard, chasing imaginary foes in their mock battle. Damatria, his wife, smiled warmly at him as he held them in view, thankful for the brief time their city would allow them to be a family. Zeuxidas, the eldest, had just turned four; his brother, Pantios, although a full year younger, stood nearly as tall and gave away nothing in their wild play. A few short years and they would begin the Upbringing and become brothers to a generation of young Spartans. Strangely, he counted them as already gone and enjoyed these days as if they were only a rekindled memory. He turned from the window and looked at her. Embarrassed by the sudden attention, Damatria rose from her chair, brushing past him on her way to the hearth where a kettle of broth steamed temptingly.

"That can wait," he said as he gently wrapped his arm around her waist.

Her first instinct was to push his hand away, but as her flesh met his, she slid her palm across his forearm in submission. She fell into his lap. Her eyes closed as she felt his lips brush the soft and fragrant curve of her neck. "The boys," she warned, "would not understand this."

"Precisely," he mumbled, through kisses of her golden tanned skin.

She twisted around and lifted his chin up with her slender fingers, tracing his lips until they curled to a smile. Suddenly she pushed him down with both hands. He slammed to the floor on his haunches as she escaped to the hearth, giggling.

"Eat first, husband. Your duty is to remain strong for your city."

"And yours is to bear many sons." He bounced to his feet. "I would never allow you to neglect your duty." She faced away, stirring the broth as he squeezed her tightly, feeling her warmth, her life, her every firm curve through the flimsy summer peplos of linen.

"Father," bellowed Zeuxidas as he crashed through the doorway. "Someone is coming." He pointed back out the open doorway with his pretend wooden sword. A figure strode up the long path, made featureless by the late afternoon sun that shone from behind. Pantios scrambled ahead of the visitor, desperate to reach the house before he did. The boy exploded through the doorway, tossing his mock shield and spear as he ran behind his father.

"Pantios," he scolded. "Do not run from strangers." He knelt, coming eye to eye. "Do not run from anyone."

With newfound courage little Pantios stepped out from his father's shadow, defiantly awaiting the visitor's entrance.

"Epitadas."

Damatria nodded politely, then called to the servants to enter. "Another setting for dinner," she instructed.

"Lady Damatria, I must decline." Now he turned to Brasidas. "We must both attend the phidition. Sthenelaidas insists that we all be present, festival or no."

"Since when did he become president of the mess?"

"Since this morning. Damonidas is dead."

At that instant his very breath fled, leaving him suspended somehow apart from everything and everyone around him. His mind raced back, past a multitude of encounters with noble Damonidas to the hidden wink bestowed upon him the day of Kratesikles' inspection of his boua almost twenty years past. He heard only Damonidas' iron-strong voice; he saw only his rugged but perceptive eyes.

She knew enough to be silent. No embrace to soothe him, not even an instinctive stroke of her hand upon his bare arm. She turned away. He followed Epitadas out of his house.

Their determined pace swept them quickly past the Skias and onto the Hyakinthia Road. A few of their mess-mates hung outside waiting, anxiety moving them to shuffling as they conversed. Brasidas and Epitadas cut through them, pushing aside the flap of the tent. As they entered, the chattering ceased.

"Now that we are all here," said Sthenelaidas impatiently, "let us sit." He nodded, his lips pressed into a forced grin as he waited for the stragglers to take their chairs.

"Keraon, the food can wait a bit," he said to the cook, sending him outside.

"Gentlemen." He stared out at the other thirteen. "Damonidas is dead." By now they all knew, but this formal announcement stirred them to chatter. "We have lost a noble comrade."

"Archidamos has one less Peer to keep watch on him," snapped Lykophron. No one else had dared to say it, but that is what they all thought, only gruff, impatient Lykophron would blurt it out amongst the mess-mates. His displeasure with Archidamos would now certainly be known to the king. With no reason to curb his thoughts, he continued. "And our allies attend the Assembly on the morrow. What will Archidamos say to them?" He stood, imitating an orator. "Be patient with Athens? Let them abuse you, steal your property, squeeze the life blood of trade from your ports and markets," he roiled on. "Your leader, Sparta, is governed by a treaty, not men. That is what he will say."

Styphon rose up. "Do we renege on our oath to the gods? Is that what you would have us do?" Styphon, hardly a religious sort, invoked the gods in a legal sense as witnesses to the treaty.

Turtle grinned at Brasidas knowingly. They could forecast Styphon; he would separate himself from any overt opponent of Archidamos and the Eurypontids. Three of the five ephors stood by the king, in policy and opinion. He would not chance it, not now, even with Sthenelaidas as one them.

"War is coming and the Athenians have summoned it," said Lykophron as he thrust his finger at Styphon like a dagger.

"I think it is Korinth that has called upon Ares, not Athens. They speak boldly with us at their side." Styphon sat back, drawing a deep breath. "Gentlemen, why don't we eat. Tomorrow we can bark politics at each other."

Brasidas stood over the table. "War is inevitable, but do not be so quick to blame Athens. There is a cost to leadership and we chose not to pay it. Now to regain it we must pay more. Delay and we may never be able to afford it."

* * *

"You stunned them all," whispered Epitadas as they shuffled forward with the crowd.

"What?"

"Last night. Your words' influence, Brasidas."

He tugged Epitadas out of the stream of Peers entering the Skias. It seemed as though every Spartiate attended, even officers of the district guards. He almost expected the exiled King Pleistoanax to appear with Kleandridas. This would be an assembly unsurpassed in importance.

"I spoke nothing more than any Spartan with eyes and ears would be compelled to say. Athens has made it plain. Domination is her plan."

"To hear Archidamos, you would think we are all bosom friends. He says the Athenians have promised to stay out of our affairs."

Brasidas shot a look of impatience at him. "Let us hear the evidence, then decide."

Like two great stairways, seats climbed the interior flanking walls; each end of the building opened to the elements and people crammed every space. Straight ahead, seated in the places of honor, he saw King Archidamos, the twenty-eight Gerontes who comprised the Gerousia and the five ephors. Brasidas recognized several embassies of foreigners seated to the right of the ephors. Some he easily discerned to be Korinthians by their lavish and effeminate accouterments. Others, more sensitive to their environs, dressed in modesty, deferring to the examples set by their hosts.

One of the ephors, Deuximachos, stood and gestured for silence. "We have called the Assembly today to hear grievances against the Athenians. In attendance also is a delegation from Athens to respond to these allegations." He waved the Megarian ambassador forward.

"I am Pamillos, son of Entimos of Megara."

Brasidas unknowingly flashed his eyes to the Athenians, catching their obvious discomfort as the man began his speech.

"Spartans, you may be lulled to a state of complacency by your distance from Athens. Make no mistake, if your city neighbored theirs, you too would suffer the indignities that these Athenians have thrust upon us.

"We are but a small city in comparison to you. Small too when measured against Athens. Like any small commonwealth, we must depend on the justice and goodwill of the larger.

"The Athenians dispense neither. They rob us of our livelihood, barring us from trading at any of their ports, so we starve. And why? Do we threaten them? Do we snatch from them the riches of commerce? Our tiny city is not capable of this. So why does Athens strangle us?

"They are a city of ambitious men, who cannot tolerate ambition in others. See what they have done to us and see what they would do to others if no one compels them to justice. We beseech you, as liberators of Hellas, to keep the beast of Athens from devouring us all."

The Megaran ceased his terse presentation, a brevity appreciated by the Spartiates in attendance. The Thebans spoke next, followed by the Epidaurans, the Tegeans, the Aiginitans, the Elians, and the Sikyonians. Everyone of them detailed the oppression suffered at the hands of Athens, mostly in trade, and usually in recompense for little more than a bit of competition. Also they chided the Spartans for not heeding their warnings of years past. Finally

Aristios, the Korinthian ambassador, stood in the center of the Skias.

"Spartans! I feel you meet the accounts of others with a bit of skepticism, due in no small part to your constitution and its long success. I too would regard others warily if I had no better experience of the outside world."

His words stirred a chorus of grumbles, especially from the Gerontes, men steeped in Spartan tradition, with little regard for the failing governments of others. They balked at the insult.

"You suspect any with regards to pecuniary interests. Petty quarrels, you think. See now that what we warned you of is true. Every Hellene here has detailed to you the outrages suffered at the hands of Athens. Look what they do to our colony of Potidaia. The citizens of this tiny city exercise independence, and what does Athens do? Choke them with a siege. While we debate the rights and wrongs of this, Athens' aggression travels. It spans the sea, cutting off trade with anyone who does not submit to their extortion." His words caused eruptions of chatter to fill the Skias, so he paused, letting his words simmer in their minds before continuing.

"And what do you do? You defend yourselves by appearing to act, while in truth you do nothing. All other Hellenes struggle against them, while you refuse to intercede." He paused for a moment to study the faces of his audience. To be sure the Gerontes were upset, but the ephors revealed little, restrained anger apparent only in their eyes.

"I pray that you will not consider these words of warning to be hostile toward you, for they are meant only to stir friends to action."

Aristios finished. Now Deuximachos invited the Athenian envoy to apprize them. Like a sempiternal hammering, his recounting of every episode, told manifold ways, relentlessly reminded them of Athens' contribution to the defeat of Persia. In this episode of his speech, he surpassed all the previous speakers in duration combined. He then went on to compare Sparta's alliances to Athens' empire. Finally he advised them not to rush to a war, but to abide by the terms of the treaty and seek arbitration for their grievances. Far from convincing them to share his point of view, his grandiloquent speech numbed them all to boredom. With the last words heard from the Athenian, the foreigners were asked to depart the Skias. When only Spartans remained, King Archidamos rose to speak. "Citizens. The wrongs of the Athenians detailed by our allies are true enough. This, I admit. But hear my advice in this matter before you vote for war."

Brasidas listened, knowing how often Archidamos had swayed the Assembly. Discouragement grabbed hold of him. Epitadas, seated nearby, merely shook his head in resignation.

Archidamos strode the floor of the Skias in momentary silence then suddenly shot a glance directly at the seated Gerontes. "This war will be fought at sea, for they are a naval power. We, of course, have no navy to speak of. And ships cost money. We require time to prepare for this war. Time to garner money, for sadly this will determine the victor.

"Meantime, abide by the treaty and submit to arbitration, while we continue our preparations. In a few years, when we have grown even stronger, attack. Consider this before you vote."

The Gerontes nodded in agreement with the king. Caution was their mantle of comfort and Archidamos had wrapped them in it. Others in attendance revealed nothing in their faces, but Brasidas knew the Assembly, by its nature, would choose prudence. Brasidas' attention was arrested by a burst of movement. Sthenelaidas sprang to his feet, brushing past Archidamos as he moved before the Assembly.

"The long speech of the Athenians I do not pretend to understand." He paused for the laughter to die out. "They said a great deal in praise of their city, but denied nothing of their transgressions against our allies. They, as always, bring up their exemplary action against the Persians in the Great War. In doing so they have made it clear that their once righteous behavior has gone bad. Meanwhile, we are the same now as we were then, and suffer no such vicissitudes at the hands of a democracy. Archidamos is right. Money fuels war nowadays, but only courage can deliver victory. Do not let lawsuits and arbitration, the tools by which Athens beguiles, be our course. By our inaction we injure our allies as surely as the Athenians do. You must vote for war so we may advance against these aggressors."

The once quiet confines of the Skias shook under the outburst of shouts. The vote, usually cast by mouth, could not be discerned in the ruckus.

Sthenelaidas stood atop his seat and shouted. "The tally is impossible! Quiet! Quiet and listen!"

Like a receding storm, the thunder of voices faded. The sudden calm induced most of them to retake their seats.

"Those who vote for war come to this side," bellowed Sthenelaidas, waving to the seats on the right of the doorway. Those for peace sit there."

Again the Skias filled with a rumbling as most made their way to the seats near Sthenelaidas. They filled in quickly, forcing many to stand. Brasidas, Epitadas, Turtle, and Saleuthos squeezed in amongst their other comrades. Across from them, sprinkled in amongst the mostly empty seats, sat King

Archidamos. Surrounding him were Kratesikles, Thrasymidas, Alkidas, Knemos, and others of the Eurypontid clan.

Suspended between the two factions, Styphon hovered. Hesitatingly he moved toward Sthenelaidas. The vote was now complete.

Athens
Thirteen
ΑΘΗΝΑ

Thukydides descended from the Pynx, Eukles at his side, neither saying much as they slipped along in the swirling current of people. The speech was short, but Perikles had convinced them quickly. Athens would not submit to Sparta's demands. Their general detailed the preparations that had already been undertaken, then read the numbers from the katalogos: Athens could field 13,000 heavy infantry; 1,200 horsemen; 1,600 archers; and hold in reserve 16,000 garrison troops. Of course he made particular reference to the 300 triremes trimmed, manned, and ready for war. And after summoning such confidence in the outcome of their enterprise, he shocked them all by advising them not to fight!

Their walls were stout and the port of the Piraios unassailable. Sparta, if she chose to invade, would be kept out while food, trade goods, and tribute would continue to enjoy unimpeded access to Athens. Like in wars past, the people of the countryside would simply retire behind the city's walls, letting the invaders snatch their harvest. In a few weeks the foe, as always, would withdraw. Perikles put it simply: "Without battle the Spartans can achieve no victory. In the meantime we keep what we have." Early spring and they knew they still had time before the invasion. Tomorrow Thukydides would ride out to his father's estate. Much had to be done.

"They would come to your property at the outset," he warned.

"Yes, Thriasia would be first, after Eleusis of course." Eukles answered in the manner of a student to a teacher, hardly realizing what they discussed would soon be a stark actuality.

"Then I suppose you must tend to your preparations?"

"Hardly. Father sent most of the livestock and servants over to Euboia. Our fleet will protect the island." Eukles bounded over one of the many puddles that the heavy rains of last night had deposited.

They continued their walk, passing the Hill of Ares and finally coming to the edge of the Agora, where at the corner of the thoroughfare, they stopped to look upon the Statues of Heroes.

"Come. The kapeleion of Teres is near. Surely you can indulge in a cup of wine to warm you." Eukles always tried to temper Thukydides' serious nature with some such diversion. Most often his friend would decline, but today was different.

It seemed colder inside than out. The place was dark, windows shuttered to keep out the wind and most stools sat vacant. From a back room the taverner appeared, gripping the weight of a full amphora of wine, hovering over it as though it were a toddler waddling in its first steps.

"Something good, Teres. Not that cheap akratos you peddle to the sailors," said Eukles, sending the hunched man away.

They stomped their wet and muddied feet upon the dry dirt floor. By habit, Thukydides swung his cloak from his shoulders.

"Better keep it on till he brings some fire."

In a few moments, Teres returned, cradling an orange pitcher decorated with the image of Herakles, club in hand, wearing a lion-skin cape. "I save this for my very best customers."

"And who do you save the heat for?" Eukles pulled his cloak tight to him. Teres lifted a single finger, requesting patience. Again he shuffled out of sight. A clatter of pottery issued from the backroom, mixed with shouts in some barbarian tongue that neither man could translate, but both were sure of the rough meaning.

"This should do." Teres shuffled toward them, toting a double handled smoldering cooker that he plopped at their feet. Inside it glowed hot, its belly satisfied with a half score of charcoal bricks.

Eukles bent over the cooker, rubbing his hands. Thukydides tested the wine, nodded with satisfaction, then sipped some more.

"So, my friend, what will happen next?"

Thukydides swirled the wine in his cup, his vision trapped by the soothing motion within. "You mean with the war?"

"Why, of course."

"Perchance nothing. Sparta, I think, will be slow to act."

Eukles gulped from his cup. "But they have promised the Korinthians to march against us, in hopes of relieving their colony."

"Potidaia? I do not think any Spartan can see the importance of Potidaia and the cities of the Region of Thrake. They will attack, reluctantly and with little vigor."

112

"Why is that?"

"Archidamos, their king, has no appetite for a fight with us. Perikles says so."

"But what of their other king? They have two, do they not?"

"He, thankfully, is in exile—" Shouting in the street halted him mid-sentence.

"Teres, what is that all about?" asked Eukles, betraying a mixture of curiosity and disdain in his tone.

The old man stuck his head out of the doorway, yelling, "Come in here." A flushed youth burst into the kapeleion. The youngster's chest heaved as he gulped for breath. "Plataia has been attacked."

Thukydides stared at him. "By the Spartans?" He thought a bit on this question, but knew it could not be them, for they would have to march through Athenian territory to get to Plataia.

He shook his head "Thebans! Last night. They took the place. Two Plataians escaped to our fort at Panakton. Word has just come from there." He went on to explain that the city was betrayed from within to a Theban force totaling a few hundred.

Thukydides fled the kapeleion with Eukles at his side, commencing a panicked hunt for information in the Agora. He searched the swirls of chattering faces until he recognized one.

"Gryllos," he yelled over the seething crowd.

Gryllos stood, one of three men in conversation outside the cobblers booth. Finally he heard his name and found the face of Thukydides.

"Is it true?"

Gryllos pardoned himself from his conversation to answer. "About Plataia?"

"Yes. Do the Thebans have it?"

"No longer. The Plataians took them all prisoner and are holding them to bargain. At least that is what Perikles hopes."

"To bargain for what?"

"For peace with Thebes, even a temporary one. That will most certainly delay a Spartan invasion."

"Do not allow Kleon to hear you," quipped Eukles. "He has been preaching war to the mob, and they are listening. As are the gods."

"If war comes, as it seems sure to be, let us see if Kleon is in the forefront of the battle-ranks, or more likely issuing commands from his tent." Gryllos' words elicited broad grins from his companions.

They milled about the cobbler's booth for more than a hour, hardly feeling the biting, damp wind that whipped in from the north. About the time the shadows of the Hill of Ares begins to spill over the South Stoa, they noticed a disturbance in the crowd, moving the people away from their conversations and toward the bouleterion. Thukydides caught sight of three of the strategoi—Generals Phormio, Hagnon, and Perikles—climbing the steep bank of steps to the building's entrance.

"A meeting of the council?" Gryllos seemed surprised.

"To discuss Plataia, no doubt," added Thukydides with a bit of authority.

They shouldered their way through the knots of people, coming to the row of newly planted willow and plane trees, all part of the civic projects commissioned by Perikles. Thukydides spotted his old teacher resting upon a bench near the steps of the bouleterion.

"Greetings to you, Antiphon," announced Thukydides with a formality that clung to him as inappropriately as a heavy cloak in warm weather.

"Ah, Thukydides. It is always good to see one of my better students. You look in fine health. And how is your father?"

"Doing well, sir."

The ancient tutor, deliberate as always, moved his eyes from Thukydides to his companion.

"Eukles! I should have known you two would be together." Suddenly Antiphon's face turned dark.

"What is it?" Thukydides was quick to discern the change.

"Did you not hear?" The old man sighed, as though his sudden grimness pressed upon his ancient chest.

"Hear what?"

"The Plataians executed the hostages. It is war with Sparta!"

Sparta

Fourteen

ΣΠΑΡΤΗ

"Two-thirds of the army marches north," Sthenelaidas announced to his mess-mates.

This invasion, as all invasions, was timed to coincide with the ripening of the crops. Athenian farms would be hostage. The noble challenge of hoplite warfare would be issued, to which Athens must respond in order to save her crops, livestock, land, and honor. This formula had defined conflict in Hellas for uncounted generations.

"And the katalogos—have the ephors posted it?" asked Brasidas.

"No, but I have seen the lists." Sthenelaidas tore a bit of bread off the loaf, then passed it to Epitadas.

"Do we go?" Brasidas waved off the loaf.

"Archidamos' heavy hand forced the composition of the katalogos."

"So—are we out, then?" asked Brasidas through clenched teeth.

"No, only you and Epitadas. The remainder of our platoon marches north with the king."

"And what are we to do? Stay here with the women?"

"You know, if it where my decision to make, you both would be included. But I have managed to persuade the other ephors to grant you a command."

"Command of what?" asked Brasidas cautiously, exhibiting no trace of disdain that had, until now, colored his words.

"You will become harmost of Methone."

His face burned. "In Messenia! To guard Helots!"

"A company of infantry is no trifling appointment, even if it is comprised of Perioikoi." He spoke of the non-Spartans of Lakonia who served in the army.

Brasidas mulled it over, keeping his outrage submerged. The unit, while not all Spartiates, would be of well-drilled hoplites from the outlying villages of Lakedaimon. He also realized that it was, most certainly, through his friend's urging that this appointment was made. He would not insult him with ingratitude.

"Do I have a choice of officers?"

"Eight have been assigned to you, including Epitadas."

* * *

The next day Brasidas stood by the Aphetaid Road, surveying the assembled army of Sparta. A squadron of horses had left prior to dawn, just after Archidamos had made his sacrifice to Zeus Agetor. Next to the king stood the pyphorus, the bearer of the sacred fire taken from the altar of Zeus and carried wheresoever the army marched. Hypaspites, armor bearers, had their masters' shields slung over their backs, spears in hand, each carrying a wicker campaign pack and bedroll. Moving through the friendly territory of the Peloponnese, a Spartan warrior wore no helmet, breastplate, or greaves, but did march with short sword hanging from his left shoulder, and xiphidion dagger on his right. He donned a scarlet chiton and triboun cloak; upon his head sat a felt pilos cap.

The entire populace turned out, lining the road or sitting perched upon the slopes of the humble acropolis, for it had been many years since so extensive a call-up had been issued. The triple files of three thousand Spartiate warriors filled the length of road from the temple of Demeter to the Babyx bridge, and following them the supply train snaked away, mostly hidden behind the hill of the acropolis. Purposely the procession would span most of the morning.

The pipers began. Starting at the head of the column, the tightly packed files stretched as movement cascaded rearwards. Brasidas grabbed the mane of his horse and with one bounce propelled himself upon its back. He waved to Epitadas and his seven other officers to follow as he peeled away from the pomp of the grand march-out toward the vacant streets. They struck off westward for the high pass over Taygetos.

"It will all be over soon," announced Epitadas, above the clattering hoof beats. "Athens will submit by summer's end."

"Only the gods know for sure," said Brasidas in a subdued and distracted tone.

"We, my friend, will be forgotten in Messenia, policing farms." Epitadas spit.

"I think this war is more then we can measure. It will surely wait for us."

116

Epitadas shook his head. "How can Athens stand up to that?" He swung his head to indicate the fading pipes of the army.

"Archidamos' sagacity is not to be underestimated. He will procrastinate, while seeming to prosecute the war with vigor."

Again he shook his head. "And why?"

"To keep things as they are."

* * *

At first appearing as faint strands of gray, the smoke advanced with the Spartans into the Athenian border towns, signaling both distance and destruction. They were all secure behind the high, thick walls of the city, watching the northwestern sky. At first it all seemed like a great adventure or diversion, releasing them from the monotony of daily routines. Men crammed the battlements. Women, unable to leave their homes, sat upon the rooftops gawking. His cavalry squadron rallied just inside the Dipylon Gate, fifty strong and waiting for the order that would propel them into the countryside.

"Captain, do we go?" asked an anxious youth who struggled to calm his horse and himself by rubbing its mane.

"It shall be at his command," answered Thukydides, pointing to an officer in the tower that flanked the double gate.

The man, helmet pushed back atop the crown of his head, waved his spear; the guards slipped the bolt free then pried open the squealing gates.

They poured out, too quickly at first, for they must ride more than a few miles before seeing a Spartan and at this pace their horses would tire. They were sent to keep the enemy in check, to dampen their boldness and prune the invading army of its straggling branches. His squadron rode past full fields and ripening groves, still untouched by the Spartans. As they rode further, the wispy spirals of smoke turned to dark, black columns, each anchored by a flame-licked structure. Like ants, the Peloponnessians swarmed over the farms of Oenoe. Thukydides stared as they torched homes and hacked down the swollen corn and barley, devastating the labor of months and years in lethal moments.

A few of the invaders pointed at the Athenian cavalry, while others collapsed into tight formation, still keeping at their methodical destruction. Quickly they hauled the stalks into high mounds, prodding them with torches here and there until white smoke began to billow from the piles; the expanding, noxious cloud dispersed them. A change of breeze allowed them back.

Crackling flames dashed through the mounds, swallowing the grain and moving the arsonists on. The ubiquitous stench proved inescapable. Afternoon turned to night under the gathering pall, spooking the horses and unsettling the men. He thought of Lord Hades and his miserable realm as he surveyed it all.

Quite unexpectedly the marauders withdrew, recalled by the blare of a salphinx. Thukydides waved his men forward.

"We will follow, for a time."

He led them past the flaming hillocks of corn to a ridge beyond. Not a single stalk remained upright, owing to the thoroughness of the Spartans. The one farmstead they passed close by had been stripped of everything, even the roof tiles, its fire-stained walls thrusting up from the rubble.

They gained a ridge quickly, cloaked by the acrid haze from any roaming parties of enemy infantry. He could hear men speaking with a Doric accent— even their laughter was edged with it—for it was unmistakable to him, but content that they were comfortably apart he sat poised, his eyes anticipating what the parting veil would soon reveal. A breeze began to lift the smoke. Before him, not but a dozen yards or so, sat a platoon of infantry ringed around a pair of wine pitchers, guzzling, weapons tossed carelessly out of reach.

He gave no order, but drove his heels hard into the flanks of his horse; it exploded into a charge, snorting and pounding—a rambling mass of muscle, flesh, and bone. Soldiers' heads spun around at the thunder of his gallop, their wide white eyes glaring at him. His kopis thwanged free of its scabbard, and with a lunge he hacked deep into the neck of one of them. His men roared the war-cry and raked through the scattering band, slicing and chopping at men who tried to fend off blows with shieldless arms and weaponless hands. Fingers and flesh danced in the air, mingled with the spray of blood. Only two managed to retrieve their shields, and these Thukydides' men avoided until they had dispatched the unarmed.

From beyond the veil of smoke he heard the shouts of many; into view came a solid wall of bronze backed by helmeted, black eyed warriors. The Spartans advanced toward them, anxious to come to the aid of their allies, but so very disciplined to the art of war that not a crease appeared between their locked shields nor a ripple of imperfection misaligned their gleaming hedge of spears.

"Withdraw!" Thukydides spun around on his mount, surveying the melee and making certain that his order was obeyed. An unstrung youth, intoxicated by the fight, continued to swing wildly at one of the shield-bearing infantry. Thukydides whacked him with the flat of his blade as he passed. "Withdraw!"

At full sprint they passed the farmstead and the smoldering mounds of grain and corn, making for the hillock above the town.

"They were not so invincible," announced the youth triumphantly as they slowed to a trot.

"And who is that?' Thukydides said, looking back over his shoulder.

"Spartans! We must have slain a dozen or more."

"You mean those drunkards we came upon without spear or shield? Those were not Spartans."

The youth's face lost its victorious grin.

"Korinthians, most likely. The bastards we ran from, the ones rolling up the hill at us like a bronze millstone—those were Spartans."

Messenia
Fifteen
ΜΕΣΣΗΝΙΑΚΑ

The village of Tragana sat in the semi-circular hollow of a large hill, like a spectator at the theatron, facing the performing sea. Here too Brasidas sat, watching the gulls swerve and dive, picking up the debris from the fishermen's nets that they only rarely discarded, this due to an unusually abundant catch this morning.

For a Spartan he had acquired a certain comfort with the sea, gained during his several voyages to the Region of Thrake these years past. Unlike the valley of the Eurotas where the steep mountains focused the season into the bracketed lowlands, here summer heat was quelled by the ocean's breath. The food proved interesting. His district guard excelled at drill. In fact, if it were not for such an inconsequential posting, he would consider himself content.

It was like biting a stone. The crabapple smelled ripe, but was tougher than old Megathon. He attacked it all the same, grinding the bitter fruit in his mouth before dousing it with a swig from his wineskin.

Below, tearing up the southern road, he spotted a horseman being pursued relentlessly by a billowing trail of dust. Beyond him the swells in the bay shimmered in silver. He stopped to speak with a fisherman who sat in the shade of a hut, mending a net; the two exchanged brief conversation, then the fisherman pointed up, directly at Brasidas. The man vaulted off his mount and began scrambling up the slope.

"Brasidas!" The man waved, stumbled but moved unhesitatingly on. "Brasidas." Sweat slicked his hair. He heaved for breath. With an audible gulp of air he leaned forward, hands on knees, resting. Finally he straightened up. "It is Methone. The Athenians have landed."

He spit out a seed, then swiped his teeth with his tongue as he mulled over the man's message. "Sit down," he commanded, "and tell me what is going on."

"Sir, I have just ridden from Methone. One hundred Athenian warships have landed there."

"Are you certain?" He asked the question, but knew the Athenians would try something—a daring sortie to get Archidamos and the Spartans out of Attika. Surely he would do the same.

"Oh yes. I counted them three times." He sucked in air deeply. His panting ceased, but the sweat still beaded and dripped off his face

"Did they land any infantry?"

"Just commenced to when I rode off."

Brasidas remained sitting. He looked beyond the messenger, focusing on nothing in particular as he ruminated on this information. With a smile he sprang to his feet.

"I think we should receive our guests properly," he said as he raised himself up. The man only returned a confused look.

Within half an hour the company assembled, all 128 of them, and commenced their three-hour trot to Methone. For most of the journey the road hugged the coast, swerving inland intermittently only to avoid a rocky promontory or steep sea cliff. The afternoon breeze had swung around to the south; they could smell the smoke before seeing it. Faint and far-off shouts echoed. Ahead of them a flock of sheep tumbled up the road, being shooed along by an old herdsman. He whacked a straggler with his crook, then turned to Brasidas. "I hope you're going to do something about them."

He winked at the old man, then turned to Epitadas. "Stay here. Have the men take water. I will return shortly."

Epitadas passed the order down the triple columns. Servants swarmed over the warriors, uncorking water flasks, relieving some of the burden of their shields, while others honed their masters' blades.

Trees spanned the ridge crest, providing him with ready cover, but he ignored it, sauntering to the ridge top and in plain view of the town. Two farm houses burned, one abutting the road to Methone and another on the far ridge that bracketed the shadowless plain. The expanse from the sea to the town was infested with Athenians, some picking the bodies of Methone's defenders, while others gathered at the wall, preparing for an assault. Brasidas' eyes danced over the scene. "Fifteen hundred," he whispered to himself.

Epitadas greeted him on his return. "How many?"

"Hardly a thousand," he said, shrugging his shoulders.

"The town?"

"Still holding, but we must go now. Form up the men. I wish to speak with them."

121

Epitadas and the officers dispersed amongst the men, whispering commands. Soon they all ringed Brasidas.

"Men, Athenians, are laying siege to the town. They outnumber us at least ten to one. That is the good news."

His officers grinned confidently; more than a few of the hoplites laughed.

"The town still stands. The enemy is scattered before it, paying heed only to the booty. We will advance to the gate in four columns at platoon depth. The primary order—maintain formation and keep moving. Kill as many as you can, but keep moving."

Each man tugged and adjusted his thorax armor, re-hefted his shield, checking its feel on the left forearm, then settled its deep concave bowl upon the shoulder cap. Some grabbed handfuls of dirt, rubbing the criss-crossed leather thong grips on their spears dry. Brasidas nodded. They all pulled their kranos helmets over their faces and began a controlled charge down the road.

At first the Athenians near them turned and gawked, awestruck at their sudden appearance, then shouting in pointed Attic dialect, burst across the fields. This elicited a grin from Epitadas. They formed in haphazard groups, rushing at the advancing Spartans. An Athenian spear clanged off Brasidas' aspis, which he flicked away with an upward swing. A quick jab and his spear found its mark; he withdrew it efficiently from the man's gurgling throat and struck another.

Like weak swells lapping against a stony cliff, the Athenians crashed frustratingly upon the Spartan flanks, then quickly receded, unable to impede the advance. A large group of Athenian hoplites scurried into formation at their officer's entreaties, heads and spears wobbling timorously. They had taken up position bisecting the road, denying the Spartans the gate to Methone.

Seeing this, Brasidas' heart raced with eagerness. He pumped his spear overhead, then broke into a full sprint, the others following while maintaining the cohesiveness of the formation. The Athenians struggled to rally around their officer, but he could see flight in their eyes. For the moment though, they held together.

Brasidas and the four enomotarchs exploded into the stationary Athenians, rolling over the first several ranks until the bodies underfoot slowed them to a walk. Six ranks deep and the enemy finally broke, some tossing away shields, for it was nearly impossible to flee while holding one. Cheers resounded from the town wall as the double gate swung open, revealing the interior and the townsfolk that lined the roadway, some waving, others shouting encouragement to hurry.

"North wall!" he yelled, pointing to the second platoon. He barked out the orders to the third and fourth, then led the first enomotai up the west wall.

Upon the boiling and confused plain, the Athenians, outraged by the audacity of the Spartan relief column, rallied every man for an assault on the walls.

Brasidas climbed the battlement flanking the main gate and commenced to assess the scene outside. More Athenians scrambled from their beached triremes, adding to the force arrayed beneath the walls. He watched as rowers became sappers, hauling ladders and rope from their ships. Three officers stood amidst several assault parties, barking at each other and the men surrounding them. Their argument amused Brasidas; their disorganization fired him with bravura.

"Tell Isarchidas to pull his men off the east wall and assemble here, at the gate," he yelled down to Epitadas.

Again he peered over the crumbling mud-brick wall to the bickering Athenians. He sucked in the salty air, then scanned the darkening eastern sky, all the while suppressing the exuberance of day. "Continue your debate," he whispered beneath his breath as he descended the ladder. The thirty-two men of the fourth enomotai lined up smartly in front of the gate awaiting his orders.

"Once outside, reform to half files!"

No more words than those were necessary. The gate swung open. The platoon jogged through it and reassembled in eight files four men deep, with Brasidas in the forefront on the right. He pointed with his spear. "Open order!"

They stepped off deliberately toward a disordered band of Athenian hoplites and rowers—the nearest of several such groups gathering before the wall—singing Kastor's hymn to the rhythm of their pounding feet.

Panicked yelling erupted among the Athenians, followed by slapdash attempts to form a battle line. The rowers cast away their ladders and sprinted toward the sea. The hoplites wriggled reluctantly into a loose rectangle.

Once to within a dozen meters or so, Brasidas sent his men into a dead run. In response the Athenians bellowed their war-cry, to chase away Spartan courage or perhaps their own swelling fear. The Spartans closed in silence. The interval slipped to nothing. Now the thunder of the bronze on bronze collision boomed across the plain like a bolt from Zeus, almost congealing the air to a solid. He felt the shield of the man behind heave into the small of his back as their formation compressed under the impact. The Athenians, disadvantaged by their lack of momentum, began to stumble backwards under the weight of the Spartan shields. The plain was dry, the footing excellent. Brasidas' men pushed forward. Spearpoints pinged and rattled, rebounding off the helmets and shields of the front-rankers. Within a fifty-meter radius, the Athenians numbered nearly a hundred, but failed to rally into a cohesive formation; some gawked disbelievingly at the onslaught, while others scanned desperately for a leader. So often when many men fight as one they stand their ground. Here the Athenians fought as individuals, succumbing to the uncertainty and fear that thrives in a lonesome warrior, a fear that paralyzes both mind and body.

Brasidas could feel the enemy before him breaking, like a flood damn against rising water. As he had seen many times before, the rear ranks, comprised of men who see escape as less elusive, took to flight first, then the flanks, leaving only a core of Athenians hopelessly locked in combat with the Spartans.

"Back!"

With only a moment's hesitation did the Spartans pause, then back-stepped, holding together while withdrawing. With this order Brasidas granted the last few of the enemy deliverance and assured his men an unchallenged retreat to the gate. He would not foolishly pursue them with the intoxication of victory, but preserve his men's lives while mastering the enemy.

Once the Athenians had fled to their ships, only then did he halt the retreat. He took stock of the plain and the battle's yield: almost a hundred dead or abandoned Athenians littered the field in eye's view; everyone of his thirty-two stood with him, although each one of them bled. His left arm, where it slipped into the porpax sleeve of his shield, had been slashed from wrist to elbow. He turned the hoplon over to view its facing. Several gashes had been ripped in its center, obliterating the crimson lambda.

Isarchidas pushed his helmet up, revealing a glistening crimson face. He swiped away the blood with the back of his hand; a flap of skin peeled down from his cheek. He calmly pressed it back into place, while shaking his head in disgust. "Lucky bastard," he mumbled.

"Yes, you are," agreed Brasidas.

"Not me. That Athenian asshole. How in Hades did he get under my helmet, I'll never know." He leaned back and pushed the slab of flesh firmly. The blood slowed for a moment.

"Let's go," shouted Brasidas, rousing his men.

Hardly in the tight and disciplined formation they had displayed earlier, the Spartans strolled back into Methone, shields wobbling with each step, spears dangling from drooping arms. Once inside they dropped their shields and planted their spears. Satisfied that his men were safely within the town walls, Brasidas took a seat just inside the gate, knees up as he leaned against the wall. Isarchidas tossed away his helmet, sat upon the fountain's edge, and leaned over, blood dripping from between his fingers as he worked to compress the wound on his face. A dozen or so young boys mingled with the hoplites, mouths gaping as they looked at each bloodied warrior with awe. Brasidas tugged one closer to him by the hem of his chiton. "Fetch the iatros."

The lad scampered off, shouting the name Kallandros. Within moments he returned leading a graying, stocky man who clutched a wicker basket like it was his very last possession. Brasidas pointed to Isarchidas. The physician knelt before the fountain and began pleading with Isarchidas to reveal his wound, but he appeared as a sculpture, frozen in pose, the only sign of life the crimson dripping from the hand clamped upon his face. Finally Kallandros the physician pulled away the bloody hand. Isarchidas folded to the dirt of the agora in a heap.

"It was only a small wound," Brasidas insisted as he collapsed to his knees beside his friend, trying to reassure both the iatros and himself.

The physician quickly unfastened the thorax armor and peeled it away. Now he probed the man furiously, patting and prodding, trying desperately to find another hidden wound.

Isarchidas coughed, then blood foamed from his mouth. "Brasidas." He uttered that single lonesome word, the name of his commander, in reaffirmation of his last thought, his last sight. His neck went limp and his eyes locked frozen upon the sky above.

"Is he dead?"

The question posed by the boy caught him by surprise. "Have you never seen a dead man before?" Brasidas cast Isarchidas' cloak like a fisherman's net; it settled gently across the corpse of his friend, revealing only the face.

The boy, staring at the body, spoke. "My uncle. But he was on a bier, surrounded by flowers and wrapped in linen. He smelled dead, though."

Brasidas grinned as he slapped the marble of the fountain's edge, signaling the boy to sit next to him. "Battle and Death are close companions. Where one goes, the other is sure to follow." The boy sat, turning his gaze from Isarchidas to Brasidas' hacked and bloodied hands.

"These will heal in time," he said, presenting them to the boy. A servant crouched before him with a sponge and small pitcher. As soon as he unstoppered it, the stinging scent of vinegar rushed to fill his nostrils, setting his eyes to tear. He poured the antiseptic over Brasidas' hands, then swabbed them dry with the sponge. The Spartan hardly winced.

"What is it like in battle?' The boy gazed at him unblinking, anxious for an answer.

He dropped his helmet upon the boy's head, then spun it 'round backwards. "What do you see?"

"Nothing"

"And what do you hear?" he said, raising his voice to almost a shout.

"My own breathing and the pounding of my heart." The boy braced the oversized helmet with his hands.

"In battle, expect no more. Between the dust and your helmet, you will be blind. Men crashing into men, steel into steel, even the screams of the dying— nothing will penetrate that helmet. But you will hear your heart. At times you may even feel it as it climbs into your throat, trying to escape."

The boy lifted the helmet from his head and presented it to Brasidas. "But I have heard the bards sing of great warriors, and how they measure their foes with taunts. How they test them with the thrust of a spear, or the swing of a sword before carrying out their plan."

"Hmm, their plan you say." He shook his head now. "That is why they are bards and not warriors. Real battle is hardly so poetic. Once the fight begins, memory and reason flee. Only emphytos, or instinct remains. Pray that the instinct you have to call on is the one implanted by training, and not by nature. I would have to think long and hard to recall any detail of things once battle has been joined." Now he rubbed the boy's head. "Anything else is just a story."

* * *

The next morning, after the bodies of the dead had been washed and anointed with oil, after they had been wrapped in their scarlet war cloaks and loaded into carts, only then did Brasidas leave the walled town and wander the fields beyond. Dogs had already been at the bodies of the Athenians. A pack, emboldened by hunger, snarled at him as he approached, hackles raised and fangs bared. He plucked a shattered sword from the dust and began swinging it overhead as he stomped his feet. The dogs scurried away, stopped once to growl at him in mock defiance, then slunk into the thick brush at the forest's edge.

It was a boy, or so it looked to him, for his beard was as down upon his smooth and chalky face. He gripped a leaf-bladed sword in his right hand, finely crafted with a hilt of bone and silver plate capped with a pommel of gold. Upon the earth lay a superb shield, fully faced in bronze with a fretted rim, the head of a gorgon emblazoned across it. His white linothorax body armor had soaked up the last of his blood, and gleamed dark from his loins to mid-section. A severed spear sprouted from his belly. Brasidas looked up at him with unblinking eyes, neither a smile nor frown upon his lips.

"They send children against us," he whispered.

Suddenly he felt the chill of sea air spill over him. The sun had slipped away, smothered by a heavy, unexpected fog.

He knelt by the boy and placed a hand on his arm while he spoke to the gods and goddesses. A hand lightly came to rest on his shoulder. He felt it but continued on with his prayer, for in this touch he perceived a kindness not sensed since he was a boy himself.

"It has been a long while since you have spoken to me."

He turned, startled by the soft voice of a woman. Her knowing eyes smiled at him. With a mere gesture from her he raised up. He could not speak.

"Dear Brasidas, you called on me. And now you cannot manage words?" She stepped slowly, circling as she studied him. Only his eyes moved to follow her.

"Oh, yes, the gods favor Sparta. My brother Apollo too has heard the prayers of your countrymen. But most of all the gods favor you, Brasidas."

"But why do you appear to me now?"

"Because you needed me. As you needed me during the Phouaxir."

He became entranced by the iridescence of her chiton and the perfection of her form barely covered by it. She grinned. Like a child once more, he stared wordless at the goddess. She placed a single slender finger before her lips to silence him, then spoke. "Remember, dear Brasidas, why you fight. Your love of honor must always exceed your hate of the enemy."

"And will I see you again?"

Without another word Artemis slipped away, escorted by the gray fog that had delivered her. The sun commenced to streak through the gloom, warming his face as he looked skyward. He took a few steps then turned, against all hope, to catch sight of the departing goddess. At the forest's edge the evanescent form of a doe bounded deep into the trees.

The great hinge pins squealed as the gates opened. He looked at his bound arm, attending to it by the sight of the wrappings, for the pain had left him earlier this morning—or was it just now that it departed?

Townsmen emerged pulling two wheeled carts, four or five men to each. They stopped at each slain Athenian, stripping them of everything: armor, weapons, articles of clothing, and even krepides boots. They rummaged about, picking fractured swords from the earth, snatching up butt-spikes or spearheads bereft of any shaft. Soon a cart rumbled up to the boy with the gorgon's head shield. A stocky, thick-armed man bent over the body, barely tossing Brasidas a glance.

"Leave him."

The man peered up, looking puzzled while gripping a ring on the boy's hand.

"Rob some other," snapped Brasidas as he raised an empty hand overhead as if to strike.

The man dropped the boy's hand, then waved his accomplices on. They halted a few meters away, hovering over three other corpses.

* * *

The Athenian raiders set sail from Methone, but instead of turning east and for home, they continued up the coast of the Peloponnese, landing here and there, striking towns and settlements, then quickly retiring to their ships. This was their answer to Sparta's invasion of Attika. With autumn came the end to the sailing season. The Athenians made for home. So did Brasidas.

"You should have returned sooner," said Sthenelaidas, smirking, "then you could have stopped to see your wife first."

"And how do you know he hasn't already." Styphon looked to his friend and winked. "He probably has been home for days. Just knows how to stay out of sight."

The rules of the mess were unbending. Only during festival time could a man dine at home with his family. All other evenings he must attend his phidition. Tonight he was doubly welcome, for not only did his mess-mates wish to hear of the Athenian attack on Methone, but so too did they wish to partake of the fresh venison Brasidas brought, enhancing the bland and meager fare. Both meat and conversation passed around the table, adding to the hearty spirit of the men. Brasidas' exploit as harmost had been the single kernel of cheer in a harvest bereft of Spartan victories.

"Brasidas, we have waited till now to take the vote." Sthenelaidas waved Keraon forward.

The cook carried the kaddichos bowl, stopping before the senior of the mess who had summoned him. Sthenelaidas plucked a ball of bread from the table and rolled it back and forth between his forefinger and thumb, then let it drop unseen into the bowl. Keraon moved from one Peer to the next, collecting each vote of bread. Brasidas, holding his ball undeformed and for all to see, dropped it into the kaddichos.

"Bring it here," commanded Sthenelaidas.

Keraon slid the bowl on the table before him to begin the count. All fourteen spheres of bread rolled perfectly across the pitched table. Only one, pressed flat, would have excluded the candidate.

"Excellent. Klaridas, son of Kleonymos, has been accepted."

With the meal and the vote complete, the phidition emptied of all but the servants and the cook Keraon. Epitadas, Turtle, and Styphon walked with Brasidas as he strolled upon the Hyakinthia Way.

"Isarchidas died bravely," said Brasidas to the others. The statement, made impulsively, did not seem out of context to his friends. Turtle looked to Epitadas, both to acknowledge his friend's words and to seek confirmation of them. Epitadas nodded tight-lipped.

"Turtle, what was Attika like in the summer?" Brasidas asked. "Did our good king Archidamos treat you well?"

Turtle shook his head. "We sauntered in, slow to take action. Archidamos wanted to give the Athenians opportunity to realize the great loss he was about to inflict on them. He made his speeches saying that we should hold their land hostage and not ravage it too soon lest they would have no reason to submit."

"And did this strategy make them compliant?" Brasidas asked, already knowing the answer.

"Ha!" popped Styphon. "He sent a herald to negotiate. Offer them peace. They would not even admit him to the city. Told him to try again when the Spartans quit Attika."

"We hacked down corn and fruit, not men. Archidamos has turned us into farmers." Turtle laughed, drawing humor over his disgust. "But you. You have fought them. And you have beaten them."

Brasidas wrapped his arm around Epitadas. "We both have." He grinned. "Now I know why they hide behind their walls."

While in their conversation they had walked far beyond the tomb of Leonidas and could see the dark groove of the moat that surrounded the Plantanista. They continued on, halting at the bridge to Lykourgos.

"Should we honor our patron Herakles, and cross by his bridge?" Styphon said.

Epitadas looked to Brasidas. "We can cross by whatever bridge we choose."

The wooden span creaked and groaned as they strode across. The sun had slipped behind the Taygetos Mountains, but a whisper of blue still lingered in the west. To the east, above Mount Parnon, stars glistened, poking holes in the purple veil of night.

"It would be so simple," mumbled Brasidas as he paced the playing field, scuffing away the dried-up memory of unshod feet that had bruised the earth.

Epitadas clamped his hand on his friend's shoulder. "Did you say something?"

He shuddered a bit as though his spirit, temporarily departed, had suddenly rushed back to him. "I was thinking, how simple it would all be if we settled it here, as when we were boys."

"You mean us and the Athenians?" said Styphon.

"I mean us and Archidamos—and his ilk. The Athenians pose but a paltry threat when compared to them."

"You come awfully close to treason," warned Styphon, "to measure both king and Peers in such a manner."

Brasidas turned to him, his eyes gleaming intently in the fading evening light. "You were there, Styphon. Did any of his actions dispute me?"

Styphon stared at him, then swallowed hard as if preparing to launch his words in defense. None came forth. He spun away, looking down, searching out the ground for something to kick.

"Why talk of this if there is nothing we can do?" Turtle glared at Brasidas. "The three of us combined hardly command more than a company."

"And how long do you think they can ignore us? How long can they ignore him?" shouted Epitadas as he pointed at Brasidas.

Styphon answered with a mock laugh. Turtle looked to Brasidas as melancholy displaced his anger.

"This war will winnow the pretenders from our ranks," assured Epitadas. "Let us hope before disaster strikes."

"Alkidas and Thrasymidas are both polemarchs, each leading their own mora of a thousand. Many Spartans may die before those dunderheads are found out," Turtle said.

"Do what you can do," Brasidas said, repeating the words of his mentor, Kleandridas. "And the gods will tend to the remainder."

* * *

The Ephorion was a runt of building, and not the harsh and imposing one he remembered from his youth. He gained the top step easily. The door swung open. Inside, five roughhewn couches of oak rose up above the tiled floor, lining three of the four walls; upon them sat five roughhewn men, the five ephors of his city. The small square windows high on the walls admitted small, tight shafts of light. Even less was thrown by the three sputtering oil lamps. One wall was pegged with several dozen sooty kranos helmets, older it seemed than ancient Menelaos' and Agamemnon's, while on the wall opposite the doorway, a snarling gorgon's head emblazoned upon a shield leered at him as he stepped into the murky interior. Immediately he noticed Diakritos, uncle to Alkidas, staring at him through icy eyes; the other four gave no indication of their demeanor. Ainisias rose and greeted him.

"Brasidas, son of Tellis, you are received with all honors." He waved him forward while the others bobbed their heads in agreement. "We await your commendation."

Brasidas balked at answering immediately, for he had dispatched his report to them months earlier, and the request caught him unawares. *Why this interrogation?* he wondered.

"We have read your dispatch in all its precision and detail. But I wish to know from your mouth the story of the Athenian attack at Methone." Again Ainisias waved him forward, this time pointing to an empty chair centered in the room. "Sit and tell us."

The bulky legs of the chair chattered as he dragged it across the tiles. He sat. A Helot presented a full kothon of wine to him. The others commenced to sip from theirs.

"Your report states there were over a thousand Athenians attacking Methone. I have been there. The walls are low and not very substantial. The plain is a highway from the beaches with little in the way of obstacles." Diakritos squeezed his eyelids with a look of pain. "Your mere one hundred repelled them?" He puffed out a mock laugh as he scanned the faces of the others. "You must be a courageous warrior indeed."

Brasidas sipped from his kothon as though he had just sat down to his own table in his own house. He smiled. "The wine is very good," he said charmingly. Now he stood and paced before the couches of the five ephors. "Courage had little to do with the fight on that day."

"And what besides courage delivers victory?" quizzed Diakritos pedantically. "You have found an attribute of the warrior that we have overlooked?"

"Discipline and audacity led us to victory. Courage, I would say, was equally distributed across the fields of Methone that day. The Athenians, to our good fortune, displayed little in the way of discipline. They substituted arrogance for it, a commodity abundant in their city—and not exactly foreign to ours," he added as he sat again.

Ainisias smiled. Diakritos grew red-faced. Brasidas retold in every detail the account of the battle, repeating almost flawlessly the original dispatch.

"And you maintain that your company overcame a force a dozen times superior?" Diakritos re-asked, desiring an answer more to his liking.

"Overcame, no. Endured is a more apt assessment."

Heads leaned from one couch to the next, the five men whispering amongst themselves while Brasidas sat in his isolated chair, sipping the last of his wine calmly, almost serenely, waiting for the discussion to end. Diakritos, still deep in conversation, would look at him with one eye, look away, then glance to him again. After several minutes, with their discussion exhausted, they released him from his chair and his interrogation. He dipped his head politely as he turned to exit. Just then the door flew open, thumping hard against the interior wall. A dust-covered man burst in, sucking the air before he spoke.

"The Athenians have attacked Megara!"

* * *

"Son, do not let pride—"

"Pride is not the issue, Father. Their incompetence will lose this war for us."

"And you will win it, then?" Tellis, like always, checked his son's hubris, for it if he did not the gods were sure to.

"This enemy will not plod along to our convenience. They act swiftly, often impetuously, and like daring and desperate thieves, grab whatever is of value."

"So we must act like thieves and abandon noble honesty?"

"A fox pelt must be used if the lion skin will not stretch," quipped Brasidas.

"You sound like Kleandridas. You would do well to remember where his words have gotten him."

"His words and his noble honesty?"

Tellis sighed. "Let us put these things aside and pretend to be a family of comity—at least for this evening."

"Of course you are right. My day has already been spent sparring with the ephors and most especially Diakritos. It irked him that we saved Methone."

"No, Son. It irked him that *you* saved Methone."

His mother, Argileonis, slipped into the room, causing both men to pause their conversation. She moved to her son, bent and kissed his forehead. "Your men did well at Methone."

"Yes, Mother." He glanced up at her. "And you have stolen back a year or two. You are certainly younger than when I left in the spring."

She cuffed him affectionately then raised her hand again, forcing him to raise his in defense. "Flattery will not take you far." Now she gently stroked his hair. "Though it might earn you a cup of wine."

She tipped the pitcher carefully, spilling the wine slowly into the hefty ribbed tankard, then filled another. The two men nursed the wine, drying their lips only occasionally as they talked of the harvest, the autumn plantings, and the more mundane dealings of the city while Brasidas was absent. Brasidas, for his part, described in detail every shrine, temple, bridge—any structure larger than a hut that he encountered in Messenia. His mind soaked up these images without incitation, while his carefully chosen words recreated them for his father.

During this, and when his cup threatened emptiness, his mother leaned to him. "Time you went home."

He rose, glancing first to his feet as he always did to watch Atlas and Herakles rouse from their contented slumber; the cold empty floor stared back at him. Since their deaths his father kept the other Kastorian hounds in the stable with the horses and apart from the household and the family. Painful memories were less often summoned.

The gate still creaked. To the west a spur of the Taygetos mountains swallowed a huge portion of the star-bright sky. Without the sun the autumn air refreshed him with its chill, conveying the damp and earthy smell of the fields—the clean and honest air of the farm and the promise of its bounty. He watched as a pair of bats tumbled awkwardly across the open space above the road, slipping into the olive grove of their neighbor, Teleklos. It all transported him back in years.

He had not seen his wife in four months. In that time he remembered her rarely, for Temo occupied his thoughts when the faces of his two sons did not. He dredged up the oath, repeating it as an inoculation against the memory of her. Guilt struck him, hard and substantial. He was certain of Damatria's love, and felt powerless to return it. Worse, he worried that he might be unable to mask his dispassion; this would injure a noble and loyal woman, a hurt that she hardly deserved.

She slept on the servant's pallet beside the kitchen door, the door he always entered by unless accompanied by a guest. She was beautiful. The faint orange light of the oil lamps swathed her face in warmth, turning her short curled hair the color of bronze. He bent to kiss her.

"Did they keep you long to sup?" she whispered in a soft, almost liquid voice. She smiled contentedly while reaching for his hand, her eyes still closed as in a dream. "Come to bed, husband."

He buried his face in her neck, then kissed her several more times. "Is this your bed now?"

Her eyes blinked open as she sat up. "Brasidas, it is you. I thought it a dream." She reached, stretching as she shook off her slumber. He slid his hand along her shoulders, slipping the short peplos free of her arms, then her breasts, down the length of her until it fell empty upon the floor.

Sparta
Sixteen
ΣΠΑΡΤΗ

Instinct compelled Brasidas to turn left at the intersection, but in a few steps he realized his error and began walking back toward the agora. The winter chill seemed to magnify the night, making it blacker, the effort more difficult, but still the shelter of his destination hardly seemed inviting. Ahead he heard laughter, then two figures slipped from the shadowed roadway. One executed an exaggerated bow as he approached.

"Step aside for the ephor Brasidas, hero of Methone, and champion of Sparta." The man, his triboun cloak pulled over his head forming a makeshift hood, remained unknown to him. Brasidas stepped closer, but said nothing. "Too important to speak with old friends?" Now the anonymous traveler whipped the cloak from his head.

"Lykophron!" Brasidas embraced his comrade, then yanked the cloak from the other. "And Turtle! Should have known it. Where you find one, you find the other." His smile left as the joy in seeing comrades subsided. "My fellows, I would gladly trade this honor for a meal with my friends, at our own mess-tent." Along with his new office came the responsibility of taking his meals at the Ephorion, separate from his own phidition, and amongst men he knew none too well. But at least Kratesikles was not amongst them. "Still. I shall never forgive you for nominating me."

Now Lykophron also lost his smile. "You can blame us for many things, but forcing this upon you was not our doing."

"Epitadas, then?" quizzed Brasidas.

"No. Not Polyakas either," replied Turtle. "Of course you deserve it, but you would serve Sparta in the field far better."

"Then if not you—?"

"It was Kratesikles," said Lykophron as he chuckled. "He put your name forward and talked you up amongst the other men from Pitane. To all it looks like he commends you, but it keeps you from a command. Keeps you under control."

Brasidas took only a moment to absorb it. "He may keep me from a command, if only for a season, but he can hardly keep me from marching with the army. I will be sure to be right at Archidamos' side."

His two friends touched their brows in unison, a salute and farewell to him as they took the road south toward the phiditia. He saw no one on the way to the Ephorion, except of course for the young boys posted as night guards amongst the public buildings. As he approached the steps, his mind whirred as it always did before entering, certain of an inquisition, a joust of words, a reshaping of the truth then a curt dismissal. He knew of the four others, the men who would serve with him as supreme overseers of the Sparta state. Three of them he would take as he found them, holding no prior opinion, but Thrasymidas would be a different matter.

Only one of them looked up as he entered. Two others flanked Thrasymidas and they carried on in conversation without pause. Brasidas walked by them, acknowledging only the wine steward with a nod to approach and fill his cup. After several minutes Thrasymidas turned slowly to face him. "Our group is now complete." He swung his feet off the couch to the floor then rose slowly. "No time for that now," he barked, shooing away the servant that was about to present a tray of food to Brasidas. "We must see the king." At these words the others stood and began to follow Thrasymidas out of the Ephorion. Brasidas grabbed a slab of boar meat from a platter and began to nibble at it as he sauntered after them. Within a quarter hour they entered the courtyard to Archidamos' house.

Two of the Royal Hippeis stood guard as they entered, Eirenes selected by the three captains of the knights. They loomed at their posts, grim and stony as statues, nodding only slightly as the five men passed. Once inside the courtyard, their path was undeniably marked out by a single lit doorway. A servant extended a hand, ushering them in. What little chatter within the andron ceased as they passed through the portal. Inside sat Archidamos, with his son, Agis, on his right. A dozen or so men lined the walls, reclined as they were upon simple couches. The five ephors approached the king.

Thrasymidas stepped forward. "Archidamos, king of Sparta, are you ready to take the oath?"

The king nodded. " I swear by Zeus, Dispenser of Justice, to uphold the great Rhetra, the laws of Sparta, laid down by Lykourgos and unchanged by any man."

Brasidas knew the words. Still they stuck in his throat. The four others began their chant. "We, the ephors of Sparta, swear by Zeus, Dispenser of Justice, to support Archidamos, so long as his oath holds true.

* * *

He walked down the steps of the Ephorion, trying to hold back his smile. He knew that their stomachs coiled like snakes, nervous as they awaited the inspection. The boys lined up, oldest to youngest, eyes staring into the dust at their feet. Knemos led them down the line, glaring at one boy, then nodding in approval at another, while passing by several as though they were invisible. Brasidas flashed a surreptitious wink here and there, to lessen the awe that Thrasymidas elicited. Oh yes, they must all learn respect, but awe, with but a nudge transforms to fright, an attribute to be cultivated only in Helots and enemies. Spartans must fear no man.

By the time they had stalked down to the youngest, the once stiff line had begun to waver: lips quivered, fists rolled up tight, and muscles twitched as they all fought against the frosty wind of autumn. Brasidas saw it clearly. "Gentlemen, I suggest we go inside," he bellowed, looking to the black doorway of the Ephorion. The other four turned toward him. "We are keeping them from their work and they from ours."

Brasidas strode up to their bouagos. "You have a fine looking troop. But can they sing?" He flicked his head toward the road and smiled.

Before Thrasymidas could add a word, the bouagos shouted the order, sending them into the Embaterion March. Their voices boomed across the agora. Brasidas hustled up the steps and into the Ephorion, and so too did the Thrasymidas and the other ephors.

"And what work is so important that it takes us away from our duty?" Thrasymidas walked to his couch, his back to Brasidas as he spoke.

"The War. What else is more important?" Brasidas stood before his couch, waiting for the everyone to settle in, then he began pacing before them. Suddenly he spun around to face Knemos directly, his posture one of combat, the timbre of his voice as pointed as a spear. "Knemos, your father, your brother, and you exert yourselves greatly against Spartan rivals, but you act otherwise when the enemy is foreign." Thrasymidas' mouth began to open, but before a word could slip out, Brasidas continued. "Stop for a moment and look beyond the mountains that surround our land. Look north across the Isthmos into the heart of Attika."

Thrasymidas laughed a bit, but quickly transformed his mouth into a snarl. "My good Brasidas, you may have missed it, but our army marched against Athens this past year. We brought war to their very doorstep."

"Did I miss their surrender also?"

"Tell us all then; what grand strategy do you propose?"

"Something beyond the summer-long picnic our king has led. We cannot breach their walls. We cannot, for now, stem the stream of ships that ferries them grain. What is left but to go to the source, to the north. Where their timber grows and where they buy their grain, their corn, and their iron."

Now Thrasymidas laughed and snickered. "Are you insane, man? With the sea our only route to carry our army there, your plan is madness." Thrasymidas stood and moved to the center of the room. "Besides, the war so far has cost little to us or the Athenians. A settlement, therefore, would come cheap to both. But you would push the price high indeed."

Brasidas threw his arms up. "The price! This war will end with victory only. Men in both cities will cry for nothing less. I mean to end it with a Spartan victory, and end it quickly. This will save not only Spartan lives, but Athenian lives as well. Their can be no half measures."

And so they argued. Finally, by the evening meal, it was decided that Brasidas' proposal be brought to the Gerousia. There the old men listened. Archidamos listened too. Then, as he always did, the old king reminded the council of the threat of Athens' navy, of her wealth, her capacity to fight, and her unpredictability. How could they send their men so far from home? What then would keep the Athenians out of the Peloponnese? Brasidas' arguments were bold. They were risky. And in the end they were tabled.

Athens
Seventeen
AΘHNA

Athens had prepared for the spring and the Spartan invasion that was sure to follow, but no one could have foreseen the ravages that Apollo, Far-Darter, would unleash. A Lemnian freighter, it was said, unloaded it along with its cargo in the Piraios. First the dock-wallopers contracted it, then the pornes. By the beginning of summer, in the month of Skirophorion, most of the physicians had succumbed also. The plague slew more than any Spartan army.

"He will be a pauper by the beginning of the new year," said Olorus to his son, pointing out the window to the townhouse across the road. "Every night he has many guests. And each night also he employs several musicians."

"Father, Glaukos is not the only one. Everyone carries on as though this day will be their last." The hoarseness in Thukydides' throat squeezed his clear voice to a growl.

"He should save his money for a physician. No doubt he will soon need one." Olorus pulled the shutters closed in disgust, barely muffling the raucous pounding of cymbals that kept time to the singing.

Thukydides rose from his dining couch. "I must be going. With nightfall the carts will be rolling again."

He spoke of the collectors, the ones who prowled the streets and alleyways after sunset, picking up bodies for delivery to the city gates.

His father, too weak to rise, waved an open hand. "Farewell." He coughed hard, then spit into a rag he persistently clenched in his hand.

Alexon handed him a torch; the fresh pitch spit the flames in crackles as he lit it with a lamp. Out here in the courtyard the music from a dozen houses blended into a jumbled cacophony, so incongruous in this city infested with death. His father's steward leaned on the gate, using it as a crutch as he pushed it shut, offering a weak nod to him as he departed.

He walked on, but could not escape the sounds. All along the road windows

139

of the houses shone bright, the air loud with celebration. A man stumbled by him, sick or drunk he could not tell for he crossed the road to avoid him and saw only a shadow of a face as he passed by, then a succession of hacks as the man vomited onto a wall.

The day had been hot but now thankfully breezes swept in from the west and the Piraios, chasing away the heat, but replacing it with the stench of the pyres. He walked by both men and women, wracked by fever, tearing the clothing from their bodies; a few had crawled into a fountain seeking relief. Ignoring them, servant-women dunked jars in the fouled water, indifferent to their plight. For two months Athens suffered under the plague; only now did it advance into his neighborhood east of the Agora.

He heard it now, that rhythmic groan of overburdened wheels grinding on the dry dirt and turned to see two men pulling a cart and smelt their cargo long before he saw it. They halted in front of the fountain, shouldering through the women that filled their jars and dragged two corpses out, tossing them into the jumble of chalky white arms, legs, torsos, and heads of the crammed freight bed. He hurried to stay well ahead of them.

Two windows cast light, but no music, so he rapped the heavy door ring into the bronze lion's head knocker. From within he could hear the soil crunch under swift paced feet. The door cracked open.

"Come in, sir," said Plades. "Master Eukles is awake still, reading."

The servant led the way though the courtyard, lit only by a single bronze lamp above the entrance to the andron. The door to the study leaned inward just a bit, enough for Plades to push his head through and announce Thukydides.

"My dearest friend, please enter," said Eukles as he let the scroll snap and re-curl. "Plades, some wine for us both."

Eukles wore a face worked over by fatigue, stripping him of his ever-present smile. He tossed the scroll to Thukydides.

"What is this?" He unfurled it, tilting it slightly to catch the light from the lamp above the writing table.

"I bought it today. A splendid copy of the book that man from Halikarnassos wrote." He pointed to the eight other wound and tied scrolls upon the table. "What do you think he would write of all of this?"

"The war? The events are too modern for him, I would say." Thukydides cracked a rare smile. He studied the scroll briefly, but tossed it back to his friend. "I can't seem to read any longer. My eyes."

Eukles stepped closer. "They are as red as your father's hair. Have you tried a poultice?"

"Cannot buy any herbs for the poultice, nor can I find a physician to treat me."

"You are strong. The plague does not take the strong," assured Eukles.

Thukydides leaned back in his chair, studying the dancing shadows on the ceiling. He sighed. "I understand you are going with Perikles."

"Yes. If you were not ill, I should insist that you come also."

"He sails to the Peloponnese?"

Eukles slid forward, resting his elbows on his knees as he spoke. "One hundred ships. We strike at Epidauros."

"I would think the ships and the men would be better spent at Potidaia. Almost three years and we haven't taken it."

"Perikles says it will fall soon. Even so that will have little effect on the Spartans. We must strike at them and their allies where they live, just as they have done to us."

He sat motionless, unable to summon the energy for debate. Finally he sipped some wine; his thoughts lingered on its coolness. "When do you sail."

"Tomorrow."

"Then I will say goodnight. The tide will turn early. Of course you will board long before sunrise."

"Of course. Midnight. He wants us at the harbor of Zea by then."

Eukles escorted Thukydides to the street. "May Apollo and his healing son walk with you," he said with concern.

The fever worked on him. It kept him from sleep, even with the smoldering burner of incense and sprigs of buckthorn tied to the lintel of his bedroom door that his father had assured him would stay the daimons of ill health. In sweaty spasms he twisted on his sleeping pallet, eyes opening in pain to watch the pale yellow rectangle of moonlight crawl across the floor as the night crept on. When he caught himself moaning, he shot up, forcing himself from the fog of delirium to arrest any cries that his servants might hear.

Unable to endure it any longer, he staggered out onto the balcony. A breeze rolled over him, clean at first until the mephitic smell of the pyres overwhelmed it. By the moon he would guess it well past midnight. Immediately he peered over the roof to the east. It was later than he thought.

Still naked and hot with fever, he stood for a moment to embrace the night's coolness, then donned a linen chiton and his riding boots. Hardly stealthy he crossed the courtyard to the gate leading to the stable. His head ached. His vision could not be trusted. Trapped by this discomfort, he would not stop to reprimand his steward for being so lax. The plague may have him also.

"Shh, Pedagos," he whispered to his horse. The animal, unsettled by this late-night visit, pranced nervously in the stall until Thukydides' gentle strokes and soothing words relaxed him.

It took awhile for him to fix the bit and bridle upon Pedagos; his fingers worked no better than his eyes. This mere effort took his breath, so he leaned against the horse, sucking air until he felt composed. Pedagos patiently obliged him.

The top of Pedagos' back seemed as high as Lykabettos, for he was unable to call up the strength to make the vault. From the ground to a stool, to the stable gate, he clambered until he could slide upon his horse. He remained upright for most of the ride, but slouched forward in intervals, hugging the horse's neck while clenching its mane. By the time he had come to the Dromos, he had vomited twice. Chills replaced the burning fever. By chance or luck he gained his senses enough to guide Pedagos through the Agora and toward the High City. As he rode, behind him Eos peeked above the horizon, bloodying the sky. He rapped Pedagos to hurry.

Their city was at war but he failed to encounter a single soldier or sentry during his ride. Even at the grand stairway leading to the Propylea, he spotted only beggars curled in sleep upon the steps. He tied up Pedagos and began his climb.

He counted each step. Three and he halted. On again. Several times three and he was halfway up. His brain felt as though it would split his skull. Dizziness forced him to a knee, and he took it, resting till his forced swallows of air subsided. Now in twos he struggled up, turned and sat at the very top. The city below still hid in darkness, while the red-tiled buildings on the slopes of the Hill of Ares caught the sunlight as it spilled over the peaks to the east. He leaned back and gazed through the imposing Doric columns of the Propylea; Golden Athena beamed in the light.

Suddenly energized, he strode through the gate, up the walkway to the statue of the protectress of the city. He swore the goddess moved, as though to re-grip the great spear she clutched in her right hand. Her eyes looked out to the northern sky, still ignoring any mortal who approached. He moved on to the western battlement.

The harbor of Zea bloomed bright with the sails of a hundred war triremes, some already cutting through its calm waters toward the open sea. Rare for him, Thukydides chanted a prayer to Poseidon, then another to the god's sister, Athena, both offered for his friend Eukles.

* * *

The biting smell shook him from a dream. He awoke to the grim face of his father, leaning over him as the iatros swabbed him with a cloth of chilled vinegar. He blinked his eyes open. His father smiled; assured of his son's apparent recovery, a scowl overtook him.

"If you had a wife I could be at home while she fretted over you."

Vinegar trickled into his eye, stinging it shut. He rubbed it open, waving off the physician. "Last I recall, I was at the High City watching the fleet. How did I get here?"

"One of the custodians of the Temple of Athena found you."

"This morning?"

"Three mornings past. You have been sleeping since."

Now the iatros stepped forward. "You are a fortunate man. The fever has subsided. Your spasms of coughing have passed. With a few days rest and some food you should be fine."

Olorus and the physician left the room together. Only his father returned.

"How did you find *him*?" said Thukydides, rolling his eyes.

"Our neighbor Glaukos sent him to me. He must be the only physician left in Athens without the plague."

Thoughts of himself slipped away. "The fleet. Any word?"

Olorus looked down at his feet for a moment, shaking his head. "They landed near Epidauros."

"Yes, I know that. What of the battle?" Thukydides asked anxiously.

"No battle. Barely even a siege. The Epidaurians did to Perikles what we have done to Archidamos. They hurried to their city and stared out at him over their walls."

He sank back into the cushioned pallet. His throat burned with dryness, so he took the cup of liquid on the table beside him, sniffed it, then sipped from it slowly.

"Do not worry, Son, that is no physician's elixir. Wine with a bit of willow bark. 'Tis my own remedy."

* * *

The prognosis proved true. Within a few days he could walk with the assistance of Alexon, the steward; his father had deemed the slave Thukydides' companion till he was well enough to return to his own home, but the steward

143

possessed neither the gentle nature or humble insight of Ataskos, his old pedagogos. He brought him little comfort. His eyes still could endure scant light so he asked Alexon to read to him—but only once. Written words loomed like the high walls of the city to the slave, each an obstacle to be overcome singly and awkwardly. Thukydides preferred the silence of his own thoughts.

Every night, as it had since the plague struck, the house of Glaukos roared with contrived merriment, until quite unexpectedly it ceased on the eve of the Kronia in the month of Hekatombaion.

"Alexon, come here." Thukydides shouted through the open door of his bedroom. The slave sometimes found it hard to slip from his role as steward and master back to one of servant; he did not hurry. Finally he poked his head in.

"Has Glaukos left for the festival?"

"No, Master Thukydides."

He cocked his ear and focused on the open window. No singing. No hum of conversation interlaced with laughter. For the first time since the coming of the plague, his neighbor's house was empty of celebration.

"Help me up," commanded Thukydides. Alexon shuffled to him and performed his part as crutch perfunctorily. Upon reaching the sill, he released the slave from his duty. He sucked the clear air while staring at his neighbor's dark house. Just before Alexon had slipped out, he called to him. "Where has he gone?"

"Glaukos sailed this morning for Potidaia."

Finally, he thought, somewhat relieved. "Is Perikles in command?"

"The strategos Hagnon. He sailed with four thousand men. More than enough to do the job—or so your father says."

Attika
Eighteen
ΑΤΤΙΚΕΣ

The army passed by its handiwork from the previous year, pouring through the devastated village of Acharnai like a winter flood, to follow a long-since abandoned track that threaded through the foothills south and to the town of Phyle. Brasidas had seen only the villages between the border of Megaris and the city of the Athenians; those sights, although many years past, stayed clear in his mind's eye, for they were so distinctly foreign. Athens was crowded. Athens was filthy. Athens was a refuge to the impious. Here in Phyle though, he saw things differently. This town sat on a ridge about eight miles north of the fort. It reminded him of Sellasia, in northern Lakonia, a town which he had adopted as his second during the Phouaxir. The few villagers that lingered here were hardly the sort he had encountered north and west of Athens, in fact many Helots would outshine them in dress and manners. He admired their unpretentiousness. To his king they meant nothing.

"Strip the buildings, then burn it all," commanded Archidamos. The three Spartan polemarchs that attended him strode away to their regiments to pass the order. The allied commanders scurried away too, hoping to set their men to the task quickly; looting always stoked their allies' enthusiasm.

Brasidas accompanied the army as an observer, for being an ephor he wielded no power of command, and could only bring concerns to the other four ephors, who must act in accord; three of the four stood firmly with Archidamos.

"Epitadas, take your company forward on the southern road." Archidamos barked his order then turned to the other pentekonteres of the Ploas regiment. "You will clear this town." Now he glanced Brasidas' way, seemingly as an afterthought. "You may find more to observe with your old company, unless you want to remain here watching Helots load wagons?"

The commanders departed, leaving only Brasidas with the king. "No cavalry?"

145

"What was that?" said Archidamos, shaken from his self-satisfaction of a command quickly obeyed by the others.

"Cavalry. Will a detachment accompany Epitadas?"

"For what? To protect him from sheep?"

"From Athenian mounted troops. The fort is at the crossroads leading to Athens, sitting upon a flat plain."

"And how do you know this?" Archidamos boiled. He squeezed his cornel-wood staff, twisting it with his white-knuckled hands.

"I asked one of them," he answered, pointing to the herded prisoners.

"No cavalry!" He spun around, and while he strode off he shouted back, "If it bothers you, stay here. It matters not to me." In Sparta he would not dare to address an ephor in such a manner, but here in the field the king held ultimate sway. Amongst the troops, Archidamos was the law.

Epitadas' men, unlike the Korinthians, Sikyonians, and other allies, stood in rank, awaiting his orders. "Platoon leaders, here." Lykophron, Saleuthos, Styphon, and Turtle stepped forward, surrounding both him and Brasidas within a tight circle.

"We are to march on." Epitadas paused, watching a squad of Korinthians fling orange roof tiles from atop a house to others standing in the bed of a wagon. One shattered, slipping through the hands of a slave.

"Stupid sheep-fucker!" bellowed a Korinthian hoplite to the clumsy slave in the wagon. "Those tiles are worth more than you."

"To where?" In disgust Turtle stabbed the earth with the butt-spike of his spear.

"South, toward Laurion."

"Ah, we get the silver," quipped Lykophron, looking to the army that swirled through the town, "while they pick roof-tiles?" He looked at Brasidas. "And you wish to come with us and leave all of this?"

The air crackled. Smoke drifted their way. Through the skeleton of one house, flames lapped the sky, while here and there flickered the orange light of arson through open, vacant windows. Rapidly the fire's voice climbed to a roar as it fed upon the town.

"He'll never know," said Epitadas. "Take command of the company— your company."

"They are your men, my friend."

Epitadas shook his head. "You command them whether you wish to or not. Take your position at the fore." He squeezed Brasidas' arm assuringly.

"Just for today," he wrapped an arm around Epitadas as the pair strode to the head of the column. With a wave of his high-held spear, he commenced the march. A thick gray rolled over them, swept by a north wind, heavy with the smell of wood-smoke and the stench of burning flesh. For almost an hour it hung with them until they began to descend from a ridge toward a scattering of small houses.

"What is that?" Styphon swung his helmet free of his face while shading his eyes. Past the cluster of huts, sticking out of a hill-slope like a huge square boulder loomed the crossroads fort.

"Turtle, find us someone." Brasidas ordered the men to stay in double column, but move off the road. Turtle abandoned shield, spear, sword, and armor, carrying only his xiphidion dagger with him. Now he turned to the men flanking the road. "Take water, if you need it." He looked down at his flask, but decided his thirst did not warrant the effort so he kept watch on the huts and the fort beyond. He caught a flash of movement; a door flung open, through which a young boy burst out, stumbling. Behind sprinted Turtle. "Stop boy!" he shouted, keeping to the chase.

The boy tore across the road into an orchard, darting in and about the gnarled tree trunks and through the tall grass, trying desperately to lose his pursuer. Brasidas tossed his gear off and raced to the orchard. Turtle, seemingly forgetting the boy, ran full-tilt for the stream that separated the tightly packed almond trees from the wooded slope behind.

"He's in the stream," shouted Brasidas as he swerved amongst the trees, adjusting his line of sprint to the swerving track of his quarry. He heard the frantic splashes of feet thrashing the stream; nearer he heard panting. Using his left hand as a grapple, he swung around the last tree and into the streambed. On the far bank stood Turtle straddling a boy. Each time he tried to raise up, Turtle slapped him down.

"I'll not chase you again."

Brasidas approached the two of them, but stopped midstream, knelt and began tossing water onto his sweaty face. He drew a mouthful or two from cupped hands, then pushed his long hair free of his face while continuing up the bank. At the top a shaft of sunlight struck him, glistening the beads of water that clung to his beard. The boy, awestruck, gawked at him.

"Let him stand."

"If he runs, you get him," said Turtle as he stepped over his captive.

He did not look like a country boy. His feet bled from the short run and his blue-dyed linen chiton sparkled with gold fretting. As Brasidas moved closer, he caught the scent of perfume.

"Where are you from?" Brasidas knelt, grabbed a bit of grass and began tearing it into smaller pieces as he spoke. "By the look of you, you're not from around here."

The boy rolled over and sat up—reluctantly. His eyes stared gray and empty. Against his efforts his chest began to convulse, prompting him to bury his face in the crook of his arm. He sobbed.

"We will not harm you," assured Brasidas as he continued to rip the blades of grass.

The boy swiped his dirt-streaked face. Emptied of tears, he wrapped his arms around his knees as he sat and began to rock, awaiting the verdict of his captors.

Turtle stood behind the boy, not so close as to upset him, but near enough to sever any escape route. "What happened to you?" He moved to the boy, staring down at his neck, then yanked on the chiton exposing his back; instinctively the boy jerked away, but something in Turtle's grip reassured him he meant no harm. "Brasidas, look here."

Gently Turtle peeled the cloth away from the welted skin. Their captive continued to shiver in the cold garment of fear.

"Who did this?" interrogated Brasidas.

The boy lifted his face. "One of the horsemen."

"A Spartan?" Brasidas' face burned with rage.

"No, sir. An Athenian."

"Why would an Athenian do this?" Turtle let go of the chiton.

"He brought me out from the city to visit his farm. He told me he had many horses."

"And did he tell you what cost in favors you would owe?" Brasidas worked to keep his anger in check.

The boy began to sob again. "No, sir. Not until we got to his farm." He sniffled a bit, then continued. "He put his hands on me and I ran. He caught me. Beat me with his riding whip."

"Where is he now?"

"Gone. He saw your soldiers as they came over the ridge."

He rubbed his beard. "What's your name?"

"Hylas, sir," answered the boy, his head dipped low in respect.

"Hylas, would you like something to eat? Maybe a bit of wine?" Brasidas tossed away the remnants of grass as he rose. "Come with us."

The boy followed Brasidas. Turtle followed him.

"The fort up there," said Brasidas. "Any soldiers in it?"

"I do not think so, sir."

"Good," Brasidas said, smiling.

They didn't carry much with them and their armor bearers and servants were still in Phyle with the bulk of the army, but Brasidas collected a half loaf of barley bread, two olives, and a handful of figs. The boy sat cross-legged and began tearing the bread into finger-sized slivers, shoving each piece into his mouth, the olives, then the figs—all before taking a drink. The Spartans towered over him smiling.

"Breathe, will you!" commanded Turtle. The youth glanced up, but his jaws worked on, until after several immense swallows, he reached up to take the flask from him.

Brasidas studied him. "Even with their ships, food is scarce," he whispered.

"Oh no, sir," replied Hylas between gulps. "The ships bring in plenty. My stepfather reserves most for his symposions. The servants and I eat what we can."

Suddenly Brasidas shouted out, "We go on." They reformed into twin columns, wriggled their shields and armor into place, then edged onto the road. Soon they passed the cluster of huts, walked in the shadow of the stone fort and continued on to the crossroads.

"That road. Where does it lead?" Brasidas finally took a swig from his flask.

Clearing the remnant of a sniffle, the boy answered, "That one leads to Athens. This one to the village of Sphettos. Beyond is Kephale, further on, Laurion."

Up until now, they tromped through wooded and undulating country, their vision limited to a hundred yards and less. As they topped a small ridge, abruptly the thick stand of trees gave way to open, flat fields.

"I do not like this," cautioned Styphon as he scanned both flanks quickly.

"Too roomy for you?" Mockingly Turtle sucked in a deep breath.

"Good cavalry country," interjected Brasidas.

"Then where is ours?" asked Styphon.

"Our king deemed cavalry unnecessary to our mission." Brasidas stopped. "Listen," he said, waving his hand, commanding silence. Immediately the march ceased along with its concomitant noise. Suddenly he swung his spear overhead, shouting, "Square!"

Smoothly and without hesitation each of the four enomotiai formed a side, four deep, shields and spears bristling outward. What had at first sounded like the approach of a distant storm, roared into view on western road.

Brasidas strained to calculate. Dust, thick and swirling, made an accurate count impossible. With his ears he could estimate better than many could with a clear eye. The wedge of galloping horses surged toward them, like a landslide tumbling down a precipitous slope, headlong and clamorous. Now he could make out individual faces of the backswept wings of cavalrymen. Not the merest obstacle of geography stood in their path, but the formation, at the edges, began to disintegrate.

"Slope spears!" he shouted, then leaned forward into the belly of his shield as one would against a gale. The other front-rankers crouched too, cocking their spears overhead. Without looking, he reached for the boy, Hylas, grabbing him by the shoulder of his chiton and flung him deep into the center of their formation.

The horsemen spilled around them like water around a stream-bound boulder, washing over the outer ranks, flinging short javelins, then galloping off. At a safe distance the Athenians collected, studying the Spartans.

Brasidas took the bend out of his knees, then defiantly lowered his shield, resting its rim on the earth before him. He tilted back his kranos helmet. With an exaggerated snort he sampled the air. "Their horses smell better than they do," he bellowed, eliciting laughter from all his men—except Styphon; he stood silent, helmet down, his knuckles white as he twisted the shaft of his spear over and over.

The Athenian commander, while tugging the purple and gold reins of his black warhorse, shouted a bevy of orders, which skimmed across the field to the Spartans as inarticulate grunts. He waved the curve-bladed kopis overhead, then swung it forward, launching another charge.

This time they did not split in two but swerved as a single body to the left and began circling, firing javelins, filling empty hands from their clutches, then firing again. Some rattled in amongst the sloped spears of the Spartans; others clanged bell-like against bronze helmet and corslet; shield strikes possessed their own unique harmony of screaming, grinding metal underscored with hollow thuds.

Brasidas flicked his heavy shield, intercepting a missile, while searching the whirl of cavalry for their commander. By his shouts he found him, now within a few meters, hunched precariously on his rearing horse at the same time twirling a fresh javelin in his hand. He was not much older than a boy, but age proved difficult to distinguish with these beardless Athenians. The cavalryman yelled for his men to keep up their volleys.

"Back step!" The Spartans compressed their square at Brasidas' word. In turn the Athenians compressed their circle. "Again!" Their formation squeezed tight, tighter than close order, and to the point that even turned sideways the men began to press upon one another. This collapse of the square emboldened the Athenians. Brasidas marked their constricting front by the churned soil where they had originally formed up. Horsemen bobbed in, then out—then closer still.

"Now! Open order!"

Like a great bronze flower, the square bloomed, expanding outward with rapidity and precision, unhorsing several of the Athenians with the impact of shields and bristling spear points. Both horses and riders floundered on the torn earth like beached tuna, and like fisherman, the Spartans, using spears as gaffs, dispatched them without compunction. Brasidas counted five riderless horses buck and sprint away from the melee, the last a gold-and-purple bridled stallion. They looked back only once as they rode west, perhaps to see if their abandoned comrades still lived. They did not wish to see too much. Almost as quickly as they appeared, the Athenians slipped over the hill and out of sight.

Spear after spear was planted in the bruised earth. Helmets were tugged free of faces. Brasidas, shield still in hand, weaved his way amongst them, checking eyes, counting heads. He came upon Epitadas sitting between two dead Athenians, legs splayed out, squeezing his hand over his wet and crimson thigh.

"Damn thing won't stop," he said in disgust, looking up at his commander. He squeezed tighter, forcing the blood to flow in sheets from between his fingers.

Brasidas rolled over one of the dead Athenians, then tugged away his chiton, leaving the corpse clothed only in blood and the muck of battle. "Bend your knee a bit," he instructed, then slipped the four-folded garment under and around the seeping thigh. "Hold that."

While Epitadas leaned on the wound with his palm, Brasidas slipped the strap free of his scabbard, then looped it just below Epitadas' groin and cinched it. He peeled back the makeshift compress, then stared at the spurting gash for only a moment before cinching the strap tighter.

"You'll have to be carried."

Others within earshot groaned. Brasidas laid Epitadas' aspis face down in the dirt beside him. Turtle and Styphon, each with a hand under his knees, lowered him gently into the deep bowl of the shield, slung their own across their backs then lifted shield and friend.

Suddenly the boy appeared beside Brasidas. "Won't you set up a trophy?" he asked.

Brasidas grinned. "Spartans do not revel in their victories. Nor do we lament our defeats. Enyalios is a fickle god." He rubbed the boy's head affectionately as he would his own son's, then barked the order to form up for the march.

"Can I come with you?"

Brasidas stopped before he had begun his first step. He turned, looking back over the rim of his shield. "What about your home? Your mother and your father?"

The boy stared at the dirt between his feet. "Sir," he said eyes still down, "'Twas my stepfather that brought me here today."

* * *

Skiritai sentries stopped them on the perimeter just before the commencement of the second watch. Brasidas knew where his wedge of the great circular Spartan camp would lie, the Ploas, regiment of his village of Pitane. As soon as they arrived at the tent of their platoon, he dispatched a runner to fetch the battle surgeon.

Menekles arrived not long after. He knelt beside Epitadas, his servant holding a lamp to work on the wound. He came with a motos of oak moss, already prepared and sponged away the blood, then taking a fresh handful, smothered the wound, leaving it now for the servant to bind it.

"It is a clean one," he said to Epitadas, but loud enough for all around to hear. "In a week you'll be running on it. Until then you will travel in a wagon."

Styphon and Turtle derided him for this. Only women and captives rode in the wagons. After today's long march, they envied him also.

Brasidas stood statue-like beside the fire while Diokles, his hypaspistes, worked to free him of his armor. In the dim light of the camp, he fumbled with the ties that held down the springy shoulder flaps of his master's linothorax. As he peeled these back, Brasidas unfastened the twin cords that met under his left arm. Thankfully Diokles did not see the splatters of blood that he would be compelled to scrub away. The weight, doubled by a day's hard sweat, fooled him; it almost slipped to the ground.

Brasidas loosened the shoulders of his exomis and let the garment fall around his feet. He kicked it away, standing naked except for his krepides boots, awaiting a dry cloak to be brought to him.

152

Across the fire from him Diokles neatly arranged the exomis and linothorax on a rack he had patched together from some trampled vine poles. The helmet he laid atop a square of linen, where sword scabbard and greaves had already been lined up meticulously. Diolkes began with the sword, the metal of its blade twanging with each passing of the stone.

Keraon, the cook, hurried toward them with a bowl of zomos broth and a loaf of barley bread. Owing to the hour, he was certain Brasidas would eat immediately, eschewing the ritual of a mess-tent dinner with the king.

"Keep it warm for me."

He stalked off into the camp, pulling his cloak tight to him, stopping at first to talk with Saleuthos, Turtle, and Styphon, then proceeding, platoon by platoon to take inventory of each body, mind, and spirit. Satisfied the men of Epitadas' company were well settled in, he decided to eat.

Keraon sat at the fire, keeping watch on the covered bowl of broth. On Brasidas' approach he gurgled a cup full of wine from a skin and presented it to him. Brasidas snatched it with a nod, then sat next to him.

"No cakes tonight?" He always looked forward to the epaikla. He swallowed hard, forgetting his manners, draining the cup quickly.

Keraon, red-faced with embarrassment, coughed nervously then said, "They took them all, sir."

"Who?"

"Servants of Thrasymidas. They said you would not be wanting them."

He tipped the bowl, filling his mouth with broth, finishing what little was left with a swab of bread. As he stood he took a hearty swig of wine then handed the cup to his cook.

"I will be back."

He strode through the perfectly laid out lines of tents, smiling to men who sat around their fires, mentioning each by name as he passed, until he crossed into the precinct of the Sarinas regiment. He heard the voice and the obsequious laughter that responded to it. Like a ghost, he insinuated himself virtually unnoticed into the tight circle that ringed the fire. One by one they recognized the spectre, and one by one voices fell silent until all talk ceased. Thrasymidas, unaware and still smiling, finally looked up.

"Brasidas," he announced, unleashing his toothless grin. "I hear you got mauled by the Athenian pony brigade."

His mess-mates responded with fidgety laughter. Brasidas snatched the remnant of cake that hung in Thrasymidas' hand so easily—so disarmingly—that he could do nothing to stop him.

"Good, very good," Brasidas mumbled as he stuffed the cake into his mouth. "Thrasymidas, let us talk." He gestured for him to rise and follow. Thrasymidas got up. Brasidas wrapped a coaxing arm around his shoulder and walked them both away, out towards the perimeter of the camp. Finally, in comfortable darkness, he turned abruptly to face Thrasymidas.

"You steal my food again and I will kill you. No ephor, no king, dare I say, no god will protect you." He thrust his hand out, clamping fingers and thumb around his Thrasymidas' quivering neck. Even in the dark he saw Thrasymidas' eyes bulge large and white. He heard the frantic gasps. He let loose his hand. A spasm of coughs followed. "And tell Archidamos it will take more than *his* feeble contrivances to kill me."

Keraon had not relinquished his seat, for he knew the meal was not finished. Brasidas returned quietly, finished off another cup of wine, and gnawed on the quarter loaf that sat in the empty broth bowl.

"Sir, I have some cheese if you would like it." The cook unpeeled a bundle of grape leaves to reveal a crumbling lump of goat cheese. He passed it, leaves and all, to Brasidas.

As he nibbled the cheese he stared at the array of armor that rested on the linen, watching yellow flames roll and dance upon the unpolished bronze. Sitting cross-legged and bent forward for light was Diokles, pressing hard upon the sword blade with honing stone, its scrape and twang the only sound between them.

From the impenetrable darkness that cloaked them, he heard a scuffle of feet and the rattle of weapons. Then into the halo of light lumbered two Skiritai guards, a boy pressed between them.

"Sir, he claims to know you," barked the taller of the two scruffy sentries. He reached down and grabbed a handful of hair, yanking the boy's face into view.

Surprised, Brasidas stared. "Yes. You can release him. He won't run. We caught him once today." The boy stumbled forward from their grip. "Keraon, go to the tent of Thrasymidas. He has offered to repay the cakes his servants took. The boy looks hungry."

* * *

The first two great summer festivals had come and gone. The Hyakinthia he had missed, for the king would release only the Amyklaians from the invasion force to return for the celebration, and he would not leave his friends in the hands of Archidamos. The Gymnopaideia too passed them by, but the army, as a whole, marched home before the start of the Karneia. Soon after he met with several visitors, men he had not seen since his trip to the Skione and Skapte-Hyle many years past. At first, officially, supping at the Ephorion, but the next day Strophakos, the proxenos for the cities in the Chalkidike brought several others from the north to dine at Brasidas' phidition. Both Turtle and Epitadas had returned from an early morning hunt with a great stag, which Keraon had quickly gutted, dressed, and roasted. Helots paraded into the mess-tent with platters stacked high.

Strophakos graciously acknowledged the Spartans' hospitality, complimenting the ample portions while finding himself unable to properly describe, without insult, the black zomos broth that his host sipped with relish.

"Gentlemen, now that our meal is near its end, I am compelled to speak bluntly of the war." Strophakos' words crashed through the several conversations that had arisen after the platters had emptied. Everyone looked to him. "Tell me, warriors of Sparta, how many battles did you win in Attika this summer?"

Saleuthos sprang to his feet. "How can we win if they do not fight?" He slammed the table with his fist, launching several cups into the air; only one settled back upon the table intact.

"Go to where they *will* fight."

Brasidas smiled at the proxenos' words. He had been to the north and seen what the Athenians valued. For him the battlefield was clearly marked.

"If you want to kill Athenians, go to Potidaia," said Strophakos as he glared across the table at Saleuthos.

"There they are no threat to us," countered the Spartan.

Now Brasidas rapped his knuckles on the table, calling attention to him and the request to speak. "Without a navy that would be a difficult undertaking. As you know, we Spartans are not sailors."

His words elicited nods of agreement. Strophakos reached for his cup of wine as he carefully pondered this response; the other foreigners from Melita looked grim, but did not enter the fray.

"I ask you, does timber grow in the sea? How much gold has been mined from beneath Poseidon's waves?"

Brasidas smacked his lips as he lowered his empty cup. "Tell me, Strophakos, the towns of Pharsalos and Melita are such a great distance from Sparta. To move an army there would require many ships, would it not?"

"Not a one," he answered tersely.

"Then how did you come to Sparta?" snapped Saleuthos.

"By land. The same land upon which the Athenians will not venture because of you Spartans." Strophakos grinned while finishing off his wine, only his smiling eyes visible above the rim of his kothon.

"Wait," interrupted Turtle. "Did you not hear? We have a fleet. A fleet of our allies, but commanded by Spartans." Laughter began to circulate about the tent. "They appointed Knemos navarch today. Alkidas as his Epistoleos. The war is won!"

The men in the phidition roared with laughter; their guests wore befuddled looks, being outside so grand a joke.

"Oh yes," said Saleuthos, gasping for breath. "The two finest commanders in all of Lakedaimon, present company excluded."

Brasidas sat grim faced amidst the banter, then spoke. "Strophakos, tell us what you told me this morning. Tell us all."

"The Thrakians have sided with Athens. This will drag the fickle Makedonians into an alliance also. Worse yet, your allies, the Korinthians, are considering an embassy to Persia to treat with the Great King. All this is happening because our enemies are convinced you will not march far from your home. Your allies are just as certain you will not move to save them."

"If we march north to Thrake, to assist you, then what becomes of Sparta? Who will stop the Athenians from laying waste to our homes." Styphon, silent until now, raged against this proposal.

"You underestimate yourselves. Send not even a quarter of your army and see what your reputation can accomplish. March north as liberators and city after city will follow you."

For most of the evening, Brasidas sat and listened as Strophakos pleaded his case. And on Saleuthos challenged him. Upon one point he agreed with the Pharsalian; the war would never be won in Attika.

* * *

Gyllipos stood like a smiling bronze, transfixed with joy at the sight of his mentor. His company had just been dismissed from the field after its victory in mock battle; naked of clothing but fully armed he did indeed look to be the handiwork of a sculptor, fashioned like a hero from the shadows of Troy's great walls. Others peeled away, saying their good-byes, or simply nodding. Brasidas, with delight in his heart, strode up to him.

156

"I have a gift for you."

Gyllipos slid his shield from his shoulder cap and leaned it against his leg, his eyes appealing to Brasidas to speak. Confidently he plunged his spear into the dry turf to free both hands.

"You are to be assigned to my company."

His face reflected the mixture of astonishment and elation stirring within. "But how—?"

"Seems the power of Archidamos is waning. Men of merit and not of family can once again be recognized in Sparta."

"The other ephors? They have consented?"

"Finally, although two block-headed cronies of the king argued, if grunting can be considered a method of debate."

Gyllipos shivered a bit as an unseasonably cool wind, like the breath of Boreas, swept down from Taygetos. The wind was indeed changing, and for the first time in his life Brasidas perceived it while in its midst. But Archidamos gave away nothing. For this unusual but insignificant favor the king had gained advancement for his friends. The people knew of Brasidas' valor, both at Methone and in Attika, and shrewd Archidamos worked it all to his benefit.

The two walked together until they arrived at Gyllipos' barracks tent. He must report, secure his kit, then bathe for supper. The commotion could be heard as men rushed about inside, some going to the river while others returned. The Karneia would commence tonight at sundown; they all would be dining not in their mess-tents but amongst members of their clan and tribe. It was a grand and holy affair.

Brasidas went off to greet his father, hoping to catch him on the road from his house. Rumors swirled through Sparta like a cold wind from Taygetos that the newly elected ephors had consulted the evening skies, as they were required every ninth year of a king's reign. Something extraordinary had been seen. Could it be Archidamos' turn for exile, or Pleistoanax's recall. Still, his father would know. His single, excruciating year as an ephor had ended not soon enough, but he wished for a moment to be there when the stars had been consulted and see firsthand the fate of kings.

Men passed by him, all heading toward the field where the tents of the three tribes had been erected. Most smiled politely to him; some congratulated him on his completed term; friends of Archidamos walked by blindly. At the turn in the road marked by a storm-beaten willow, two figures appeared, nothing more than black shadows mixing in the fading light of the tree-swallowed path. A voice he recognized.

"Father," he called out. He hustled toward the pair. Now he made out the face of his neighbor Anaxandros and greeted him first, announcing his name politely, then turned to his father. "I had hoped to catch you on the road." He walked between them now. "Have you heard the rumors?"

Tellis grinned knowingly. "About the reading of the stars? They are not rumors. Facts hard and cold as the iron of your sword."

"Is it Archidamos?"

"Better. Pleistoanax is to be recalled."

His mind raced with this news. Pleistoanax would end this war quickly. And Kleandridas. He too would be reinstated. Gyllipos would have a father once more. "When?"

"After the Karneia. In fact, the ephors will appoint you as royal escort."

Brasidas' smile stole his voice. Anaxandros nodded in agreement—for certain he would know, for he was a Gerontes, and elected to the council for life. His words were much valued because of their scarceness, but also because they never failed to ring true.

Arkadia
Nineteen
ΑΡΚΑΔΙΚΑ

Epitadas spoke softly to his horse, rubbing its neck to calm it. Turtle's family had bred racers and they were high-strung, athletic beasts—a challenge to handle by even an expert horseman, and Turtle had selected the most spirited lot from his stables to impress his comrades. Brasidas murmured something into the animal's ear. It neighed a bit, shaking its head, then trotted off out of the stable-yard and onto the road. Turtle and Epitadas followed.

Dawn had slipped over the eastern peaks like a golden ribbon, fleeting but brilliant against the retreating purple sky of night. Frost crunched under hooves. Their breath boiled and faded in the chilly air, like the fast-moving wispy clouds exhaled by gods. He thought this the best part of a day.

"Is it not odd that they send only us?" said Turtle.

"A large contingent might draw undue attention," offered Epitadas.

Brasidas said nothing.

They passed a troop of young second-year boys who had been sent to forage on the banks of the Eurotas. Further on, mingled in with the trees of a gentle slope, they came across more boys, but they were older and gathering firewood. Their bouagos shouted orders, shaking them all to high-pitched action.

"Where is our friend Styphon?" asked Turtle.

Brasidas stared ahead as he spoke. "You know he does not care for horses."

The three continued on amongst the long shadows of early morning. Suddenly Brasidas pulled up, eyes focused ahead as he waved for silence. At the next bend in the road, beneath a canopy of arching chestnut trees, a fawn stood frozen, black eyes searching for movement. The deer blinked directly at him, then bobbed its head before bounding off into the thick of the forest.

The cool dampness quickly fled, whisked away by the climbing sun and hot breath of a south wind. In the heat, morning ripened into midday. Through the haze they could see the small bridge that spanned the Oinos River, where

159

the road bent to the west to Sellasia. Brasidas scanned the ridges, reminiscing.

"Is this where you met her?" asked Epitadas respectfully. "The first time, I mean."

"The goddess?" Brasidas would not give his answer so easily.

"Why, of course. Who else would I mean." Epitadas rolled his eyes. Turtle kicked his horse to come between the two, bent on hearing the answer.

"Not exactly. Further up the valley, near Karyai."

In Sellasia they bought three loaves of flatbread, a dried flank of venison, and two pints of wine. They ate as they traveled. By dusk they had reached the mountain village of Arachoa in the territory of Skiritis. The inn was small with only a few guests, so they ate a leisurely supper and lingered in the hall to keep warm and sip wine.

"So tell me, men of Sparta, what is going on up north?"

The peddler of votives, a Sikyonian, threw out the question to stir a bit of talk from the stolid trio.

"North? What do you mean?" Epitadas walked over to the brazier, palming the hot, rising air as a mystic might summon a daimon.

"This morning a troop of horsemen rode through. At first glance I took them for Spartans. As dour and tight-lipped as the three of you, although none wore your scarlet cloth." Epitadas perked up at his words; Brasidas remained unconcerned. "You know nothing of this?" The Sikyonian tapped the dregs from his cup into his yawning mouth. "No embassy these fellows, girded for battle as they were. All hard-looking men in their prime."

The innkeeper dropped another lump of charcoal into the brazier while nodding in agreement. "They talked with no one, watered their horses, then rode off."

Brasidas glanced at Turtle, yawning, who in turn looked to Epitadas and said, "Does it not seem strange that they could not spare more than the three of us to go to Tegea, yet a whole squadron of cavalry rides out before us?"

"There is a war, you know," Brasidas interjected.

"But you think they would tell you—"

"If you mean the ephors, dear Turtle, they tell me only what they must." Brasidas walked over to the brazier, joining Epitadas.

The peddler continued with his talk, it now maundering to gossip circulating in the allied cities, then suddenly he blurted out, "They were in a great hurry too."

Brasidas, ignoring the conversation, slipped into a chair beside him. "May I have a look?"

The peddler beamed. He reached into a large wicker-work basket and withdrew several highly polished figurines. One by one he lined them up on the small table as though they were in a miniature procession. Brasidas' expression did not change. The man pulled out more.

"That one," said the Spartan. "How much for that?"

The peddler glanced at his hand with a sour look. "But I have many finer ones," he said apologetically.

"That one will do fine." He slid an obal on the table, replacing the figure in the procession.

"Thank you, sir," said the Sikyonian as Brasidas excused himself of their company with a nod.

"That is not like him," said Turtle through clenched teeth, trying to cloak his words.

"No, he is awake much later than usual," answered Epitadas, grinning.

Turtle turned to the peddler. "Why aren't you laughing, sir? Have you not heard Spartan humor before?" He spun the chair hard against the table as he rose and strode out of the room. The Sikyonian remained in his seat, cradling his cup with both hands, flummoxed.

"A good night to you, sir," said Epitadas, "and thank you for your conversation." He nodded politely, then slipped through the black doorway, his footsteps fading quickly.

* * *

Turtle rode through the whole morning simmering, unwilling to talk to either of his comrades. He hardly appreciated their complaisant manner of the prior evening and he surely did not like being ignored, especially in so serious a matter. Brasidas, on the other hand, welcomed the silence. Most times he drew conversation out of men, his confidence spreading to those around him, his interest genuine, and his opinion highly sought. Epitadas kenned his attitude; he rode in silence also.

By mid-afternoon, when the sun had drained the horses of their bounce and stripped the men of their sharpness, they left behind the spacious track that meandered along the River Oinos and plunged into the dark of thick woods. Here the oaks grew tangled in intimacy, turning bright day into dusk. Quickly the horses recovered their buoyant gait in the shadowy coolness. Quickly too the men regained their edge. Turtle scanned the gloomy wood furtively, certain they were not alone. In him men conjured no fear, but the stories of mad nymphs and wild gods who dwelled here unsettled him. What good would his sword be against an immortal?

"The road, it splits in three ahead," cautioned Epitadas.

"Ah, my friends, what would you like to see today? The sanctuary of Zeus Skotitas perhaps, or the statue of Herakles?" He turned right, then left, looking to each of his comrades.

Turtle answered, not amused in the least at his casual manner. "Neither. Which is the road to Tegea?"

"Follow me." Brasidas galloped off to the right, following the path that sliced deeper into the forest.

Turtle slapped his horse to bolt, while Epitadas urged his to pursue. As the forest collapsed around them, the two became unnerved by the absence of sky above; only a hint of sunlight filtered through the stooping walnuts and oaks.

Suddenly, as though Zeus himself had pushed the forest aside, they broke into bright and open country; planted fields sprawled ahead of them, and beyond the clustered buildings of a large village. "That is Karyai," Brasidas announced as he turned around to check on his friends.

While they rode along the narrow road that writhed over the undulating fields like a great serpent, he related to them of the festival of maidens and their choral dances that he, during the Phouaxir, had the pleasure to watch from a nearby hillside. But he did not tell that in every maiden he saw Temo. These recollections he preserved for himself.

Around them men toiled. Here the clime was cooler than in their valley, so the harvest did not run as deep into autumn. Barley stalks leaned cut and piled, awaiting the train of wagons that wended their way from a farmhouse to the east. The road carried them through the village proper, past a modest agora and the few inhabitants that loitered there, on by a wooden temple to Demeter and out to the countryside beyond. On the far side of the village the land was scoured of any soil, only fields of boulders spreading out and up the slopes of the high-climbing hills to the north. Above, in the pale blue of the sky, carrion birds swooped in lazy circles, searching for a meal.

"Something's dead up there," said Epitadas, pointing.

"I heard a lion roaring one night," reminisced Brasidas. "Might have been from those very hills. Unfortunate we do not have time for a hunt."

"In all these years, Brasidas, you have never told us why you came so far during the Phouaxir?" Many years past, when the three had ended the Fox Time, Turtle thought Brasidas' talk of the north—Sellasia, Skotitas, Karyai, and such—was an invention of imagination. This tour and firsthand recollections proved otherwise.

"To keep out of trouble," he answered. He did not make mention of the goddess, nor his warnings about Epitadas.

For most of that afternoon they followed this rock-hard, heat-tempered land, seeing no one until they began to descend through the gorge cut by the Sarantopotamos River. Before them the valley fanned out; rising from its center, the city of Tegea.

The walls here were modest when compared to the Athenian's, but in Sparta they possessed nor required nothing of the sort; walls proved a novelty to them and admitted weakness. In and out from the gateway surged the traffic of heavy grain wagons, men on foot and teams of panniered mules, kicking up a pall of stinking dust. The three rode above it, but not above the noise; the clamor shook them. As they entered, a figure hidden in the shade of a stoa called out.

"Brasidas, son of Tellis."

They turned. Brasidas leaned out, shading his eyes, searching the shadows. A tall figure emerged, hardly dressed as a Spartan in a bright turquoise chiton of embroidered linen. Brasidas stared incredulously.

"Do you not recognize me?"

After the man took three long strides toward him he knew. He vaulted from the horse, his emotions teetering between past sorrow and present joy. They embraced, stood apart for a moment measuring each other, then embraced again.

"Kleandridas, the years have been good to you."

"Much better toward you, Brasidas." Now he looked up to his companions. "Epitadas! Turtle! Splendid to see you both."

Brasidas glimpsed the sunlight as it reflected off the welling tear in Kleandridas' eye. Unconcerned, he let it roll down his cheek, and only wiped it later, instinctively.

"Come, gentlemen. The king is anxious to see you." He led them through the crowded street, shouldering his way, making a pathway for the men and their horses. Abruptly he halted and turned around. "And where are the others?"

"What others?" returned Epitadas.

"The guard for the king. Where are they?"

Brasidas locked his eyes to Kleandridas'. "We are all they sent."

Kleandridas smile fled. "And you thought nothing of this?" he said, shaking his head in disbelief. "You should have demanded at least half of the Knights—one hundred and fifty. That is the what he deserves," shouted Kleandridas, waving towards their unseen destination.

Dismounted and leading their horses, they threaded their way through the teeming agora, beyond the stalls and booths until arriving at the bouleterion. Kleandridas entered first.

"Brasidas," said Pleistoanax as he rose from his chair. "I am glad it was you they sent." Others, men unknown to Brasidas, remained in their seats that flanked the king. "The journey uneventful?"

"Yes. Not a single traveler did we encounter until well into Skiritis."

"And how is your father?"

"Unchanged, I would think, since you last saw him," answered Brasidas with a hint of disdain.

"So seem you." Pleistoanax laughed. "We shall dine at the home of my good friend Hippias. With first light on the morrow we set out for home."

* * *

Brasidas rose before any of them, wanting to check the horses and watch the sky for the light of a new day. The stable boy, huddled beneath a pile of blankets and deep in slumber, heard nothing as he crept in. The horses swayed mildly in the numbness of sleep, from their nostrils wisps of vapor stroked the cold morning air. The stable boy tugged the blankets tighter. Something unseen flitted by the edge of his vision.

"My house is your haven," whispered a velvety, unseen voice—an immortal voice.

He spun around, his heart drumming so loudly it was certain to wake the stable boy. Nothing, not even a shadow.

He swung open the double doors, scanning the stable-yard and the gray expanse of the open field beyond. At the edge of the woods a doe froze mid-track, then sprang for cover.

"Sir?" In the doorway, rubbing the sleep from his eyes, the boy spoke. "Do you want your horse now?"

"Go back to sleep," he said, pushing the doors closed.

The rest began to stir. Pleistoanax made sacrifice to Zeus Protector just as the sun slipped above the hills to the east. Afterward they took their first meal of the day, the akratisma, with their host Hippias. It consisted of nothing more than a bit of bread dipped in wine, for they were more anxious than hungry. Pleistoanax thanked Hippias warmly, embraced him as a brother, then extended an invitation to him as a guest-friend to visit Sparta. Kleandridas spoke with him apart from everyone, embraced him, then hustled them all to depart.

During the ride Kleandridas did not pose the questions Brasidas had been prepared for. He asked little of his son, Gyllipos, nor did he speak about his wife, mother, or kin. When Brasidas offered any information, Kleandridas dismissed it politely, his interest being confined to Archidamos.

"No change, although he did take the army much deeper into Attika this summer past."

"Yes. Word of this came to us. Word also of your little victory," Kleandridas added. "Seems you have upset him again no matter how closely he watches you."

Pleistoanax, hearing their talk, interjected, "He banishes you to Methone and you deliver Sparta's only victory the year prior. He locks you within the Ephorion, and still you disappoint him with another lone Spartan triumph." Now the king chuckled. "How dare you exhibit such competence!"

"Nothing more or nothing less than any commander would have done."

"Except his chosen ones," interrupted Epitadas. "They are in supreme command of the allied fleet."

"Archidamos owes the families of Knemos and Alkidas much." Kleandridas spoke for all to hear. "More, it seems, than he owes our country."

They had entered the narrow, dark road of Skotitas, forcing them to ride no more than two abreast; Brasidas paired up with the king. Several of the escorts hung their heads napping, lulled by the rhythmic clop of hoof on the hard-packed road. He wriggled his sword-strap and scabbard till it again fell comfortably on his hip.

At first they heard nothing. Brasidas felt something through his horse, for the animal's ears pricked up and its neck tensed; it snorted nervously. Then, exploding from the trees on either flank, helmeted men on horseback charged, screaming while spinning their swords and javelins wildly overhead.

"The king," shouted Brasidas to Turtle, who knew without another word what to do; he grabbed the bridle of Pleistoanax's horse, tugging hard. Kleandridas moved in beside his friend, filling the void left by the king, each covering the other's back as they parried and struck at the enveloping melee.

Kleandridas' short sword proved difficult to wield from horseback. He had nearly to embrace a foe to employ its stubby iron. Brasidas' single spear had snapped in the abdomen of a foe, where the leg joins it, its splintered end wobbling frantically with each whirl of the man's horse. Smoothly he emptied his scabbard and began to hack away at the poking javelins and spinning enemy horses.

Repelled at first the attackers gathered, severing the road and escape to Tegea. They glared at the Spartans as hunters do when they come upon a stunned boar caught in a snare, confident—heartless. Meanwhile Brasidas, Kleandridas, and the four others formed up, weapons drawn, ready to defend. Beneath him his horse cantered nervously; Brasidas could feel the power coiling in the beast. Behind him hoof-beats faded.

Two lay dead across the road, both members of the ambuscade, men whose lifeless eyes seemed to stare only at him. His left arm felt wet; a sword cut, slicing only flesh, ran the length of his forearm. Like their foes, both pain and blood paused, overwhelmed by the swiftness of the action but assured of an inevitable return.

Suddenly Brasidas kicked his heels hard. "Ride!"

Using this momentary respite they bolted after Pleistoanax and Turtle.

"How many?" shouted Kleandridas over the thunder of hoof-beats.

"Twenty at least." Brasidas snuck a look back over his shoulder. "Maybe thirty!"

Ahead of them a bright patch of sunlight cut a swath through the forest; soon they would emerge into a clearing—more advantage to their pursuers' greater numbers. Dust hung in the air, low and thin, but quickly gaining in height and density as they closed the distance with Turtle and the king. Beyond the clearing he spotted their obscured forms.

"Turtle!"

One figure turned around, slowing his horse. The other two looked back to them.

Brasidas and the escort tore across the bright open patch of road, but with each passing moment, he could feel them closing. A javelin whistled by his ear, kicking up a clod where it struck. Another tore the air. From behind he heard the thud of a body hitting the earth. He turned. Kleandridas still rode. So too did Epitadas. As he passed a hedgerow that framed the road, he looked quickly right, then left, searching for a trail, some obstacle to turn, anything that might impede the raging pursuit that began to overtake them.

Without warning crimson waves surged up from the hedges, half a hundred Spartan horseman inundating the road. Horses snorted and wailed in the collision while riders fought to control their wild estrapades. The scene boiled with dust and the wails of dying men and beasts. Brasidas pulled hard on the reins, spinning his horse to face the fray, the rest following as they added their weight to the hammer of cavalry that struck the anvil of the road. Horse slammed against horse, the very weight of their muscle and bone conveyed by the heavy sounds of combat. Men screamed as they were hacked off their mounts and into the mill of hooves beneath.

"Take them alive!" shouted Brasidas as he rode into the whirl of combat, pulling down the sword of a trooper ready to strike. "I want them alive!" The man, his face full of rage, transformed at these words until an incongruous smile appeared. "Styphon!" Brasidas stared for a moment, then barked the command again. "Take them alive!"

Quickly the Spartan cavalry circled the five survivors, threatening them with weapons held ready to strike. They lowered their swords, a gesture of false submission, before each one of them reversed their grip. Eyes rolled back into their heads as they plunged their blades deep into their bellies. Clutching, swooning, then tumbling over, each one of the five fell dead to the ground.

Epitadas flew from his horse. One by one he frantically turned over each body, but life had abandoned them. He wiped the blood from his hands upon the cloak of a corpse. "Twenty dead. Only two of ours." A rider cantered up to him. He glanced up. "Styphon?" He, like Brasidas, stared long and unbelievingly. Finally he added, "I thought you disliked horses?"

Brasidas said nothing as he looked to his friend. Epitadas stood over the bodies in silence, awaiting an answer.

"It was Temo. She warned me of this," he said, swinging his unsheathed sword about, indicating the dead highwaymen.

The mere mention of her name sent his heart racing. He was certain she had forgotten him, lost in the hard, short life of a Helot. "But how—?"

"Talk amongst Strangers, near a well. She had even overheard the name of the place."

"And what place is this?" asked Epitadas, shrugging his shoulders.

"Why, the sanctuary of the Huntress." Turtle pointed with his dripping blade to the gleaming image of Artemis tucked in the open-sided shrine."

Brasidas slid from his horse and walked to the painted wooden statue of the goddess. He reached into the satchel slung over his shoulder and pulled out a small figurine, one of a young woman, quiver and bow slung gracefully over an arm.

"Thank you," he whispered, placing it upon the small roughhewn altar.

Kleandridas, with King Pleistoanax riding next to him, reined up over the bodies of the five. "Would have liked to talk to them," he said as he spit upon one of the corpses. "Although, we would learn little more."

"You must know who sent them. Only a handful of men would benefit from your death," said Brasidas as he looked to the king.

"We can prove nothing. And even if we could, what would you have us do? Provoke a war in Sparta itself?" Kleandridas jumped from his horse, then began poking a body with the tip of his sword. "An Achaian. Couldn't understand him anyway."

Athens
Twenty
ΑΘΗΝΑ

Perikles stepped to the bema, brushing by Kleon as though he had no more substance than a shadow. Kleon had passed the better part of an hour before the Assembly, deriding his war policy of restraint; prior to this he had spent many weeks in the same endeavor, but jawing at citizens in small groups at symposions. Perikles and the more seasoned statesmen of the polis despised him not so much for his opinions, which encouraged rashness, but for his uncouth manner in delivering them; he spoke to the worst in each man, slapping his thigh in mockery to make a point, stirring thought-numbing emotion in place of reason. Perikles turned to look out upon a sea of rage.

"Truth be told, I was not quite prepared for the indignation which this man has," he said, pointing down to the departing figure of Kleon, "aroused in you all toward me. He reminds you of everything you have suffered. Remember, it is a better thing when our city is on the right course, and it is likewise better for each individual than for private interests to be satisfied while the city goes down in ruin. What good is your wealth if your country and security are destroyed?"

Now he looked beyond the faces that crowded around him, beyond those standing upon the wall of the Pynx and to each side where boys hung in the trees gawking. He stared off, as though he pondered something great and distant, stretching the silence as a potter stretches clay; like the potter he was ready for his idea to take form.

"Now you are angry with me. For certain it is folly to go to war if one has the free choice and can live undisturbed. But given a choice between submission and safety, or freedom and its companion danger, I choose freedom. So did you all when our city followed my advice, embarking in this struggle. I have not changed; it is you who are not the same."

Presently he turned his gaze to Kleon. "It is because your own resolution is weak that my policy appears to be mistaken. Granted it is a policy which entails suffering—and surely each of you knows what suffering is. But when something unexpected and against all preparation happens, it takes the courage out of men. The plague has done this to you."

He looked upon the crowd. Silent faces stared back. Some even nodded. He liked the shape of things.

"If you are the people who I think you truly are, then I know each of you will ignore his own troubles and join with the rest for the survival of all."

The shape now matched his imagination, although he must work to smooth it all, fashioning it to completion.

"When Xerxes and his hordes posed the same question—submit or perish—what did our fathers do? They chose neither but forged victory for themselves. You must never fall below these standards that generations past have set down for our city.

"Every event that has unfolded we have anticipated save the plague. But remember it is right to endure with resignation what the gods send—but face what tribulations man delivers with steadfast courage. That is the Athenian way."

Heads nodded in agreement. Kleon spun around and began shoving through the crowd.

"Do not send embassies to Sparta. Do not give the impression that you are bowed down under your present sufferings. Stay behind our walls. Neither peace, nor outright battle with the Spartans will ensure our prosperity. Summon patience! Summon fortitude! Things will turn our way." He stood poised upon the bema, looking over the crowd to the gleaming temples on the Akropolis. Perikles re-emphasized his points, adding the finishing touches, then stepped off the bema, not waiting to receive the judgment of the Assembly. In his heart he already knew.

By evening, when he had retired to his home and had commenced the evening meal, a messenger arrived from the Assembly. He was to be fined, to appease their pride, but his arguments were accepted. Two months later he was re-elected strategos, general of the army.

To celebrate, Thukydides held a dinner in Perikles' honor, feasting his re-instatement as military leader and also his hold on the opinion of the demos. The following week he received command of a company of heavy infantry.

Attika
Twenty-One
ΑΤΤΙΚΕΣ

With the approach of the summer harvest, the Spartan army and its allies streamed across the Isthmos, past Megara and into Attika. Like a leashed dog this great army bounded up to Athens' wall, reaching the limit of its tether, barking fiercely at an enemy beyond its bite. Again Brasidas marched with them, and once more he railed at the impotence of this strategy of devastation.

Now in command of a battalion, he found himself encamped outside the town of Leipsydrion. The heat of the day moved aside, every so often, to allow the breezes from the slopes of Mount Parnes to slip by. Behind him an Elaian trooper hacked away at an olive tree.

"What is that all about, man?" he yelled to the Elaian, over the crack of iron clefting into wood.

The man dropped his hands to his side, still clutching the ax. "Orders. Destroy anything that can feed them."

"You can hack at that all day. Tomorrow too if it pleases you. It will grow back—unless you mean to dig it out by its roots then burn it. Meanwhile, all you do is dull your blade, and it seems your wits."

He dropped the ax. "Then why such orders? It is your king who issues them!"

Brasidas declined the man's invitation; he would not disparage Archidamos, at least to a foreigner. Epitadas walked toward him, the rim of his shield clanging against his bronze greaves. He planted his spear, then himself next to his friend.

"I don't think there is anything left to burn," he said wryly, scanning the remnants of walls that once made up the houses of the town.

Something shiny caught his eye, so he scratched at the soil, revealing a bronze clasp, the type women used to fasten the shoulders of their peplos gowns. With his fingernail he scraped the black from its surface, revealing the embossed form of a swan. The pin at its base was snapped off.

"What is that?"

"Something that serves no function," answered Brasidas. He tossed the relic to Epitadas. "That is the only thing left here. We have stripped the countryside of anything of value. Only useless fragments, like old memories, remain."

Out of sight, they heard the rustle and clatter of an armored man running. From the other side of the hill, Turtle bounced into view.

"News from home," he said, puffing with exertion. "Knemos has sailed for Zakynthos with a thousand Spartiates!"

He spoke of the island off the west coast of the Peloponnese. They had declared for Athens at the start of the war, and now with Archidamos away the ephors encouraged action.

"Knemos—ha!" snapped Epitadas. "It should be you leading that expedition."

"We do not decide such things, but I shan't disagree with you." Brasidas laughed. "One thing is certain; we will find no victory here in Attika. The Athenian empire is like a great cake, much too wide for any mouth to chew. We must nibble at its edges, in Zakynthos, the Chalkidike, Ionia—wherever it harms her interests."

"But what else need you do to prove your abilities? You should be in command, not that dull wit, or his toothless brother."

Turtle fell in beside the two. "Whoever commands here, or at Zakynthos for that matter, is nothing more than a herdsman tending a flock. We do not fight, we graze." He grabbed a bit of grass and began chewing. The Elaian stopped his work on the olive tree to stare.

"Hylas," Brasidas shouted, waving to the boy.

He approached, shuffling awkwardly under the weight. Upon stopping he slid the basket down the length of him, straining, finally settling it in the dirt. He turned back the leather apron and reached in to pull out a bundle wrapped in oily linen.

"Ah, let's see how he has cooked it," said Epitadas as he studied the parcel anxiously.

Hylas peeled away the linen; inside sat a steamy quarter of boar, slain this morning by Brasidas and Epitadas—gutted, skinned, dressed, and cooked by Hylas this afternoon.

"Excellent," announced Brasidas. He slipped his xiphidion dagger from its sheath and carved off a palm-sized hunk, repeating this until he had cut and distributed a portion to each of them, Hylas included. "Bring the rest of our meal here. I would forgo my tent on such an evening."

The three friends and the boy Hylas finished the plank of boar-meat, Brasidas ordering the remaining portions to the officers of his battalion. Across the hills smoke wafted in the breeze, redolent with the aroma of well-cooked food, a smell easily distinguished from the harsh scent of war.

"It reminds me of home," mumbled Turtle through a full mouth as he outlined the mountain with the blade of his knife.

"Yes," concurred Epitadas. "In this light it does look quite like Taygetos. Even the high summit takes on its shape. Don't you agree, Brasidas?"

His question fell to no one. Brasidas walked in the darkened glen, away from the meal and his friends, his thoughts carrying him home. It angered him. He reminisced not of his wife or two boys, but of her. She had saved his life while risking hers. He knew where she lived but avoided the place, fully occupying every moment, certain to leave no time to reflect. Here in this war of boredom that was impossible. In all things but this he could call on his courage; with her he doubted it.

"Hylas! My horse."

The boy returned shortly, tugging the stallion behind him, shouldering a leather pack while fumbling with an unruly triboun cloak that refused to stay wrapped about his arm.

"Epitadas, you are in command of the battalion."

"What about Archidamos?" he shouted after his friend.

"I ride to tell him now."

* * *

The farm of Kratisikles appeared much the same as when he was enduring the Fox Time, except on this occasion a mob of Helots swarmed over the fields, bringing in the harvest of barley and corn. He rode through the twin stone pillars that bracketed the trail, past the outbuildings and toward a cluster of women who hacked at the few upright stalks with iron sickles. As he drew nearer, one by one they uncoiled from their laborer's stoop, glimpsed at the Spartiate, then quickly looked away. One woman straightened, dropping her sickle, gaze locked upon the approaching stranger. She shuffled forward a step or two. Next to her clung a little girl.

"Temo?"

She did not speak, but nodded.

Anxiously he slid from his horse, stepping forward to embrace her, but she stood frozen, wordless, the only movement discernible a trickle of tear flitting down her cheek. Repulsed by the awkwardness he withdrew. He stared. The hope-filled glow of youth had faded, replaced by the lusterless veil of a hard life. Although still beautiful, age had begun to etch away the natural perfection of her face.

"You saved my life," he said, searching her eyes for some acknowledgment, something comforting and reassuring; he found nothing.

"You abandoned mine."

Unsure of what to say or do he lashed out at the other women. "Leave us. Leave us now!" His words sent them scurrying. The girl sobbed as she ran.

With the back of her hand she rubbed the tear-streak from her face, composing herself. "You have two sons? Are they well?" Bereft of words, he nodded. Now he paced restively before her like a wolf in a cage. "The girl you chased away. That is my daughter."

From the far edge of the field, he caught the movement of figures. Warily they moved closer, eyeing him, while brandishing gleaming sickles. Memory flashed; he distinguished the same two who had trapped him in the barn. Worn old by working the fields, they did not seem so formidable now.

"You have wedded," he blurted out.

"As did you," she answered, turning her glance to the approaching band. "That is my husband, leading them all. In many ways he is much like you. His name is Xenias."

Brasidas studied Xenias boldly. The other Helots noticed this and began to flock around Xenias. They chattered. Xenias simply stared back. "Is he a good man?" She nodded. He paused, then suddenly whipped his cloak back to reveal the gleaming handle of his short sword. The group of Helots crept forward, their sickles flashing in the bright sun as they twisted in their grips. Brasidas lowered himself into a crouch, plucked some grass from the earth at his feet and began tearing it, letting the tatters waft from his fingers.

"He is always there for me." Not a trace of a tear lingered in her eyes now.

He wanted to explain himself, to talk away his callousness, to blame his father, Kratesikles, even Sparta. But it would change nothing. He looked around from his crouch. No grass, only powdery, dry soil and a few stones. He said his good-bye with a glance, then bounded upon his horse.

* * *

"Archidamos returns and this happens." Brasidas tossed the scrap of bread on the floor of the phidition in disgust.

Sthenelaidas raised his hand off the table, high enough for Brasidas to see his gesture of restraint.

"Maybe if Knemos and our vaunted one thousand had slain more than cows on Zakynthos, there would be no need for such dealings in perfidy."

"It is only an embassy, a warrant of talk, not action." Sthenelaidas lost his usual coarse and gravelly speech, transforming it with a tone of subtle patience. "Nothing will come of it, I am certain."

"I cannot believe such men as Aneristos, Nikolaos, and Protodamos would agree to this commission—an audience with the Great King!" He stared up at the trophies of captured armaments pegged upon the posts of the tent, trophies of enemies defeated at the cost of Spartan lives. The light from scattered lamps danced over the polished bronze and iron armor. "That," Brasidas said, pointing to a purple-edged corslet of gold-scaled armor, "belonged to a Persian, cousin of Xerxes. Slain by your grandfather. Now we chat with these barbarians?"

Sthenelaidas could not find a word. He grabbed his cup, burying his mouth in its wide rim.

"This is to placate our allies, is it not?" Styphon dropped the question, more as a distraction than an inquiry.

"The Korinthians would sell their mothers to best Athens. So would the Thebans. What favor would the deathless gods bestow on us if we cozied up to the Medes?"

"Dear Brasidas, the Athenians would do the same, if given the opportunity. We do not covet the Persians' friendship, only their money," Sthenelaidas said reassuringly.

"There is a cost for everything, my friend. The cost for their money would be too high."

"Brasidas, you linger too long in the past, thinking of the Great War when the distinction between enemy and friend was drawn with stark clarity. It is different today." Styphon, as always, sought the smoother of two roads, even in conversation.

"I would rather grant Athens here empire than side with Artaxerxes."

"And have Sparta perish in the process?" Sthenelaidas raised his hand higher, as if to caution against any quick response. "We argue for naught. The Great King, if he has a brain beneath his jeweled tiara, would see to it that neither Sparta or Athens dominate affairs here in Hellas."

This logic calmed Brasidas; he pursued the matter no further. The mess-mates spoke of the coming autumn, and the time they would spend in company with the youth of the Agoge. The campaigning season, now at an end, gave way to other duties of the army. Battle veterans worked with the older boys, drilling them in formation evolutions, marching and counter-marching, instilling the binding element of community to their war skills. It was a pleasant season.

* * *

During the month of Diosthios, in the middle of the year when the days were their shortest and the snow crept down the slopes of Taygetos and into the valley, the Assembly of all Spartiates convened. Tellis and his son, enduring the cutting winter wind, hustled along the road toward the Skias.

"Do you know what this is all about?" shouted Brasidas over the roaring wind as he brushed the hair from his face.

"Must be word from the embassy to Persia."

As they drew closer to the agora, the road began to fill. Epitadas, Turtle, and Styphon fell in with them, this thin trickle of crimson-clad Spartans eventually thickening to choke every road leading to the Skias. Relieved to finally be out of the weather, they looked about for a vacant seat and others of their village. As they sat Archidamos called for silence. Beside them sat the senators of the Gerousia. Kratisikles, again elected ephor, rose up to address the assembly.

"We have here Erasinidas, a companion of the Korinthian emissary Aristios. He accompanied the embassy to Persia and has returned with sorrowful news." Kratisikles waved the man forward, encouraging him to speak.

"Spartans, I know many of you think you fight this war for Korinth. You say we despise Athens because of her infringement on our trade. This, I admit in the beginning, might have been true. For what wrong did Athens perpetrate against mighty Sparta? To many the Athenians were merely aggressive merchants, tough traders, and wily businessmen. Surely nothing that would endear them to a Spartan heart, but nothing evil either." He looked out at the faces, catching himself. These are Spartans, he reminded himself, and need no embellishment of speech, no preening of the orators art to sway them—only truth. "To cut to the quick—our ambassadors, yours and mine, have been slain."

Groans, then chatter spread across the Assembly. A single voice shouted out, "Death to the Mede." Quickly others echoed him.

Erasinidas lifted his arms, quelling the commotion, then continued. "Was not the Persians who committed this foul deed, but the Athenians. They murdered your citizens and ours."

The Skias erupted in shouts of rage, streams of threats pouring from the mouths of more than a few. Epitadas turned to his friend, cupping his hand by his mouth to protect the whisper. "What do you think of the Athenians now?"

The Korinthian waited for the outcries to subside. "That is only a portion of the tidings I was sent to deliver." Silence fell like a great stone, quashing the last mutter. "The Athenians have taken our colony of Potidaia."

Brasidas spun around, shouldering his way through the mass to exit the Skias. Epitadas followed. Behind them shouts rose and fell, mingling with desperate oration.

"Where to in such a hurry?" the question landed in concert with a hand on his shoulder.

"Kleandridas, I hurry to nowhere," Brasidas answered.

"Come with me. The boys are practicing at the Plantanistas today. I'm sure your sons are there."

"And Gyllipos? Will he be instructing them?"

"Most certainly." Kleandridas tugged him through the press of men until the bodies thinned and the road opened wide. They did not speak on the way. The howl of the wind discouraged conversation, but when they finally arrived at the grove, the two found shelter amongst the plane trees and sat to watch the boys and to speak.

"What has to happen?" asked Brasidas. "What more do the Athenians have to do to show us where their interests lie?"

Kleandridas grinned at him. "Look, there is Pantios." He gestured toward the scrum of boys fighting over the stitched leather ball. Brasidas' son had emerged from the pile momentarily, long enough to be spotted before he was drawn back into the tumble. "You mean Thrake?"

"Of course," agreed Brasidas. "They laid siege to Potidaia for how many years? A costly endeavor. Athens expended much more on that single episode than on the rest of the war entire."

"And—?" Kleandridas kept his eyes on the match.

"Take it from them! March our army up there and take it. Then they will crawl out from behind their walls and fight."

"The Athenians, always innovators, have conjured a new type of war, a war which will not end until either our city or theirs lies trampled beneath Ares' feet. The old and honorable ways are gone forever." Kleandridas looked off, as if recalling a dream.

"Then why do we continue to fight as our fathers and grandfathers did? Surely more than you must see this change."

The match ended. Some boys rolled from the tangled mass, others bounded up with energy, invigorated by the competition and anxious to try again. The paidonomos dismissed them. Gyllipos ushered Pantios and Zeuxidas away from the field and toward their father, urging them on with a hand on each back.

Kleandridas' manner grew dark and grave. "They will be the ones to suffer, lest we adapt to this new world."

The two boys, naked and filthy with the grime of mock combat, approached the two Spartiates with eyes downcast as manners dictated. Gyllipos stood behind the two.

"And which one of you crossed the line with the ball today?" Kleandridas asked with mock sternness.

Gyllipos nudged Zeuxidas forward.

"I did," replied the boy.

"You can both look up," instructed Brasidas.

The boys slowly lifted their heads, working hard to hide the smile that simmered just beneath the surface of each face. Brasidas knelt, opening his arms. His sons fell into the precious embrace. He gave them a squeeze, then released them both.

"Your troops will be expecting you both at the river," he said, looking them up and down, measuring the dirt, mud, and streaks of dried blood that mottled their skin. "Go!"

They left him after one long glance, then exploded away through the grove to the river beyond.

"They seem fit," Kleandridas said as he watched them slip through the trees.

"Most certainly. Fit in both mind and body," assured Gyllipos.

"Of the two, which exhibits leadership?" Kleandridas rubbed his beard, awaiting an answer.

"That is a most difficult question," Gyllipos said, looking a bit uncomfortable.

"Answer your father—with the truth." Brasidas found a perverse enjoyment watching the young man twist.

Gyllippos ruminated a bit. "Pantios is the stronger, and the boys in his troop look to him for his strength." He paused, then cleared his throat. "But it is Zeuxidas who they rally to."

"And why is that?" Kleandridas wore the question on his face like an actor's mask—exaggerated and plain to see.

"He decides with confidence." Gyllipos glanced to Brasidas, hoping the answer was well taken.

"Let us eat." Brasidas put one arm on Gyllipos' shoulder and one on Kleandridas', moving them toward the road and the phiditia.

Attika
Twenty-Two
ΑΤΤΙΚΕΣ

Thukydides leaned over the edge of the battlement, gazing north at the plumes of smoke that writhed from the plain like uncoiling black serpents. The corn had ripened. The Spartans marched again. On the road a train of carts rumbled, fleeing the yearly invasion. He yelled down to a driver.

"How far off?"

The man, aroused from a daze, stared up to the wall, shading his eyes from burning Helios, searching out which face had called to him.

"The Spartans—how far off are they?" Thukydides repeated.

"Who knows? They burned a few farms then headed north, toward Mount Kithairon and the Oaks Head Road."

Eukles turned to his friend. "Maybe they have had enough of their allies the Thebans and are invading *them*!"

Thukydides spun away, then scrambled down the ladder.

"Where are you going?"

"For a ride," he answered as he paused midway down. "To Kithairon."

"Wait."

The two men gathered their horses, weapons, and three day's food, riding for the mountains that walled off Attika from Theban Boiotia. They took the road toward Acharnai, following the Kephisos River, which at this time of year hardly could be called a river, passing the fort south of the town, arriving a little more than an hour after their departure from the city. Acharnai, like the road, was vacant except for a pack of stray dogs that had claimed it as their own. The animals trotted along at a distance, keeping watch on the intruders, until disinterested they peeled back toward the town.

"We may just make Phyle before sunset," said Eukles as he glanced up, measuring the height of the sun.

All around the grain stood tall and full, the air clear of the mephitic odor of burning wood and flesh. Everything in sight lay untouched by the invaders for the first time in two years.

"I am surprised that Perikles did not order all the cavalry out. At least then some of the fields could be harvested under their protection." Eukles sipped from his water flask. Satisfied, he jammed the soft willow plug back into its mouth.

"Sometimes I think he actually welcomes the Spartans—to take the crops, I mean." Thukydides remarked. "To show us all how little we truly need the land. To him our destiny lies in the sea."

The lofty towers of the fort stood dark and ominous, spiking the ridge like the hairs on a boar's back. Not a single lamp glimmered through the small, deep windows cut into the stonework or on the flanks of the gateway; only the last of the day washed the western flanks of stone in its soft, fleeting light.

They brought no fire with them; neither was skilled in conjuring it from stone and iron, so they climbed up through a skylight of a tower onto the crenellated roof to take advantage of faint moonlight. It reminded them of their days as epheboi, guarding the frontier.

They ate. A half loaf of flatbread, some wine and a handful of olives each, which they took seated, backs against the cool mud-brick that lined the rooftop wall. Against the soft violet glow of the western sky, they watched a string of bats tumble by and into the black of the wooded slopes beyond.

Eukles began counting stars. "Look, there is Herakles' club." He pointed with his last wobbling bit of bread.

Thukydides, glanced up out of politeness, then stared out at the stand of trees where the bats disappeared.

"Don't the heavens interest you?"

"What goes on up there only affects the gods. I prefer to keep my eyes to what affects men."

"Dear, serious Thukydides, eventually even the gods will affect you. Show more interest in them, or you will bring their wrath down on you—and me!"

"I give what the gods require, as any pious man does. But I keep my mind to the affairs of men. Beyond those mountains," he said, gesturing northward, "is what concerns us. I wish I could fly like a bat or bird, and perch on Kithairon to see where our foe has gone."

"Plataia, of course," Eukles said bluntly. "They are not audacious enough to march much beyond that." He flipped the last of his bread into his mouth, chewed awhile, then continued. "Did you think they would march to Thrake?"

Thukydides pulled his knees up to his chest and leaned his head back against the wall, staring up. "You are right. No such inspiration exists in the army of Archidamos."

"I will check on the horses." Eukles slipped through the open hatchway into the blackness of the tower, his booted feet slapping hollow on the wooden stairs.

With his friend gone, Thukydides snuck a long stare, watching a solitary tongue of a cloud drift by the crescent moon. He chided himself for indulging in such a pastime, even as brief as it was; to him dreams, unless inspired by the gods, served no purpose.

"They are tied up and fed," announced Eukles while still unseen in the tower room below. He emerged onto the rooftop, still talking about the condition of the horses, their makeshift stable and the lack of water. His friend gave no response. He unrolled the blanket and draped it over the hunched, sleeping form of Thukydides.

* * *

The last hour up the pass they walked the horses, spelling them from the steepness of the road and the thinning air. At the crossroads, where a trail veered off to the left and toward the quarries, a single block of stone still wrapped in its wheel-like wooden frame lay abandoned. At the beginning of the climb the air hung hot and stifling, but now hints of a breeze stirred. A few minutes more and a gusty wind swirled over them. They had topped the pass. Visible now in the plain below sprawled the camp of the Spartans and their allies.

"Where are the Spartans?" quizzed Eukles as he scanned the plain in front of the small town of Plataia.

"There. See the tents arrayed like the spokes of a great wheel, precisely spaced. That is the Spartan camp."

The two gazed with a certain admiration upon the order and design. The bright tents of the Spartan allies peppered the drab fields randomly, as though the hand of a god had picked them up and scattered them like seeds.

"I told you it would be Plataia," reminded Eukles.

"Do you remember when we were boys, listening to the man Herodotos in the Agora as he told his story of the great war against Persia?"

"Barely," replied Eukles.

"Come now—he described in perfect detail the landscape you see before us. The River Asopos. That marked the front-lines of the Persian army."

Thukydides displayed rare excitement now as he explained further. "That ridge there, beyond the shrine to Hera, that is where the Spartans stood. Cannot you picture all of it?"

"Sorry, my friend, but I do not remember."

Thukydides shook his head in displeasure. "But I know whom to ask if I want to know what star is in Herakles' club."

"What are they doing?"

Thukydides leaned forward, shading his eyes, straining to make out actions of the men closest to Plataia. "They are building a stockade. Sealing off the town, I would think."

"Good news I say."

"And why is that?" Thukydides asked.

"It means the town did not submit."

* * *

Brasidas paced before the temple of Hera while surveying the progress of the army. Helots had been dispatched to the slopes of Kithairon to fell timber for the stockade, the echoes of their axes cascading from the high forest to reverberate amongst the scattered knolls on this side of the Asopos River. Only partially completed, he estimated another five days before the wood and earthen noose would tighten around Plataia.

"Good evening, polemarchos."

"Epitadas," answered Brasidas without turning away from the stockade. "Have the men completed their exercise?"

"Done, sir, and preparing themselves for the evening meal. But that is not why I am here. Archidamos has sent for you."

"Is he cross because I avoid his mess-tent?"

Epitadas lifted and plunged the butt-spike of his spear, poking the turf over and over unconsciously. "A courier from Sparta has arrived. He has summoned Timokrates and Lykophron also."

Brasidas called for Diokles; the Helot appeared as if he had been hidden like an actor behind the skene bounding onto the orkestra floor on cue.

"My shield."

The two Spartans strode off, followed by Diolkes, who wore his master's battle shield like a turtle wears its shell, all hurrying to the summons of their king. Archidamos paced ferociously before his tent, looking down at the furrow he had scoured out. Sensing their approach he glanced up for a moment.

"That idiot Knemos!" He blurted it out, then began to pace once again.

Brasidas drew himself up before the king, helmet cradled in his left hand, spear clenched in his right, moving next to Lykophron and Timokrates. "Did you say something?"

Archidamos threw a dark-browed scowl at him. "You heard me quite well. Knemos has been beaten!"

He went on to detail the expedition of Knemos, appointed commander of all the Peloponnesian forces sent to assist their allies the Ambrakiots against the Arkananians; the enemy routed them. A second fleet was dispatched to reinforce Knemos and this was attacked and turned back by the Athenians stationed at Naupaktos. Now the Gerousia and the ephors demanded that "advisors" be sent to Knemos. The Spartans resisted the urge to recall him outright, preferring instead to provide a last chance at redemption.

Brasidas said nothing. He prayed silently to the memory of the still unknown Spartan dead, for his first thought was not the disrepute that had befallen Knemos, but the injury and loss to his city; as a youth he had quickly fathomed the responsibility of command and now it rang loudly in his mind—errors are paid for with lives. Knemos was not someone to vilify. Simply, he was an impediment to victory, with no more life than a mountain, river, stretch of sea—any obstacle. He must be overcome, swept aside.

"You must be wondering why I would tell you all this?" said Archidamos, his anger quenched by the talk and the pacing. "As polemarchs and commanders of the Spartan regiments, the ephors are sending you three to Elis to confer with Knemos. They seem to think we are wasting our best officers here when carpenters would seem more appropriate to the task at hand." He waved furiously at the work details on the stockade.

"We should all abandon this," added Brasidas with disgust. "Our fathers, after the defeat of the Mede on this very plain, took an oath to protect and defend Plataia. Now, at the urging of Thebes, we forswear this sacred pact. Remember it was these very Thebans who fought with the Persians against us. How long will it be before they turn enemy once more?"

"Out of my camp!" Archidamos turned. His face, seething red with anger glared at them, but he kept silent, only the flick of his hand emphasizing his order to depart.

* * *

Epitadas remained outside Plataia with the army while the three polemarchs and their orderlies rode for Korinth and the trireme that awaited.

Quite unexpectedly they were met by two ephors, sent to convey in person the orders of the Gerousia. Kratesikles, wrapped cocoon-like in his scarlet triboun cloak, stepped forward to address them. Sthenelaidas stood back in deference.

"No doubt you have heard of the defeat in Arkanania, and no doubt you have already passed judgment on Knemos."

Brasidas listened stolidly, revealing nothing but an aspect of attention. So did Timokrates and Lykophron.

"One lone Spartan commander among our many allies is overburdened. You three are being sent to assist him." Kratesikles leaned into Brasidas' face, the odor of black broth and onion thick upon his breath. "You especially," he whispered in a growl, "best not take advantage of this, but offer only help."

Brasidas' face grew hot. He stepped to within a hair of Kratesikles. "Sparta is my first concern—not your incompetent son."

Sthenelaidas, sensing but not hearing the exchange, pulled Brasidas aside. "You are going because of your abilities, and Pleistoanax's influence. He," whispered Sthenelaidas, flicking his head toward Kratesikles, "will reshape whatever you do to suit him and Archidamos. Beware."

"I will tell you what I told him. Knemos is irrelevant. Victory paramount. That is my answer as a polemarchos. He paused, shedding his anger like a soiled cloak. "Now as a friend I thank you for your advice." He turned and bounded quickly up the gangplank of the Korinthian trireme, looking back only after the lines had been cast and he felt the ship reluctantly surge forward.

Their voyage took them along the north coast of the Peloponnese where they set ashore their first night at Sikyon. The three Spartans loitered near their ships, avoiding the city, sending servants for food. Diokles bent over a robust fire on the beach stoking the flames and keeping warm. Indistinguishable voices aboard the triremes soon became erased by the rhythmic advance, collapse, and retreat of the gentle surf lapping the beach.

"Is there a spot for us?" Brasidas smiled as he approached his hypastpites. Diolkes sprang upright waving the three men to the warmth of his fire.

"Cups and wine to fill them," said Timokrates, dispatching the man. Diokles sped off across the beach toward the black-hulled ship that sprawled upon the sand like the carcass of a great whale. Aboard a flickering lamp darted to and fro across the deck, held no doubt by a crewman aroused to a task.

"There is an allure—" Timokrates said as he lowered himself into a seat near the fire.

"Allure?"

"The sea, Brasidas. On evenings such as this, when it is calm and the crisp breezes roll in, there is something about the sea that calls to men. Don't you agree?"

"You sound like an Athenian," he answered, smiling.

"Come now, you have been to sea quite often. You do not have to be an islander or an Athenian to appreciate it."

"I do appreciate the sea, my friend. From this beach it is a benign realm, abundant with appeal and adventure, but I have seen it when it casts away the actor's smiling mask to reveal its true and cruel nature."

Timokrates shook his head. "Dear Brasidas, for once, do not analyze, but simply enjoy it."

"Our wine is coming," said Lykophron, attempting a distraction.

Diokles filled three twin-handled tankards, then returned to tending the flames. Timokrates held his cup with one hand while fanning his other over the fire, warming it. Lykophron leaned back to catch the stars. Brasidas stared into the flames.

"How do we handle Knemos?" said Lykophron, his eyes still bent skyward. "He will hardly accept our advice."

"True. We are being sent to share the blame." Timokrates switched the cup to his warm hand. "Unless we take command, he will fail again."

Brasidas looked up from the whirling tongues of flame. "We will force success upon him." He tossed the dregs from his tankard, rose and walked off into the darkness beyond.

"He will do it, somehow," assured Lykopron. "He will do it for Sparta."

"Knemos is an ass. You know it. I know it. I am sure even Knemos knows it, but perhaps that is straining expectations. May we hope that he also places his city first and listens to us."

* * *

The next day they kept to sail well past sunset, hoping to slip past the Athenian squadron stationed at Naupaktos, then sail through the narrows between Panormos and Rhion. Before midnight they beached near Patrai. The next evening they docked at the Eliain arsenal port of Kyllene.

No one from the command staff greeted them. The docks were noticeably empty of the activity of war. One lone Korinthian captain strode the deck of his ship anxiously bellowing orders to his crew, taking to the lines himself when they moved too slowly for him. He paused for a moment at the sight of three scarlet-cloaked figures as they passed by.

"Ahoy, Spartans! Do you lead fresh troops?" Hanging on to a mast-line he swung from the far side of the deck to the near railing. He leaned over. "By the gods, we need them!"

"Where is the commander?" shouted Brasidas.

"Cozy in his house. Haven't seen him in days."

Stopping just beyond the bow of the ship, Brasidas pulled his two companions closer. "You two go on to Knemos. I will wander about here for a time."

"And why?" Lykopron knew what his friend was about, but asked just the same.

"I would see the condition of these men for myself. Then I will join you."

He walked amongst the sailors of the warships. None worked upon their vessels save the single Korinthian crew, and they begrudgingly, their captain the only individual of purpose and energy on the entire waterfront. Lining the main street from the docks, brothels and taverns seethed with activity. Not a single officer did he find along the way. No sentries at the crossroads, no mounted patrols either. A man staggered and bounced along a wall in the narrow street, brushing by, the smell of stale wine following him like a shadow.

"Where is the Spartan camp?" Brasidas clutched the man by his shoulders.

He pointed while his cheeks puffed. Vomit spewed. Then he swiped his mouth with an arm, shook his head looking at the Spartan. "Outside the east wall." He stumbled away.

The Spartan wheel was laid out properly, tents lined up like spokes radiating from the center stack of arms. A lone Skiritai stepped into the path. "Hermes!" he shouted the challenge.

"Slayer of Argos," Brasidas returned confidently.

The flap of a tent snapped open. "And how do you know the password?" A tall, trim figure emerged wielding a spear and a scowl.

"Not very difficult. Knemos knows so very few," Brasidas responded.

The man hefted the spear, measuring its weight casually. Suddenly he strode forward, lowering the blade. "I know only one Spartan that would speak such, in the very camp of Knemos." He stepped forward into the torchlight of the sentry.

"Turtle!" He swatted the spear-point aside as he stepped to embrace his friend. "I did not know you had left Sparta."

Turtle nodded to the sentry dismissing him, then led Brasidas toward a lonesome fire tended by a young boy. "Sit and have a bit of wine."

"I will sit, but no wine. I must meet with Knemos tonight. The others are already with him."

"Others?"

"Lykophron and Timokrates. We three have been commissioned here as advisors to our navarch." He spun his cloak around his arm several times, gathering it up neatly.

"Word had it that only you had been dispatched. Lykophron is a good man. Timokrates too, except that he is even more impatient than you, if that is possible."

"What happened at Stratos?"

"You waste little time." Turtle handed his empty cup to the boy. "No discipline. Knemos divided the army into three parts: we formed on the left, the Leukadians on the right, the Chaonians in the center." He turned to the boy. "Where is my wine!"

The startled boy scurried off, returning quickly with a small black pitcher with a likeness of Apollo, bow strung and aimed, emblazoned in orange upon it.

He sipped. "He gave his orders and that was that!"

"What do you mean?"

"Brasidas," he said, shaking his head in disgust, "as you have said to me often times, free men do not blindly follow orders. They must know why they do a thing. Knemos has yet to learn this fundamental of command. He barked his order and walked away. Of course they did not listen."

"The battle—what happened?" Brasidas gestured for the boy to fetch him a cup.

"The center broke and ran ahead, with the idea that they alone would take the city, the loot, and the victory." Of course the Arkananians routed them." He paused, grinning. "Knemos has learned how to retreat though."

"I must go to our commander. I will see you at exercise in the morning." He tossed the emptied cup to the boy.

He passed through the Anaktorian precinct on his way back to the town, it looking more like the pilgrims' ramshackles at Delphi than an army's encampment. He came to a large house surrounded by a wall twice the height of a man. The single Spartan on guard recognized him as he approached, and fumbled nervously with the gate ring until he finally wrested it open. On each side of the courtyard, hanging from the floors of the surrounding balcony hung triple-spouted bronze lamps, sputtering their orange light up the walls and across the white limestone walkway. Ahead the largest and only open doorway beckoned; the talk of men rolled out of it. As he stepped through, the chatter ceased. Across from him, lined up on one side of a makeshift table stood Knemos, Thrasymidas, and the other Spartan officers, like the front-rankers in the phalanx, grim-faced and ready to do battle.

"Greetings, Knemos," Brasidas announced cheerfully as he stepped into the room and moved in beside Lykophron and Timokrates. Knemos reluctantly nodded. Thrasymidas, his brother, honed his scowl while trying to stand a bit taller; he kept his toothless grin hidden.

Lykophron pointed to the map inked upon an ox-hide. "The Athenians have a squadron stationed here at Naupaktos. They patrol to the narrows off the two Rhions and beyond. They will surely spot us when we try to cross to Arkanania."

"And what is your plan?" Brasidas directed his question to Knemos.

"Sail at night, if needs be, to avoid the Athenians, then land in Arkanania to help our allies."

Brasidas studied the crude map. "How many ships do they have at Naupaktos?"

"Twenty," answered Timokrates. "No more than that." The Korinthian admiral, Machaon, affirmed the count.

"I saw only fourteen warships in our harbor." His eyes left the map.

Knemos frowned. "Twenty of our allies' triremes are on the beaches in repair."

"We came across only a single crew onboard their vessel. The rest are crammed in the streets, drunk and puking." Knemos seethed, but remained silent. Thrasymidas opened his mouth to speak but Brasidas cut him off. "My advice to you, commander, is this. Send to the allies for ships. Send the couriers tonight and without delay. Ask for exactly what you need, no more or no less. Set the repair crews to work on the twenty."

Brasidas took a small lamp from the table, hovering it over the map as he stared. No one talked. A cough. A sniffle. No other sounds. Carefully he replaced the lamp. "All captains will meet here at dawn."

Lykophron caught up with him as he swung open the gate, brushing past the sentry like a breeze. "Your plan—what is it?"

Brasidas halted. "I have no plan."

"Come now, I saw it in your eyes when you studied that map. You most certainly have a plan."

"Until we have a fleet, there is no plan."

He strode off toward the waterfront, leaving Lykophron and Timokrates. Although night had fallen, the single crew and its diligent captain were still laboring on their vessel. A pair of drunks mocked them as they wobbled by.

"Korinthian!"

The captain spun away from his task. "Spartan. Find our admiral, did you?"

"Exactly where you said he would be." Brasidas scanned the dock for a gangplank. "May I board?"

The captain waved impatiently to a crewman, who dragged a plank to the rail, then slid it until it teetered over, one end slamming against the dock.

* * *

The first light of the new day struck the masts of the swaying warships in the harbor. The last of the captains, bleary-eyed and grumbling, squeezed into the courtyard. Brasidas stepped atop a bench, above them all.

"Gentlemen, I am Brasidas, son of Tellis. My city has commissioned me to offer what advice I can to help you in the coming battle with the Athenians." Knemos stood behind him flanked by two columns, conspicuously silent as the grumbling continued. "Give me a moment of your time, then you may go eat."

A few smiled at the remark. Most looked up, scowling.

"The first thing you must know is that more ships are on the way to us." A few scowls faded. "The second is that every warship here must be ready by the time they arrive."

A bowlegged Anaktorian with matted black hair and a wine-stained chiton edged forward. "Spartan! What do ye know of ships? We need shipwrights, pitch, hemp, and nails to repair them, not fancy words."

"Then I will offer you no more of my words. But know this, supplies—hemp, pitch, timber, sailcloth—are being carried to the beaches. Carpenters have been hired and more sent for. But I will let your own superintendent of refitting tell you of these details." Brasidas jumped down from the bench. Up stepped a Korinthian, the very same captain he had met the evening prior.

By mid-day the harbor was empty of triremes, each and every one had been dragged ashore to dry the swelled wood, caulk every seam, and hammer the bronze war-beaks back into their deadly shapes. Brasidas wandered amongst the black hulls, delighted with the symphony of focused labor that resounded across the long, sandy crescent. A stream of barrow-men lumbered

190

along the tidewater road, halting where the sand had swallowed its hard surface. There stood the Korinthian, barking orders, sending the supplies to where they were needed, keeping every man in motion.

"Spartan!" He paused only for a moment to acknowledge Brasidas, then returned to his keen supervision.

"How many days to refit them all?"

The Korinthian answered without looking. "Three days at most, if they keep to this pace. We surely have enough in the way of supplies."

"Good. In three more days our reinforcements will arrive. I have word that the Athenians too have called for more ships. We will have little time for delay." Brasidas winked. "Keep them to it."

He left the beach behind, choosing instead to walk a narrow path through the woods that took him by a small pond on his way back to Kyllene. A rustle. Now elusive movement. The sleek form of a deer bounded through the underbrush, speckled by light that filtered through the trees. Here, then gone.

"Brasidas," purred a soft and silky voice. The huntress glided into view, sharing both sun and shadow, keeping her form purposely obscured by the riddle of light. "Tell me, Brasidas, why do you still revere me above all the others? Most Spartan boys outgrow me, preferring my brother as patron." She slipped into a shaft of sunlight, revealing a smile of perceptive satisfaction.

"Dear goddess, your brother knows I honor him, but it has always been you who have protected and comforted me."

"Still and always. But remember this; the coming battle is not yours to win or lose. It belongs to Knemos."

A gust of wind shook the trees, mimicking the sound of rainfall, causing him to look up briefly. In that moment the goddess vanished.

The agora of Kyllene played host to a dozen sailors, strung together like pack animals—a punishment inflicted upon them by Knemos for leaving their guard posts aboard ship the night previous. Brasidas strolled by them, shaking his head, unable to fathom why men should invite such ignominy. The bunch glared at him when he passed, their faces pained from the sun's hammering away the last of the wine from their skulls. From across the span of market stalls, he saw Turtle slicing through the crowd. He had spotted Brasidas as he entered the agora proper and moved quickly toward him.

"The ships?" Turtle asked.

"The work is well under way. But tell me, where is Knemos."

"Busy meting out punishment." He pointed to the bound criminals.

"There are more?"

Apparently, for he is with the allied captains now holding trials."

"I would have fined them, not let them avoid the work they are so needed for. Men do what they are expected to do by their commanders. Why does he not tie *them* up, himself included!"

The two walked together to Knemos' house, to see for themselves the trials. Neither interfered, but quietly attended, keeping count of the number of men charged. By mid-afternoon fifty had been brought before Knemos and the allied commanders. All fifty sentenced to public display with food and drink withheld for a day. Fifty men, commented Brasidas to his friend, that could have been engaged in repairing the ships.

* * *

On the third day after his arrival the anticipated reinforcements from the allied cities rowed into port. The next day, well before dawn and while the tide was favorable, ships were loaded with bronze-armored marines, stocked with provisions and launched north toward the mouth of the Krisaian Gulf. It would be another day till they expected to see the Athenian fleet. By the information garnered from spies, traders, and fishermen, they expected to outnumber the Athenians twice over.

The following day they landed at Panormos, across the waters from Molykrion and the Athenians. Both fleets eyed each other; neither launched. Knemos held council with the officers of the fleet, issued his orders—which had been conveniently formulated by Brasidas and the two other commissioners of war—and retired to his tent to dine with his staff. Brasidas deferred the invitation. He instead ordered the herald of the fleet to assemble the men on a hillside facing the harbor, not far from where the sixty vessels had been pulled up for the night. Brasidas stepped up onto a white boulder that stuck out from the hillside, affording him view of all the men who had gathered. The herald waved his staff high, silencing the assembly.

"Allies! Fellow Peloponnesians!" commenced Brasidas, calling them to attention with his distinctly confident voice. "Some here are full of apprehension about the coming battle, based on your last acquaintance with the Athenians. This is a mistaken thought. I know before this first encounter you had just recently gathered, men new to commanders and each other. Too, your preparations were for battle on land, not at sea as it had happened." He paused, scanning their faces, seeing agreement.

"Your defeat was not the product of cowardice, but happenstance. Remember that brave hearts must always be brave, never putting forth excuses of inexperience. Remember too that all the benefit of experience is lost if accompanied by a faint heart. Art is useless without valor.

"True, the Athenians might possess superior experience, but you possess superior courage and superior daring. Here too, you will be fighting off your own coast, supported by your own infantry, so unlike the last battle. Mistakes were made, yes, but I am sure we have all learned from them. So steersmen and sailors attend to your duties; the marines certainly will do so, as will the landed infantry, watching from shore. Tomorrow there will be no excuse for misconduct. Any man failing his duty will be known to all, while the brave shall be honored."

He went to explain that for security's sake no details of their plan would be divulged until all were on the water, and that he begged their indulgence in having not revealed all; this precaution would save lives, he reassured. He told them also that he would sail with them sharing the outcome, good or bad. They shook the hollow beach with cheers when he ended his speech. The men surrounded him as he tried to depart, shouting his name, raising their clenched fists high in the air

"Do you look to steal my brother's command?" Thrasymidas said, stepping into his path.

"Steal—no! Someone must pick it up from the dust where he has cast it. I merely brushed it off for him, returning the abandoned item in better condition then when it fell from his grasp."

Thrasymidas shifted his feet to block the pathway. "I know you, and you would do anything to bring dishonor to my brother and me."

"I have grown beyond our boyhood rivalry; you have not. Your true enemy is at Naupaktos, not standing before you." Brasidas pushed him aside and continued on. Thrasymidas whirled away.

* * *

Brasidas outlined the simple plan. The fleet would sail east from Panormos, four abreast, exposing their fifteen-deep formation to the Athenians to the north of the strait. If the Athenians permitted them to sail on, they would land at Naupaktos and take the port city; if not they would wheel to the left and engage the enemy squadron. Brasidas would be on the exposed flank, commanding a trireme. Knemos would lead in the center, Lykophron with him. Timokrates would command the far-right wing of the fastest ships; his task would be to intercept any Athenians trying to make a run for Naupaktos.

Off the point of land known as the Fingers, they drew up; across the narrow waters, on the northern shore of the straits, the Athenians scrambled aboard their vessels, anxious to be at the ready should the battle begin. The Peloponnesians, keeping to orders, set a course parallel to the shore, heading east. The Athenians with their thirty triremes shadowed them.

Brasidas stared out across the glistening swells; the enemy reminded him of the pack of dogs he encountered in Attika—prowling just out of reach while keeping him in check. The Athenians edged farther from their shore, most probably to stay clear of the shallows that could trap an unwary crew. The interval compressed. The Athenians maintained their slow, mimicking maneuver.

The Korinthian captain looked at Brasidas. "Now would be a good time," he shouted anxiously.

Brasidas waved to the trumpeter. The man blasted a series of notes on his salpinx; the fleet pivoted smartly, veering left and reforming to a line three deep and fifteen across. A fourth line sped off to seal the trap. The Korinthian barked out the order to quicken the stroke. In response the flute players sped the cadence of the pipes. The oarsmen heaved and drew, lurching the sleek, low ship forward. Ahead the Athenians swept in broad arcs, trying desperately to turn their bows into the coming storm, crews pulling their oars to the rhythm of panic. Marines on their decks moved forward while archers loaded their bows. In uncoordinated volleys, arrows flew from the enemy ships, most overshooting, swallowed by the sea on the far side. A few rattled in amongst the rowers. Only a single man on Brasidas' ship was struck, catching one atop his bare foot, pinning him to the deck. He snapped the shaft and tossed it overboard, then took up his oar once again.

With each stroke the warships lurched toward collision, the piping of the Athenian flutes mingling with the frantic redeployment of oars skimming over the swells to them. A chorus of shouts following, in forecast of contact. Upon impact every man on deck flew forward, unable to maintain purchase with the sudden loss of forward motion. Brasidas, under the weight of seventy pounds of a hoplite panoply, struggled to regain his feet; when he had, he looked over the railing to the enemy vessel. So violent was the collision that the Athenian, although broadside to the hit, carried many yards back, and rode up now on an unseen reef. It began to tip, rolling away from the impact. Its crew slid helplessly across the deck. Oarsmen, placing all chance of life on their ability to swim, leapt free of the groaning, twisting hulk. The marines, heavily armored, had no option but to stand and fight, so the dozen or so that could rally moved together, shoulder to shoulder to receive the assault.

Brasidas, followed by his Korinthian marines, clambered aboard the listing Athenian, moving cautiously until the pitch of the deck steadied. They strode across the slick cedar planks, helmets lowered and shields up. Without thought they all chanted the hymn to Kastor.

From behind the small cluster of Athenian marines, an archer raised up, aiming his bow directly at Brasidas. At this short distance the arrow tore through the bronze and wooden shield, slicing past his forearm within the shield before plunging into the array of bronze scales on his linothorax. Unflinchingly he moved forward.

The thud of hollow bronze shields colliding echoed across the dying ship, soon replaced by the frenzied stab and plunge of overhand strikes of iron-tipped spears. Targets abounded: an open slit of a helmet, the exposed flesh of the neck or bare arm, the unprotected back of the fleeing coward. Each strike landed. Brasidas pumped his arm furiously. With each withdrawal of the weapon, blood chased after its glistening warhead, washing the deck in crimson.

One fell, then another. Soon the valiant phalanx in miniature eroded, allowing the Spartan and his men to slice their way in and finish it. Behind the disintegrating cluster of armored men, an enemy archer knelt, arrow loaded and bowstring drawn. Fear shook loose his aim. Brasidas stepped forward and lowered his war-worked spear. The man flung the bow aside, gesturing submission and begging mercy. The Spartan retracted the spearhead. Without warning, the archer's eyes grew wide—pleading—then blood exploded from his mouth. A Korinthian marine placed one foot on the archer's back and twisted his spearshaft, struggling to free it.

"Snagged on his fucking spine!" cursed the marine.

With a crackle of bone, the archer's lifeless body released the spear; his eyes stared up at Brasidas.

"He was through!" barked the Spartan at the marine. "He asked for quarter."

"See how many of our men they spare." The Korinthian marine poked his bloodied spear out to sea. There, a lone allied vessel surged ahead, in pursuit of an Athenian. They both watched. They both saw the trap.

"That is Timokrates' ship," mumbled Brasidas as gazed across the heaving sea.

The Athenian sped off towards an anchored grain-lighter. Timokrates' Leukadian trireme raced blindly after. When the Athenian had cleared the merchantman, it pivoted quickly, using the anchored vessel as a hinge point, circling around it to reverse its direction. Suddenly it had turned about and was bearing down, bronze beak leading, right into the broadside of the Leukadian. The noise of the impact reverberated over the waves, the screams of twisting planks and wail of torn cedar ribbing filling the air. The Athenian drove its ram deeply, withdrew and surged ahead once again, rolling Timokrates' ship into the wind-whipped swells of late afternoon. The several allied ships that straggled behind the Leukadian were swarmed by a dozen or so Athenian triremes that had hunkered down temporarily on a stony beach near the temple of Apollo. Heartened by the sinking of the pursuer, they burst into the channel to strike at the disarrayed Peloponnesians.

Damn Timokrates, Brasidas thought. *And damn Knemos for not attacking with the remainder.*

Brasidas looked out over the tossing sea—his left wing had run nine of the Athenians aground while Timokrates' right wing had lost cohesion in their pursuit of the fleeing survivors. Knemos and the center columns drifted on the tide neither moving eastward to help Timokrates nor north to assist Brasidas.

He gave the order to attack. His Korinthian pilot, the captain who he had appointed to oversee the refit of the fleet, ran across the pitching deck upon hearing the impossible order.

"That will happen to us too, unless our Spartan admiral launches his ships into the fray," he said in disgust. "Can you count on him!"

The command was withdrawn. The allied sailors and marines scurried aboard the captured Athenian ships, slicing the throats of the living, and tying off lines in preparation to tow the prizes into the port of Panormos.

The captain of marines, drenched in saltwater and blood, stepped before Brasidas. "If you have no objections, I will set the trophy."

Brasidas stared at him blankly, pausing for a moment to recall the odd custom of other Hellenes to erect a trophy of captured armaments in celebration of a martial victory; Spartans disdained such practice. He nodded. The man sped off and began barking orders to some of the oarsmen to follow him. They rowed a single captured trireme to a small, rock-strewn island in the channel, one not more than the width of the ship they rowed. They anchored then assembled a pile of arms, tribute to their valor and an offering to Nike, goddess of victory. To their surprise, on the shore near the temple of Apollo, the Athenians did the same.

* * *

"I will go with the herald," demanded Brasidas.

Knemos argued with him no further, but waved him off while shaking his head. "Go, if you must, if you think that herald's staff will protect you."

Their single trireme caused no enemy ships to launch. The Athenians on shore simply gawked at them as they approached the harbor, their ship's top deck empty of marines. A few armed men ran across the undulating quay to where they reckoned the vessel would dock. The herald stepped forward, holding his staff and stating his aim while invoking the protection guaranteed to him by Hermes and the Olympians.

They were led a short way from the waterfront to a two-storied house of whitewashed mud-brick, its exterior wall decorated with living statues of armed marines, each leaning on a spear, shields at the rest against a knee. A short man with a wispy chestnut beard emerged from a darkened doorway, his attire common; his bearing was not.

"I am Phormio, commander of the Athenians." He paused, waiting for the herald to state his name and business.

Brasidas stepped forward. "I am Brasidas of Sparta. I come to ask for an exchange of prisoners—and our dead."

"Then you concede defeat?" said the Athenian, grinning.

"I concede nothing, save the bodies of your slain countrymen."

"Then I have nothing but dead Peloponnesians to offer in return." He waved to a subordinate. "Take them to the beach near the temple." He spoke briefly with the officer, then spun around haughtily and departed, offering no more words.

A few slaves roamed the shoreline, dragging bodies that bobbed in the surf up onto the rocks, discriminating quickly enemy from ally; the former they tossed amongst the bloated corpses, while the latter they laid respectfully in wagons. Three armed men—light infantry for they stood equipped only with javelins and small hide shields—watched over the entire beach, keeping the human scavengers from the detritus of battle.

Brasidas, the herald, and their guide walked from the residence of Phormio, through the tight and shadowed streets, onto the beach without dropping a single word in conversation. Finally Brasidas turned to the Athenian.

"You are a long way from Thasos, are you not?"

The Athenian, a look of puzzlement upon him, turned to the Spartan.

"You are Brasidas," he exclaimed, less than confidently.

"And if I recall correctly you are Thukydides, son of Olorus and a dealer in fine Thrakian timber."

Thukydides nodded. The stench of rotting flesh arrested his speech. The three men halted on the low ridge that overlooked it all, disheartened by the product of war. Gulls circled above; some pecked and tore at the corpses, snatching a fast meal before one of the slaves chased them off with a flurry of swings of a splintered piece of oar.

"Phormio says you may inspect them if you wish."

Brasidas slowly walked down from the ridge, past the wagons, stepping over the debris that once belonged to exquisitely crafted vessels of sea warfare. He could easily discern to which ships the larger timbers and planks belonged, but the tidal flat was strewn with hundreds of indistinguishable bits of wood, sailcloth, and cast-off garments. A lone sandal crept up the beach with each meek wave, only to be drawn back with the water's retreat. A slave ran by him, splashing up to his waist, hurrying to drag another corpse from Poseidon's dreadful realm.

The herald stood unmoving upon the ridge. Thukydides followed the Spartan, staying respectfully behind him till he halted amongst the dead.

"Do you have a friend here?"

Brasidas looked up. "Yes. He was on the trireme that was sunk near the grain-lighter."

Thukydides frowned. "I was onboard the ship that took her. Only a handful of your men were able to cling to the rails once the hull turned up from the water.

"The commander, did you see—?" He stopped mid-sentence. He reached down, pulling on the shoulder of a dead man whose face was buried in the soft, wet sand, then turned him over. Now he knelt and gently whisked off the clinging sand from his friend's face.

"He fell on his spear before we could take him," Thukydides said before leaving the Spartan.

Brasidas slipped the wooden arm token from his dead friend and stared at the name—TIMOKRATES—carved upon it.

Panormos
Twenty-Three
ΠΑΝΟΡΜΟΣ

For a month or more the Peloponnesian fleet loitered at Panormos, relishing their qualified triumph over the Athenians. Knemos strutted about the town, playing the part of an architect of victory. Brasidas, on the other hand, mingled with the men, learning their names, of their homes and families, all the while measuring their demeanor for war. He encouraged competitions of athletics, and races for the squadrons of warships. Even the crews of carpenters, shipwrights, and sawyers found themselves pitted against one another in contests of repair and refitting. Finally, with the end of fair sailing weather, the recall was issued. The fleet would be dispersed for another winter.

"Take this message to Sparta!" Brasidas handed the skytale stick—that Spartan invention of twisting a band of leather around a precisely sized stick, writing on it, then unraveling the leather, rendering it unreadable until it was matched with the proper size skytale at its destination—to the courier.

Lykophron shook his head. "They will not allow it."

"What?" Brasidas sipped from his kothon.

"Your request to keep the fleet assembled."

"And why not?"

Lykophron rubbed his raven beard. "Because Archidamos is back in Sparta. He will sway the Gerousia against this request."

"Oh, I think Archidamos will approve, after all it was by Knemos' order I made the request," said Brasidas, grinning.

"Knemos petitioned for this?" Now Lykophron swigged a hearty portion of his wine.

"Why, yes, except he does not know it yet."

* * *

Within the week a Spartan messenger arrived bearing a single skytale with an order to present it to both Brasidas and Knemos. The navarch took possession of the dispatch, carefully wrapping it around the stick, until aligned properly. Deliberately he studied it, then handed it to Brasidas. Lykophron and Thrasymidas waited eagerly to hear the pronouncement of the Gerousia.

"They have approved our plan," said Knemos, nodding to Thrasymidas.

"They most certainly have, so let us review the particulars once more." Brasidas tossed the leather-bound stick to Lykophron so he could spread out the hide map with both hands.

"We take forty triremes to the port of Lechaion. Our Korinthian admiral, Machaon, assures me he will have forty more for us on the opposite side of the Isthmos. One day's travel overland and the oarsmen will board these warships." He poked his finger at the Saronic Gulf, the island of Salamis and the gaping harbor of the Piraios. "But we must strike out quickly, giving the Athenians no time to prepare their defenses."

"Should we not send out scouts first to test the Athenian patrols?" Knemos warned. "If they catch us in the gulf, we may lose all."

"Reasonable men take reasonable precautions. That is what the Athenians are counting on. Here we must be unreasonable. Here we must show unequaled daring. Only then will the plan succeed."

The four Spartans labored over the details of the impending campaign, keeping apart from the allied generals. They would chance no disclosures of so risky a venture. Only on the day of the planned assault would they divulge the particulars.

Two mornings passed and the fleet spread out from Panormos, dotting the azure sea with resplendently decorated sails of fully rigged triremes. The final few vessels received their crews. The marines boarded last. Brasidas, followed by his hypaspites, Diokles, waded out to their waiting trireme.

"Brasidas!"

He turned to see Turtle racing after him. "Diokles, get aboard. This should not take long."

"Brasidas, a messenger has just arrived from Sparta." His friend gulped for air. "He said it was urgent."

"Hold the ship," he said, waving to the captain who leaned impatiently on the balustrade. "What could be so important? They knew we were to sail today."

Away from the breeze that rolled in with the tide, the air grew stale and stifling in the empty alleyways; most of the town stood out on the beach or lined the docks, watching the departure of the fleet and their precious income for another winter. Without a word the messenger handed him the strip of leather. Brasidas wrapped it deftly around the skytale he carried with him. He read, dropped the stick from view, sighed, then read it again.

"I have been recalled."

The messenger lingered. Turtle, noticing the discomfort the man felt, turned to his friend. "I think he is waiting for you."

Somewhat distracted, he snapped a glance at the courier. "Tell them three days."

With that the man sprang upon his horse, inciting it to a full gallop. What few townsfolk that ambled the streets swore and cursed at him as he tore by them, waving clenched fists and tossing stones as an answer to his rude exit.

"Why now?" asked Turtle.

"Because the plans have been laid, the fleet readied, and the men stoked for war. Now it is Knemos' opportunity for glory. An opportunity for both him and his king."

"What do you speak of?"

"I am sorry, dear friend, but I could not confide even in you. The men aboard those ships," he said, pointing out to sea, "will be in Athens in a few short days. We have provided Knemos with the critical occasion to win the war. Even he would be hard-pressed to fail now."

* * *

"The charges are quite detailed." Archidamos crossed his arms as he spoke, his head tilted while studying Brasidas.

"They are also ludicrous," blurted out Kleandridas.

"And you were there?" Kratisikles' voice sang from behind a smirk.

"No, but *he* was," fumed Kleandridas, thrusting his finger like a spear toward Brasidas. "I would take his word over the remote accusations of a thickwit."

Kratiskles, as old as he was, flew from his chair, striding toward Kleandridas in a rage. Pleistoanax, quicker still, intercepted him.

"There will be no fighting here," the king admonished. "And you, Kleandridas, shall refrain from insults."

Kratiskles, the flush red of his face slowly fading, turned back to his chair.

Pleistoanax continued. "I see by this dispatch that the charge of misconduct can be substantiated by witnesses. That is good. We should hear all sides. Brasidas too has witnesses he would like to call upon."

Kratisikles fell back into his seat. "What! One of his mess-mates perhaps. Or maybe his cousin or father."

Pleistoanax grinned. "Why no, sir. Several allied captains, it seems, have seen things differently. They informed me they would be happy to come to Sparta to testify—to the deportment of other Spartans besides Brasidas here."

Archidamos coughed conspicuously, clearing his throat and gaining the attention of all present. "Comrades, what good would come of this trial, bickering before our allies like laundrywomen?"

Brasidas remained uncomfortably standing before the five ephors and two kings. They exchanged glances, whispers, and finally nods.

"Then this matter is settled," announced Archidamos.

Just as he finished the heavy door groaned open; through it stepped a mud-splattered courier. Pleistoanax waved him forward.

"A message for the kings," he said respectfully, handing the roll of leather to Archidamos.

An attendant hurried to the king bearing a skytale. Archidamos fumbled with the stick and the message, finally giving up and passing both onto Pleistoanax; he quickly decoded the missive.

"The forty triremes launched undetected into the Saronic Gulf. Attacked the Athenian fort on Salamis. Retired to the port of Nisaea." Pleistoanax dropped stick, shaking his head.

"That is all?" Brasidas asked incredulously. "Knemos did not attack the Piraios?"

Pleistoanax continued to shake his head in disbelief, while Kleandridas jumped from his seat, glaring at Kratisikles. "My opinion of your son still holds!" He spun away from the others and burst out of the Ephorion.

Kratsiskles sank deep into his chair, locked in a trance of despair. Archidamos too did not stir. Brasidas and Pleistoanax exited the room together, emerging into the bright and noisy street at the edge of the Spartan agora; the chatter of the crowd and scorching sun overwhelmed them momentarily. Brasidas halted at the foot of the stairs. "You did not tell me there were witnesses willing to testify to Knemos' conduct at Naupaktos."

"I know of none," answered Pleistoanax with a laugh. "Though there must be. Archidamos was certain of it."

Although surely disappointed by the failure of the plan to capture the Piraios, the Spartan Gerousia adjourned the following day to review the details of the expedition. The entire armada of forty ships had embarked undetected by Athenian spies or patrols and advanced as far as the fort on the island of

Salamis. Induced by their weak defenses, Knemos attacked, capturing then sinking four Athenian triremes. But by then signal fires had warned the Piraios of their approach and the impending assault. All available Athenian warships launched. Knemos withdrew.

Kleandridas recounted it all to the men of his phidition.

"And what did Archidamos say to all of this?" Saleuthos asked as he waved to the cook for more bread.

"The king sat rubbing his beard." Kleandridas held his hand up as if to ward off additional questions while he snatched a mouthful of cheese. Done chewing, he lowered it, initiating another rampage of inquiries.

"And Kratisikles?" Styphon blurted out. Others echoed the question.

Brasidas rapped his kothon atop the table, inciting silence. "More importantly, what did Pleistoanax say?"

"He thanked Knemos for his attendance, then dismissed him." Kleandridas said while tearing a bit of bread from the loaf.

The gravel in the pathway leading up to the mess-tent crunched under the weight of an approaching visitor. During a pause of conversation, the flap swung open.

"Here is the man who can tell us all what happened." Saleuthos stood welcoming his friend. "Turtle, sit, eat, and tell of the raid on the impregnable fortress of Salamis."

They all laughed—except Turtle. "What is to tell. He had his chance—a magnificent chance—to take Athens' harbor."

"What of the allied commanders?" Styphon, normally quiet, grew more curious as he continued swigging his wine.

"They were all happy to go home—content with another small victory. I did not know Nike was a dwarf."

"Some men are intimidated by success. Knemos shits himself when he is confronted with it," Saleuthos said, stoking laughter once more.

"We may make light of this," admonished Kleandridas, "but Knemos, Alkidas, and their brethren will hold the highest offices of command while Archidamos lives."

"And King Pleistoanax—he holds no sway over the Gerousia?" Epitadas asked in a voice of impatience and desperation.

"The Gerontes, our senators, still defer to Archidamos—and to Kratisikles' influence," lectured Kleandridas. "But things will change. They always do."

Attika
Twenty-Four
ΑΤΤΙΚΕΣ

Mid-winter and finally Thukydides had been released from Naupaktos to return home. On the day his ship sailed east toward Attika, Phormio and the squadron of triremes launched in the opposite direction, heading for Arkanania in support of their allies. The voyage proved swift, although stormy, for they made landfall at night far from any settlements and masked from the Spartan coast patrols by the incessant squalls. At the same time he landed at the harbor of Zea in the Piraios, ships from Thrake were docking too.

Tired from the voyage and still unsteady due to the sea-tossed passage, Thukydides roamed the quays seeking news from the north. The place seemed unusually void of activity. He had lost count of the days while in Naupaktos and realized it was the third day of the Anthesteria, the Day of the Pots—a day of ill-omen and dread; most huddled in their homes, performing sacrifices to Hermes of the Underworld, while leaving the streets to the spirits of the dead. Amongst the several grain ships that had docked, almost lost in the press of the wide-hulled vessels, he came across a single old penteconter—a fifty oar—the crew moving indolently to off-load its scant cargo of hoplites. A dozen or so disembarked, each grasping a spear, cradling a crested bronze helmet while others, servants most likely, wrestled with bagged shields, baskets, and tattered bedrolls. The last one shuffled down the gangplank painfully. There was something familiar in his gait. Thukydides approached, gawking.

"Sir, what is your name?"

The tired hoplite lifted his face, his eyes in a tight squint. "I am Glaukos."

Thukydides, shaken at first by the sight of him, clasped the man's shoulders, bringing his face close, still staring, a smile forming. "Glaukos! It is Thukydides, son of Olorus—your neighbor."

The man's lips quivered. He craned his neck, still squinting, straining to recognize the face that had recognized him. Tears welled. He wiped his nose with the back of his scarred hand, sniffling.

Thukydides awkwardly reached out to the trembling man and embraced him. "I will take you home."

They walked mostly in silence, a Thrakian slave following behind, toting Glaukos' armor and bedroll. Thukydides caught himself several times outpacing his worn-out neighbor and slowed, trying not to stare at his gaunt and withered form.

Suddenly and without prompting, Glaukos spoke. "It was the plague, you know. Killed more of us than the Potidaians did. Almost two thousand lost."

"But the city is ours now."

"I would trade it all back for the lives of my comrades. For my life also."

Thukydides grabbed the spear and helmet from him, but his friend's legs still wobbled as though a great weight pressed down upon him. Every so often he would fall against a dwelling wall, using it to keep to his feet as he sucked the air, wheezing.

"I remember when you had it," Glaukos said between coughs. "You were stronger than most."

"And so are you, Glaukos. Look, you are almost home."

A single window glowed with the flickering light of an oil lamp. Thukydides called out, "Your master is here."

From within the walled courtyard a door whined on its hinge-pins as it swung open, followed by the slap of shod feet on hard tile. The gate cracked open—just enough for a pair of eyes to peer out at them.

"Come here and help," Thukydides barked.

The servant rushed to Glaukos, pulling his master's arm over a shoulder to prop him, as he led them inside. "I am sorry, Master Glaukos. I thought you were one of them. It is their day, you know."

"Not yet." His feeble grip tugged the servant's chiton as he clung to him, his strength failing. "No, not up the stairs," he pleaded, foregoing the comfort of his bedroom for immediate rest. "Take me directly to the andron."

Once they had settled Glaukos onto a couch, Thukydides sent the servant to fetch a physician, while he tended to gathering what he could for a meal. Wine, still plentiful in three large storage vessels, he quickly found. The kitchen was bare of any relish; only three loaves of stale flatbread and a single onion sat in a basket. He soaked the bread in wine, offering small portions to Glaukos, intermingled with slices of onion. He too sampled the fare, but only in small doses, preferring the wine to the brittle loaf and pungent onion. After a bit of food Glaukos seemed to recover his strength, for now he raised up, leaning upon his arm, still wrapped in the single blanket the servant Abas had covered him with before departing.

"Why did Hestiodoros keep you at Potidaia so long? The city fell last year."

Glaukos wriggled the blanket, pulling it tighter to fend off a chill. "We did not come home directly because of Kleon. He accused us of negotiating too lenient a surrender. Threatened Hestiodorus with a trial on our return. So we did not return—until now."

"And I hear our Thrakian ally, Sitakles, has failed in his bid to conquer the Makedonians."

"A pity they did not annihilate each other. I do not trust either of them, even if they be our staunch friends today." This bit of talk incited a fit of coughing, which Glaukos could not halt. He trembled as he hacked, trying in vain to muffle the outburst in the folds of the blanket.

From outside the sound of two men arguing rang out. The gate slammed open. Again the shouting commenced, but this time in close proximity. Abas strode into the andron, carrying a man across his burly shoulders like a hunter carries a prize stag. He dropped him at the foot of Glaukos' couch. "Your physician, sir."

Thukydides sprang from his seat, pulling the man up from the cold tile floor. "I apologize for Abas and the zeal with which he carries out a task." He snapped the purse free of his belt, fingering it before the iatros' face. "But we will be sure to compensate you for this inconvenience."

* * *

By the month of Thargelion, Glaukos had regained his health and accompanied Thukydides and Olorus to the festival of the goddess Bendis. She was a Thrakian god, but the Bendideia had become popular, due mostly to the torchlight race on horseback, which Thukydides had won several times previously. This year he played the role of spectator. The morning after, patrols scampered into the city, bringing with them the undeniable news of late spring—the Spartans were coming.

"It will be the same as every year," said Eukles, yawning. "They will come, they will burn our farms, then they will leave. Why do we gawk from walls at them? This year will be no different."

Even Thukydides began to chafe at the policy of patience that Perikles had established. One battle and it would all be over. Victory or defeat in a single afternoon would settle it all. *With Perikles things will never change,* he thought, scanning the plain and the worms of smoke that squirmed into the hazy sky.

Below them, at the base of the walls inside the city, where the refugees of the countryside had set up their shanties to endure another summer, a voice called up to them.

"You two. Come down here. We are called to the Strategion." Gryllos waved vehemently for them to hurry.

A crowd had gathered outside the building, forcing the summoned officers to shoulder their way through, fending off shouted questions and indignant tugs as they tried to ignore the mob. Inside, and surrounded by nine other strategoi—generals of Athens' army—sat Perikles, illness or worry had snatched his normal countenance of optimism. The company commanders squeezed into the confines of the hall, anxious to hear his address. He spoke briefly, reading a message sent by the Athenian proxenos in Mytilene. Within the hour he dismissed them.

"This sounds like Spartan jugglery." Eukles hurried down the steps to keep pace with Thukydides. "If false, and we act upon this information, it would turn an ally into an enemy."

"I fear it is true."

"Why is that?"

"Perikles himself told me; he told us all. I have never seen him so downtrodden."

"It is only one of many cities that our fleet will handle easily."

"It must be far different. Why else would he divert the fleet from attacking the Peloponnese to sail?"

Olympia
Twenty-Five
ΟΛΓΜΠΙΑ

Olympia. The first day of the games. They had strolled the precincts of the temple of Zeus, amused by jugglers, acrobats, and magicians, while the athletes met inside the temple, pledging to the god and the judges to abide by the rules. Still morning but they could feel the heat of mid-summer gathering like a rising ocean swell that would soon inundate them—by afternoon the very hills would sizzle. The temple doors groaned open. The athletes emerged.

"We must follow them to the altars," instructed Kleandridas.

Away from Sparta they held to associate as they did at home, preferring to keep to the mates of their phidition. Saleuthos, Lykophron, Sthenelaidas, Epitadas, Hippagretas, Styphon, and Brasidas slipped through the chaos of charm vendors, entertainers, and bettors to the six double altars of Zeus—constructed they say by Herakles himself. The white marble of the altars, streaked with the dark, dried blood of its victims gleamed in the hot sun. Two boys clad in white chitons led a bull forward. Beside the altar stood the mantis, sacred dagger in hand; next to him a burly man rocked nervously, his two paw-like hands wrapped around the grip of a huge ax. The mantis reached into a shallow wicker-work basket, scooping out a handful of barley, sprinkling it over the bull; it shook its head in affirmation. There was no pause in the ceremony; the ax drove hard, cracking the animal's skull, collapsing it quickly in death. With dagger and bowl the mantis collected the sacrificial blood. Attendants spirited the carcass away. Another bull was led forward.

"How many poor beasts must be sacrificed to Zeus-Averter of Flies?" Epitadas shook his head.

"By the third day you will wish many more sacrifices than these would be offered to him," said Brasidas.

True, the Games were not known for their attention to hygiene, particularly for the spectators. The local people—Elaians—joked that the games were held every four years because that is how long it took for the stench to subside.

Now a procession formed that would bring the officials and spectators to the tomb of Pelops. Here libations were poured, concluding the ceremonies of sacrifice. The remainder of the morning the group of Spartans traipsed the grounds, searching out acquaintances while gawking at the scores of hucksters that plied—to them at least—totally superfluous goods. Here among the other Hellenes they drew stares, their ancient style of long hair and beards now abandoned elsewhere, marking them for comment.

"Kleandridas!"

From the swirling crowd emerged Turtle. "Pleistoanax summons you," he said in a guarded voice as he pushed his way through to them. "It is urgent."

Sthenelaidas smiled. "I thought for a moment sensibility had afflicted you, and you had come to ask me to drive your chariot tomorrow."

Turtle scowled. "He insisted you hurry."

It proved troublesome moving through the abounding crowds, the eddies and currents of men shoving them from their course until almost half an hour later they filtered out of the temple precincts and into a field where the Spartans had erected their tents. A small hill rose up behind the camp, and there upon its slope they saw Pleistoanax, Agis—son of king Archidamos, and several score Spartiates seated before six foreigners.

"Who are they?"

Turtle leaned to Brasidas. "By their speech, I would guess islanders."

Pleistoanax rose up upon seeing them approach and waved them forward anxiously. "These gentlemen seek our help," he said while directing them to sit.

The eldest of the strangers wiped the sweat from his brow with the half-sleeve of his chiton. "Gentlemen, as I told your king, we are from Mytilene and have come to petition for an alliance." This statement incited a whirl of muffled comments amongst the Spartans; the Mytilenean, an ally of Athens, stunned them with this proposal. "Remember Spartans that we did not become allies with the Athenians to subjugate Hellenes but to liberate them from the Persian. Athens has since forgotten our common enemy and worked this alliance to her own devices. Given this we could no longer trust her to lead us, nor could we expect them to allow us to determine our own course. That is why we have come to you."

Instantly Brasidas comprehended this opportunity. Patiently he listened.

"Mutual fear of the Persian brought us together, sympathy the basis of our friendship, but the Athenians have replaced this sympathy with terror."

The Spartan faces, far from exhibiting interest in his words, shouted indifference. He re-thought his words. "This war will not be decided in Attika, but in the cities and on the islands from where Athens draws its sustenance. There are many like us who only need the slightest encouragement to come over to you. Become what the Hellenes believe you to be; become liberators!"

Even Agis, son of Archidamos, understood the opportunity presented to them. Without subjects and allies to sustain her, Athens could no longer hide behind her formidable walls. She must fight or starve.

For the remainder of that day, while thousands sought the entertainment of the festivities in anticipation of the games, the Spartans and her allies discussed this proposal. In five days they would march into Attika. In five days they would launch the fleet.

* * *

Alkidas, navarch of Sparta and admiral of the entire Peloponnesian fleet, displayed unusual vigor in assembling the armada at the Isthmos. But the Athenians had been warned of the Spartan expedition to Mytilene and fitted and manned an additional one hundred warships, ships that neither friend nor foe thought existed in their arsenal, and deployed them off the Isthmos. The two fleets, embraced in a standoff, studied each other for weeks. Meanwhile the Mytileneans mustered what strength they could on their own, testing the Athenian blockade with daring sorties both by land and sea, but the Athenians would not release their stranglehold. Pleistoanax, frustrated by these events and anxious to assist their new ally, argued his plan before the ephors.

"We must send advisors to them. Men who can rally them until we can dispatch the fleet when the weather turns. They must see our alliance, as solid as a man, before them."

* * *

"Take care, my friend." Brasidas stepped forward to embrace him. "You will be far from home and your comrades."

Saleuthos, his eyes gleaming with eagerness, spun away. "Brasidas, if the gods are with us, this war will be ended by next summer. I will do my part to hasten it."

"Your mission is simply one of encouragement. Assure them that we will attack Athens with the full weight of our army and fleet. They must persevere. Spring will come soon and with it our fleet."

"I will be waiting for you at Mytilene, my friend."

Saleuthos along with two Helot servants rode south for Gytheion, from there setting sail aboard a newly outfitted Korinthian trireme, landing on the island of Lesbos at Pyrrha, not far from Mytilene but outside the Athenian blockade. The voyage, affected during this most turbulent of sailing seasons, assured he would avoid interception. His discreet party moved overland, bypassing the Athenian line of siege by scrambling along the dry course of a stream directly to the city's wall; his arrival proved more than propitious.

The Mytileneans, although reduced to apportioning their food, man for man received more to eat than any Spartan soldier; still they complained. Saleuthos, perceiving that what the townsfolk lacked was not victual but leadership, rallied them, setting them to tasks, improving their defenses, gathering caches of weapons and exhorting words of encouragement to the men of fighting age. He knew activity bred confidence and purpose. He also knew, by careful calculation, that the grain reserves would not last the season.

With the end of spring approaching, the Spartans launched their double-edged plan; Kleomenes, brother of Pleistoanax, would lead the invasion of Attika, while Alkidas would command the contingent of forty warships destined for Mytilene.

Pleistoanax, forced by illness to remain in Sparta, sat wrapped in his triboun cloak before a waning fire, his houseservant scurrying to collect more charcoal to feed it. Brasidas sat opposite him. His right foot tapped rapidly, keeping in time to the music of anticipation. Finally he sprang to his feet.

"I should be with the fleet, not sitting here impotently in Sparta." He sat back down, drawing a deep breath as he realized what he had uttered. "I am sorry," he added, "but I fear time is a currency we have in short supply. It is also a currency that Alkidas squanders."

"I do not like the man either, but it is our allies, not him, who have lost enthusiasm when it comes to a sea fight with the Athenians."

"Why invade Attika again? What is to be gained? We strut our army across their empty fields, boasting of our prowess in war and their incapacity to challenge it. Still they endure, safe and sound behind their walls."

"It keeps them busy. And us too, although my brother will leave no field, farm, or vineyard in Attika untouched. He is a thorough man." He shivered a bit as he smiled. The servant tossed a few more bricks of charcoal into the fire. "If it were your decision to make, what would you do?"

"For certain I would send more than forty ships to Mytilene. The Thebans press us for help and we respond all too quickly. The Elaians, Leukadians, Korinthians, and others clamor for us to lead them and we run to the fore. These are people who have insisted that we risk all to defend them while they forfeit little. These are men most unreliable. Yet, when a city comes to us, as Mytilene has, staking her very existence upon friendship with us, we wait nearly a year to respond—and then with a meager fleet, timidly led."

"Would you speak such if it were Thrasymidas at Mytilene and not your friend Saleuthos?"

Brasidas stared intently at the king. "If Thrasymidas were at Mytilene, I would have pressed the issue sooner."

"Who can argue with that? I can think of no better man to have sent to Mytilene than Saleuthos—unless, of course, it were you."

* * *

Brasidas loitered in Sparta, apart from the war in Attika, meeting with Pleistoanax when he could to glean information from the official dispatches that the king was privy to. News detailed Kleomenes' exactitude in his devastation of Athenian territory. Like a wound that refused to heal, sore and throbbing, Plataia still withstood the siege. Nothing from the fleet, Alkidas, or more unsettling still, not a word from Saleuthos and Mytilene—that is until one morning during the summer month of Karneios.

"I used to watch you from up here." Kleandridas lowered himself into the cool, tall grass that spilled amongst the cluster of oaks.

Below, in the dust dry field, a herd of boys lugging battle shields and mock spears ran in formation from one end to the other, their bouagos screaming the command to maintain close order. For several laps it all held together, but the heat, fatigue, and meager rations tugged and pulled at their disciplined ranks, at last disintegrating the impressive block into a tattered train, cruelly partitioned by age and stamina. The tail of the train scattered further. The smallest youth fell to the earth exhausted. Another tumbled from his feet.

"He is pressing," observed Kleandridas.

"Gyllipos is learning—look."

Gyllipos the bouagos, who until now had been screaming at the boys to keep to their feet and formation, let the drill continue on, carried forward by its own momentum. He knelt quietly beside one of fallen. Obviously he spoke to him, but whether the lad could hear Gyllipos or not, they could not tell. Slowly the prostrate youth rolled over, gaining a knee while pushing up against his spear and shield. He shuffled off to catch up with the others. Soon after several such conversations, not a single boy lay on the ground. The formation was less than perfect, but it was cohesive and in motion.

"See. He has learned the lesson," said Brasidas triumphantly, "that free men are led by ideas. The whip is suited only for animals."

"Ah, but cannot it be said that some men behave like animals and therefore deserve the whip?"

"You sound like Kratisikles. He would gladly decide which of us are animals. I prefer to let each man decide for himself."

Now Kleandridas, aroused by the discussion, straightened his back in preparation to draw a deep and thoughtful breath. "And how do men decide?"

"By their choices. We choose to shun the animal in us, that aspect that would force us to act on hunger, lust, or greed. These things are poor substitutes for virtue." Brasidas pointed to the field. "Look. They all run now, slower but in tight formation."

"Do you restrict your definition of virtue to our prowess in battle?" Or is it the devotion to our city?" Kleandridas looked furtively to the herd of boys, his glance quickly returning to Brasidas as he awaited a response.

"Virtue of any sort wrings the animal from man. An athlete may be virtuous, for he shuns comfort in pursuit of perfection. Why even the sculptor or potter may be virtuous, striving to craft the perfect form."

"Then virtue is not a gift exclusive to the warrior?"

"No—although above all others, he discards the urges of nature—the desire to avoid death and pain—for his city. But there are those who call themselves warriors who only postpone these baser impulses to achieve some personal goal, some reward. The sculptor is far more virtuous than such a man."

"Brasidas, you speak as though you know of such a warrior?"

"In truth any *warrior* is such a man—one who fights for his own glory. But it is the *soldier* who is virtuous, for he is nothing by himself, but everything as part of the greater whole, subjugating his animal to the law of the polis."

"Then the barbarian is not virtuous. Is he not as brave and competent a soldier as any Hellene?" Kleandridas raised his chin as though he were inviting a blow to be struck.

"Bravery is not the measure of a true soldier. You and I both have stood by men while they shit themselves—or vomited their last meal as the phalanxes converged. Are these brave men?" Brasidas paused only briefly, for he knew his question required no answer. "Duty is what they relied on, not courage. The barbarian, once ensconced in battle, is duty-bound only to himself. I have encountered many barbarian warriors, but not a single barbarian soldier."

"But we fight Athenians, do we not? Would you count them as virtuous?" continued Kleandridas.

"Yes, but their virtue is in the pursuit of success."

Emerging from the dust-obscured field stalked a tall figure, followed by two smaller ones.

Kleandridas smiled. "Well done."

Gyllipos trudged the final steps up the hill while Pantios and Zeuxidas marched behind triumphantly, bearing their mock shields and spears.

"It is more difficult than it seemed at first." Gyllipos halted before his father.

"That is?"

"Keeping a clear head when things go awry. Even small things like a herd of boys." Gylippos smiled as he rubbed Pantios' head affectionately.

Meanwhile Brasidas' two sons stood poised before him, shields up and spears planted, trying with all they were worth to appear like Spartan soldiers. Before he could speak to them, he heard far-off shouts. Hylas, his attendant, ran toward them, waving his hands and shouting in his Attic dialect that, for the moment, alluded his understanding.

"Calm yourself," commanded Brasidas.

Hylas swallowed air, pausing. "Sir, Mytilene has fallen!"

* * *

Kleon strutted before the Assembly of Athens, pointing to the captured Spartan. He had spent the last hour stirring the crowd with the tale of the near-disastrous defection of Mytilene and detailed how such treachery should be dealt with.

Others tried to speak, but as always Kleon trampled their words with his marketplace bellow. "Leniency now will exhibit weakness. We must make an example of Mytilene and any agents of sedition." Now he glared at Saleuthos. "Beginning with this Spartan!"

From the throng a voice yelled, "Death to the Spartan!" Another repeated the cry. A man leaned past Thukydides and shouted the same. He scowled at him, wincing from the uncomfortable proximity to his outburst. Eukles turned to his friend. "They are all his cronies—every one of them."

Thukydides nodded. Suddenly, with the cry for death multiplying throughout the Assembly, he felt his stomach tighten; he was unnerved at this truancy of justice and how easily Kleon dispatched it. The Assembly, urged on by the demagogue, had substituted anger for thought, expediency for truth.

"We all know what penalty the Mytileneans must pay—the very same as him!" He stabbed at the Spartan with his bony finger, then waved for the guards to come forward. Two men armed only with spears bracketed Saleuthos and led him off through the taunting crowd to an empty street that took them north to the prison. As they distanced themselves from the Pnyx, the words of Kleon merged unintelligibly, punctuated occasionally by cheers of affirmation. Saleuthos turned to one of the guards, looking deeply into his eyes. "He is more a danger to you than any Spartan could ever be."

* * *

For most of the summer, Brasidas tended to his instruction of Gyllipos, and on occasion organized mock battles of the older boys in the Agoge. Unusually he ate at home; the members of his entire phidition save Kleandridas and himself were either serving with Alkidas aboard the fleet, outside Athens, or engaged in the siege of Plataia.

His wife, Damatria, like any woman of Hellas, supervised the meal's preparation, but so unlike women of the other cities, sat to eat with her husband and Kleandridas. She stared out the window blankly to where her sons had played, perhaps recalling their boisterous games—games that she had not seen in several years. Still staring, she tore the loaf of wheat bread; wisps of steam leapt from it. She nibbled in silence.

"Have the ephors sent to Athens yet?" Brasidas dipped his bread into the bowl of zomos broth, swirling it 'round and 'round to moisten it.

"The Athenians would not speak with them while our army encamped in their fields."

"Tell me. You have spoken with the king often. Does he think they will release Saleuthos?"

Kleandridas shook his head. "With Perikles dead, there are few men of reason left in Athens. Fickleness rules that city now."

"And Alkidas? What is to become of him?" Brasidas gulped his cup dry. "If he had—"

"—arrived sooner at Mytilene," interrupted Kleandridas. "Is that what you were about to say?"

"If he had arrived at all!" Brasidas flung his empty cup into the hearth, jolting Damatria from her trance of nostalgia.

"That is why you are here and not in the field?" Kleandridas paused, gathering in his temper. "It is your candidness that has cost you allies in the Gerousia. You forget your schooling. Think much. Say little."

Quite by accident he caught sight of a single tear as it rolled down his wife's cheek, illuminated by the orange light of a fading sun. He too gathered in his temper. Summoned by the crash of pottery, Hylas peered through the open doorway.

"An accident," said Damatria through a sniffle.

The boy ducked away.

"I am sorry, have I upset you?" Brasidas, calmed now, asked her.

She swallowed hard. "No dear Husband, it is not you."

"Then what? What has disturbed you so?"

She left her pleasant vision of the window and twisted to look at them both. "A messenger rode in from Athens today, the son of our neighbor Anaxandros. He stopped to visit with him before he continued on to the ephors." She wiped the tear from her face, blinking. "They have killed him."

"Who?" said Brasidas as his friend mouthed the same word.

"Saleuthos is dead. The Athenians have killed him."

For a brief moment, he suspended his thoughts, then erupting from his chair, tore out of the house. Before he had gone halfway to the gate, a hand tugged at him from behind.

"And where do you go now?"

"To the ephors." He flung the hand of his friend from him and strode down the path, through the gate, and onto the road. Kleandridas followed in silence as they covered the distance quickly. At the foot of the stairway of the Ephorion he paused.

"Brasidas, remember what I have said," he cautioned.

He nodded, then bounded up the stairs, his cloak billowing out behind him as though he were in a gale.

"Ah, Brasidas," said Kratisikles as he looked up from his platter of bread and cheese. "We were about to call for you."

"Yes, please join us," said Tantalos.

Kratisikles called for a couch to be brought from an adjacent room, and cups, plates, and the other appurtenances of dining also. The Helot responded swiftly.

"Our fleet," began Kratisikles, "having narrowly escaped an overwhelming force of Athenian warships, is bound for Korkyra. It seems even in failure the Mytileneans have inspired others to leave the fold of Athens. The exiled Korkyraians have petitioned for our help to recover their city from Athens."

His first impulse was to remind them that it was these very Korkyraians that had ignited the war when they called on Athens for help against their mother city of Korinth. But he heeded Kleandridas' advice and sat silent, merely nodding.

"By chance Athens has retained Mytilene, but if we can detach Korkyra from them, then the west becomes secure. This coupled with the fall of Plataia may bring them to terms."

"Kleomenes has taken it?"

"Why no. He is still in Attika. Knemos stands as master over Plataia now," said Kratisikles, glowering.

His mind whirred with the possibilities: Knemos and Thrasymidas were at Plataia; Alkidas, through his procrastination, had allowed Mytilene to fall; no doubt he would finally receive command of the fleet.

"Brasidas, you are to proceed with haste to Kyllene. We have commissioned you as advisor to Alkidas."

Instinctively he leaned forward from his couch, preparing to spring upon his prey as a lion does. The hand of Kleandridas restrained him. Uncoiling, he reclined, passively listening to his final instructions from the ephors, then was dismissed curtly. Upon exiting the Ephorion both he and Kleandridas halted in discussion before the Bronze House. That is where Tantalos found them.

"Again I must advise!" he launched the remark at Tantalos like a javelin.

"I had put forward to them that it was you who should be navarch. Kratisikles twisted it to suit his nephew."

"Don't you see? If we succeed then Alkidas will be honored. If we fail, the blame will rest with me. Like his cousin, he is too deliberate to contend with the Athenians. Like his cousin, he will not heed my advice."

* * *

Before dawn the morning next, Brasidas departed, accompanied by Diokles, his battle servant, and the boy, Hylas. In a few days he arrived at Kyllene, engaging in cool but detailed discussion with Alkidas on their plan to help the Korkyraians. Once final preparations of fitting the warships had been made, they sailed to Sybota. The mere sight of their fleet instigated several enemy vessels to desert, but led by the Athenian triremes the *Paralos* and *Salaminia,* the remainder formed up for battle. Duplicating the encounter at Naupaktos, Brasidas attacked aggressively, scattering one flank of the enemy fleet to rout; Alkidas, acting with trademark fugacity, was slow to realize his advantage on the opposite flank, allowing the bulk of the Athenians to slip away. This battle ended, not in defeat but in hollow triumph. Again the Spartans and their allies drew up their long-hulled warships for the winter, pondering what might have been. Again Brasidas, compelled by rage and spurred by his innate temerity, delivered a tirade upon his superior. Again the ephors removed him from his posting.

Sparta
Twenty-Six
ΣΠΑΡΤΗ

The tolling of cauldrons resounded throughout the village of Pitane. The death knell—but which king? Now he hurried along, anxious for home or to come across anyone who would tell him. A Helot wearing a dog-skin cap turned away as Brasidas approached, cowered it seemed, by a cold breath of wind. When he was certain the Spartan chose not to pass by he lifted his face and uttered, "Archidamos."

Thoughts poured through his mind: relief at first that his friend Pleistoanax still lived; a shiver of dread for his departed foe; the uncertainty of a new king; shifting alliances. All these things and more disabled his focus on the war. He sought out Kleandridas.

When the door to the temple swung open, its smoky ether engulfed him, reminding him that he would soon be in the presence of Lord Apollo, the Far-Shooter. Slender tongues of light from the flanking tripods lapped the interior walls. High above, where the small windows cut through the stonework, smoke swirled in the shafts of sunlight. Before the image of the god stood his friend, sowing the flame with incense. The offering crackled then billowed up, stinging his eyes.

"I have been waiting for you," said Kleandridas without turning around.

"You should be offering to Hermes." Brasidas moved next to him, entranced by the dancing embers in the tripod.

"If you mean Archidamos, I make no such offering. This, my friend, is for you."

Surprised and honored by the gesture, he now felt a bit uneasy too, for the god's sister had been his patroness. "For me?"

"Our king's death will smooth no paths for you. Kratisikles holds sway over the ephors. And Archidamos' son owes much to him also."

A rattle echoed. Behind the image of the god an attendant fumbled with a stool as he moved it aside to sweep. The two edged closer to each other.

"You once told me that war winnows out the weak." He paused, waiting for the slave to move by them with his sweeping. "Why is it not so now?"

"Unfortunately weak commanders may survive while their own men do not. But in time they too will be culled out."

"Count the Spartan and allied troops that have perished under Archidamos. How many more will find themselves in Hades Hall under the command of Alkidas and Knemos?"

"Patience, dear Brasidas. We must suffer defeat before we can celebrate triumph."

Pylos
Twenty-Seven
ΠΓΛΟΣ

"May Artemis protect you." Brasidas embraced his friend, then stood back. "Because Thrasymidas surely will not." His quip echoed in his mind, ringing with dreaded truth, for Epitadas and his two companies of hoplites would indeed need the protection of the fleet. The island stretched barely over a mile in length and was much narrower, barely a few hundred yards wide, forming a plug to the harbor at Koryphasion. With their ships stationed at either end and infantry on the island, they would seal off the harbor and the Athenians from their allies. Or so that was the plan.

Over four hundred heavy infantry boarded the transports that would ferry them across the bay to Sphakteria; Epitadas would be in command. Following him up the wobbling gangplank came Hippagretas, then Styphon. Crewmen moved leisurely in the heat of a perfect day, stowing the ramp and securing the lines. Sails spilled from the mast, quickly gorging on the breeze. The troop ships creaked and groaned as they lumbered forward, moving at first imperceptibly, until at last they sliced through the meek swells of the harbor.

Brasidas, instead of watching the departing transports, looked to the Athenian fort at the thumb of land called Koryphasion. Men atop the walls scurried about, thinking perhaps the approaching ships moved against them. They snatched up their arms, packing the crenellated walls with their armored bodies, spears swaying like wind-raked grain, every one of them set to motion by anxiety. *A strange turn of events,* he thought. *The Athenians defend a piece of our land while we attack them from the sea.*

When word came of the Athenian landing several weeks past, no one in Sparta thought much of it. Another raid along this isolated part of their coast. In a few days, when the Spartan army marched, these Athenians would quickly retreat to the safety of the sea. It had been a pattern repeated many times up till now. The place they had selected was convenient for defense: the landward side of Koryphasion—or as it had been called in Homer's day, Pylos, home of King Nestor—was secured by a stout wall, which the Athenians reinforced. The portion facing out to sea was ringed by a narrow rocky strand, difficult to land upon in tranquil conditions, a supremely hazardous feat in the contest of battle.

The transports veered left, beaching upon the mid-point of Sphakteria. Filled with curiosity, the Athenians clung to their walls to watch the disembarkation; heads bobbed; necks craned. In a short while the empty ships struggled free of the island and catching the breeze, slipped back toward the Spartan camp.

He looked down the length of the crescent-shaped beach, counting the ships and scanning the clusters of heavy infantry that mingled restlessly on shore. *Many more ships than beach*, he thought as he looked across the bay to the Athenians.

"He calls for us," said Turtle as handed his spear to his hypaspites.

Thrasymidas climbed upon a glistening limestone boulder, helmet tucked under arm, his blood-red chiton sizzling in the shadowless sun of midday. His mouth stayed clamped as he glared out at the assembly, only to be forced open by the necessity of speech.

"At the sound of the salpinx we shall attack the seaward side of their fort between those stony pediments that bracket the beach. At that moment our infantry shall assault the eastern wall from the inland road." He indicated these places by jabbing at them with his walking staff.

Now Thrasymidas covered the specifics of his plan and the sequence of attack the squadrons of ships would follow. Brasidas listened. With immeasurable restraint he fought the urge to challenge the plan. *That is exactly what I would expect if I were the Athenian captain*, he thought after listening to the assignments. Now his mind whirred in cerebration, developing his own plan for defense, as the Athenian ought to be doing. He tallied the numbers. He recalculated. Five to one; that is what he would require in weight of numbers to overcome the advantages of terrain and fortification—especially without engines of siege—that the Athenians possessed. Thrasymidas continued to speak. Brasidas stared across the harbor to Koryphasion and the enemy, half-listening until one single crucial word was uttered.

"Archers? What did he say of the archers?" he whispered to Turtle.

"They are to go with the infantry to attack from the landward side."

"I must have loosened more than a few teeth from his head." Brasidas surged forward a few steps until the strong grip of his friend clamped upon his shoulder.

"You open that mouth again and your next command will be the grain mules." Turtle stared at him till he saw the rage drain from his eyes. "Our enemy is there." He pointed across the bay.

"Are you so sure?"

The two hurried to the beach, where sixty triremes lay, bows drying while their sterns wallowed in the sea. With the arrival of the officers, activity erupted: heavy infantry, fighting as marines, wrestled with their linen or bronze breastplates, squirming into them as servants assisted; crews scrambled at the water's edge, heaving their shoulders into the black, pitched hulls of the warships as they worked to float them before the weight of the boarding marines pinned them to the beach.

Brasidas pulled down the shoulder flaps of his scarlet-and-white linothorax as Diokles quickly tied the waist and chest stays on his side, pulling them tight to eliminate any gap. The six rows of bronze scales that encircled his abdomen reflected back the sun in orange flashes upon the hypaspites face as he finished securing it. Hylas snapped both greaves upon his master's legs, his eyes fixed all the while upon the snarling faces of twin gorgons that formed the kneecaps. Diolkes then held out the high-crested helmet, expecting Brasidas to snatch it. Instead his master pushed it back into his grip.

"Wait."

Stiffened by the accouterments of war he trudged away, up a dune and across the road, slipping into a shady grove of willow and oak. He peered into the shadows. A light breeze shook the trees high up, distracting him for a moment, but quickly his eyes searched the forest once more. He prayed to her. "Dear goddess protect him." No sign. Nothing to confirm his invocation.

"Master Brasidas!" The boy's voice sprinted with concern. "They are launching." He looked at him with pleading eyes, then scampered toward the beach, stopping after a short sprint to turn back, jogged, then turned back again, making sure Brasidas followed.

Brasidas, even under the weight of his armor, bounded up the gangplank like a boy on the way to supper. There beside the rail stood Diolkes, helmet, shield, and spear at the ready. Brasidas, in a manner almost ceremonious, reached for the helmet first, which he settled atop his head, but tilted back to clear his face. Now he took hold of his spear. The weighty shield he would leave in his armor bearer's hand until moments before the landing.

At the midpoint of crossing, their grounding site appeared so very narrow, and hardly grew as they approached, keeping in scale the aspect of something distant. From the gate of the Athenian fort poured companies of heavily armed hoplites. Hardly sixty, but they covered every meter of stone that lay dry above the waves. He reckoned they might land three triremes at best on this scanty stretch—seventy-five marines, disembarking haphazardly against a dense formation of heavy infantry almost equal in number. He wished for his calculations to be mistaken. As he shouldered his way forward to the bow, he glanced at the two vessels which cut the swells beside his; the rest, intimidated by the absence of a clear landing spot, hung back. Suddenly the pilot screamed the order for the rowers to backwater. The enemy infantry, lacking missile troops, instead fired insults at them. A bowlegged hoplite, his feet wedged securely between two knee-high boulders, waved a spear at them. "We are waiting for you, my darlings." He kissed the air. Another stroked his spear shaft obscenely. Insults melded with ribald laughter.

Brasidas looked to the two warships closest. He recognized neither captain, then spun around, looking astern. Back more than fifty meters trailed the ship of his friend Turtle. He pushed his way through the press of marines toward the pilot.

"Why are you stopping!" He loomed over the man, enraged, muscles twitching beneath his armor.

"Take a good look at that beach," he snapped back indignantly. "It'll rip a hole in us as wide as that asshole's mouth," he said, pointing to the loudest of the Athenians.

Brasidas leaned into the man's face. "We can't swim. Ground this ship." He nailed the butt-spike of his spear into the splintered deck. Gripped by fear or stubbornness, the pilot stared back in silence. Brasidas shouted, "Ground it now!"

The pilot shouted the order. The oars dipped and pulled, heaving the trireme forward. Brasidas yelled across the glinting swells to the nearest warship. "Ground your vessel!"

For a moment the captain, a Sikyonian, stared at him as though his thoughts froze like a stream in winter, but then barked out the order to his pilot. The third ship had drifted out of earshot.

They would have to make due with fifty.

On the beach before them, arrayed in files not more than five men deep, the Athenian infantry slid their helmets down and hefted their shields, readying for the assault. Their captain, waving his spear overhead, shouted encouragements; his men acknowledged these with robust cheers.

The trireme heaved forward, inexorably, toward the enemy while the rising sea-bottom scraped and thumped the keel and ribbing, prompting the rowers to withdraw their oars, and setting the marines to an uneasy shuffling. With each passing moment the hull ground harder into the rocks, until with one painful groan it stuck fast. Prepared as they were, the marines lurched then tumbled across the narrow top deck, losing precious time in regaining their feet and lost weapons. Brasidas spun to his feet while snatching his shield from the pitched deck; with a reassuring glance he spotted the figurine of the goddess swaying frantically from the cord that secured her to its inner rim. Behind the bronze of his helmet, he smiled.

The Athenian infantry stampeded toward the single beached trireme, hacking to pieces, a dozen blades to a man, the first three marines that disembarked. Brasidas shoved his way to the rail near the bow, all the while wedged in a tight formation with four other marines. With shields tucked into their shoulders, they slammed the mob of attackers that had spilled over the rails and had begun to establish themselves upon the decking; some continued to lunge and strike with their spears while others extended hands to help their comrades scramble aboard. Brasidas quickly found himself outnumbered on his own trireme.

Only the narrowness of the deck kept them from being overwhelmed. The Spartans, shields still interlocked, strode into the enemy, striking down with their high-held spears into the faces, necks, and shoulders of the surging Athenians; many fell, but many more took their places.

Even through the insulating qualities of his heavy bronze helmet, the sound of metal striking metal thundered deafeningly. The marine to his right crumpled under a fury of blows from several of the enemy, exposing his vulnerable unshielded side. First he heard then felt a rapid succession of iron blades smack his helmet, shield, and corslet, driving him rearward against his will, causing him to stumble and fold under the onslaught. He felt his shield being torn from his grip. His vision blurred. His chest burned. Dark silence engulfed him.

* * *

The storm had passed, leaving the air heavy, moist, and scented with resinous pine. Although wet from the rain, he felt a pleasing warmth and stood to accept the breeze that filtered through wood melodically. First he stared up, watching the remnants of clouds gently scud over the high peaks of Taygetos, then glanced down into the sleeping trench lined with leaves and boughs and saw the three game snares that he had carefully wound around a stick, his water flask and xuele knife. Shafts of sunlight sifted through the foliage, speckling the ground in yellow; it urged him to walk.

A rustle of leaves. His eyes moved to the noise, and there half hidden by a straight-trunked pine posed the goddess, smiling. She slipped out into plain view and moved effortlessly toward him, placing a slender finger across his closed lips, and with a touch commanded his silence.

"He is safe." She turned and strolled away, slipping amongst the shadows....

"You must drink."

He blinked open his eyes painfully, the glare of the sputtering lamp forcing them shut again.

"Master, you must drink this."

He peered through the tiny slit of his parted eyelid; a small black bowl hovered over him. Behind it the worried face of Diokles came into focus. He felt a hand slip under his head. Unable to resist, he bent forward and allowed the warm liquid to flood his mouth, swallowing cautiously.

"You have lost very much blood. Please drink. It will help to restore it."

The only objects that came into view were the seemingly suspended faces of Diokles and Hylas. His hypaspites continued to gently tip the bowl to his lips while the boy propped him up. Surely it was night, for everything else lay in blackness.

Weakly he pushed the vessel of broth away. "Koryphasion—did we take it?"

Diokles shook his head.

"Master, you have been in sleep for three days, away from the world of men and in the care of the gods. The battle-surgeon pronounced you all but dead."

"And what has happened in those three days?"

"More Athenians arrived yesterday. Sunk or ran aground a dozen of our ships and scattered the rest."

Brasidas swallowed painfully, his voice crawling through his dust-dry throat. "And our men on Sphakteria?"

"Cut-off by the Athenian fleet."

The room whirled as he tried to lift his head from the pillowed fleece. The wound in his side burned angrily, reminding him of its depth as Diokles pushed him firmly back into the pile of linen and hides; he shook his head.

"If you die now, it will not be the doing of the Athenians, but of a single willful Spartan."

Brasidas' hand gripped the soiled chiton of Diokles, in anger at first, but as much to steady him as he crumpled into the fleece. "We must make a landing there." His words hissed from him like steam from a lidded pot.

Hylas, eyes red from fatigue, stared until he trapped his master's glance. "The Athenians," now he spoke of his countrymen as some men of an unknown city, "circle the island. No ship dare challenge them."

Brasidas slid his hand atop the boy's and smiled. "Fetch Lichas for me."

Hylas exploded through the hide flap of the tent. Soon two pairs of feet pounded the hard earth of the encampment, growing louder until they stopped just outside. Again the door snapped open. Turtle knelt beside his friend.

"What is he doing?"

Before answering, Turtle dismissed the pair with a mere glance. As soon as he was sure they were out of earshot, he leaned to Brasidas. "He does nothing until the ephors answer his dispatch."

Brasidas rubbed his eyes, trying to clear them. "Ships. How many do they have?"

"Twice as many as we have, but they still dare not land on the island. They have instead, sealed it off from us, hoping we will launch what ships we have to relieve our men."

"What about at night? Do they patrol after dark?" More than by water or food, his appetite would be satisfied only with information. A head peeked in through opening in the tent wall. Diokles mimed sipping from a cup, then pointed to the bowl of zomos. Turtle acknowledged with a wink. "I will answer no more questions till you finish your soup." He touched the bowl to his friend's lips. "Now drink." Before he emptied the bowl, sleep took him.

* * *

Kleon, as always, roused the crowd to fever pitch by tossing aspersions at any convenient target; today he derided the generals at Pylos.

"How many months has it been?" He slapped his thigh in an exaggerated gesture. "Our great generals cannot take a tiny island from a handful of starved Spartans while our men at Pylos suffer depredations because of their leaders' inaction."

Eukles lifted his eyebrows. "He cares only that it is costing us money to maintain our fleet there." Thukydides nodded.

Now Kleon turned to general Nikias. "You purport yourself to be a leader of men. Go to Pylos, take Sphakteria, and the Spartans!"

227

Nikias stepped up to the speaker's platform in a dignified manner that underscored Kleon's crassness. "I would not endeavor to dispute the logic of your argument, my dear Kleon. But how could I—as you have so eloquently pointed out in the past—a man so inadequate in purpose, attempt to execute this bold and exquisite maneuver that you suggest. Only the author should recite so grand a story. I nominate you to lead the expedition to Pylos."

As grave as Thukydides' face remained, he could hardly contain the satisfaction he now felt as Kleon squirmed before the entire Assembly. *Never,* he thought. *He will never take the field against the Spartans.*

Kleon, at first stunned into silence by this nomination, worked his words in desperation to coax Nikias to captain the expedition. The more he spoke, the more the crowd cried out for him to trade his talk for action. All the while Nikias stood back, gesturing with open arms for Kleon to answer the call. Finally, after minutes of mock cheering from the Assembly, red-faced Kleon motioned for silence. "Not only will I lead this campaign against the Spartans, but I will deliver Sphakteria to you in less than two weeks!"

Nikias grinned. The crowd exploded with laughter. Furious, Kleon jumped from the bema as he pushed his way through the taunting throng of citizens, not even noticing Thukydides as he passed.

"It will be interesting," commented Eukles as he watched the tumultuous wake of Kleon's departure through the Assembly. "He argued against peace with Sparta a mere month ago. Pity, for it all could have ended then and there."

"The war or Kleon's career?" Thukydides, hardly imbued with humor, brought laughter to all around who heard this remark; he directed it with all seriousness. A man standing nearby, by all appearances a potter, for his gray exomis was smeared brown with dried clay, let the last trickle of laughter roll from his lips. "Let us see if he wields a spear as deftly as his tongue."

"He will talk the Spartans to death. I am sure of it," said another.

"Will you dine with me tonight?" Eukles asked as he led Thukydides down the stairs and away from the Pnyx. His friend, thoughtful as ever, meant to keep him from his father's empty house; only recollections of death stirred there now, a house as empty as his neighbor Glaukos'. All the while they walked, the name of Kleon lurched from the milling throng, chased after by a string of laughs.

Tucked within the columns of the stoa, workmen unwrapped from their linen coverings a collection of weapon-scarred armor. Both men halted then stepped into the shade of the building to watch, lured by trophies of war. One slave lifted a beautifully crafted war-helmet, complete with a crimson-haired crest up to another who hung it from a square-headed nail. Next they uncovered a meter-'round shield of polished bronze, its surface rippled with dents. Still its red lambda, emblem of their foe, glared defiantly at them; upon its surface were punched holes that crudely formed letters: *Taken from the Lakedaimonians at Pylos.*

Thukydides grabbed the shield before it was hoisted to its nail. He flipped it over. The armband hung by one of its eight bent rivets, flopping uselessly in the deep bronze bowl. From the rim swung a small wooden figurine of a woman, barely the height of his hand, fashioned with bow in hand; a lacing of thin sinew secured it. Hardly the elegant workmanship of a sculptor, it reminded him more of the handiwork of a pious child. The slave, with but a look, asked for it back, then hung that too with the other captured armaments.

"Will he go?" Eukles said as he jumped the gutter that split the narrow street in two.

From behind a closed door that faced the street came the sound of rattling metal. "Ho!" The yell preceded the door cracking open. A bear of a man peeked out, making sure the open door would not strike some unaware passerby. He slipped out, bouncing along the wall till he regained his elusive balance, still clutching a half-empty wine-cup in his hands.

"They ridicule men like that."

Eukles, startled by his friend's comment, turned away from the drunkard. "Who?"

"The Spartans. They purposely allow their slaves to drink themselves into a stupor, then take them before their children, making examples of them."

"And do you suggest that it is a practice that we adopt in Athens."

A rare smile formed on Thukydides. "Athens would have many more drunks than pupils."

They halted before the gate to his house. Eukles tugged on his arm. "Come with me and forget them for tonight."

Thukydides stared up at the hollow black windows of his father's bedroom. From within the walled courtyard, he heard his servant approach, moving quickly to unlatch the door and greet him. The gate squealed open.

"I will be home later."

The servant slowly pressed the door closed. The two men walked off, neither looking back.

* * *

Damatria, at first overcome with dread on the day they carried her husband, Brasidas, into her home, now quietly thanked the gods for his wounds. She loved him, and that is why she thanked them, for in their ten years of marriage, this had been the longest time he remained with her, although he proved to be a most difficult patient.

Almost three months to the day of his return, and he could begin to walk without her beside him, using only a walking stick and slow shuffling steps to get himself about. It irked him: Brasidas could not walk or ride to the Ephorion; his father refused to visit, for he knew his son would only rile them both with talk of Sphakteria; his closest comrades lingered still at Koryphasion with Thrasymidas in command.

"Now you must rest." Damatria eased him into a fleece-covered chair, while disarming him of his walking stick.

He gritted his teeth as he descended, settling into the curved seat, then kicked out his legs, while rubbing his bound ribcage. "I think I have had enough of this." He fingered the knot of linen, trying to unfasten the bandage, but she pulled back his hand like that of a pilfering child's, slapping it in admonition. "Are you my new commander?"

"Until you are healed—why yes!" she replied sternly.

"You must take me to the Ephorion, to Kleandridas' home, anywhere I might find out about Sphakteria." The pain erupted. Sweat seeped from every pore on his head. He squeezed his right hand into a tight fist.

"No wonder that they risked the journey in bringing you here from Koryphasion. You must have been unbearable there, even with your wounds, you have forgotten how to take orders." She daubed his forehead dry. "Lichas told me, you know. Ordering your friends about to bribe both Helots and freemen to swim with food to the island. He told me you tried to hire a trireme to sail there yourself."

He said nothing, but fought to bury the pain. "I think I will rest," he said. "If you will not bring me word of the war, at least tell me of the harvest. Take Diokles with you and tally the yield of barley."

"On your state kleros? Why that is more than half a day's ride. Who will tend to you?"

He eased himself onto the couch, and pulled a blanket of fleece across his chest. "Send the boy Hylas to me. He is more than able." He tucked his head into his chest. His eyes closed. He did not watch her depart, but when the door opened for the second time, he snuck a peek from his half-closed eyes.

"Hylas, come here." He tossed the blanket aside. "Get me my stick."

Without thinking, the boy handed him the walking staff. "Master Brasidas, your wife forced me to take an oath to keep you here undisturbed. I dare not break it?"

"And what about your oath to serve me? Does this new one take precedence?"

"Sir, either choice puts me in peril with the gods—if you force me to make one."

"And how long?" he asked as he leaned on his walking stick while rising deliberately from the couch.

"Sir?"

"Your oath. How long are you to keep me here undisturbed?" His legs barely bent as he shuffled to the door.

"I do not understand."

"A week? A day? An hour? Surely if you undertake so solemn a thing as an oath before the gods, you should at least know what you are swearing to."

The boy, clearly unsettled, said nothing.

"You have kept me here, to the credit of your oath. Presently you shall help me to Kleandridas' house, then I shall return here so you can again maintain your oath, with only a minor lapse." He unlatched the door. "Now get the wagon."

He despised riding in it, like a girl-child, woman, or Helot, but it was the only way to travel even this short distance without his wounds scolding him for this bit of insubordination. Hylas held the reins while he sat stiffly upright, forced to this unnatural posture by the tight bandage that embraced his chest. He had never taken notice of the ruts and boulders that scarred the road before; every one of these rocked and bounced the wagon, causing his side to throb. He began to sweat again.

"Sir," said Hylas with concern, "the fever again?"

"No! This vise that the iatros calls a bandage is squeezing the very breath from me." He drew in some air, expanding his chest, then winced.

"Do you want me to stop?"

"Keep going."

They passed three Helots who pushed barrows of manure along the road, men who worked on his neighbor's farm. The trio stared for a moment at him, but soon cast their eyes down to their work, hoping this momentary balk in manners had gone unnoticed. The smell of dung faded as they rode on, encountering no one until, at the turn in the road that slithered through a dale of willow, they heard the gallop of a single rider. Tearing into view rode Kleandridas; he yanked hard on the reins, sending his horse into a rearing spin before halting.

"Brasidas?" He slapped his horse affectionately on the neck to calm it. The beast snorted with approval. "You look in no condition to be riding—even in that!" he said while glancing at the wagon scornfully. "I must take you home."

"I will go, but you must tell me of Sphakteria." Brasidas let slip a wince as he spoke.

"I will tell you all I know—at your house."

Hylas swatted the mule with a cornel switch, talking to it while clicking his tongue and at the same time steering them in a wide about-face turn that he artfully negotiated within the narrow road. Kleandridas led them. He glanced over his shoulder now and then, forcing their mule to keep pace with his eager horse, making it a short trip back.

Brasidas, using every bit of strength he could muster, stepped from the wagon unassisted, determined to show his friend that he had healed well and glanced down, making certain of his balance only to see blood drip onto the chalky soil. He reached for the bandage and felt the sopping linen, which he worked to hide by clamping his arm to his side. Once inside he ordered Hylas to fetch wine for them both, not pausing to ask his guest first.

"Aren't you going to have him change that dressing first?" Kleandridas shook his head. "That should have scabbed by now."

Brasidas moved his arm away and studied the wet linen. "It did scab. The ride worked it open." He pressed his hand onto the wound. "It will close again."

Hylas presented full cups to them both, then without any prompting, worked on Brasidas' dressing while he and Kleandridas spoke.

"I can breath once more," sighed Brasidas as the unfastened bandage slid from his chest. "Now tell me of Sphakteria."

Kleandridas stared grimly at his friend for a moment before answering. "We have lost the island."

"When?"

I found out today. But a few here in Sparta know."

"They are all dead?"

"Not all." Kleandridas gulped his wine now. "Over one hundred have been captured by the Athenians."

Brasidas heard, but refused to comprehend. "Surrendered? With Epitadas in command?"

232

"He was not, it seems, in command when our men did submit."

"Neither would Hippagretas surrender."

"Neither was he in command. Epitadas was killed, rallying his men as they were being surrounded. Hippagretas fell too, although they recovered him alive from the piles of the slain. Styphon capitulated."

He allowed himself but a moment to grieve his dearest companion before his mind began whirring with the ramifications of this disaster. He sat looking at nothing, sucking his wine slowly.

"The ephors are in a panic. I know, for I got this news as they did, before the kings this morning. They were certain that Athens would accept the peace terms they offered, in exchange for our men on the island."

He lifted his head slowly to look into his friend's face. "And why did they not?"

"Aristokrates was there as one of our emissaries, and says their assembly was all but ready to endorse the treaty as proposed. One man turned them all against it. A man named Kleon."

Not long after, his friend departed, leaving him to ponder Koryphasion. The sun arced across the unblemished afternoon sky, finally slipping behind Taygetos; through the open window he followed it, neither moving nor speaking. Hylas, sensing his master's need, sat on a stool near the empty brazier, waiting—available. Returning finally to his house in mind, Brasidas looked at the boy.

"You may leave if you so desire. I require nothing."

Hylas leaned forward. "Are you certain, Master?"

"Is it so obvious?"

The boy wrinkled his brow.

"That I need—something?" He studied Hylas for a moment. His mouth curled into a smile. "I think it is you. You need something, and it is talk. Bring us both some wine and come sit here," he instructed, pointing to the table near him, "and we shall talk."

First he splashed wine into the hollow cups, then dragged his stool to the table. Both drank; he waited for Brasidas to speak again.

Unusual for late afternoon, a blustery wind stirred up dust outside the open window, shivering the trees in the orchard beyond and the latched door of the house. Only the very tops of the trees pushed high enough into the retreating light, everything else steeped in shades of gray shadows. It was his favorite time of day.

"You have a question for me, Hylas?" He shifted in his chair, feeling the wound with the tips of his fingers.

"Come now. You Athenians always have questions. You ask and I shall answer."

The boy squeezed his wine cup in the palms of his hands. "Your friend Epitadas, sir. When Kleandridas told you he was slain you seemed—"

"Content? Is that the word you are groping for?" He spoke gently, his manner urging more conversation.

"Yes," Hylas responded, stumbling a bit over the word. "Are you not sad at his death?"

"I am saddened that I will never see him in this life, but rejoice at the way he met death. You may think it strange, but we Spartans define our entire life by how we end it. His was a beautiful death, a *kallos thanatos*."

"Then what upsets you now?"

Brasidas grinned. "You are perceptive. My distress is for the living, our men made prisoners."

Hylas swallowed loudly, emptying his mouth of wine. "In Athens we would rejoice that the lives of our soldiers were spared and would have grieved over the dead. Here, in your city, things go quite opposite. It is a difficult thing for me to grasp."

"But we Spartans understand you Athenians. We certainly understand that you measure your success in life by your acquisitions. Horses, money, land, slaves, even your citizens' support in politics. All these things you work to acquire. Look at us. We own very little, and even this meager portion does not invoke us to be miserly. But of all things you possess, it seems to me what you covet above all is a love of life—as do most men. Remember, it is the nature of possessions to possess their owners. We have learned to exploit this in others, while never succumbing to the same trap—until now."

"You mean Sphakteria?"

"Yes. Our one hundred that live will, by their very survival, kill thousands of us. Like Leonidas before them, 'twas better if they perished, free of possessions."

Hylas, encouraged by the wine and his schooling in rhetorika, prodded further. "Master, you say you have no possessions, but look around you. You have a house, and your farms, and," he added, slapping his chest, "a slave. Are not these things that you own."

"You have been here for years, but still you do not understand. This farm, this house, and you," he said jabbing his finger at the boy, "belongs to no one, yet everyone. Like me they are possessed by my country, Sparta."

* * *

Autumn, disguised as summer, slipped into Lakonia unnoticed, but by the time it had departed became known by its true face. Cold rain buffeted the valley of the Eurotas. Snow began its march down from the peaks of Taygetos while the trees on its slopes cowered in their nakedness. Winter, raw and bitter, finally arrived. Unlike winters past, the ephors spent no time calculating which age group would be called in the spring; the kings and polemarchs did not counsel over plans of their yearly invasion of Attika. This great machine of war had become disabled by a mere one hundred men— the men held prisoner in Athens.

Sparta
Twenty-Eight
ΣΠΑΡΤΗ

"And how many embassies have we dispatched to Athens? Are we any closer to peace?" Brasidas, moving stridently before the ephors and the kings, dismissed the pain in his still-unhealed side. He locked eyes with Kratisikles. "I do not want your precious office of admiral that you crave for your sons and cronies. Keep it! Give me a regiment of Spartiates to command and I will bring Athens to terms. Only then will we see our comrades alive again and freed from Athenian prisons.

Kratisikles leaned back in his chair, looking down his nose at Brasidas. "How do you propose to accomplish with a few hundred men, what we and our allies could not with thousands? I know you hold intimate council with the gods, but do they now bestow their powers upon you?"

Brasidas stepped to within a foot of him. "Simple intelligence is not an Olympian trait, though it seems to have been very scarce in our own commanders."

Agis glared at him. Pleistoanax grinned foxily. The others, even Kratisikles, seemed undisturbed by his comment.

"The Athenians have threatened to execute our men if we invade Attika. Is this is a gift from Olympos? We have ravaged their farms, burned their grain, and hacked their groves down to the very roots, and what has it gotten us?" Brasidas drew a long breath.

Pleistoanax lifted a single finger in the air. "Specifically, what do you propose?"

"Thrake! That is what I propose. The cities there cry out for liberation. One regiment of Equals. That is all I ask, and I will pull the Athenian suckling from Thrake's breast. Without Thrake and its cities, Athens will starve."

Kratiskles leaned toward Agis, then mumbled a word or two. In turn he spoke quietly with Pleistoanax. Finally he addressed Brasidas. "We shall consider what you have said. You may take your leave." Finished with him,

236

Kratisikles again whispered to Agis.

He departed, somewhat surprised that they did not reject his proposal out of hand, for Kratisikles and Agis surely would undermine any attempt to draw power from them or their confederates. For some unknown reason he turned and walked away from Pitane and toward the Eurotas and upon passing the Persian Stoa—that long portico constructed with the treasures of the Spartan victory over Mardonios and Xerxes—he heard someone call to him from deep within its columned shadows. He walked up the few steps, halted at the top to listen. The voice called again. He walked further. There upon a long marble bench and quite alone, sat Turtle.

"Come and sit." His friend patted the gleaming white stone seat. "I know where you have been, so I suppose you need to talk."

"Why is it," he said as he folded to a seat, "that when I am silent both you and Hylas think I need conversation?"

"Because, when you do not speak with your friends, we know something is amiss. Now what did they say to you?"

"Nothing. It is what I said to them that may be of more interest to you."

Turtle rubbed his beard between his forefinger and thumb. "Hmmm—might it be about Thrake?"

"Yes. We have talked of it so often, the words seemed put to memory."

"And?"

"They said nothing."

"And why were you walking down to the river? To swim perhaps?"

"Perhaps indeed. I would think its waters less chilly than the place I have just come from." He looked up at the modest hill that formed Sparta's acropolis, catching sight of the last bit of daylight that washed upon the temple of Athena. "It will be cold again tonight," he added with a tone of preoccupation.

"They just may be desperate enough to allow you to win the war, my friend. Now we must make our way to supper or our comrades will be cross. Sthenelaidas, in particular, has shown scant patience with tardiness, and I for one would like a full portion tonight."

They left the stoa, turning right onto the Aphetaid Road, skirting the agora until coming to the Hyakinthia Way. Soon they were over the Knakion River and onto the Amyklaian Road, directed by the smoky aroma of the cook-fires of the phiditia. Luckily they found a few others of their phidition and fell in with them as they hurried into the tent. Brasidas swung open the flap; the hearty smell of zomos and roasted venison greeted him.

237

"Good evening, gentlemen." Stenelaidas waved them enter. "We are blessed tonight with a fine meal, compliments of Lichas."

Brasidas, trying not to appear at all surprised, smiled and leaned to Turtle. "Little wonder you did not want to miss dinner tonight. When did you bag this deer?"

Turtle smiled at Sthenelaidas, while talking through his teeth to Brasidas. "Why do you think I went looking for you? I would not hear the end of it if you missed partaking of my contribution to our dinner."

As soon as the men were seated, Keraon entered, leading the small procession of food servants. Loaves were passed the length of the table while the Keraon directed the placement of twin steaming platters of meat. With the wine poured, each man began to pluck a slab of venison with his dining knife. Upon the pole from which the door flap hung came a polite, faint rapping.

"Enter!" barked out Sthenelaidas.

In meekly stepped a Helot messenger, waiting to be acknowledged before revealing his mission.

"You may speak." Sthenelaidas studied the platter before him with deliberation, then stabbed at it. Steam billowed from the meat as he raised his portion free from the stack. The single thick piece filled his plate entirely.

"The ephors require Brasidas, son of Tellis, to attend them." As abruptly as he finished his announcement, he departed.

Brasidas pushed his plate away with one hand, while hurriedly filling his mouth full of wine from the cup he held with the other. In a moment he flew through the doorway.

"Wait!" Behind him jogged Turtle, cramming a greasy string of venison into his mouth. He pulled up beside his friend. "You may need someone to restrain you."

They covered the distance quickly and without conversation, catching up to the messenger as he entered the Ephorion.

"We thank you for your promptness," said Kratisikles.

Both men stood silently before the five ephors; the kings, it seemed, had departed to their phiditia and the evening meal.

"We have considered your proposal, Brasidas, and agree." Kratisikles looked to the other four, nodding affirmation. "But, we think your plan needs to be altered a bit—for the benefit of the polis."

"I am pleased that we seem to agree. Now on which points do we differ?"

"You shall have your command, and your commission to lead an army to Thrake—" said Angenidas.

"—but," interrupted Kratsikles, "you will lead no regiment of Spartiates. We can spare none."

Brasidas felt his face growing hot. Turtle jabbed him with an elbow. "Who am I to lead?"

"You may go to the cities of our allies to recruit your army. With your reputation, many men will join you." Angenidas spoke in a manner almost apologetically. He too worked to restrain Brasidas.

"No Spartans? None at all?"

Kratiskles pushed up from his chair. "None."

Before the word had left his lips Angenidas interjected, "No Spartiates, but you may take Helots."

"Helots? What incentive will these slaves have to follow me—and obey me once outside of Lakedaimon?"

"Threat of punishment. Death, in fact, if they fail to obey. That is why they will follow your orders." Kratisikles lowered himself back into his chair, grinning satisfactorily.

"You would make a fine Persian. Xerxes whipped his soldiers to fight against us and failed. The whip hardly produced men of spirit—or virtue." Brasidas maintained his poise.

"Then what do you suggest?" Angenidas opened the door for his friend.

"Freedom. If they fight with distinction, grant them their freedom."

The five spoke amongst themselves. Kratisikles lifted his face. "Agreed," he said with reluctance laced in his voice.

"And I will be allowed to choose these Helots."

"Agreed."

"And one final point. Then I will leave you to your supper. I demand your solemn oaths before Zeus, that whatever treaty or alliance I propose to the Thrakians, you will not renege on. Agree to this also, or find another to lead the campaign."

He exited the Ephorion with less than he had hoped for but much more than expected. They swore the oath, granted his selection of officers and also promised to deliver to him the catalog of Helots which the Krypteia had selected for extermination. He insisted upon this list—the names of all exceptional slaves—men too smart, too strong, or too virtuous to be held down in peaceful subjection. In his mind these were the most fit to become soldiers

The next morning, one in which the frosty winter sky took on the luster of an iron sword blade, he spent with Damatria, putting in order all the things of his family and kleros that would weigh upon his mind. His sons would be well cared for, supervised by Gyllipos. His mess dues as he detailed, would continue to be paid. The devotions to Artemis in his name and paid for in advance would continue at her shrine. While Hylas worked diligently packing, Diokles secured his master's armor to the mule before garlanding the animal in celebration of the campaign.

The hard gallop of an approaching rider drew him to the open window. The man, wrestling with the reins to bring his horse to a stop, rolled off and to his feet just outside the gate then sprinted to the door. Brasidas hustled to greet him.

"From the ephors," he announced curtly, before turning away.

Brasidas unrolled the hide and quickly scanned the catalog of Helots. "Continue," he said to Hylas, then he looked to his wife smiling. "Something important." He re-rolled the hide then rapped it against his thigh as he strode off. Within the hour he arrived at Thrasymidas' farm.

No one worked the crop-bereft fields, but he caught sight of several Helots lugging stones to a broken section of the boundary fence. Outside a stable a single Helot pitched hay from a wagon into a manger. The stable door swung open. Out came a woman leading a cow, which she walked to the trough of hay.

"Temo?"

The woman, shading her eyes from the unexpected sun that had just pushed out of the clouds, leered at him for a moment, then walked away toward the stable's door. He kicked his heels, sending the horse to a trot, cutting across her path and forcing her to halt.

"Will you listen to me?"

She slid the cloak from her head, revealing her snowy hair and tired face. For a moment it repulsed him. Nevertheless he slid from the horse, never taking his eyes from her while he approached. She fumbled with the ends of the cloak, her work-swollen hands shaking from the wintry gusts. Beyond the fields, where they worked on the fence, a group of Helots ceased their task and stared at the pair; one stared at them most intently.

"Temo, I am leaving on a journey that most likely will never return me to Sparta."

"And this means something to me?" Her voice and bearing carried a disconcerting vigor. He expected bitterness.

"Yes, for Xenias—your husband—is coming with me."

Her look went blank, as though she surrendered that strength. "Why? Is this to purge your slaves of any man of mettle—and of worth? Are you Spartans so afraid of us that when any dare behave as men you kill them?"

He thrust the roll of hide before her face. "This is a list," he said through clenched teeth, while holding it in clenched hands. "The Krytpeia's list. Every one on it has been marked for death. If you could read I would show you his name." He pointed with the roll directly at Xenias.

"You would let them do this?" Her voice, quit of anger, implored him.

"Only if he comes with me will he live." He placed both his hands upon her shoulders, feeling more bone than flesh beneath her soiled cloak. "If he does, he will earn his freedom, and yours."

She stepped back. His arms fell from her. She pulled the cloak back up over her head, squeezing it tightly beneath her chin with both hands. "I am to be grateful? To celebrate this gift you offer, a gift which you Spartans have stolen from us. Keep fighting your wars, and when you are all dead, that will be a gift to celebrate." She ran through the open door of the stable, pulling it shut in her wake. He did not follow, but stood for a moment, mulling her words. From within the stable he heard sobbing. Unthinking he stepped toward the sound, but halted after a few steps, bounded upon his horse and rode out across the field to the Helots at the fence.

"Xenias, you have been given a great opportunity. If you prove you can fight like a free man, then maybe you will become one." Before the slave could answer, Brasidas sprinted his horse across the empty field and onto the road south.

* * *

Their static column stretched from the Eurotas back into the agora and beyond. Amongst them only the Spartiate officers stood appareled in battle dress of crimson chiton and tribuon cloak. The Helots, on the other hand, wore only their dirt-gray tunics and held a variety of cloaks and blankets to complete their kit; they gave the appearance of a procession of dirt farmers on their way to the shrine of Demeter. Wagons laden with weapons and armor rocked forward and back, tugged by mules anxious to move away from the impinging crowd. In perfect formation the boys of the Agoge filled the north slope of the acropolis. Beaming and wide-eyed with untested courage, each anticipated the day when they would march out of Sparta to battle. Brasidas searched the hill until he found his sons; they sat amongst the others, but their grins of pride gave them away.

241

With satisfaction he sucked the cool spring air while studying the feathery clouds that scudded by overhead; the sun warmed him quickly as it slipped into view. Carefully now he took inventory of everything familiar to him, every building, tree, statue, and shrine—any object that fell under his gaze. Finally he found her. She held a garland of myrtle and phlox and wore a solemn face. Beside her stood his mother, Argileonis, cold as the statue of Athena that loomed behind her. His father said farewell with his eyes only while Damatria stepped forward, presenting the garland. Brasidas dipped his head to receive it. She pressed her cheek to his as she dropped the ring of flowers upon his shoulders, holding this subtle, discreet, and final embrace.

"Be strong for them," he whispered.

Now the pipers struck up their shrill marching tune, spurring the squadron of mounted scouts along the column like a shudder on an enormous serpent. Before he could mount his horse, Kleandridas moved to him.

"There is no one else in Sparta that could do this," he said buoyantly, his manner quite distinct from the others. "You, my friend, have been endowed with a *kharisma*—a divine favor. The goddess will certainly be with you."

In silence he embraced Kleandridas before vaulting upon his horse. At first he kept to a slow canter, studying his men, each face, every step of foot and sway of arm, searching for any distinction to be stored in memory and summoned when needed. They would fight as a collective, but be attended to as individuals. His role expanded far beyond commander. Teacher, drill-master, priest, and jailer—he would be all this and more. He rode up through the agora, keeping the column to his left while passing the House of the Gerousia, then the Shrine of Lykourgos, until he came to the Babyx bridge. Here Turtle, Lykophron, and Polyakas waited, along with a handful of junior officers who would now assume command of Helot companies.

"Well, gentlemen, are we ready?"

He led them across the river, by the meadows where as boys they trained and on past farms of gawking Helots that paused their sempiternal toils to watch them march by *their* training fields. Wives, sons, and daughters, granted this brief respite from their tasks, ran up to the road, offering garlands, meager bundles of food, and hasty embraces.

By mid-afternoon, after the sun had sapped the bounce out of their legs, he ordered the column to halt, calling together his officers. He rode up to a small knoll, one which overlooked the road and his men, and leaned forward on his horse to stretch his back a bit before commencing to speak.

"We will camp on the north side of Sellasia, where a stream crosses this road. They will think this a very satisfactory march. Almost fifteen miles. Today will be the very last day we cover so meager a distance. Each day we must increase the pace while decreasing our respites. Where we go, we will have few friends. Indeed, where we go, we will need to move quickly."

His speech now ended, he skidded his horse down the slope, pulling up before Turtle and Lykophron; a few dozen yards away, Polyakas sat silent beneath a lightning-cleft plane tree, using this holy place as a refuge and lost in thought. The company commanders dispersed. He said nothing until the last of them was back amongst his men.

"I will ride ahead, to Sikyon in fact, to begin recruitment there. In three days we shall meet at Korinth." He glanced to the tree and Polyakas. "Keep watch over him?"

Turtle nodded curtly as did Lykophron, who paused just long enough to give the impression that he did indeed take heed, before asking, "How are we to control these Helots?"

"They are not Spartans, but neither are they Helots any longer. Treat them as you would any other ally."

He rode north past Tegea and into the territory of Mantinea, the boy, Hylas, his only companion, rapidly covering the distance before sunset. Although he had many close acquaintances in the town, established through both his father and Kleandridas, he decided to camp beyond it at the threshold to the pass called the Ladder. In doing this, he thought, he would not be detained by hospitality, or be noticed by Athenian spies that surely lurked in the city. Upon stopping, Brasidas tended to the horses while Hylas prepared a meal of warmed, salted boar-fish, a barley loaf, and a few olives.

Through the trees they watched another's fire dance in the wind that had picked up since dusk. Hylas scooped up a handful of twigs and snapped each one, paused, then laid it carefully upon the flames to a distinctive and mesmerizing tempo.

"Do you miss your home?" Searching for something to say, this question emerged from Brasidas' lips as though someone else had posed it.

Hylas kept to his ritual. "At times, sir," he answered but only after he had broken the twig first. With it now in the fire he could manage a word or two before the cadence demanded another. In steady time and deliberate manner he fed the fire, one rent twig after another until, with his reserve almost spent, he began to search for more in the retracting halo of firelight. The ground flickered empty.

"Fill your cup, then sit and we shall talk."

No doubt the boy was thirsty for without hesitation he unplugged the wine-skin and poured till his cup was politely less than full.

"Why only at times?" Brasidas recommenced his questioning once Hylas had resumed a seat beside the fire.

"Because I have to think back quite far to recall it as a pleasant place."

Brasidas grew curious at this answer. Cities did not change; at least Sparta did not. "And what was the city like during the war?"

Unsettled by his absent supply of twigs he now began to trace figures in the dust, sitting cross-legged, looking down. "Master, I can answer you with one word—plague."

Brasidas had heard stories of the plague, the vast numbers of people affected, and the suffering and death of so many. But to him it seemed only as a story, told by the age-old poet, something so removed, so unimaginable, that it must be an exaggeration, enhanced in the retelling. "Tell me what Athens was like during the plague."

Hylas' attitude transformed somehow from slave and servant to equal. "Your invasion forced all of Attika to flee into the city. The first precincts to fill were between the Long Walls. You must know of these. They stretch from the city proper down to the harbors. Families patched together huts there using the walls as one side and their neighbor's as another. By mid-summer of the first year, thousands encamped there."

Brasidas listened intently and in silence. Indeed this was unimaginable, he coming from a city that prided itself on its broad streets, spacious agora, and widespread dwellings across its five villages. He grew up in a polis where he never saw his neighbor's cottage from the windows of his own.

Hylas licked the wine from his lips. "They say a ship from Libya or Egypt brought it. Started in the Piraios, then raced toward the city using the Long Walls as its roadway. Over three years it killed many more than you Spartans could have." He stared at the scrawls in the dirt. "We should have come out and fought you."

Brasidas sighed. "You Athenians would be just as dead."

"But at least quickly and in a struggle with men—not a god."

"Come now. Do you truly believe that Apollo brought the plague to Athens? How could an Athenian believe such a thing when a pious Spartan such as myself does not?" He laughed a bit after speaking, trying to relax the boy's spirit, which had become both dark-browed and agitated, replacing his usually solicitous manner.

"Because the oracle said so."

"The oracle says many things. People only remember the predictions that suit them. You stated clearly why the plague killed in Athens, and by your stay in our city must also see why it does not kill there."

"You Spartans are safe because you venerate the gods. Some in Sparta say that you, sir, even speak with them."

"And who told you this?" Brasidas threw up a most stern demeanor as a shield to hide his amusement. "Only priests and soothsayers speak with the gods, not simple soldiers like me."

"You are hardly a simple soldier," replied Hylas, his schooled fashion of rhetorika emerging.

"In the end that is all any Spartan can hope to be." With scarcely a pause he asked, "What is it you strive to be?" The question tumbled into the boy's path, an impediment to his surging and fiery discourse.

Hylas' voice became subdued. "That question can no longer be answered by me, sir."

"The answer may not be in words, but in deeds. This army that I lead to Thrake, when it returns to Sparta, will be comprised exclusively of free men. Any slaves will be left behind, slain by the enemy."

"Do you mean to kill us all?" Again his voice burned.

"No! Cowardice and disobedience will be the sole agents of death. Any and every man who possesses discipline and valor will both live and be set free."

The boy swirled the dregs 'round and 'round, gazing into his cup, seemingly detached from the moment. "Then I will tell you when I am free."

* * *

Crammed into Sikyon's agora were sundry merchants and anxious buyers, all chattering the banter of commerce. He stalked about, eyeing their wares, occasionally handling an odd item or exquisitely crafted one, and returning it once the seller launched into his pitch. Hylas moved about more comfortably than his master, seemingly revitalized by this stew pot of trade so reminiscent of his former city.

"There are several items," stated Brasidas coolly, "which I am told the Sikyonians produce, that are considered by many to be of the finest and most unique quality." So uncharacteristically he used many more words than usual. Hylas grinned at him. "I want you to find a stlengis each for my sons, the bracelet they call a Sikyonion, and a pair of slippers by the same name, both for my wife. I will be there." He pointed forcefully to the shield painter's shop, then slipped a handful of Aiginitan obols to the boy.

Hylas edged through the crowd, bobbing his head above the sea of people to catch a glimpse of his objectives. Soon he was lost from view. Brasidas, meanwhile, moved slowly through the agora, peeking sideways at stacked bronze bracelets, vials of perfumes, and wagons groaning under the weight of sykos squash. Now he moved amongst the armorers' booths, the smell of oiled iron and bronze smothering the dainty fragrances of the agora proper; he felt at ease. Beneath a slung canopy of linen, the painter squinted, dipped his brush into the flask of pitch and lampblack, then began to outline the glaring red eyes of the Medusa upon the shield.

The painter never turned, but cleared his throat and said, "You are in no need of my services, Spartan. You all have only one device adorning your shields." With an up and down stroke of his brush he painted an imaginary lambda in the air. "Even you could paint so simple an emblem."

He studied the horrible face of the monster upon the polished bronze facing, its fangs bared and its serpent hair swirling wildly. "I wonder, my friend, which shield an enemy might fear more—your gorgon or my lambda?"

"I fear your lambda more than you know," he said, finally turning to face him. "For here in Sikyon—in imitation of you Spartans—these figures that are my livelihood will soon be replaced by an austere sigma."

"Then it looks like your trade will take you abroad."

"As does yours? You are the Spartan sent here to recruit for the campaign in Thrake, are you not?"

"Practice your letters, friend." He said nothing more, but began to stroll amongst the makers of swords, spear tips, and bronze butt-spikes; he lifted first a wide-bladed spearhead from the shelf near a forge, testing its edge with a careful run of his thumb. A spear butt-spike, double the length of a typical Spartan one, caught his eye. The armorer, busy until now hammering the ribbed blade of a sword, grinned at him. "Heavy bastard, isn't it?"

Brasidas nodded, turning the long, tapered butt-spike in his hands to measure its weight.

"A Theban merchant ordered them. Must be for a mighty long spear." Sparks burst from his hammer-strike.

"Master Brasidas!"

He turned. "Did you find everything?"

"Yes, everything—and with money to spare." He thrust out a hand and slowly uncurled his fingers, revealing three coins.

Again he heard his name. Not far off a hand waved high over the heads in the swarming agora. Ableros, a Sikyonian general, emerged wearing a worried look. "Brasidas, the Athenians are attacking Megara."

* * *

Not waiting for the turn of a new day, but after sending word north to the Boiotians to join him, he gathered up the six hundred volunteer Sikyonian hoplites, along with the four hundred Phliasian heavy infantry—the contingent already assembled at Sikyon—and marched speedily on to Korinth. There the Korinthians eagerly provided him with nearly three thousand more. Here too Lykophron, Turtle, and Polyakas arrived with the Lakedaimonian force. By the day next they proceeded north, past the Isthmos and over the Diolkos slipway and to the town of Tropodiskos. Here, in the shadow of Mount Geraneia, he waited. A day passed. Not a word from Thebes and the Boiotians.

"Polyakas, assemble two companies of our Lakedaimonians—the most fit of them. I want to march in full battle order within the hour."

Brasidas hurried to his tent. Hylas, somehow anticipating the order, scurried about inside, pulling together his personal kit, while Diokles daubed the rim of his hoplon shield with an oily rag before sealing it away in its leather sack. He smiled at their efficiency.

"Will I be going?" said Hylas as he watched Diokles secure the armor upon the skittish, prancing mule.

"Yes, but not as my servant." He now addressed Diokles. "He is to be issued armor and weapons."

The hypaspites nodded, then summoned the boy with a single glance; they both hurried away, seeking the quartermaster of arms.

"Will I be going?" The words mocked absent Hylas. Leaning on the twisted and swollen trunk of an olive tree was Turtle, grinning.

"You will not!" answered Brasidas with stark brevity.

"We finally get a chance at them, and you will not let me tag along."

"What chance do you speak of? I march to grab the city proper before the Athenians do. Megara's gates are shut to them while they linger in the harbor of Nisaia. I mean to keep them there."

"And what are we to do?" challenged Turtle.

"Your attitude is distinctly Athenian today," snapped Brasidas, more than disturbed by his friend. Recall your heritage and follow orders. That is what you should do."

247

Turtle cast away the casual air of a friend and became a soldier once more, stiff-standing, attentive, and silent.

"You will remain here under Polyakas' command and greet the Boiotians." He spun around not pausing for confirmation from Turtle, fading quickly from his friend's view in the dying light of dusk.

Brasidas, along with the three hundred picked men, came to the northern gate of Megara, announced his intentions to defend their city from the Athenians and requested entry, but within citizens became wary to choose sides when the outcome of the impending battle seemed in doubt. They would not let him enter, but neither would they grant access to the Athenians, who now stood south of the walled harbor town of Nisaia. Assured by the canniness of the inhabitants, he marched back to his encampment at Tropodiskos. As he cleared the final ridge that separated him from his destination, he heard the din of horse and infantry on the march echoing from the slopes of Mount Geraneia. Soon he could make out the chatter of Boiotians, their broad and tedious accent marking them out.

He passed the sentries, abruptly hurrying to his tent where he was sure to find Polyakas, Turtle and the other allied commanders.

Turtle, seated adjacent to a smoldering and exhausted fire, snapped up from his seat. "Victory so soon?" he said, smiling.

"No, but neither defeat. We must call to council all the officers."

The night sky crept away, nudged aside by the impending day, which turned the early morning mist chalky; still they talked. The Boiotians had marched daylong and well into the night to hasten their arrival, but Rhexenor, their commander, exhibited scant fatigue; the enthusiasm of adventure kept sleep at bay. With Brasidas it was simply the task that urged him on. He explained, in detail, the situation to them all, answered their questions, then explained it all again. He insisted that his officers be well informed. Finally it was decided; they would march after the morning meal and take up position north of the Athenians, between Megara and the harbor town. There they would test the enemy's appetite for battle.

* * *

They marched toward the sea, keeping the long walls which connected Megara to the harbor of Nisaia on their right. Scattered about the narrow coastal plain, Athenian light infantry scurried about, foraging. Rhexenor galloped up to the front rank of the infantry; his squadron of Theban horsemen followed with the obedience of a shadow. The two commanders met without a word exchanged between them. Brasidas merely nodded. Rhexenor spun his horse around and kicked it to a full sprint. In perfect mimicry his men followed.

The Thebans swept over the plain like a hot wind, smothering the unarmored spearmen and acontists of the Athenians with a blistering charge. The killing came too easy and in abundance; they raced blindly after the fleeing survivors, not aware of the proximity to the Athenian battle line. A salpinx blared. From behind the enemy heavy infantry, dust churned. The ground shook. Suddenly Athenian cavalry roared out as though the ranks of hoplites exhaled them with a single deadly breath. Brasidas, knowing that to advance out into the plain would jeopardize his advantage of terrain, could only stand and watch.

Like the light infantry before them, Rhexenor and his cavalry spread thin across the flat, grassy table of land that stretched inland from the sea. And so like that infantry, doom, swift and deadly, descended upon *them*. Only their horses could save them now. After the initial shock of the assault had been absorbed, both in mind and body, the Thebans withdrew, galloping for the safety of the deep ranks of Brasidas' infantry. The Athenians pursued, but only to maintain their form and add to the humiliation of the encounter. Brasidas stared across the plain; there amongst the fallen lay Rhexenor.

"We advance!"

With his command the pipers commenced, and the men bellowed out the paian as they stepped off. Their formation rolled forward—cohesive, deliberate, and coldly ominous. The invitation had been extended.

But the Athenians declined. They stood in their phalanx, twelve men deep, their lines stretching almost a mile. An order echoed out, causing their extended front to compress and retract as they evolved to close order, shields overlapped, anticipating the assault.

Brasidas, seeing that they shied from combat, barked out the order to halt. The salpinx blared again. His phalanx held to.

Turtle slid his helmet up to clear his face, letting it rest atop his head. "Why stop now? They have no fondness for battle with us. Victory is but a few hundred yards away."

Brasidas too pushed his helmet back. "Look where they are." He pointed with the tip of his spear.

Turtle squinted through the glare of midday. "The walls!"

"Yes, my friend. They hug the walls of the harbor, for the ramparts are full of archers, slingers, and men with rocks and javelins. A hard rain would fall on us if we move further."

"Then what do we do?"

Brasidas smiled tight-lipped while wiping the sweat that had streamed into his eyes with his empty spearhand. "We stand here for a bit looking fierce, then march into Megara."

Turtle's face puckered with incredulity. "But the gates are bolted to us."

"Not for long, and especially after this little show we have put on. The shrewd Megarans sit atop their walls too, watching all of this, watching the tentativeness of the Athenians. They know we will not allow them to move on the city. They know the Athenians dare not move against us."

He gave the signal for them to ground their shields. The files roared with the clang of hollow bronze as each man slid his weighty hoplon from shoulder to the earth, letting it lean comfortably and upright against his knee. For an hour they stared at them, almost defiantly. The Athenians embraced the safety of their walls. By evening Brasidas entered Megara.

* * *

"Now that we are all fast friends," Brasidas said with an air of satisfaction, flanked as he was by two fully armed Lakedaimonian hoplites who stood like a pair of looming scarlet pillars. "I urge you good men of Megara—councilors and magistrates—to gather those fellows that seemed less than enthusiastic about allowing me entry." He spun the end of his cloak about his left arm as he paced the floor of the bouleterion, occasionally looking up at the anxious faces of the attendees, the numbers of which barely filled half the available seats. "Are all your council meetings so poorly attended?"

Most of them just sat. Several whispered in pairs, some in threes, until finally a lone figure sprang up conspicuously from his seat. "We expected allies. This meeting, called by you and by its very nature, can hardly be termed a discussion amongst friends." His courage fleeing quickly, the man slunk back into his seat.

"Ah, you expected allies. And what are we? Remember, it was your messenger who came to *my* camp, panicked and pleading." He strode coolly in silence now, from one end of the floor to the other, wrapping and unwrapping his arm within the cloak, until finally he had made his way back to his starting point between the two unmoving guards. "We marched here without delay, unsettled by your pleas and anxious to assist an ally. And what hospitality was shown to us?" He searched the faces of the assembled. "You barred your gates to us—your allies!"

Now he stepped to a small table, which he made use of as a convenient and appropriately high seat, contemplating the less than forthright gathering. "I will keep my words bold and to the point. I have no inclination to burden your city with us. But I will not leave knowing that the cowards among you—men that dare not even show their faces here—will infest and disable this good city. In one hour I want them here."

"And you will do what with them?" a voice shouted anonymously from the seats.

"I will take them with us. And you will bolt the gates to them, if they ever seek to return. And inevitably when they want in, let them do as the Athenians and fight for the place. It was my men who stood out there, shield and spear in hand, ready to do battle with the enemy. Not one of you dared join us. You have hardly earned it, but you have your city again." He slipped off the table, gesturing to the two hoplites to follow. "Remember. I want them here in one hour."

The interval he spent with his commanders, sampling the fare that the Megarans had presented in hopes of softening his heart with a full stomach. He, on the other hand, found the food too plentiful, much too seasoned for his liking and corrupting, as he put it to Polyakas and Turtle. He declined the relishes and spiced fish in favor of a disc of bread and a bowl of broth.

Brasidas, with the hour passed, departed the company of his officers. Turtle, alone amongst them, bolted up and followed him.

"Why do you even care about the rabble-rousers?" Turtle caught up with him at the gate to the courtyard.

"It is much easier to possess something than to strive to obtain it. We possess Megara. One man, in the dark of night and with the turn of a bolt, can accomplish what even the mightiest army cannot. This I will not allow. I will not fight for the same place twice."

Again hoplites accompanied him, not a pair but an entire platoon officered by Lykophron. They strode into the lamplit hollowness of the council room, his arrival smothering instantly all chatter. A dozen men, makeshift bundles in hand, stood in the center of the room and apart from the others. Brasidas stalked the collection, peering at reluctant, denying faces until he recognized one—the man from the gate tower.

"*You* should have opened the gate."

At these words his platoon surrounded them and ushered the lot out into the cool night air, through the agora and toward the north gate. As he passed a small tile-roofed house near the gate, he heard the muffled sobs of a woman. She said nothing, her eyes following one of the exiles until they had passed through the gate and beyond.

Thessaly
Twenty-Nine
ΘΕΣΣΑΛΩΝ

Brasidas squinted, shading his eyes from the low morning sun that just now shattered the tranquil sky over the forest ridge. Thessaly, even when attended by native escort, always proved a difficult country to traverse, and he and his army had managed to march as far as the River Enipios before being challenged. Only a single bridge spanned it, a narrow and ancient span that stretched out feebly over the snow-fed torrent. His mind, speaking only to him, repeated the words: *No other way.*

"Sir, they dispatch a herald." Lykophron leaned forward, pointing to a single horseman that broke away from the mass of cavalry smothering the far riverbank; their horses pranced anxiously as riders tugged on reins to keep them to station. A few thousand men on each side watched in silence, while the clatter of a single horse's hoofbeats upon the bridge echoed up the valley walls.

"Stay her e." Brasidas then rapped his heels into Allaios, sending them both down the slender track and toward the river. The two approached each other, Brasidas slowing to a trot while seemingly gazing up and down at the high valley walls, the river and the crystal sky; the Thesasalian, on the other hand, never took his eyes off the Spartan, gripping his herald's staff before him as though it were a shield meant to deflect some anticipated blow.

"Beautiful day." The herald, like his comrades across the river, fought to keep his horse still while pondering the comment. "I said it is a beautiful day, is it not?" Brasidas rubbed Alleios' glistening neck while the horse browsed on a bit of mountain clover.

The herald cleared his throat. "I had not noticed." He snapped a glance over his shoulder. "We are here to stop this illegal march."

"Illegal?"

"Spartan, we have neither been asked for or dispensed permission for you to cross our frontier. By all the laws of Hellas, this is an illegal act."

"Fine cavalry," he said, looking across the Enipios to the skittish formation, "but you have no need of them, friend. My war is with Athens, not you, for my journey takes me beyond your frontier to assist friends in Thrake. In the same way if you were to cross into Spartan territory, we would let you pass, for as I have said we have no quarrel with you." Again the herald looked back across the river before speaking. "Tell your commander that if all the Thessalians wish us to depart, then we shall do so, but if you do not speak for all of them, then we shall wait for their answer. We are in no hurry. But let us at least send wagons to the nearest village to purchase food and other necessities to tide us over while we wait." He spun his horse around and galloped back to his officers. The herald, obscured by the dust, sat staring until finally he recrossed the bridge.

"What do they want?" asked Lykophron when he barely came within earshot.

Brasidas said nothing until he brought Allaios up to nudge the other horses of his comrades. "They are showing us that this is their land."

"But we cannot cross the Epinios in the face of that," Polyakas gestured to the Thessalian horse.

"And we will not." Brasidas tugged on the reins. "Come, let us make camp and enjoy the remainder of the day."

"Camp? We broke camp barely two hours ago." Polyakas' voice carried and this disturbed Brasidas, for he knew that the Chalkidians who rode with them heard the comment and the tone of dissent. "If you are impatient, we can fight them right now. But we will still lose the day. Let us lose the day— not our men."

Lykophron, Polyakas, and Turtle rode after him, dismounting as quickly as he, scurrying after their commander like chicks after a hen. He walked up to a clearing that overlooked the river below.

"I want huts built along here. Have the men pile their arms and get to it."

"Here? In the open?" Again Polyakas challenged him.

"You are due no explanation, nevertheless I shall give you one." Now he strode across the open ridge like an actor across the floor of the theatron. "I want the Thessalians to see what I want them to see. They will see disarmed men preparing a substantial camp. They will see hunting parties dispatched, supply trains sent to their villages, and the smoke of a hundred fires. Meanwhile, be prepared to march on short notice."

Lykophron and Turtle departed carrying the orders with them, but Brasidas called to Polyakas before he could follow. "I did not realize that you were so stupid that you needed every command explained to you?"

"Every command, no. But yours—yes!"

"And why mine only?"

"Because they are yours and not Sparta's."

"Why else do I march here but for the sake of our city? Why else do I take us on a campaign that can only end in death far from home?"

"Sparta! If you had no country, you would fashion one as an excuse for your glory hunt."

"Why did you put in for this campaign, if you doubt my intention?"

Polyakas' eyes widened. "I did not! I thought you requested me."

The fire of his gathering anger, dampened momentarily by this revelation, began rising again—a fire he had learned to suppress many years ago, for it is a fire that would consume reason, the one ally he must retain. "You—" he said with an air of discovery. "You speak, but the words belong to someone else. When *you* have something to say, I will listen. Until then follow my command."

Polyakas broke into a march of rage, shoving through the line of officers that had inadvertently blocked his path. Brasidas watched and grinned.

"Master, do you wish to eat?" Hylas, out of sight till now, pointed toward a cloak spread at the base of a pine, a platter, cup, and pitcher precisely arranged along its edge. Beyond it Diokles wrestled the pannier loose from a mule, stumbling away from the beast under the weight of the bundle. The supply train oozed into the clearing. Slowly at first, but growing in volume and frequency, the thwack of axes smothered all other sound. Activity was abundant. Soon the dust of men moving, and the smoke from damp wood fires shrouded the ridge.

"The orders have been passed," announced Lykophron as he strode into view, emerging from the anonymity of the bustling encampment. "And they seem to be enjoying it."

Across the valley on a bald slope of white stone, several mounted Thessalian scouts watched, each with one hand on the reins and the other shading his eyes from the sun. For hours they observed, the intensity and diligence they exhibited amused the Spartans. By late afternoon, when the roof staves had been fashioned and the thatching commenced, the Thessalian scouts departed. Shortly afterward Brasidas summoned Nikonidas, a Thessalian guide sent by the Makedonian king, Perdikkas.

"Do they always travel in such large parties?" Turtle laughed only loud enough for Lykophron and Brasidas to hear, then quickly transformed his smile to a snarl for the arrival of Nikonidas and his entourage.

"Nikonidas, my friend, you of all the men here in my camp should know best what they intend to do. Will your countrymen fight to stop us?"

"Brasidas, honor has compelled them to challenge your crossing of their land. It seems, at least for now, honor has been satisfied."

"Will they let us pass?"

"Most certainly not. But they cannot stop you either."

Turtle slammed his cup upon the table. "You speak like a fucking Athenian. You cannot have two different answers to the same question.

Brasidas tugged on his friend's shoulder. "Of course you can. But only if you ask the question at two different times."

"King Perdikkas has risked much in silver and grain with this Spartan alliance. You must not delay. The Thrakians, allies of Athens, will undoubtedly attack, as will the Athenians once they launch their fleet. By your delay you are gambling with lives of your allies in Makedonia."

"Sir, I never gamble. But if I were to wager on their actions, as of course I would never do," Brasidas said, pausing until the laughter amongst his officers subsided while pointing across the river to the anxious enemy cavalry, "I would bet my horse that by nightfall most of them will be gone to their homes and villages, their leaders seeking consultation and the body as a whole a warm dinner and a comfortable night's sleep. By our very preparations they need not worry about us moving across soon." Now he looked out, across the dark void toward the sound of rushing water. "Understand this; I would show no compunction in marching across that river to do battle with them, for I know my men and their abilities. But, as I said before, I am not a gambler, and will not wager the life of one of my men to fight these Thessalians when the enemy of your benefactor, King Perdikkas, the same enemy of my city, waits beyond. We will cross."

Nikonidas nodded and turned to leave, followed by his sullen-faced retinue, each and every one of them wearing a mask of indignation to please their leader.

"First Polyakas, now him." Turtle slapped Brasidas on the back. "Keep to this and we can look no further than our own camp for enemies."

"Perdikkas is an ally of convenience—nothing more. He moves with the breeze, first this way, then that, hardly reliable. Therefore we must remind our Makedonian friend that for *him* it will be profitable to hate the Athenians more than us. Polyakas, on the other hand, troubles me."

Strophakos, his friend and envoy from the Chalkidike, trotted up the slope, ushered along by Lykophron, moving with speed under a summons of concern. "Something urgent?"

"Your assessment of Nikonidas. Can he be trusted?" Brasidas said, locking eyes with him in search of the truth.

Strophakos grinned. "Why of course not. But neither can you." He laughed. Brasidas too. Lykophron wrinkled his face in puzzlement.

"For today, and I remind you that I mean precisely what I say, he is the agent of Perdikkas. So if he speaks for the king, believe him. Tomorrow," he added, shrugging his shoulders. "—who knows?"

The sun slipped below the westward ring of mountains as both men gazed into the darkening valley and at the victual wagons that Brasidas had dispatched, with the Thessalians' permission, to replenish their stores. They spotted only three mounted guards on the far bank, each bestowing a cursory glance as the column passed, then they quickly resumed their conversation.

Brasidas drew a deep breath of cool evening air, holding it within, savoring it, then exhaled with a nod. "Get them all a hearty meal, a few hour's sleep, then we will be off."

Brasidas and his officers gathered in a large, still-roofless hut, peering at a crude hide map by the flickering glow of a single oil lamp. Darkness brought with it damp and icy air, washing everything in steely blue, only the brassy tongues of flame from the scores of cooking fires marking any contrast. For several hours they continued to huddle around the faintly lit map. The first watch ended, then the second. With the commencement of the third the entire encampment seethed into hushed motion.

Diokles handed the honed short sword to Brasidas, its blade reflecting what scant moonlight shone through the thickening mountain mists. Lykophron pulled up beside him.

"Twenty men with horses will stay behind to tend the fires as ordered. The rest are ready."

"Excellent. And Turtle?"

"Probably across the bridge by now."

They stared off into the blackness and fog toward the sound of the river, knowing that they could not see him, but imagining they could, waiting for the signal.

Below, riding silently between the tall pines, Turtle and his party of picked men approached the bridge. Through the darkness the glow of only two campfires, blurred by the mist, marked the far bank. The twelve Spartan horseman floated across the bridge, suspended, it seemed, by a magical ether, the rushing waters beneath them overwhelming all sound while they closed upon the Thessalian pickets. Like a shadow Turtle slipped from his horse and moved to the first sentry. He loomed over the curled up man, drew his sword slowly, producing only the slightest twang of metal as the point scraped across the scabbard throat. He paused. Over each drowsing Thessalian hovered two or three Spartans, swords in hand awaiting the order. Turtle thrust his sword, then withdrew it quickly, its point driving into his victim's haunches. Startled, the man cried out.

"It's only your arse," said Turtle as he flicked the blanket off the man with the point of his sword. The four other sentries, aroused by the cry, tried to get to their feet, but sharp Spartan iron kept them in place.

Turtle slapped his captive with the flat of the blade. "Get up."

"What will you do with us?" The man rubbed his rear end, hunching with the stiffness of a poor sleep on cold ground.

"Talk a bit." Turtle, sword still drawn, gestured for them all to sit—even his Spartans.

* * *

Above the peaks, the indigo of night became streaked gray, the gaining light giving form to the shapeless shadows, stirring the elements of day; the breeze swept away the mist as the chorus of larks echoed from the tall pines; high over the peaks, a hawk screeched and circled; gnats swirled in the shafts of light that poked into the forest. The four men sat atop their horses, steamy breath rolling from the beasts' mouths as they clustered together on the hill crest, looking back at the bridge and the last of the wagons that had just crossed.

"And your new acquaintances. What did they have to say?" Lykophron asked, breaking the silence and Turtle's mental napping.

"The Thessalian guards? They proved most agreeable fellows. We shared some wine. I suggested that they depart. To find their leaders, of course, and tell them that we were moving north."

"And what did they say to this?" Polyakas pushed the hilt of his sword back to clear his cloak.

"At first they seemed dismayed. But then I explained that we had to move on because of lack of supplies, but would move slowly so they and their cavalry could catch up with us if they did indeed decide not to let us pass.

For at normal marching pace through these mountains it appeared reasonable that we could cover no more than ten miles a day."

"Reasonable," repeated Brasidas, picking out that single word from his friend's response. "Then we must be unreasonable with our pace."

So they raced through the serpentine roads of Thessaly, covering the distance from Melita to Pharsalos on the first day, by midday next Phakion. On the third day, they marched into the shadow of Mount Olympos, arriving at the Makedonian border town of Dion at nightfall. Turtle reminded them all that only one army had covered such a distance at more rapid a pace; the Spartans who, seventy years previous, had sped to aid the Athenians at Marathon; although arriving late to battle, they had covered 140 miles in three days. Brasidas assured them, that unlike their predecessors, glorious battle still awaited *them*.

A pair of Makedonians, each armed with twin javelins and a heavy-tipped kopis sword, rode up to greet Brasidas and his officers as they entered the city. The place, surrounded by a wall four meters high and spiked with towers, seemed more of a trading post than true city; they saw no gymnasion as they entered, and in the market-place could glean no sign of a council hall, place of assembly, or other civic building; even the shrines, statued with crude wooden figures, smacked of the makings of barbarians. Surprisingly, the guards addressed him in comprehendible Greek.

"Spartan Brasidas," announced the older red-beard. His partner held a sputtering torch above them both.

"The king invites you and your officers to dine with him. Follow me," he said hesitating, then added, "if you please."

The Spartans rode the narrow streets, keeping behind their escort and trying to avoid the streams of waste water, piles of swill and comatose drunkards that impeded their way. Deeper into the town, a curtain of quarried stone rose up, gated and bracketed by a pair of square towers. A squad of light infantry milled about the entrance, glanced disinterestedly as they passed, then returned to their ribald talk and gaudy laughter.

"The king waits in the citadel for you." The red-beard did not dismount to guide them further, but merely pointed with his clutch of javelins to a lit and opened doorway. A conglomerate of music, howling, and women's screeches emanated from within. Brasidas slipped from his horse, smacked his cloak several times to beat away the dust, then followed by his three companions strode through the portal and into the glowing, lamplit interior. There he spotted Perdikkas reclined upon a sumptuous divan. The king gripped a substantial horned rhyton cup in one hand and groped wildly at a flute-girl with the other. The attending Makedonian nobles—lords by right of their own districts—emulated their king. Even with the strategically placed pots of incense, the place reeked of stale wine, vomit, and the spoiling scraps of food that littered the blue-tiled floor. Abruptly the hall fell silent.

"Greetings to you, Brasidas, and your fellow Spartans." Perdikkas gestured him forward and to a couch adjacent his, which he had emptied of occupants with a stare and flick of his hand. "Are you in the habit of arriving sooner than expected?"

Brasidas approached. "With friends, sometimes; with enemies, always."

Perdikkas bellowed with laughter, then swung his rhyton up to his mouth, wine running through his beard as he gulped furiously. His chiton glistened wet from his neck to belly. He swiped his mouth with his hand. "Sit. We have fine venison tonight. And the wine is Thasian. Enjoy it while you can, for the Athenians have declared war upon me, and I will not be drinking much of this for awhile."

Brasidas folded his cloak, handing it to a servant as he lowered himself onto the pillowed divan. Immediately the wine steward, attended by a pair of boys, presented him with a rhyton of wine. Others placed several bowls of food on a table beside him. He sipped, perusing the fare: steaming pink slabs of venison caught his eye first; another bowl brimmed with goat cheese; one high-stemmed dish glistened with figs; oddly he found no bread.

"Eat, Spartan, and I will talk," Perdikkas said, propping his head with one hand while the other stretched out, holding his empty cup. A slave rushed forward to fill it. "Tomorrow we march together to Lynkestis. Their king, Arrhabaios, has declared himself my enemy. He shall be the first."

Brasidas smacked his lips, savoring the vintage. "Then Arrhabaios has put in with the Athenians?" He snatched a fig, waiting for an answer.

Perdikkas' smile left him. "Not yet, but as I said he is my enemy, and shall be held to account."

From the adjacent couch Turtle glanced with concern to Brasidas, who returned the look with one of casual dismissal. Lykophron ate wolfishly, saying nothing but nodding on occasion in cursory acknowledgment of the conversation around him. Polyakas, on the other hand, ate little, holding his cup before his lips like some sort of shield, watching and listening.

"Remember this, Brasidas." Perdikkas swung his feet to the floor, sitting erect. "I fund this army of yours. I feed them and pay your mercenaries. I summoned you north." He halted, stopped by the glaring eyes of Brasidas. "I requested you and this army to vanquish our common enemies, Arrhabaios foremost amongst them."

"Friend Perdikkas, have no doubt that we come here with full intent to band together with your forces and confront *our* common enemies. But let us first be certain who these enemies are." Perdikkas snarled at Brasidas, who in turn smiled, sipped some wine, then asked for examples of Makedonian courage, to which his drunken hosts quickly obliged. One boasted, recounting his first kill, emphasizing both his slight age and the superior size of his foe. The next, of course, slew an even older, larger, and stronger adversary, and this before his beard came to show. For an hour or more the drinking and self-praise continued until Brasidas, assured he had endured what manners required, stood. "King Perdikkas, I must ask your leave of us. I am tired, as are my companions, so forgive my ungracious behavior, but excuse us." Perdikkas, now deep into a story of his own youth, nodded then returned to his tale, punctuating each and every sentence with a gulp from his rhyton.

Hardly acknowledged by the Makedonians, Brasidas departed, followed unhesitatingly by Turtle and Lykophron. Polyakas lingered for a moment, then followed too.

"Arrhabaios is no threat to us," whispered Turtle as they passed into the courtyard. "We cannot attack him on the order of that barbarian."

"Of course not." He stopped to face his friends, waiting for Polyakas to catch up. "I promised to march to Lynkestis with him, nothing more."

The Spartans conferred with Strophakos and the other envoys from the Chalkidike, telling them of Perdikkas' designs and soliciting their thoughts. Each one of them held a deep distrust of the Makedonian, but especially Torylaos and Strophakos. They also cautioned Brasidas that it was their cities, all so close to the sea and within easy striking distance of the Athenian fleet, that would suffer an attack and not the inland kingdom of the Makedonian. Brasidas assured them that their march to Lynkestis would be of quick duration, the return even quicker.

At noon the next day the combined forces of Brasidas and Perdikkas paraded out of Dion, led by the king's Companion cavalry, which consisted of his high-born Makedonians, men whose families had controlled the rich pasture-lands and lowland farms for uncountable generations. The Spartan contingent, at the insistence of Brasidas, brought up the rear of the armed troops. Behind them trailed the wagons of camp provisions and the inevitable, mobile brothels.

Three days out and heading deeper into the mountains they neared the limit of Perdikkas' realm. Brasidas summoned Turtle.

"Come walk with me, friend." Brasidas wrapped his arm around Turtle's shoulder, leading him away from the bustle of the encampment. "I need you to take a little trip for me."

"Where to?" Turtle grinned, relishing the surreptitious nature of the discussion and the mission to follow.

"To Lynkestis."

"Perdikkas would not like that," scolded Turtle in jest.

"That, my friend, is why I ask you to go." They stood near a chattering brook, the noise loud enough to mask their conversation from unwelcome ears. He looked around, making certain no one watched. "Last night a messenger arrived from Akanthos."

"The Athenian city."

"Yes. There are many in Akanthos that are ready to come over to us. But they want Spartans there to protect them. We are in the wrong place. We are marching against the wrong foe. You must parley with Arrhabaios. Find out his true intentions. If he joins with us, I will not march against him. And without us, neither will Perdikkas."

"Guides?"

"Strophakos himself will ride with you. I will do my best to delay the advance."

* * *

"They appear more likely to flee than fight."

Brasidas, stretched out on a blanket, wincing as Hylas rubbed the warmed oil across the old wound in his side. "The Makedonians?"

"Why, yes. I do not trust men who ride horses into battle. Too quick in, and most certainly the quickest out."

Hylas reached for the curved bronze stlengis and began to scrape the oil from his master's back. He wiped the dripping blade dry, then commenced another stroke. Brasidas, made drowsy by the warm sun, closed his eyes.

"You are not going to sleep, are you?" Turtle shook his head while standing over Brasidas. "Give me that, boy. I will show you how to keep your master alert." He snatched the stlengis from Hylas.

"No need of that. He is through with it. And I have my morning exercise." Brasidas bounced to his feet.

Turtle roared. "You never moved that quickly in the Agoge."

The two walked off to join the loose gathering of platoons and companies, the men mingling casually before the start of gymnastics. Brasidas and Turtle paired off, ready for a bout of wrestling.

"I think I will seek another partner today." Brasidas straightened from his crouch. "Turtle, I think Lykophron will accommodate you." Now he yelled to Polyakas. The man turned at the calling of his name, then slowly approached. He said nothing.

"We will pair up for the wrestling today."

Polyakas' vacant expression transformed at these words. His eyes gleamed. His muscles visibly tensed as he barked for his servant to fetch some oil. While the servant worked on him he knelt and scooped up some dry earth, a poor substitute for the fine sand of the gymnasion, and ground it relentlessly into his hands. Within moments he entered a crouch, arms extended, ready for the match.

Brasidas stalked closer, undulating his fingers like a lure, keeping his feet to a wide stance. "That is the first order in weeks you have obeyed without question." He raked Polyakas' arm, his fingers sliding free.

"The first sensible order you have issued in weeks." Polyakas dipped his right shoulder, snapping out his hand toward Brasidas' thigh. It grabbed at air.

They circled each other with predator-like intensity, muscles coiled, pulsing and ready to explode. The others around them stopped their bouts, sensing somehow the escalation of this contest; they would watch their commander be tested and revel in it.

He stared into Polyakas' eyes. "What have I done to stir such anger in you?"

Polyakas lunged at him, falling to his knees, and at the same time wrapping both arms around Brasidas' thighs, sending them both into a tumble. Brasidas kicked his legs free, then sprang to his feet, pushing with both hands on Polyakas' back to propel him. With Polyakas, anger replaced reason. He scrambled on all fours, charging like a wounded boar, while churning up the bone-dry earth. Brasidas shuffled easily away.

"This rage rules your mind." As Polyakas lunged again, Brasidas slipped an arm around his neck while driving a knee into his back. Polyakas slammed brow first into the ground. "I have brought you to dust, now answer me." Polyakas convulsed like a netted lion, but finally exhaustion compelled him to rest. Not until he felt every muscle of his adversary surrender did Brasidas release his grip, shoving Polyakas' shoulder to turn his face toward him.

He lay there, chest heaving and lips clamped. The red-clay dust clung to him, tinged here and there with the blood from fresh cuts. His eyes relayed his defiant answer.

Brasidas rose, rubbing the soil from his arms, then called to Lykophron. "*He* will be going home with the next messenger."

Diokles came running, a water flask in hand, pushing through the mob that ringed the impromptu arena. Seeing his master unharmed, he offered up the flask to him. Brasidas snatched it gladly, then emptied it atop his head. From far off he heard the shouts of men, then above the trees where the trail cut across the ridge he spotted the dust of approaching riders. Naked and wet he moved through the crowd toward it, Turtle, Lykophron, and Diokles in tow. Three riders, surrounded by the perimeter sentries, fought to hold their skittish horse to station. The guards turned, pointing to Brasidas while screaming at one of the men on horseback.

"Let them through!" Brasidas waved them forward.

The three reined up, all clad in thick bearskin cloaks. The oldest of them, a man brandishing a magnificently fashioned kopis sword, its horsehead hilt gleaming bright with jewels, spoke first. "We have been sent by King Arrhabaios to meet with the Spartan commander Brasidas."

Brasidas slicked back his glistening wet hair. "You have met him. Now let us talk."

The two Lynkestians dismounted, following Brasidas with some reluctance and only after they were satisfied that their horses had been well tended to. Both men were tall, taller to be sure than Brasidas and the other Spartans, and their skin glowed ruddy, with beards the color of weathered iron. Beneath the canopy, Diokles worked along with several other Helots, hastily arranging tri-legged stools and small tables into a setting for conference.

As they walked, the Lynkestians stared at the Spartan. He turned and grinned saying, "Pardon my appearance, but we were engaged in our morning gymnastics." He waved to Diokles, who scurried off from the canopy, returning promptly with a scarlet chiton in one hand and a pair of krepides war-boots dangling from his other by the untied lacings.

As soon as they ducked under the edge of the canopy, servants moved to fill their cups where they sat. Brasidas tugged his chiton overhead, then sat as Diokles fitted his boots.

The one with the jeweled kopis nodded perfunctorily then spoke. "I see you are getting accustomed to our mountain air."

"I come from a land of mountains too," said Brasidas. Lykophron entered, then Turtle, who shrugged his shoulders as though responding to an unspoken question, upon which Brasidas introduced both to the Lynkestians. They chatted awhile of trivial things—discussing the beauty of the forest and which gods, goddesses, and nymphs resided in these parts—all this verbal prodding shaping the way for the talk of substance. By mid-afternoon laughter spilled out from the conference. The three envoys, escorted to the camp perimeter by Brasidas and his officers, departed much less formally than they had arrived.

"Now I must go and convey the bad news to Perdikkas."

"Bad news?" Turtle's smile transformed quickly to a scowl.

"Yes, for we have ended the quarrel between him and Arrhabaios, only he does not know that yet." He glared at Lykophron. "Find Polyakas. Have him report to me on my return." Then he directed his attention to Turtle. "A quarter hour after I go to Perdikkas, come with the message."

* * *

Perdikkas, surrounded by his nobles, reclined on a splendid couch, and well into his cups, even this early in the day, turned black-browed upon the entrance of the Spartan. With a flick of his chin he gestured for a couch to be emptied, clearly exhibiting his displeasure. "I hear you meet with my enemy?"

"If you speak of the Lynkestians, yes, although they are no longer your enemy."

Perdikkas' ruddy face boiled with blood. "I choose my enemies, not you, Spartan," he snapped back with disgust.

Coolly a servant presented him a full cup, then backed away. Brasidas sipped a bit of wine. "Likewise I choose my enemies—and my allies also. As friends I place the Makedonians above all." He paused, gauging the faces of the Companions; many grinned, some nodded. "But also the Lynkestians came to me, not proposing a separate peace, but to act as an arbitrator."

"And what are their terms? What do they offer me to turn away from their frontier?"

Brasidas, drawing on every shred of rhetorika taught to him by Kleandridas, commenced his bluster. "We spoke at length of King Arrhabaios' intentions, of his desire for peace between these two lands of a common people. He most certainly does not want war with you, King Perdikkas."

"Then will he cede that territory in question?"

Brasidas, embracing his cup with both hands, swirled the wine while staring within it, hoping Dionysos would inspire him. "Again, as I have said, we spoke long about your grievances, and his—"

The tent flap snapped open and in strode Turtle. "Lord Brasidas, a messenger has arrived from Akanthos."

Brasidas nodded, exhaling a sigh which he hoped had gone unnoticed by the Makedonians, but apparently observed by his friend; Turtle grinned. "Tell us all," he said with mock impatience.

"The Akanthians are calling on us to help them. If we march to their aid now, they will break away from the Athenians."

Brasidas stood looking up to the heavens as though the tent had become transparent. "Only the gods could bestow such good fortune on us." He now looked at Perdikkas. "Whether you believe Arrhabaios or not, accept this postponement of battle. Let us march to Akanthos together. Liberate this city, then if the intentions of Arrhabaios prove false, I will gladly resume the campaign against him."

The Companions, as before, appeared to agree with his words. Perdikkas waved Brasidas to approach and extended his hand in a show of friendship, but tugged the Spartan closer and whispered, "I know what you have done here, even if they do not. You can go to Akanthos, but without my men, or my money."

* * *

The Chalkidike stuck out into the sea like the trident of Poseidon; at the base of the northern prong stood the city of Akanthos, tributary to Athens and supplier of timber and silver to this enemy of Sparta. Here Brasidas would begin. Here he would nibble at the giant cake that was the Athenian Empire. Their march, minus the Makedonians, would take the better part of seven days; on the sixth a single rider met them. Brasidas conversed with him briefly and alone. On the departure of the messenger he called an assembly of his officers; all except one attended.

Brasidas summoned the enomotarch of this first platoon. "Find Polyakas!"

The platoon leader marched off and commenced to shout orders after exiting the tent. The officers within maintained quiet conversations, passing the time until their commander would initiate the meeting. From far off they heard the shouts, then the rumble of several men jogging—armed to be sure, for the clang of bronze and iron accompanied the pounding of their feet. Abruptly the ruckus ceased. Polyakas, urged forward by the enomotarch, burst into the tent, chiton disheveled and his face still red with fury.

"Here he is, sir," growled the enomotarch as he backed out.

"Becoming forgetful?"

Polyakas stepped forward, rearranging his garment. "No, sir. I understand this is a council of your officers."

"And you are one."

"No, sir, I am not. By your own order you have discounted me."

"Until you leave for home, you are still an officer and under my command." He moved to within inches of the man. "Do you understand me?"

Polyakas glared back defiantly, saying nothing.

Again Brasidas edged forward, bumping him. "Do you understand me?"

All present seemed to suppress every movement, sound—even breath—awaiting the outcome of the confrontation.

"Yes," replied Polyakas half-heartedly.

Brasidas turned from him, stepping to the center of the gathering. "Good. Now that we are all present, we shall discuss Akanthos."

Lykophron pushed the lamp clear of the hide map that spread upon a table near his commander, revealing their position and the city of Akanthos. Now he looked up at Brasidas.

"As you can see we are but a day's march out. Today I spoke with a messenger from the city. Seems there are many who are ready to come over to us," spoke Brasidas, his eyes never leaving the map.

"But are there enough?" asked Turtle. He too had grown to be wary of the fickleness of these cities and their shifting alliances within.

"Enough I think to gain me entrance," assured Brasidas.

"Sir," began Lykophron, "we all know you to be a formidable fighter, but you must admit that even you would be hard pressed to capture the town single-handedly." His words initiated an outburts of laughs, some more hearty than others; Polyakas merely scowled.

"Some talk, that is all. I expect these Akanthians are reasonable men."

"I see," said Lykophron, coaxed further by the laughter. "You embrace the Athenian fashion of warfare."

"I choose what is successful—and prudent," said Brasidas. "If we can liberate Akanthos without a single death, as we did at Nisaia, we protect our most precious resource—our men."

"I apologize, sir. No Athenian would ever place a man's life above his money."

"Gentlemen, we are here to fashion plans that I hope we will not need to implement." Now hovering over the map, he swept his index finger around the marking for Akanthos. "If I fail in my negotiations, we will burn their farms, orchards, and vineyards. This we will do without delay. Examples must be made."

The officers crowded around the table, watching and listening as each received his orders; at first light they would march; they planned to torch the croplands by midday. As the discussions now dwelt on detail, Brasidas called for the messenger, and only when he entered the tent did Polyakas' stony expression change. With Brasidas' dispatch he would be bound for home. He watched him carefully mark the letters upon the skytale, encoding the message before unraveling it from the stick, then handed it to the messenger, who after acknowledging its receipt, turned to go. Polyakas began to follow.

"You have not been dismissed."

"The messenger leaves. And by your order so must I."

"I have changed my mind. You will remain in command of the third lochus. Now study the map and prepare."

* * *

Hylas rode with him, not as slave, attendant, or armor-bearer, but filling the role as the single guard and chosen companion on the short journey to Akanthos.

Unusually, Brasidas kept to himself, pondering the Akanthians, friends and foes alike within their impregnable walls. His army would find no entrance without invitation. And without invitation he would be compelled to bring the city to its knees—hardly the act of a liberator.

"Commander, why did you not send him home?" Hylas immediately peered down to the road, presenting a most complaisant manner.

"Polyakas?"

"Why, yes, sir."

"Because he wanted to go." Brasidas chuckled.

Hylas looked up. "It must be more than that."

"Yes, I would say so. I wish to know what has set him so against me. We have been companions since the Agoge, comrades in battle and time-tested friends. Someone has turned him from friend to foe. I would know who."

Hylas grinned. "Why, sir, it is you who turned him against you."

"What!" Brasidas reined up on his horse. It pranced nervously, coming to a halt.

"I said you."

"But I love the man as a brother. How could I have caused this rift?"

"Because he loves you, but not as a brother."

"Then he is more dangerous than I had believed. True hatred is spawned in love." His words rushed visions of Temo through his head.

Brasidas kicked his heels hard into the horse, setting off on a gallop toward the looming walls of Akanthos. Men stirred in the pair of towers that flanked the gate, their newly lit torches blurring with movement in the gray of early evening. Even from this distance he heard the grind of the gate bolt as it slid into place then locked. He halted below the tower to the right of the gate.

"Will you allow us entry?" He craned his neck as he called out to the guards above.

"No one may enter." He barked his reply, then ducked back into the black of the tower room.

"Send for one of your council. Tell them Brasidas the Spartan wishes to speak with him. Inside, or out here. Either will do."

The guard stared at him for a moment before ducking back into the tower room again.

"Will they meet with us?" said Hylas, pulling his cloak tightly around him against the chill of the coming night.

"We shall see."

For nearly an hour they sat atop their horses, glancing every so often at the men in the tower, the slightest noise within, they hoped, was a prelude to the gate swinging open.

Finally the unmistakable sound of the iron bolt scraping as it slid free fired them both with anticipation. The gate groaned; it swung open by only one of the two sides, but it did not stop till it slammed hard against the tower wall inside. A man bearing a torch followed by a dozen others stepped into the yawning gateway. "Follow us." The unnamed spokesman said nothing more, but turned and led, bringing them to a small square stone building fronted with several columns. Three steps led up to the open door.

"This must be their bouleterion," whispered Hylas as they dismounted. "Seems you will address their entire council."

Inside, scattered around the stepped seats of the interior sat about one hundred men. Brasidas stepped to the center of the room, still accompanied by the man who had met him at the gate. "Spartan, we would hear what you have to say." Now he left Brasidas' side and took a seat among his fellow councilors. Brasidas freed his cloak with a flip of the clasp then handed it to

Hylas. He took a moment to look at the men who looked at him. "Akanthians, the Spartans have sent me out with an army. This army exists not for conquest, but for liberation. Since the beginning of the war you and your neighbors have called on us to free you from Athens. I apologize for our tardiness, but we tried, at first, to subdue our enemies by challenging them to fair and honest battle. This they refused, so the war has dragged on. But we have never forgotten you, or your plight.

"But strangely I come here and find the gates locked to me. We thought of you as allies, eager to have us, and with this in mind have undertaken a long and risky march through a strange country. This because we thought your zeal equal to ours. I would remind you of similar circumstance at Nisaia. Their inhabitants were unsure of our ability to protect them from a substantial army of Athenians. Our smaller force prevailed, as we shall prevail here.

"As I look up at the faces here in your council chambers, I see doubt. Let me assure you that I am not here to help this party or that, and I do not consider that I should be bringing you freedom in any real sense if I should disregard your constitution, and enslave the many to the few. What sort of liberator would Sparta be if I did this?

"But remember this also. If you fail to see the benefit of these considerations, and through fear remain slaves to Athens, I will compel you to become free, for I cannot allow you to lend aid to an enemy that destroys the liberty of all Hellas. Unlike the Athenians, we Spartans do not aspire to an empire; it is what we are laboring to put down. Endeavor to decide wisely, and strive to begin the work of the liberation of Hellas with us, and gain for yourselves an endless renown."

Finished with his speech, Brasidas exited the silent bouleterion, Hylas with him. A single armed man escorted them both to the very gate that they had entered Akanthos. By this time the army had encamped on the outskirts of the city; their campfires lit a sparkling swath over the low hills, in amongst the ripening vines. As they passed through the gate, men above in the tower pointed out and murmured to each other. The escort stopped just outside the walls, arrested by the sight. "I will bring their word in the morning."

Once comfortably out of earshot of the Akathian guards, Hylas resumed their hours' old conversation. "What will you do with Polyakas now?"

Brasidas did not answer immediately, but kept his horse to a lazy canter while fixing his eyes on the heavens; he rocked and swayed with each step. Still, he looked to the sky.

Athens
Thirty
AΘHNA

The ten generals sat upon their couches in the Strategion, chattering away with the news from the region of Thrake. Kleon pounded his fist and slapped his thigh, wound up in an argument with Hippokrates. Eukles and Thukydides sat silent.

"Demosthenes is ready. The plan is ready." Kleon spun from the couch to his feet. "Fortify Delion and we can control the border. The Thebans can do nothing to stop us."

Thukydides rose from his couch also, still clutching his empty cup as a speaking prop or baton, waving it to call attention. "And what if Demosthenes is delayed? What if any of our agents in our enemies' cities are delayed?"

Kleon faced him. "If this plan succeeds, Thebes will be out of the war."

"The plan, in the best of times, would prove risky. Now with this news of the fall of Akanthos to the Spartans—"

Kleon, as he was wont to do, replaced eloquence with wild gesturing. He pounded his fist upon a table, sending a pitcher and several cups careening across the mosaic-tiled floor. "Without risk we can gain nothing?"

"Whose risk? Certainly not yours. It is Hippokrates here who will carry out this fragile plot. And what about Akanthos? Do you think Brasidas will stop, having gained the allegiance of only one of our tributaries?"

Kleon leaned his spindly frame forward, his face projecting toward Thukydides like the figurehead of a trireme. "Then I suggest you proceed to Thrake and secure it against this Spartan. The rest of us," he said, waving at the other strategoi, "will remain here and attend to the risks that you seem most reluctant to undertake."

Thukydides returned to the embrace of his couch. A scribe toiled over his wax tablet, detailing the orders of the war council. Thukydides, along with Eukles, would sail immediately for the island of Thasos in Thrake. Hippokrates, not Kleon, would lead the invasion of Theban territory, relying

271

on the betrayal of key cities by agents of Kleon and by a diversionary attack by Demosthenes. Only if all these elements fell into place would the march to Thebes succeed. Thukydides and Eukles spoke in private of this plan, their doubts and on what required preparations should take place before their departure. Two days later they looked back at the Piraios as it faded into the pre-dawn mists. Sound replaced sight as the fog swallowed the faint lights and harbor boom, leaving only the rhythm-keeper's flute and the slap of oars to accompany them.

In several days the trireme docked at the harbor on Thasos. Overhead the sky hung heavy and dark, full of winter, and threatening to disgorge itself upon the island. The wind raked in from the north. Thukydides gazed across the leaping waters to Skapte-Hale.

"Do you know I met their commander once. Over there, on the mainland."

Eukles shooed a servant from his path as he bounded down the gangplank and onto the shivering quay. His sea-legs steadied him. "The Spartan Brasidas?"

"Yes, but we were both young men at the time, and our cities at peace." Thukydides stopped mid-stride to direct a disembarking marine to the arsenal; the rest of his squad followed.

"What sort of man was he?" Eukles hurried to keep pace.

"Not what I expected."

They continued on, past the military berths and toward the few merchant ships that had been dispatched to ferry supplies from the mainland. The crews unloaded their cargoes leisurely. Thukydides, impatient at the progress, shouted to the captain of the nearest vessel, a square-bodied, balding man with an untamed beard and a glistening wet leather jerkin. "Have them hurry it up!"

The captain swung on the rigging and leaned out over the dock below. "For what? It be winter and no one is going about."

"I think you should sail across to Akanthos and remind the Spartans that it is winter. They seem to have forgotten." His eyes squeezed to black slits. "Your cargo will be off by dusk."

"Why only Akanthos? I can go up and down the entire peninsula. The cities of Thyssos, Olophyxos, Dion, and Sane—they have all gone over to the Spartans," said Thukydides.

"Sane? Dion too?" Eukles shook his head in disbelief.

Thukydides hurried away, only halting when it became apparent that his friend did not follow but stood fast upon the dock in front of the merchant ship. Above him and still alarmed, the captain chuckled then slunk out of view.

Now the wind picked up, whipping the gray clouds angrily and forcing the two men to lean into it as they pressed on through the waterfront toward the city proper; soon it swept the streets clean of people. As they passed by, shutters slammed. Doors shook in the grip of the surging gale.

"Look!" Eukles stuck his hand out from beneath the cocoon of his snug cloak, spreading his fingers. "Snow!" The flakes clung to him, then dissolved, extinguished by his warm flesh. "I think we have time."

"You think wrongly. He began waving his hand through the descending flakes. "This will not stop him."

They reached the house of the magistrate of Thasos and took up their quarters. Their evening meal, taken with the captains of the triremes and company commanders of hoplites and marines, ostensibly became a meeting of strategy. Most dismissed Thukydides' notion that the Spartans under Brasidas would make any further moves until spring and proper campaign weather. Others, who might not have wholeheartedly agreed with this, hoped that this was the case. None wished to leave the sanctuary of Thasos until the stormy season had passed. This was not the weather for war.

Thukydides called to the servants to suspend the hide map against the wall, covering the mural of Apollo in pursuit of Daphne. "This river—the Strymon—is the only natural barrier left to the Spartans. Because of the defection of the cities on the peninsula they can now march their troops through Hellas unchecked. But at this river they must stop, for we hold Amphipolis and the city guards the crossing."

"Have no fear, General. Their paltry force could never take Amphipolis," assured Lykas, captain of marines.

"The cities that have fallen before—Akanthos, Sane, and the rest; do you know how many men took part in the assaults?"

"No, General."

"I will tell you," he said, glaring at Lykas. "I will tell you all." Now he held a lone finger in the air before the map of Thrake. "A single Spartan, without escort, snatched all these places from us."

Lykas chuckled in disbelief. "Is he a hero or a god?"

"No. He is but a mere Spartan."

"And who is this mere Spartan that wins cities single-handedly?"

"His name is Brasidas." Thukydides left the map and returned to his couch, where he reclined, sipping from his cup, poised to listen.

273

From outside and heard even above the howl of the gale, a pounding followed by the squeal of an opening gate drew their attention. Voices. The door to the andron swung inward admitting a man, his cloak caked in wet snow; he peeled it off as he entered, tossing it to a waiting servant.

"General, I have a message from Athens." He handed the bundled wax tablets to Thukydides, nodded politely then departed. The room, previously humming with several conversations, fell dead silent, all watching as Thukydides peeled away the oil-skin to expose the tablets inside. He read for only a moment before his expression betrayed the message.

"General," Eukles said, being the first to read the dread upon his friend's face, "what is the matter?"

Thukydides tossed the tablets upon the table; they skidded over its polished surface, crashing upon the tiled floor. "We have lost a great battle. Delion has been captured. Worse news—Hippokrates is dead."

Several of them sprang up from their couches. A few stared, bleary-eyed. Thukydides held his head in his hand for a moment then sighed. "Gentlemen, be prepared to launch by week's end." He pulled Eukles aside. "You, my friend, will sail for Amphipolis with the tide."

* * *

"Doesn't this concern you?" Lykophron craned his neck, looking up into the swirling flakes.

"The snow? Not at all. They will march all the quicker." Brasidas stood motionless upon the hillock, mocking the cold while surveying the column as it passed beneath him. Lykophron uncharacteristically shivered. Beyond the distant hills, the lights of Amphipolis shimmered, marking warmth, shelter, food, and their prize. Now in gusts, the wind raked across the hill, buffeting them on the exposed crest, snapping the loose ends of their cloaks like pennants.

Lykophron stamped his feet to chase away the cold. The others hunkered in the protection of the slope. "What about the Athenian garrison?

Still staring out across the plain, Brasidas answered, "I will allow them to leave. Any one of them may depart. I only want the town."

"What about the fort at Eion. Without it we have no access to the sea."

"First things first. Amphipolis is the key." Brasidas scrambled off the crest, passing his officers who, gathered in conversation, leaned into the wind as they would lean into an enemy in battle. He vaulted upon his horse and galloped alongside the columns of slogging infantry, urging the men on, encouraging some by name, but reminding them all they had been through much worse. He knew that talk from without would reinforce, while talk from within, the conversation all men have with themselves when discouraged, would weaken resolve. This private conversation isolated men from each other and from courage. He must emphasize that they are not alone, but part of something greater. Tirelessly he kept to it as the column passed. From the stream of marchers a face turned up, eyes locking with his. Brasidas went silent. The infantryman, squinting against the wind-whipped snow, gazed back unblinking.

"Step out." Brasidas reined up, back-peddling his horse away from the road. The soldier slipped from the column.

"You are Xenias?"

He nodded in reply.

"Husband to Temo?"

Again he nodded. "But how do you know this?"

Brasidas did not answer, but slid from his horse to stand face to face with Xenias. So unlike a Helot, the man returned the glance, unflinchingly. He pulled tight on the cords that held his dog-skin cap, the sign of a slave, to his head.

"Throw that away," commanded Brasidas, as he pulled his own pilos cap from his head.

"But, sir, that is the cap of a free man."

"And by rights so shall you be. Take the cap and hurry back to your platoon."

He snatched the hat without further question, working it tight to his head with a free hand as he trotted off to his place in the column. Brasidas watched, his long hair swirling like the snake-locks of Medusa in the blustery wind.

"Who was that?" Lykophron tugged hard on the reins to keep his horse still.

"A warrior."

"What! A spear and shield alone do not make a warrior."

"In time he will prove himself."

"And how do you know this? Have you been speaking with the gods again?"

Brasidas vaulted upon the horse. "Assign a junior officer to him. He is to be instructed."

"Instructed?"

"In the technique of command."

"You cannot make a Helot into a commander. I doubt if you can even get him to fight, once the time comes."

"He will be instructed." Not waiting for confirmation, he smacked his horse into a gallop; Lykophron sat atop his, shaking his head.

Their column slithered past Lake Bolbe and by dusk had halted outside the town of Argilos, where a troop of horsemen rendezvoused with them— men who had just been to Amphipolis. Men who despised Athens. Brasidas dined with them alone. He quizzed them on the number of Athenian colonists, the size of the garrison, and the total of non-Athenians within the city. At commencement of the first watch he departed, geared in the accouterments of battle and making for the bridge over the Strymon that led to Amphipolis.

"See," said one of his guides. "The guards are not at station. Some huddle around fires while others are inside sleeping." He marked out several houses with the rusty tip of his sword.

Brasidas studied the bridge and the few houses that lined the road on the far side of it. Beyond lay Amphipolis, a city partitioned in two by a high stone-and-brick wall. Immediately he knew he could take the portion of the city outside the walls, but if they roused quickly and locked the gates to him, the center of the town would be denied to him.

"Form the company by enomotai—four columns."

Silent as death they streamed down from the heights, the first two platoons racing across the bridge, ignoring the defenders as they pushed through. The trailing enomotai swarmed over the bypassed defenders, slaying them as they tried to form a pitiful line. Screams echoed from the houses. Suddenly a door swung open; out crawled two guards chased by a single Spartan, both disarmed and pleading for their lives.

"By the Holy Twins!" Brasidas slammed the butt-spike of his spear into the ground.

"What is it?" Turtle slid his helmet free of his face.

"If I had brought the entire army with us, we could take the city now."

"How could you know this fight would be so easy."

"We could have had it, and cheaply. The cost rises with each passing moment." Now he plucked the spear free of the icy turf. "Send a messenger to Lykophron. Have him march here at once."

"And what do we do in the meantime? Prepare to attack them when the rest of the army arrives?"

"Certainly not," he answered, grinning. "I think I shall ride to the city and talk with them. Let me see how well I can bargain to keep the price of Amphipolis low."

* * *

"There is little to pack, so let's be quick about it." Eukles barked at his officers, who all stood numbed by the cold and the sudden order to depart the town. They shuffled off, all except the marine captain, Lykas.

"I warned you and General Thukydides. Now Amphipolis is lost."

Eukles cleared the phlegm from his throat. He spit. "And what warning was this? You are like the cock who crows at noon, announcing the obvious."

"Do you trust him? Why does he allow us, his enemies, to depart?"

"Lykas, do you not see that is the ingenuity of his plan. He offers any and all who wish to leave Amphipolis five days to do so, with any property they can carry, along with his personal guarantee of safety. Friend and foe alike praise him for his generosity; by comparison we Athenians appear as brutes and bullies."

Eukles rolled a hide map, slid it into a wooden tube, capped it, then slung its cord over his shoulder. A servant hastily tossed the remaining items from the table—several styli, four wax tablets, and a smoldering oil lamp—into a satchel at his feet. Cowered by its weight, he waddled out of the room to the courtyard, sweeping the floor with the bag like a broom as he went. Eukles shook his head.

"At least he had the decency to chase us out before we were fully unpacked." His words echoed off the stripped walls. He scanned the empty room before exiting. Another servant, holding a palm-sized lamp and the last to leave, never looked back as he and the light slipped out.

The Athenians, easily the minority in the city, gathered in the agora; less than a hundred civilians herded together, some pulling laden carts, while others hunched under the weight of overstuffed bundles slung over their shoulders. The few soldiers of the Athenian garrison meandered into the marketplace, drawn to the pile of arms near the steps of the bouleterion; here woefully, each tossed down his spear, sword, and shield.

Eukles, exhibiting hardly the demeanor of a defeated man, bounded up the stairs, his cloak flowing behind him, slowing only when he had made the doors at the top. He pushed one open and entered. Three men stood in the center of the meeting hall. Several lamps sputtered, painting the cavernous room in pale orange. To him it felt colder inside. As the door swung shut behind him, the tallest of the trio turned to him, flipping back his scarlet cloak to reveal an open hand; still in the shadow of the cloak, he caught the glint of a polished Spartan short-sword.

"You must be the Athenian commander?"

Eukles nodded as he approached. "Am I addressing Brasidas the Spartan?"

He clasped Eukles' hand as he would in greeting a long-absent friend. "Commander Eukles." The faint pleasantness that had appeared on his face quickly faded. "Are your people prepared to depart?"

Again he nodded. "You will not keep this place," he said defiantly. "Our fleet—"

"Your fleet! You speak of the ships that have landed down river at Eion; I know of them. I saw them from hill just south of the town. I also know you do not have the men needed to recapture this place."

A deep breath summoned composure. "Why so generous in your terms?"

"Because your demos—your people—will do for me at no cost what my army would pay dearly for."

"And what is that?" Eukles said, scowling.

"Eliminate you. Your democracy is a hungry beast that must be fed. Fiery talk will be the appetizer. Then they will devour you. It is because you Athenians admire men of rhetorika, those who speak of patriotism but ostracize the men, who by their very actions, exhibit it. Look no further than the life of Themistokles. He delivered Athens from the barbarians. Before him Aristides. These men were patriots, and your democracy—your mob— rewarded them with exile."

From behind Brasidas, two men stared grimly at him. Eukles saw no point on speaking further, so he turned to leave.

"Pass my greeting along to General Thukydides."

Eukles did not turn to acknowledge those last words but instead flung open the twin doors and flew down the stairs to his waiting officers. They all took to their horses and began the gloomy procession through the agora toward the Argilian Gate. The Amphipolitans that stood along their route stared at them, smiling. A few taunted the garrison troopers as they passed. A lone woman, nearly full-term, huddled in a doorway sobbing. Near the gate a pack of boys swirled about, imitating the march of soldiers, pointing and laughing as the once proud Athenians trickled out of the city.

Eukles, struggling to keep his eyes ahead and his head up, looked out to the plain in amazement: hundreds of campfires smoldered, burned out after their usefulness for the morning's meal hand been expended; four squadrons of cavalry, assembled smartly, polished helmets glinting golden with sunlight, snapped to attention as the Athenian approached; the infantry, company upon company formed in scarlet and bronze blocks, bracketed the road to the bridge, no aspect of humanity apparent through the full-visored helmets that hid their faces in shadow. Not a single word, no, not even a breath, interrupted the silence of the procession. A defeat without death, trophies, or the entreaties of heralds. A battle decided without struggle. No glory, courage, or cowardice defined the outcome. Eukles thought deeply on Brasidas' words. Indeed would their own assembly prove more lethal than any Spartan spear.

Not until he had passed over the Strymon and turned south to follow it to Eion did he look back; on the nearest ridge, the Spartan cavalry loomed, monitoring their retreat. He could barely make out the infantry columns that slithered through the city's gates. The frozen blue above, void of any clouds, disarmed his thoughts. He gazed up, forgetting the gnawing cold, lulled by hoofbeats and creaking wheels. An hour passed. With the coming of afternoon, the rock-hard mud that had paved the road turned soupy; snow melted into glistening puddles. Along with the mesmerizing warmth of the sun, it all worked to slow them. Hills occasionally altered the pace of their column, rushing them downward, then compressing them on the ascent, until a failed cart wheel or wagon axle compelled them to halt. Soon he spotted the walls of Eion that stood like dark shadows against the glimmering swells of the sea beyond; they rode into the naked winter fields that checkered the plain. Summoned by the sight of the fort, the cavalry galloped off, while the foot-soldiers continued on with their tedious pace. Another wagon slipped a wheel, but no one stopped to repair it; they trudged by, barely acknowledging its presence as it foundered in the roadway.

Eukles, his spirits hardly elevated by the sight of his destination, kept the horse to a slow canter and rode amongst the straggling infantry. The troopers on the walls stared down at them in silence as though they watched not an army but a funeral procession pass beneath them. Finally one leaned out and shouted, "What of Amphipolis?" Blank faces stared back at him.

As they entered the fort, others mingled with them, assaulting each with questions, setting the main square humming with a hundred frantic conversations. Eukles rode through it all, halting only when he had come to the guarded doors of the citadel. A servant snatched the reins from him, leading his horse from the doorway while he worked to clear his thoughts as he attacked each step. A figure moved across his path in the brightly lit entranceway.

"Hurry in, my friend. We must talk." Thukydides tugged on his comrade's shoulder, leading him into the hall filled with officers of the Athenian fleet. They read the look on Eukles and it set them all chattering.

"How many Spartans?" quizzed a trirarch, captain of the Eleusinia.

Eukles collapsed into a divan. A servant rushed to present a kylix of wine, which he quaffed empty before answering. "One!"

Now the hall rumbled. Loud voices, carrying indiscernible words, swirled ubiquitously. One pierced the banter with its clarity. "Silence!" Thukydides waved his hands angrily. "Let him speak."

"Only one Spartan entered Amphipolis. He met with their council for but a short time. They handed the city over to him."

"What of the garrison?" barked out the trirarch. The question echoed over and over by a dozen others. "What of the battle?"

"The garrison has returned here safe and intact. All Athenian citizens also have retired. He wanted nothing but the town."

"Who is this Spartan that beguiles our allies? Is it Brasidas whom you spoke of before?" The trirach hounded him.

"It is. And I am sure you will meet him yourself very soon."

Again the room erupted in chatter. Eukles fell back into the cushions and swung his arm over his eyes as a shield. The empty kylix clattered upon the floor, loosed by fatigue from his grip.

Thukydides approached his friend. "How large is his army?" he whispered as he sat down on the edge of the couch.

Eukles slipped his arm free of his eyes. "About a thousand with lambdas on their shields. Several thousand more without, and a good number of cavalry."

"What did the Spartan say to you?"

"He knows our people very well, my friend. He counts on them to act as Athenians. He knows what will happen to both you and me, and he thanked them for it."

Thukydides paused for a moment as he gazed into Eukles' sorrowful eyes. "Is that all?"

"He sends his greetings to you with respect."

* * *

For several weeks Thukydides put the men to work; soldiers and townsfolk labored on, repairing the walls; scribes and clerks scurried about inventorying foodstuffs; armor-bearers and smiths toiled over weapons and shields; ship crews dragged their triremes up onto the stony beaches and re-caulked the hulls. All this in anticipation of an assault. Four weeks after the fall of Amphipolis, the state trireme, Saliminia, put ashore at Eion. A single messenger called on Thukydides.

Eukles, his mind occupied with the duties of preparing the fort for battle, dwelled little on Amphipolis. Outwardly he regained his good humor, exhibiting the most encouragement of all the officers in his day-to-day dealings with the men until the messenger arrived. As was his routine, he called on Thukydides early, expecting to take their meal together while consulting on progress. He passed by the single guard at the citadel's entrance, and hurried along through its columned yard until he came to the hall. Finding it unexpectedly vacant, he passed through it and on to Thucycides' quarters, where he rapped on the partially open door.

"No morning meal?" He asked the question before digesting the scene inside. Two servants scurried about, one emptying the shelves of folded garments while another wrapped fleece around a banded pair of greaves. Thukydides looked up. He shook his head.

Eukles stepped deeper into the room. "What is going on?"

This time Thukydides did not look up. "I have been recalled."

"For what?"

"For Amphipolis." Thukydides slipped a bound scroll into its leather case.

"This smacks of Kleon!"

Now he glanced at his friend. "Kleon, yes. But if not him, someone else would be crying for my head. Remember, my dear Eukles, that victory is a feast that feeds many; defeat provides but a solitary meal, a meal that I am forced to partake."

"I lost Amphipolis, not you. Why have I not been recalled?"

"I am in command, therefore I am at fault. It is proper." He continued sorting out his belongings, at the same time directing the two slaves in the packing.

"Proper!" Eukles grabbed him by the shoulders, glaring at his empty eyes. "They will execute you."

Thukydides said nothing. His eyes fell back to the items that littered the table before him. He picked up a silver stylus, the one his father had given him on the day of his appointment, twirling it slowly between his thumb and forefinger before presenting it to Eukles. "You may have more use for this than me."

Unconsciously he took the gift. "That Spartan was right. We are our own enemy."

Amphipolis
Thirty-One
ΑΜΘΙΠΟΛΙΣ

The men did not appreciate the exercises, especially during the squalls that swept in from the northern Aegean. Gales interlaced with wet snow struck with regularity through the winter, but every day he stood outside the walls of Amphipolis, his small army with him, drilling incessantly. Brasidas strode before the assembled ranks and files of the phalanx, shouting encouragement to them. As he passed, men who had otherwise been downcast and shivering straightened up while some shouted out his name with affection. No one dared disappoint.

"Ground shields. Breastplates off."

The plain reverberated with the clatter of armor being removed. Spears, now spiked into the partially frozen earth, formed a leafless forest. He waited until every man had his shield leaning against a knee and his armor spread upon the ground before him. At first glance it seemed a random placement, casual and without plan, but when he shouted the next command, its intention became clear.

"Gear up!"

In contrast to the deliberate removal of their kit, the men of the phalanx plucked up their breastplates and thorax armor and slipped them overhead and into place, while armor-bearers scrambled about, fastening them tightly. They heaved their shields off the earth, and plucked free their spears. Not a head wavered in indecision. All the while Brasidas' lips moved in silent countings. "Two hundred," he whispered to Lykophron. "We must get to one hundred."

Not until lengthening shadows of dusk had enveloped them did he dismiss the men. Tomorrow would again bring more drilling.

"Excellent work." He smacked a hoplite on the back as he passed by. The man returned a grin.

"I thought I saw you napping out there," he yelled to another.

"Just concentrating, General," the man yelled back. Energized by the brief exchange, he broke into a jog.

Turtle caught up to him as he continued to speak with each nearby man. "Look!" He pointed to the Thrakian Road. "Your dear friend Perdikkas has come for a visit."

He stared out, but only for a moment. "We must prepare for him." He slung his hoplon upon his back then broke into a trot. Turtle and Lykophron, reminiscent of past Agoge races, trailed after him.

"What does he want?" Turtle said, coming shoulder to shoulder with Brasidas.

"He is here because we have Amphipolis. He wishes to celebrate our good fortune."

Turtle laughed. "That Makedonian wolf wants to nibble on the carcass of Athens."

"Carcass! We have only the tail. We must be certain to not loose our grip."

Once inside the walls, they surrendered their armor to servants before enjoying a pre-dinner bath. The three men lay together on benches in the gymnasion, while servants kneaded warm oil into sore backs.

Brasidas turned to face Lykophron, who drifted toward a nap. "How is Xenias faring?"

"Why such an interest in a Helot?" interjected Turtle. He groaned under the weight of the slave's massage.

"Shows promise," answered Lykophron. "And by Kastor and Polydeukes, you know we need officers."

"Now that you say this," said Turtle, "I have noticed that he has lost his submissiveness a bit too easily. If we were at home, he would be fodder for the Krypteia."

Brasidas pushed his servant aside and rose up onto an elbow. "Thank the gods we are not in Sparta. Fearful men like Kratesikles would kill all of them. These men are patriots like us. More so I would think, for they have none of our privilege but would still fight for Sparta."

"Is it Sparta they fight for or their own gain?" Turtle buried his face into a wad of linen.

"Matters not," said Lykophron. "They are our men now. Treat them that way."

A courier entered. "Commander Brasidas, I have a message for you from King Perdikkas." He flicked an abbreviated salute with his fist. "The king invites you to dine with him tonight in his encampment. He extends this invitation to all your officers." The man stood frozen, poised to accept the response.

"Thank the king for his hospitality, but instead ask him if he would join us here at a dinner in his honor."

The servant's face puckered in confusion until acknowledgment finally transformed his complexion. He nodded, then spun around to depart.

"Why invite him here?" Turtle asked, shaking his head. "As guest of honor? He abandoned us."

"If he dines here, we ration the wine. That alone will be punishment enough for him." Brasidas sat up. "We may need this Makedonian. Our funds run low. We require his silver to pay mercenaries and armorers and purchase victuals for our men. Come, gentlemen, we have guests to prepare for."

* * *

"Spartan, you have done remarkably well." Perdikkas drained his cup quickly. Now he waved it, summoning the wine-servant. "Hardly a man lost and you have taken the whole peninsula from Athens. I hear you have agitated more than a few in that glorious city." He grinned.

"I would not know about that. I am here to liberate Hellenes and persuade as many as I can to join our cause."

"The Athenians are in a panic about you. Much as Sparta was when Sphakteria fell." The servant filled his cup. All but his eyes hid behind it as he sipped. "Why some have even proposed peace with you."

Brasidas shrugged his shoulders. "I leave that up to statesmen and diplomats. I am a soldier. Peace comes to me only in victory—or death."

"Brasidas, I think peace will kill you. But peace is unavoidable, at least between Sparta and Athens. And if this peace comes to fruition, I propose a separate campaign for you, Spartan—and a lucrative one at that."

"Arrhabaios again?"

"This Lynkestian has broken the treaty—your treaty—and attacked Makedonian towns." Perdikkas' eyes gleamed, not with anger but delight. Now his face turned stony. "Spartan, I know your predicament. Sparta has sent you neither men nor money. The men, I think for the time being you can do without, but the money? That is a different question. You need food and you have many mercenaries whose allotments are due."

"So, King Perdikkas, what is your proposal?"

Again his eyes gleamed. "March with me and I will pay your men. It will be a short campaign and we both will be the richer for it."

The king, supported by his nobles, detailed the incursions perpetrated by the Lynkestians into Makedonian territory. Perdikkas was sure to emphasize it was Brasidas' treaty that had been violated, that the Spartan had trusted a conniving barbarian and had he listened to him at the outset his villages would not now be in cinders. Brasidas, for all the talk and the head bobbing of the Makedonian lords, listened but said little. Well into the third watch, a time by which the Makedonians had usually succumbed to hours of wine, the still-sober Spartans concluded the symposion.

"King Perdikkas, you present a tempting offer, one I would be hard pressed to decline. But my officers and I must talk on this. By midday you will have my reply."

The Makedonians, bloated on tankards of thinned wine and remaining uncommonly lucid, reluctantly departed. The Spartans too left the andron in the citadel of Amphipolis, anxious for sleep; they would be rising soon for their morning gymnastics.

Just before dawn the gallop of a single horse tore through the silence of the sleeping city. Diokles tugged on his shoulder to wake him; Brasidas released his grip when the sharpened xiphidion poked into the flesh between his ribs.

"Master, a courier has arrived from Sparta." He backed away, rubbing the hole in his chiton.

Brasidas bounced to his feet. "Bring him here." He hastily wrapped his cloak around him, discarding any semblance of fashion as he pulled it tightly around him. The man entered the dark room, escorted by Diokles and a single tongue of flame from a small lamp. With a curt nod he handed the skytale to Brasidas.

Diokles moved beside his master, trying his best to keep his shaking hand steady as he illuminated the message; the smoke from the lamp stung his eyes. Brasidas read, dropped the inked leather to a table, stared a bit then picked it up and read again, this time muttering the message aloud. "As of the twelfth day of Kerastias, all hostilities between the Spartans and Athenians have ceased. This decree to be upheld and enforced for one year."

He tossed the message upon the table. "Diokles, assemble my staff."

285

Athens
Thirty-Two
AΘHNA

Eukles stood before the Assembly now, his throat incapable of swallowing the last trace of spit that lingered; it felt as though he were at the palaestra, his neck squeezed tightly by some giant opponent. He sucked nervous and shallow breaths now. His friend Thukydides' sentence for incompetence had just been handed down—twenty years exile; he now awaited his. Kleon strode the bema and gestured for silence.

"Citizens of Athens, your punishment is both swift and just. General Thukydides, as commander in Thrake, must pay the price." He waved his hand as though he were casting away an olive pit. "But I would request leniency for Eukles and the others."

Eukles expelled a breath that startled the few around him. He felt a temporary respite, like an animal at the slaughterhouse who watches the butcher secure his knife, only moments later to see him return with a heavy-bladed ax. He winced now, awaiting his ax. None came. Kleon ended his harangue. The Assembly, at his suggestion, attenuated all punishments for the Amphipolis debacle with Thukydides.

"Where will you go?" Eukles said to his friend who stood flanked by two fully armed hoplites.

"To my land in Thrake. Who knows? A year's peace between Athens and Sparta may afford me some travel." With a shove the two guards moved him off, cutting through the swirling disinterested crowd quickly.

Eukles watched as the Assembly began to disperse, first acquaintances and accomplices melded together, forming distinct clusters, all chattering away. Kleon, surrounded by his entourage, finally departed. Near the edge of the road leading to the Areoupagos, a foreigner, Makedonian no doubt by the cut of his clothes and the gaudiness of his gold-embroidered cloak, passed a few words to Kleon, who in turn passed along a small leather pouch. They separated quickly, walking in opposite directions.

* * *

"The gods must be with us," announced Lykophron. "The war with Athens ends and we have another one waiting for us."

"The war is not over. We have stung them, but they are hardly injured." Brasidas turned to look at Turtle. "You have said nothing since we left."

"I know we need his silver," Turtle said, pointing ahead to the boisterous cloud of Makedonian cavalry that led the column, "but I do not trust him." They rode on a bit before he spoke again.

"For now I think we can read his intentions. Arrhabaios has been a boil on his ass for years. He wants us to lance it for him. So long as his ass aches, he needs us." Lykophron lifted his pilos cap from his head and swiped the sweat from his brow with the back of his hand. "And his money keeps our mercenaries content."

It reminded them of Skotitas, but a distilled essence of the place, darkened by the illimitable stands of pine and blackened further by looming peaks. By mid-afternoon they came to the only blemish in the landscape—the string of lakes and ponds that marked off the frontier. Beyond lay Lynkestis and battle. Here the army slowed, enticed by the prospect of refreshment at the lakes. Here too Brasidas launched his scouts.

He allowed the men to drink their fill, but urged them to march on; a chain of lakes at his back and sky-grasping slopes on either side kept him beyond alert. If he perceived this, so did Arrhabaios. Hours later he marked out the encampment with the aid of torchbearers. About this time the scouts returned.

"We counted into the thousands, and that, sir, is what we *could* see. The forest hid the rest." The cavalry scout rubbed his hands down his chiton, scraping away the mud that had dried upon his chest. "We hid at the edge of a swamp. Saw them clear enough." Now he scratched his left arm, back and forth, maintaining a subtle rhythm. Welts rose into sight as the dirt fell off him, exposing the flesh that the mosquitoes and gnats had dined upon.

"How much infantry?" Brasidas asked.

"Hard to say, sir. Many with spears, but hardly any with armor. Considerable cavalry though."

"Your estimate?"

"Double what we have, sir. At least." The scout shook his head. "At least," he repeated under his breath.

Perdikkas questioned him now, asking much the same, hoping for contradiction. The answers did not change. The king huddled with his entourage of Companions while Brasidas recommenced his interrogation.

"Spartan, we are returning to our camp. Battle seems as sure as the next day. We must prepare." Perdikkas and his nobles departed, declining an invitation to sup and converse. "We will be ready," he assured as he whirled his cloak over his right shoulder, not looking back to confirm receipt of the words.

"Not like a Makedonian to refuse a drink." Turtle twirled the hair of his beard.

"Sight of the Lynkestian army seems to have sobered him. I hope he keeps his men out of their cups too." With a nod he dismissed the scout. His officers contracted around him. "Two things tonight, and two things only—eat and rest."

Immediately the Spartan officers dispersed, but the commanders of the allied contingents lingered, unsettled by the scarcity of orders on the eve of battle. Brasidas paced before the fire ignoring them, until the Amphipolitan general spoke up.

"Orders?"

Brasidas took four more steps then halted. "I issued them."

"For the battle, sir. For tomorrow."

"Eat and rest. Nothing more."

Instead of resuming his circling of the fire, he walked straight off, discarding the Amphipolitan to follow some unnoted path that led him toward the muffled roar of a stream. Above light flashed. The sky rumbled. "Zeus," he whispered, looking up.

"Men!" A disappointed voice announced. "Your first thoughts are with him."

Brasidas snapped his head from side to side. The voice emanated from all around, like a cascade of echoes in a cave.

"My dear, let your eyes see."

On the far side of the stream what at first appeared to be a shadow slipped between the trees, moving closer. He attacked the darkness with his sight, fighting for clarity. A hand lighted upon his shoulder. He turned. There a woman, taller than he and clad in chalk-white garments smiled at him. Her hair floating in an unfelt breeze, lit by an unseen moon.

"Why do men always call on my father first? He hardly takes notice of you mortals at all. That is unless it is a beautiful woman." Her look of disappointment faded. "It has been many years since you have called on me."

He stared at the goddess, but for only a moment. "Artemis, I am grateful to see you again, but I did not call on you."

He had never been this close to her. He studied her, not as a traveler would gaze upon a strange landmark or novel animal, but with his heart, like a sculptor admiring a work of great beauty. He saw what he wished and discarded the rest.

"Oh, but you did. You prayed as you walked rings around your campfire. You prayed—not for you, but for your men."

His eyes widened in agreement. He said nothing.

"There are wolves and there are lions. Wolves, although small in size, fight together to bring down much larger adversaries. The lion, on the other hand, hunts alone. Tomorrow you must be a lion."

Again his eyes widened. She nodded, confirming his understanding. Above, the tree tops swayed, chattering in conversation with a rushing wind. The sky flashed. Thunder crackled.

"He is calling," she said, looking up.

He too gazed up at the bursts of light that in brief moments bombarded him with the overwhelming detail of complexities of branches, swirling leaves, and precarious shadows. In that instant she was gone.

The rain lashed them all night, unsettling the horses and inflicting its usual misery on the sentries. Brasidas sat before his fire, cloak pulled overhead, contemplating the flames until the servant tending it finally conceded, after an hour-long struggle, to the wind and rain. With the flames at last extinguished, Brasidas retired.

Just before first light the rain had withered to a mist. The wet remained but the sentries could hear again. Paths now became streams, streams torrents and every depression, large and small, a reservoir. He tossed aside his cloak as he rose and stepped out of his tent to measure the new day. The ground beneath him bubbled, water oozing up with each step, sucking at his boots. Outside Diokles hovered over the fire, dunking Brasidas' helmet in its flames, then drizzling it with a bit of oil. He rubbed till he could see his face mirrored on it. Men moved, but slowly. Most clung in small bands around their fires, the infrequent clang of armor the only sound. Across the soaked earth echoed footsteps.

"Brasidas!" Lykophron shouted as he ran. "The Makedonians." He bent over, fighting for breath. "They are gone. Deserted us in the night."

"Is that all?" He accepted the wine cup from Diolkes. "It is time for the sacrifice."

"Did you not hear me? Perdikkas has fled."

Brasidas walked off with his sword and cup, out to the field where the other officers awaited. He heard the bleat of several goats. Lykophron tromped behind him; he tugged on Brasidas' shoulder. "We are outnumbered six to one. And with our backs to the lakes." He raged against the unconcern of his commander.

"Our men remain, do they not? They should be your concern, not the Makedonians." Losing the mask of commander, he smiled at his friend. "Attend the sacrifice, then we prepare."

A garlanded boy led the goat to him, while another took his cup. The Spartan officers stood to one side, the allied generals opposite, all tight-lipped and unknowingly leaning toward Brasidas in anticipation. Every morning he sacrificed before dawn, but today a special solemnity permeated the service; today there would be battle and their very lives would depend on it. Brasidas, on the other hand, treated it as any other day; he strode up to snatch the goat, holding it while the mantis sprinkled water atop its head; the beast shook in approval. Brasidas quickly pinned its hind legs with a knee while drawing the blade deeply across its neck. The goat kicked, wriggled, then rolled from his grip, its last breath of life escaping as a gurgle through the wound in its neck. He left it now for the mantis, not lingering for the reading of the signs. Turtle lumbered after him.

"They are worried."

"Good, it will put an edge to them. They will need to be sharp today." He hurried along, sloshing through the wet grass with Turtle jogging to keep pace. "Assemble the army."

Turtle ceased the pursuit of his commander and friend, hurrying back to the clearing and the assemblage of officers. Word passed. Eat and arm. Within an hour the army, men clinging together by unit, crowded into the field. Brasidas in the bed of an open wagon, cradling his helmet, watched the men squeeze around him. Some of the younger ones climbed into trees, perching close to hear. At the edges of the field men jostled forward, eyes wide open, mouths clenched shut. The morning's hush magnified his thoughts. He scanned the faces of the nearer ones, hoping to find the usual calm that these veterans unknowingly exhibited. In the past this set him at ease. Today he gazed at unfamiliar faces. Fear had seeped in with the damp fog, for they looked to him not as men, but children pleading to be delivered. They knew everything combined against them; he knew it too. Chilled by it, he stared at the sopping crest on his helmet; a drop of rain slipped over the braids of horse-hair, expanding as it swallowed up smaller drops until, under its magnified weight, it plummeted free, exploding upon his helmet, swelling the rivulets of water that laced the bronze. He swiped it dry.

"Comrades!"

Now it seemed that every man swayed forward a bit.

"If I did not suspect you of being dismayed by the flight of our trusted allies the Makedonians—" He paused, letting the scant laughter peter out. "I would have kept to my usual Spartan brevity, free of any elaborations. But I can see an uneasiness in your faces. We have been deserted by the very men who we have come here to help. The barbarians who would do battle with us far surpass us in numbers. These facts are undeniable. But remember too that your courage is undeniable. You have never chosen to fight because of the allies at your side, but because of the bravery in your hearts."

He jumped to the ground and began walking amongst them. He needed no platform. Every soldier looked to him; every soldier heard.

"To us the enemy is bold because we do not know him. With ignorance comes uncertainty. Let us take stock of what we do know. Yes, they are large in number, and yell loudly while brandishing their weapons high in the air. These sights and sounds are frightening. But when has a mortal been wounded by a noise? Forgetting Medusa, when has a mere gaze slain a man? To me they look and sound a rabble. No rabble can defeat an army which stands its ground."

He passed the Spartans, moving on to the allied Chalkidians, looking each in the eyes as he passed, stopping before an ashen-faced youth. He wrapped an arm around him, and felt the trembling. Now it seemed he spoke only to him.

"To them, there is no difference between fighting or deserting, since they do both alone and as individuals. But we fight together." By his gaze alone he emboldened the youth. He walked on.

"Stand your ground when they advance. Retire when ordered, and you will all reach safety soon enough. The Lynkestians, by their bluster, are brave at a distance. We shall test their courage at close quarters, and we shall prevail."

His officers now closed around him, Lykophron moving closest, catching Brasidas' eye before he spoke. "I have passed along your orders. The youngest and swiftest of our Lakonians, with Xenias leading them, will be formed into a strike force; the steadiest will take up the rear under your command. We each will lead the remaining sides of the square." Lykophron and Polyakas nodded in affirmation. Turtle, conveying his displeasure with a covert shake of his head, took Brasidas aside.

"Are you so sure of him?"

"Xenias?"

"Of course Xenias. You would place the fate of our army in the hands of a slave?"

"He is no longer a slave. But he has always been my brother."

Turtle's jaw dropped like the gangplank of a trireme, his eyes as large and round as platters. Now his mind whirred in calculation as he kept silent. Finally he spoke. "Strange that I, or someone else, had not made that connection. But then again, who looks at Helots?"

"Only you and I know of this, and by Zeus, it will stay this way. He especially must never know I am his brother." Brasidas stared into the eyes of his friend. The look returned confirmed the oath.

By now they could feel the heat of the sun even though it still lay smothered by the dwindling mist. The shouts of the Lynkestians rattled up the valley, surrounding them, this war chorus punctuated with the clang of iron on bronze. A pause, then the commotion swelled up, this pattern repeating as they marched on. The huge square rolled southward, flowing through the narrow gap between the lakes. Beyond lay low rolling hills, still further level ground— war ground. Mid-afternoon and the roar of the Lynkestians marked them out as they rumbled into sight on the hill crests. The sun had burned its way through the gloom, causing the waving armaments of the enemy to gleam and dance as they swarmed forward.

"Close order!" Brasidas stood outside the ranks, looking at the approaching enemy, then turning to study the formation of his men. He shouted to a front-ranker to edge left. He slipped into the cavity between two shields, tucked his shoulder into the rim of his, then shouted, "Slope spears!"

Three hundred ash spearshafts snapped forward with hardly a ripple. To the right, he watched as Xenias coiled his strike force, waiting for the order.

The first wave roared at them. Stones clattered off their shields; javelins, arrows, and sling bullets rattled amongst their sloped spears and bronze helmets. The barbarians came within range with their missiles, then confident that the heavy infantry of Spartans posed no threat, casually retired. Xenias and his men exploded from the square, sprinting, while holding their formation intact. They struck down the panicked Lynkestians, chasing the survivors briefly before returning to the safety of the square. Only twice more did the barbarians attack, and both times Xenias and his band exacted a heavy price. By late afternoon the army stood on the threshold of Makedonia and safety.

"They are moving around us," cautioned Lykophron. He shoved his helmet clear of his face. His hypaspistes relieved him of it, then handed him a water flask, which he promptly emptied atop his head. "We must be very close to the pass. And if they were Spartans, they would be racing to get there before us. They must be going for it."

Brasidas swung around, searching out the crests of the hills; they rose from the plain like two bristle-backed boars. One, he gauged, they might take before the Lynkestians. He ordered one last charge by Xenias and his men, then bolted with his three hundred for the nearest of the two hills. For a moment he was at Methone again. Like a huge bronze-clad catapult shaft, they tore up the path, slicing through the stunned Lynkestians. He did not see the ones he had slain, but could only hear them as they screamed or moaned or sighed, falling beneath his spear and shield. Worse than the impediment of enemy soldiers, the steep slope of the hill slowed them to a crawl. By now the weight of their armor and weapons became amplified by the climb, not half each man's weight but now seemingly doubled. The wounded began to stumble. Halfway up and even the unscathed bent low, resigned to scrambling on all fours. He flung his helmet off, his eyes dancing across the cluster of men around him as the count echoed down the files from each platoon leader. All but four stood atop the hill. Cheers swelled up from the plain. *His* thoughts, for the moment, lingered with the four.

Like snow under a spring sun, the Lynkestians melted away, the cost of battle too high, the outcome far from certain. With the coming of night the Spartans and their allies encamped, light infantry posted around an expanded perimeter, as the remainder of the army, still formed into a square, ate what they could and rested. The next day the army squeezed through another pass, emerging into a valley of thinning pine. Several fire-scarred rectangles of stone marked where houses once stood. Here the stench of death mingled with wood-smoke. Upon the slope, the remnants of a herd of goats browsed; one looked up at the approaching army, mouth churning, then rubbed his nuzzle into the ground once more. As they sank deeper into the valley the incidence of manmade structures increased until the frontier village of Arsina, a Makedonian outpost, came into view. Townsfolk, most clothed not in wovens, but animal skins and hides, tossed garlands of flowers as they marched in. Many offered up what little food they possessed. The Spartans had secured them, at least for a awhile, from the Lynkestian raids.

Brasidas' men marched in with more food than the town could offer, but still they camped here to the relief of the villagers. Here too the wounded could be treated. By evening, and after all had taken their meal, he dispatched scouts to the next village for word. The period of truce with Athens neared its end, and he would know of Perdikkas and his army. It seemed his only allies were these shabby mountain herdsman.

"I am sending you home."

Polyakas' jaw clenched, but he said nothing.

"You must convince the ephors to dispatch reinforcements quickly, before the Athenians gather in Thrake. Furthermore, Perdikkas may have thrown in with them, and will do what he can to stop any relief force from arriving."

"Why send me? Lykophron is a far more persuasive." Now his face twisted with anger. "You do this to rid yourself of me."

"And why is that?"

He looked up at the sheep grazing on the slope; they moved to chase the gentle clang of a ewe's bell. "Because I do not embrace you as bellwether— as they do." He pointed to the herd. "The gods have given me a mind. I will make use of it, unlike those in your circle of friends."

"I have always considered you within that circle. But consider this. Spartan men are not sheep. They follow because their reason compels them to, not some empty, clanging bell."

The frantic pounding of hooves forced them to pause their talk. The rider pulled up before them. "Sir, Perdikkas is marching to the coast to meet with the Athenian Kleon."

"Ah," mused Brasidas while rubbing his beard. "The loudest bell in all Athens has come our way."

Polyakas ignored the scout. "When shall I leave?"

"First light. I will give you the dispatch then."

Amphipolis
Thirty-Three
ΑΜΘΙΠΟΛΙΣ

"He wants only one place—Amphipolis!" Lykophron slammed the table with his fist, toppling the empty wine cups. "Mende, Skione, and all the other towns he uses as bait."

Brasidas glanced to the map, but only for a moment. "Are we to abandon them? They have placed their trust, and their lives, in us."

"If we try to take back these towns—and believe me, I gravely doubt our success in this venture—they will surely attack Amphipolis. They have the numbers to do all of this."

Now he locked his eyes on the map. Lykophron rocked on his feet while Turtle crossed his arms, both waiting for a response. Brasidas leaned on the table, hands pressing down the anxious edges of the map; his eyes danced as he glanced from Amphipolis to the three-fingered Chalkidike, then northward to Thrake.

"They will come to us." He pushed up from the table, smiled, then grabbed his kothon of wine. "They must come to Amphipolis."

"What of Polyakas? It has been two months, and we have heard nothing. Sparta must send reinforcements." Lykophron fell into his chair, massaging the cup between his long, thin fingers.

Turtle shook his head. "Of us all, why did you send him?"

"Simply put—if Polyakas delivers my request, it will be granted."

"And why should he?" said Lykophron. "Agis, Kratisikles, and the others have influenced him against you. He could easily forget to deliver your request." Turtle nodded in agreement.

"He will not forsake his duty." Brasidas snatched his cloak from Diokles. "The morning's drill will commence shortly. We must go."

He emerged from the quiet of his courtyard into a stream of townsfolk that filled the narrow street. They all moved west toward the agora; he shouldered his way against the current, making for the eastern gate with his officers hurrying behind. Persephone had escaped Hades, bringing with her the warmth of spring, for the streets were soft and muddy, and the iron gray of winter absent from the sky, replaced by a perfect azure. The chill still pooled in the shadows, but once in the uninterrupted sunlight of the plain outside the walls, he began to sweat. This simple pleasure, denied to him throughout the winter, elevated his spirits. Flinging back the edges of his cloak, he broke into a jog. Lykophron looked to Turtle. Both smiled. They caught up to him at the edge of the assembled army.

The allied officers, huddled near a cluster of white boulders, moved to greet the Spartans. Talk was brief and with their abbreviated meeting over, the salphinx blasted out the call to form up, causing each contingent to whirl, then collect into ordered rectangles of men twelve deep. Aside from their lambda-emblazoned shields, the Spartan and Lakonian companies stood out by their impeccable order. The allied companies shuffled about, unsure and a bit intimidated, but soon they too fell into proper alignment. Once all motion had ceased, the orders were shouted along, carried on their way by each platoon leader.

Brasidas studied them carefully, making note of which companies lacked cohesion, singling out those commanders with conversation while stalking the front line of the phalanx. For two hours they drilled. At noon they ate, then they drilled once more. Not until late afternoon did he allow them time for gymnastics.

"What is that you are so interested in?" Turtle squeezed his beard into a taper. "Do you see something upon that hill that I do not?"

Brasidas flicked his head as though he had been awakened from a dream. "Walk with me."

The two ambled across the matted fields, crossing a swollen stream that fed the Strymon. They plunged through the icy water that numbed their ankles and stiffened their knees, but the ascent up the hill called Kerdyllion warmed them quickly. Soon they stood atop the crest. From here they could see the town to the north and the road from Eion as it squeezed through two pine-clad hills to the south. Only one other prominence poked above the plain, an unnamed hill east of Amphipolis skirted by the road.

"How many men would you say can fit atop this hill?"

"Five hundred," answered Turtle without rumination. Then he added, "Maybe six hundred. Do you mean to hold this place against the invaders? To what advantage?"

"The advantage, my friend, lies in the fact that men grip their shields with the left hand."

Turtle grinned knowingly. They trotted back to the army, dispersing the men for the evening meal. Brasidas eschewed the company of his officers and food, choosing instead to wander the agora. There he sought out traders, merchants, fishermen—anyone who had been in or near Eion. A ferryman who had his boat confiscated by Athenian troops became his dinner-mate. The man gladly exchanged information for a hot meal and a dry, warm place to devour it. Brasidas patiently sat and listened to the bitter recounting of the man's loss, the lawlessness of the Athenians and their ever increasing numbers. He asked about soldiers and the types of armaments, but received only vague replies until he quizzed him about the ships. The man described in painful detail the types of ships, their draught and tonnage, and whether they were fitted out for war or commerce. The vast bulk transported troops. For sure triremes had docked, but by his count comprised escorts for the troop ships and not part of any assault. The Athenians knew it would take little for an enemy to blockade a river.

"And the troop ships held at least a hundred men each, with stores of grain. Not many horses though." He stuffed the crumbling cheese into his mouth then deftly plucked up what crumbs had fallen onto the table, daubing them onto his tongue.

"Any talk of when they will attack?" Brasidas motioned for the wine steward to refill the man's cup.

"Not really. I have seen their commander, a strutting peacock of a man, ranting his orders, prancing around the town as though he owned it." Wine gushed from his overstuffed mouth as he quaffed. With a reflexive stroke of his beard, he went on. "A bag of bones and wind he was. His name is Kleon."

Brasidas knew he must hold Amphipolis. The town protected the road from the south—the lifeline that would deliver his supplies and reinforcements. "Have you heard anything of a Spartan army marching north?"

The man shot a frozen glance at him. "Did you not hear? They have been in Lamia, near Thermopylai, for nearly a month. Don't seem they wish to march further north."

Brasidas felt his stomach coil like a snake. In his mind too formed the likeness of a serpent and it wore the face of Alkidas.

Two pitchers dry and the words poured out from the ferryman faster than the wine going in, loosed in torrents and punctuated by deep gulps from his ever-filled cup. Brasidas found it difficult to separate the strings of chatter into something comprehendible. Minutes later fragments emerged, left exposed in his mind like the detritus of a receding flood. Now *he* drank.

After an hour of this the man slammed his forehead into the table, wine and exhaustion stealing consciousness. Brasidas sat there, staring, his head cradled in his two hands. He filtered out all the dribble from the net that his mind had cast and that name floundered singly and most noticeably in it. *This Kleon thinks you, Brasidas, are still in Makedonia.*

He left his dinner-mate collapsed in a chair, paid the owner of the kapeilion more than he should, then slipped out into the night. The influence of the wine fled, chased away by a slap of cold air that struck him on the edge of the agora. As he maundered about the streets with no destination, his mind wrestled with his two greatest fears: he feared battle with this sizable Athenian army; more deeply though, he feared the prospect of no battle at all.

The town itself is bounded on two sides by the Strymon, its steep banks and deep, rushing waters securing it from assault, but to the east and south rose up the stonework walls. Here he found himself where he began tracing the base of them, walking south to the small bridge that connected Amphipolis to the hill of Kerdyllion. Above him, on the battlements, he heard on occasion the grind of a sandled foot upon gritty stone, the mechanical walk of a wind-numbed guard as he paced behind the crenallations. Torch-fire whipped like pennants, almost snuffed out before a respite in the wind allowed them to sputter back to life. Only when he reached the foot of the bridge did anyone challenge his stroll.

"Zeus!" barked out the sentry, his voice hardly clear.

"Agetor," returned Brasidas. He stepped into the torchlight, anxious to see who issued the challenge, for the voice rang familiar. "Hylas." He embraced his friend. The two other sentries gaped.

"Commander, why are you about so late?"

Brasidas turned to address the guards. "You will remain on duty here. Hylas will attend me."

Hylas shrugged his shoulders at his companions then stepped after Brasidas, who slowed his walk, but did not stop. The last of the wall left them as they crossed the bridge, but they were greeted abruptly by the steep slopes of Kerdyllion. He was told the climb would be an easier one from the bridge than from where he and the army had approached the same afternoon, but to him the difference seemed unmeasurable.

"Sir, why are we here?" Hylas poked the turf with the butt-spike of his spear, unconsciously forming a lopsided rectangle.

"I am trying to see tomorrow." He sank down, sitting cross-legged at the pinnacle of the hill, looking east to the hill across the river, then south to the

Eion Road. "Your countrymen will be here soon."

"I hear tell their army swells with each passing day. Many times the men we have."

He stared out into the darkness. "It is not lack of men but the scarcity of weapons that concerns me. I sent to Sparta for reinforcements, but also for new weapons—spears, shields, helmets, and swords—all these lost on our retreat from Lynkestis. We can hardly arm two-thirds of the men we have."

"Can we defeat them?" Hylas asked, expecting reassurance.

"Any army, like any man, can never predict what fortunes are in store."

"Then why are you here? Why do you search for tomorrow?"

"Because I truly believe you can only realize a thing if at first you can imagine it. I look to see what I would do if I were Kleon. His army, he knows, outnumbers ours. His weapons and supplies are inexhaustible. Ours we garner like tight-fisted misers. These things will form his actions. But most of all what he sees when he marches up that road will determine what he does."

"We have few cavalry, and fewer missile-men. How do we keep him from our walls?"

"Give him something else. Two hills dominate the river and the town. We, my friend, will sit upon one while offering the other to Kleon. I think he will accept his seat."

Beyond the eastern hills the gray of new dawn pushed up from the horizon, flicking away the stars and adding shape to the murky landscape. The river, betrayed by its throaty voice, lay hidden beneath the mist. Wood-smoke began to fill the air.

"Morning. Time I left." He moved stiffly to his feet, the damp earth recalling his wounds. From the road came the rumble of horses, but nothing could be seen, for it still hung in pools of lingering night. A golden band of sunlight swathed the hill tops; illuminating five riders as they gained the crest.

"Not Athenians," declared Hylas. "They come from the north. Makedonians, perhaps?"

Brasidas shook his head with a smile then scrambled down the steep path. By the time he had reached the bridge, flexibility returned to his limbs, the pain had faded and he exhibited a bounce to his step that delighted Hylas. Only peddlers moved about the streets, pushing their carts to the agora, readying their wares for another day of trade. As he passed an open gate to a courtyard, a hen tumbled out cackling, followed by a wiry old woman wielding a cleaver. He bent, arms outstretched, preparing to herd the fugitive back to the courtyard. Seemingly ignoring his assistance, the woman swept her hand across the ground and snatched the hen by her feet, sending it into paroxysms of fear as she retreated into the courtyard. One thud and the clucking ceased. He heard the splatter of liquid on the hard stone, like someone emptying a pitcher or basin. The woman heaved her shoulder into the gate, then rattled the latch to secure it. He hurried on. As he approached the main gate he saw men gathered about five riders, all wearing smiles and offering skins of wine to them. The tallest slid from his mount and strode toward Brasidas.

"Commander," said Polyakas without a tinge of emotion. "I apologize for my failure."

Brasidas, ignoring these words for the moment, embraced him, then spoke softly. "It is Alkidas."

Polyakas stepped back. "How did you know?"

"Seems everyone knows. I learned it from a ferrymen last evening."

"It goes deeper that Alkidas. Kratisikles, Agis, and the rest had come to an arrangement with the Athenians and Kleon."

Brasidas, rarely surprised, staggered backward a bit. "Until now I have only suspected them of stupidity, not treason. Is this speculation or fact?"

"Fact as hard as if were chiseled in that stone," he waved at the huge blockwork gatetower. "You forget. I was in their confidence. Their plan was to dispatch the reinforcements from Sparta, to divert any suspicion of collusion. Upon reaching our outpost at Heraklaia, Alkidas would assert his authority over the force. He could delay it indefinitely, as he has done."

"To what end? Why risk such treason?"

"For the men of Sphakteria. Kleon has guaranteed their release if Spartan reinforcements were denied to you."

"It would have been better if they all perished. These mere one hundred prisoners have done more harm to Sparta than any ten thousand Athenians."

"They are our countrymen. We must value their lives."

"Our strength from times long past has been that we value honor more than life. What would Leonidas say to this? What would your Grandfather Amompharetos say? They chose honor over life. By their action they preserved Sparta. And by the actions of Alkidas and the rest, we shall lose our city."

Polyakas walked away from him, back toward his horse as though he we preparing to depart, but instead of vaulting upon it, he snatched a saddle bag and returned to face Brasidas. "I failed in my charge to return with men and weapons, but I have brought what I could carry." He handed the weighty sack to Brasidas. "There should be enough to buy more than a few panoplies."

Brasidas unfastened the ties, then plunged his hand in amongst the clinking drachmas. He hastily sealed the bag then handed it back to Polyakas. "You will go to the allied towns with this for weapons. You are the only one I could trust with such a task."

"Leave Amphipolis now? Kleon may attack any day."

"Without those weapons, we have little chance against him. Out of courtesy we will be sure to stall the battle until you return. I am sure Kleon will oblige."

Polyakas had changed. He laughed at these words instead of raising his hackles. Where before he had seen ridicule in him, lightheartedness now dwelled. His confident grin comforted Brasidas. Both men hurried off for the morning meal, where Polyakas drew center stage amongst the officers, passing along greetings from friends and relatives in Sparta, and relating the ever-shifting tides of loyalties within the polis. To the simple man they were all heroes of Sparta, outnumbered and fighting far from home. To the ephors and King Agis, they were a bargaining chip, and one already counted as lost.

Well before noon, on a day which the wind had stilled and the sun began to work its magic on the newly sown fields, coaxing green from the gray vines and olive groves, Polyakas left, carrying with him the hopes of the men of Amphipolis. On this day too Brasidas doubled the frequency of patrols, and set up a signal station within sight of Eion and the gathering Athenian army. Meanwhile, they drilled. Then the signal fire sputtered on the southern ridge. The Athenians were on the march.

Amphipolis
Thirty-Four
ΑΜΘΙΠΟΛΙΣ

The dusty wake of a single horseman smudged the road from Eion, both man and horse still cloaked in a pall of dust as they pierced the twin hills near the river. Every morning Brasidas climbed up here, to the tallest of the towers on the southern wall and watched. In his mind, he had formed the vision of a vast horde of gilded bronze warriors pouring through those hills, decked-out Athenian lords leading battle-hungry commoners, hurrying to claim a victory that their numbers all but guaranteed. He had not imagined the solitary rider. It shook him from his dream. From the northern towers he heard a voice bellow out his name. He turned around to catch sight of a man on the battlement waving and pointing out to the plain beyond walls. He knew what the rider from the south conveyed. His heart took to wing at the thoughts of what might be approaching from the north. Turtle stood at the bottom of the ladder, waiting for his commander to descend. Together they hurried to the twin gates; the hinge pins wailed as the keepers shouldered them open. The rider from the south galloped up the rising slope and into view. He yanked his horse to a halt, vaulting off at the moment the beast stopped.

"Two hours away!" He spit out the words in a string, inhaled, then continued. "Three at the most." Another breath. "Thousands of infantry."

"Any ships?" Brasidas pointed toward the river.

"None."

A clang and clatter bade them pause their talk and look north. There another river flowed, one of wagons, carts, and men on horseback, and leading it all, Polyakas. He stopped to allow the convoy to pass by him, so he could shout encouragements, insults, or swing his whip—anything that might hasten them along to the gates of Amphipolis.

"Two hours is more than enough." Brasidas smiled. He stood outside the walls waiting for his friend.

In less than half an hour Polyakas had unpacked the arms; nearly three hundred full panoplies, several hundred javelins, and a good number of replacement shafts for spears. He did not waste an obol on arrows or the bow; he knew his commander, and there would be little need for them. Men lined up, ones who had lost their weapons in the great retreat from Lynkestis, and others who had tried in vain to repair what was beyond repair. Brasidas prowled the stacks of arms, hustling the men to choose quickly and form up by company in the agora. He came to a small hill of shields and noticed Xenias hefting one to his shoulder. "Let me see that one." Brasidas surprised him with his request. Xenias said nothing as he handed the shield to him. With one smooth motion, he slid his forearm through the central band and clutched the grip near the rim. "Not bad. A bit light, but not bad." He tipped the interior to view. Expecting to find a seamless and smooth facing, instead he stared at a medley of repairs. "I prefer this one," he said. "Diokles, give him mine."

Without protest Xenias accepted the trade, then hurried off to his company. Diokles grabbed the old patchwork shield and trotted off shaking his head. Brasidas, summoned by the cry of a sentry, bounded up the stairway to the battlement tower.

At first he spied the dust, then the rumble of advance cavalry reverberated up the valley from the south. Brasidas looked out from his perch in the watchtower toward the hill of Kerdyllion where a company of his men stood to arms; sprinkled atop the hill with them, farmhands attacked the soil with their hoes as though they were preparing the ground not for planting but for the coming battle. Across the river the high ground to the east of Amphipolis lay empty and inviting, for the few men Brasidas had posted there scrambled down and into Amphipolis at the first sight of the Athenians. The enemy scouts thundered up the road, paralleling the river, taking a slow accounting of the walls, towers, and gates, then finally roared up the far hill where they stopped and watched. Half a hundred mounted scouts whirled about the hill crest. Their leader motioned for them to dismount, dispatching only a pair to trace their way back to their advancing comrades. Soon the great procession of arms unfolded between the twin hills; they marched up, grander than in his dreams, armor glittering in the afternoon sun, all shields braced to port, facing the river and Amphipolis. As the last of the Athenian hoplites marched into view, Brasidas started counting; the numbers proved greater than his most exaggerated estimate. Their would be no margin for error. Salpinx trumpets blared. Now into view rode a cluster of brilliantly appareled riders, the leading officers no doubt, for the speeding scouts halted to meet them.

"Very nice," said Turtle mockingly. "I like the gold and purple on that one." He pointed to the Athenian who seemed to be the center of the storm of activity.

One of the scouts pumped his javelin frantically at the hill. Words were exchanged. The column moved along the same route of the scouts, swarming over the high hill, forming terraces of shields that faced back toward the city.

"Come. We must be sure they keep to their hill and us to ours." Brasidas departed the tower to the ranks of men that waited for him in the agora. Their pace through the streets proved neither hurried nor casual, but one of confident determination. In formation they streamed over the bridge, up Kerdyllion and into view of the gathering Athenians. By comparison, their force was meager and ill-deployed—precisely what he wished Kleon to think. Once upon the crest of Kerdyllion, he ordered his men to prepare an encampment, erect their tents, and kindle fires. They would settle in for the night. Across the river so did the Athenians.

The steady wind that had swept in from the northeast dwindled with the approach of dusk. Behind them, in the west, the clouds hung like glowing embers, suspended in a bed of purple ash. He watched the flicker of campfires dot the heights, and without thinking, counted, calculating the enemy's numbers by them. "Six times over," Brasidas muttered.

"Say something?" Turtle asked.

"They outnumber us six to one."

"Oh," Turtle said, somewhat surprised, "I reckoned more." He flicked the dregs of wine from his cup, then ambled to a waiting pitcher, waving the wine servant off. "I savor it more in the face of the enemy." He sipped, then sighed with satisfaction.

"Tomorrow he will send his herald." Lykophron eased past Turtle to snatch the pitcher. With a nod he flashed it to Brasidas, then filled his comrade's cup before filling his.

"I think we shall send ours to him this night." Brasidas emptied his cup, then made his way down from Kerdyllion and into the town.

* * *

"A herald!" The scout waved back over his shoulder as he reported to Kleon.

Barely lit by the guttering campfires, a figure approached, bearing the herald's staff and flanked by armor-clanking hoplites. As he came closer to the circle of Athenian commanders, the herald pushed away the hood formed by his cloak. "I enter your camp under the protection of Hermes."

"And by his protection and mine you shall leave it," answered Kleon, almost boastfully. "Do you come to seek terms? Is your commander a sensible man, a compassionate man, ready to spare the lives of his men?"

"Yes to all your questions. And he would strive to spare your lives too. Simply surrender to him now."

All the officers roared at his words. All except Eukles. Kleon, his face clear of any remnant of a grin, stepped forward. "Is it you or your commander who levels such insolence? If I did not know that Brasidas were still in Makedonia, I would say those were his words."

The herald presented his staff, almost as a shield, and certainly as a reminder of his immunity from harm. "Kleon, my commander is Brasidas, and to your sad fortune, he is not in Makedonia but encamped upon that hill." He thrust his staff out like a spear at Kerdyllion.

"And how do you know my name?" Kleon stared through the dying light at the herald.

"Sir, I would ask, how do you not know mine?"

"How should I?" Kleon nervously wrapped the end of his cloak about his arm, loosened it, then wrapped it again. All around him stared at the herald.

"I think you would remember your own step-son." Hylas moved into the light.

The officers opened their tight circle, easing away from Kleon and Hylas; none spoke. Kleon's hand flew to the grip of his sword, but Eukles stepped forward clamping his arm. "Do not provoke the gods."

Kleon tugged free of his grip, lifting his open palm skyward, as if to show Zeus it held no weapon. "I will save my blade for your Spartan—and for you."

Hylas turned 'round and strode off. He heard them as he departed, not the meaning of their words, but the timbre of them. He smiled, knowing he had completed his task.

* * *

The sun filtered through the oaks atop Kerdyllion, turning the earth to gold and kindling the tree-tops with its shimmering light. He stood amongst the stand of trees straight and motionless as them, whispering a prayer. A servant approached. Brasidas passed the order to him; they would move off the hill and down into the city. The salpinx tore the silence of dawn, then the hill itself seemed to swell, expanding as the men rose from their sleep. Across the river the Athenians too were roused by the call, but they moved more quickly; the rattle of their iron and bronze echoed across the interval.

He delayed his departure, choosing to survey the column of his men as they descended the hill, and to be entertained by the Athenians as they scurried about, heads bobbing, spears shivering like wheat in a gale. Officers spun their arms above their heads, trying to rally them, screaming orders and shoving the recalcitrant, until at last they formed their great phalanx parallel to the river, facing the main gate of Amphipolis. Finally, as the last of his men crossed the small bridge at the base of Kerdyllion and seeped into the narrow streets, he lumbered down, rejoining them as they reassembled in the agora. Before the ranks, Turtle, Lykophron, and Polyakas hung in conversation and hurried to him on his approach.

"Orders, sir?" said Lykophron, he being the closest and most impatient.

"Disperse the men."

Lykophron and Turtle both stood before him, stunned to silence. Finally Turtle opened his mouth to speak, but Brasidas cut him off. "They will not attack, for they fear we will, so let them stand and quake upon the plain, waiting."

With the order given, they dissolved away from the agora—all but Polyakas. Brasidas said nothing, preferring only to wave for him to follow. The pair climbed the steps of the gate-tower, startling the drowsy guards that had propped their chins on the block-sill of the window. They jumped up; one dropped his javelin, snatched it up then dropped it again. Brasidas bent down coolly, lifting up the fugitive weapon, then held it out steady for the guard to accept. "Worry not, friend. They are waiting for us." He shouldered between the two guards, who both withdrew nervously from their perch into the depth of the tower room. Polyakas draped his arms on the sill, staring out at the gleaming, jostling formation of Athenians.

"I expected you to say something." Brasidas too draped his arms and craned out, mimicking the posture of his officer, looking not at him or the enemy, but something great and distant.

"I understand you now."

Brasidas turned, but only for a moment, then gazed out to the enemy beyond. "Do you?"

"Yes. I once said you fought, not for Sparta, but for yourself. For glory.

For reputation. But I was mistaken. You fight because you love this." He swept his hand out as though he were a god creating all before him.

Brasidas again looked to him, but could find no words to offer.

"I loved you from when we were youths. I accepted your friendship with Epitadas. I wept with you when he died upon Sphakteria. And with him dead I was sure you would feel as I did, but your indifference poisoned my heart against you—until now."

"And what has changed you?"

"The fear in their eyes." Now he pointed to the Athenians. "Not them," he said, shaking his head, "but it was in Sparta where I saw the real fear. Men follow other men into battle for many reasons. Some because they hate an enemy. Others because they fear the rebuke of their peers. Many for glory, loot, and plunder. And some for redemption before the gods. But the men in this town follow you because you love them all. The weak-minded in Sparta fear this love and you more than they fear Athens."

Brasidas withdrew from the ledge into the black of the tower-room. Only the glint of his eyes suggested any detail to his face.

"Do you know what name they have chosen?"

"Who?" Brasidas asked, still staring out at the plain.

"These men who followed you here. They are no longer Lakonians, Tegeans, or Helots. They call themselves Brasideioi—Brasidas' men." Brasidas turned now and faced his friend but could say nothing. Polyakas continued. "Every Spartan learns war as a profession, but you embrace it as a thing most dear. I do not mean that you love war as a possession that gratifies or as flesh that satisfies. You love it like you love your sons. It is a very part of you. There is not a man in Sparta or out there in the plain who could contend with this."

"You see more than there is." He spoke from a mask of shadows, motionless as a statue, his tone even cooler. "I do not relish battle, nor do I shrink from it. It is a thing which must be done, like tilling a field, drawing water, or casting a fisherman's net. But you are indeed on the mark when you say I love these men. The gods demand a cost for battle, a toll if you will, that must be paid. I shall ensure that the burden of this toll is with the Athenians."

The two exited the tower, meeting with the remaining officers who had collected near the gate. He assured them that there would be no battle today. But tomorrow—tomorrow would be a different matter.

Amphipolis
Thirty-Five
ΑΜΘΙΠΟΛΙΣ

Brasidas huddled in the trench just outside the gates along with his picked three hundred. He looked at the graying sky, then down the length of his men, his eyes stopping at the figure of his brother. He smiled. Vaporous breath rolled from their mouths, and it came to him that if he saw it, the Athenians might well spot it too, giving away their position and their plan.

Polyakas leaned into him, whispering, "Are you certain they will withdraw today?"

"They brought no supplies. Expected the city to fall at the sight of their great procession. Without the machines of siege they can do nothing." Brasidas tugged his helmet free of his head, then peered out across the interval. Their trench cut through ground lower than the Athenian camp, but was screened by a snarl of olive trees skirted in brambles. Still, he had a good view of the road to Eion. Again he surveyed his men, catching the eye of Heirax and waving to him to cover his burnished shield with his cloak. The sun would soon wash over the hill behind the Athenians; he wanted no glint of bronze or iron to alert them. He watched the night sky retreat, stars overwhelmed by the dawn, black to violet, violet to bright crimson, then like the blade of a golden sword, the sun sliced the horizon, dividing land from sky; in an instant, light tore the mantle of shadow from the plain.

Polyakas crossed his arms, hoping to capture a bit of warmth from this meager embrace, then glanced to Brasidas. "You do know how few men you have here in this ditch?"

"More than enough, if we remain undiscovered. And if not, only a handful of us will die."

Polyakas recrossed his arms. Still, he shivered. Behind him metal struck metal, like the sound of a cook beating an empty pot. He jerked his head to see. Someone had dozed off, and in a swoon of slumber struck his helmeted head upon another. Three hundred heads peered over the edge of the trench toward the Athenian hill. Here and there figures rose up through the dawn mist like legless ghosts. Men shouted at men, horses neighed as their master's fought to bridle them while the sound of armor and weapons rattled over the hill.

"They have heard us!" The words hissed from Polyakas as he fought not to shout.

Brasidas hunkered back down into the trench, rubbing his hands while blowing warm breath into them. His legs ached from the damp and cold. "They are packing up." Brasidas did not move, but continued rubbing his hands. "It will be a while yet." Now he looked up at the walls of Amphipolis, to the tower men and guards stalking the parapets, and felt satisfied at their safety. He waved for Hylas and the other officers to attend him. Now with the clamor in the Athenian camp at its height, he felt little need to whisper, but spoke as loudly as one might at dinner among friends. "When the head of their column passes, be patient. We will strike at the center. They have no choice but to march on the road with their shields facing away from us. But this advantage will be short-lived. We must strike quickly and without pity. There can be no shirking—by any man." He took role call with his eyes, waiting for a return glance of confirmation, stopping at Polyakas. "It is time for you to go. You have a boisterous lot of men. Be sure Kleon knows it too. When he hears you gathering near the northern gate, it will hurry him south. Once he is on his way, I will strike at the center. You must then hit the tail of his column or they will hit us."

"I will see you there." Polyakas glanced out at the road before scrambling up and out of the trench. Silent as a shadow, he slipped through the postern gate.

Across the road, the Athenians began to roll down the hill in loose formation, with no more care than if they paraded for the crowds in the Agora. Kleon watched and waited upon the crest as the front of the column began its march southward toward the Twin Hills. From within Amphipolis the sound of horses snorting and pounding their hooves rose up above the clatter and clang of the Athenians. Kleon pointed to the Thrakian gates, then waved to his section of the army to descend to the road.

"He doesn't want to be left behind," said Turtle, smiling.

Just as the Athenian contingents led by Kleon spilled onto the roadbed, Brasidas stood up. Three hundred spears poked up into the air with nary a waver. With several short steps they heaved up and out of the trench, walked slowly through the grove and into plain view of the road. Once reformed beyond the trees, he gave the order for the pipes to be played. At first they stepped off, then strode at long paces, keeping to the cadence set by the flutes, until their momentum had gathered. Now each stride expanded till they rumbled forward at a sprint, the landscape shivering as they peered out of the narrow eye slits of their helmets. Still dozens of meters away, each man selected a target, looking at faces blank with dread. The Athenians turned, some to their right, some to their left, trying to spin around and bring their shields to bear, as a ship's pilot might steer his vessel at the last moment to turn headlong into storm-driven waves.

The Spartans coiled their legs and tucked their shields tight to their shoulders, then exploded into the reeling Athenians, the thunder of bronze upon bronze jarring them to the bone. Feet slipped. Legs twisted as each Athenian struggled to hold his ground as the Spartans heaved forward. Now spear-points rattled a thousand fold against the armored heads and chests of the front-rankers. A howl of death, then the tumble of a warrior. In an instant another filled the gap; this repeated up and down the line. After the collision a macabre equilibrium set in, both phalanxes void of momentum and stalled. Here and there, as front rankers fell, the Athenians surged into the gaps using their greater numbers to attempt a breach. To his left Brasidas saw the arm of a single Spartan reach up over the melee, spear twirling overhead in a gesture to advance. The others around the figure rallied, pouring into the gaps while shouting the name—"Xenias!"

Around Brasidas a sea of hacking and hacked limbs whirled, while men screamed in terror or shouted for their comrades to advance, but unlike past battles, the chaos slowed, making all movement predictable to him, as though he could see the future just a moment ahead. Before him and across this tumult, he eyed Kleon; the man swung his spear wildly while back-stepping, shoving his own men to fill the void formed by his retreat. Brasidas drove his spear downward, ripping through the eye-slit of an Athenian, sending the man spilling backwards, casting off shield and spear, empty hands clutching the gaping, eye-less wound.

As though it were a play, a pantomime or oft-learned dance, he smacked one of the wounded aside with his shield while driving home his spear into another, hacking deeper into the Athenian ranks with smooth, confident strides, and perfect aim. Again he looked up to check his prey and survey the advance around him; his line of men stood shoulder to shoulder, solid, inexorable, and shoving forward. Kleon, made obvious by his triple-crested helmet, tossed away the splintered remnant of his spear, but instead of drawing his sword, he used his free hand to grab and toss adjacent men into the path of the Spartans. Brasidas, frustrated by the seemingly endless supply of Athenians, kept to his advance by carving them away until the very weight of bodies, both living and dead, checked his progress.

Brasidas' leg felt hot and wet, his chiton soaked and his booted feet heavy, but he bled not; the mire of battle—the blood of the fallen, the butchered, the dying, and the dead—sloshed onto him as he pressed forward. Traction began to fail him, so now he transformed his spear from weapon to crutch, plunging it deep into the slop at his feet, bracing against its shaft to slog on.

Like the flaming eyes of an animal at night, Kleon's glared at him out of the tempest of death that enveloped them. Brasidas saw in them recognition, certainly of him and also of impending fate; the panic that had filled them transformed to rage, compelling Kleon to grab for the hilt of his sword. As in a moment when the gods grant perfect clarity to the philosopher, reveal a cure to a physician, or the telling landmark to a wayward traveler, all distractions fled. With the interval clear, there stood each man, each commander, each progenitor of war, tugging at the same thread of fate, pausing momentarily to appreciate it.

Kleon strode forward and reared up, bringing himself a head and more taller than Brasidas, his sword cocked high over his shoulder, eager to plunge, to thrust, to overwhelm. The blade whined, slicing the thick air before glancing off helmet, then shield. Brasidas circled his spear hand upward, shoving the pointed blade under Kleon's shield and into his groin. Kleon froze, eyes looking to nowhere, body recoiling rearward, shuddering, his mouth gaping as though he would vomit; blood foamed out. All around suspended their combat, entranced by the figure of the Athenian commander stumbling backward. First his heavy shield slipped from his left arm into the churned and muddied earth. His sword he hung onto, twirling its downward-pointed blade in shrinking circles until it plopped into the muck at his feet. His eyes flew back into his head. He twisted, folding upon the bodies of his own dead. At this the remaining Athenians melted away. Only the rumble of their armor as they cast it off competed with the thunder of hoof-beats. Brasidas turned to see Polyakas and the cavalry riding up the road, scattering the last survivors before them. Some rode the stragglers down, while others bent low, embracing the necks of their horses as they fought against the irresistible fatigue that threatened to unhorse them.

Suddenly his throat filled, hot with the sting of salt and iron, each breath hissing through blood. He spit. His mind brought him back to the Plane Tree

Ground, but now the faces were shadowy and the chants of victory muffled and fading. As he tried to lower his shield he found it caught, snagged upon something, his corslet, he thought, or the scabbard of his sword. He fumbled with it, coughing red, bending over till his helmet fell off. Polyakas jumped from his horse, lunging to his support, while Turtle knelt beside him, looking up into his pain-wracked face.

"Get the surgeon," Turtle shouted. "Get the surgeon now!" Gently he lowered Brasidas to his knees, resting the rim of the shield on the earth. A spear had torn through shield, corslet, and abdomen, plugging the wound temporarily. He dare not remove the shaft, but instead carefully slid the aspis free of the splintered stave, then rolled Brasidas onto his back. He looked into the eyes of his friend. He did not see the commander, the warrior, or the man, but the boy who led them to victory on the Plantanistas so many years ago. "Rest. The surgeon is on his way."

Brasidas smiled, squeezing a trickle of blood from the corner of his lips. He coughed weakly. "Is she with us?"

"Who?"

"Nike, my friend. Is victory ours?"

Xenias stared across the litter of bodies to Kleon. "Yes. Yes, she is." He slipped his hand into his brother's, a comfort to both, letting slip inadvertently a word or two of his prayer to Apollo.

Hylas, dragging shield and spear, staggered toward the huddle of men, his dented helmet still covering his face. He emptied his hands, then cleared his face of the bronze. Brasidas summoned him with a glance.

"You owe me an answer, my friend."

Hylas swapped his look of concern for one of puzzlement. "An answer?"

"To my question." Each word came with more difficulty now, but coughed his throat clear and continued. "I once asked you what you wanted from your life."

"My freedom, which you have granted. And your friendship."

"Then you have both." His face contorted with pain. He fought it off quickly, allowing a faint smile to form.

From beyond the pall of battle, two men rode toward them, one wielding a herald's staff, the other clad in armor but carrying no weapon. Polyakas stepped forward to challenge them. The armored man slipped from his horse.

"I seek Brasidas. I come to ask for the bodies." The Athenian, no doubt in the thick of things, was covered from foot to brow in splatters of drying mud and gore. He wore the look of a lost wayfarer, longing for home.

"Who asks for this?" Polyakas growled.

Brasidas worked to lift his head, but Turtle pressed him gently back. "Bring him here," he whispered.

"Wait!" Turtle barked it out like a command, then waved over a battle servant. "A cloak," he said quietly. The servant returned quickly with Brasidas' triboun cloak. Turtle rolled it up, grabbing a corner of it to gently daub away the blood from his friend's beard, and dried his lips before pillowing the cloak under his head. He waved the Athenian forward. "Who are you?" Brasidas said in a sigh.

"I am Eukles, General of the Athenians. I come to ask the victor for the bodies of our dead."

He tried to smile, but the pain clamped his lips. Still Eukles saw it in his eyes and nodded. Brasidas' mouth moved, forming silent words over and over, like a child memorizing a poet's line, until finally he had summoned the strength to make them heard. "I am glad it was not Thukydides." He pointed with his eyes to the limp form of Kleon.

Eukles bent low. "So am I."

Brasidas' chest heaved, not with pain but with laughter, but it sent him into a spasm of coughs. He spit to clear his mouth of the blood, then tried to prop himself up with an arm, but fell back staring up at the blue, his chest rising and falling less noticeably with each breath until it moved no more. Turtle knelt, slipping the cloak from beneath his head, then unfurled it across his body, curling the edge beneath the chin of his comrade.

Sparta
Thirty-Six
ΣΠΑΡΤΗ

The three men, appareled in battle armor as a sign of respect, solemnly approached the house. Like an alarm bell the creaky gate set the dogs to barking. A figure bobbed in the frame of the black window. The door yawned open. Two of them proceeded down the path, paused in the doorway, then slipped into the house, while the third man stood sentinel just outside the gate.

"Greetings," said Tellis in a hollow, empty voice as he dispensed a curt nod to each.

Turtle, clutching the red triboun cloak which was so neatly folded in his arms, cleared his throat, then spoke. "Sir, he died as he lived—with courage."

Tellis drew a long breath, then smiled. "Wine?" Not waiting for an answer, he ushered them through the courtyard and into the andron. Argileonis did not follow, but stared out an open window at the man by the gate; for a moment, her eyes saw Brasidas. Tellis waved two servants forward; one carried a tray with a pitcher of water and three cups, the other a heavy bowl of wine. Once mixed, the wine filled the cups. In silence they emptied them. While the servants replenished the wine, words began to slip free.

"Sir, on our journey home, as we passed through the towns and cities of our allies, people cheered us, exclaiming the war is over, waiting for an answer.

"This very day I leave to meet with the Athenians. To sign the treaty. Amphipolis must be very dear to them."

Now Turtle, still clutching the war cloak, replied, "Both our cities have lost something dear."

"Master, they are waiting." The servant hovered in the doorway, waiting for instruction from Tellis.

"Bring my horse." His words sent the man off. Tellis rose, placing the empty wine cup upon the plain and polished table. "I must go and finish the

314

work my son has started." Turtle and Lykophron followed him as far as the courtyard, watching Tellis slip through the gate that led to the stables. Argileonis, her head covered in a black shawl, loomed like a statue in the columned shadows as she watched them all. Turtle walked up to her and presented the cloak and the wooden wrist token of polished olive wood.

"Did my son die bravely, and with distinction?" Argileonis embraced the bundle, staring at her son's named carved upon the token

"He was the best of us all," replied Turtle.

Slowly she turned and gazed out toward the stranger at the gate. "I thank you for your words, but Sparta has men braver."

Glossary

Agelai - a regiment of youths in the Agoge representing one of the five communities in Sparta.

Agoge - the state-sponsored education system of Sparta, focusing primarily on military development, thought to begin at age seven and continue to age eighteen.

Akratisma - breakfast, or the first meal of the day.

Anapale.- A dance-like exercise, the movements of which mimicked maneuvers of pankration (boxing) or weapons handling.

Anathesteria - the three-day festival of Dionysos; the first day, the Opening of the Jars, the new wine was tasted; on the second, called the Choes, or Wine Jugs, a procession of the image of Dionysos ended with a ceremonial marriage of the god to the wife of the king archon, and was accompanied by drinking; on the third day, considered an unlucky day, sacrifices to the dead were made.

Apothetai - the chasm outside of Sparta where male infants were cast if they failed to pass physical inspection.

Aryballos - a small flask used for storing oil.

Aspis - a shield; the hoplite shield was constructed of a bowl-shaped wooden core with an offset rim, and was often covered with a thin facing of bronze, although leather was also used; it was held in the left arm by a central armband that moved the weight from the wrist to the forearm, while the left hand gripped a handle just inside the rim.

Boua - literally a herd; a company of boys in the Agoge.

Bouagos - a herd leader, usually an older boy put in charge of a troop of younger boys.

Bouleterion - the civic building in a polis where the boule or council held session.

Chiton - a tunic made from two rectangles of cloth, pinned at the shoulders.

Daimon - a spirit.

Eirene - in Sparta, the age between 20 and 30, the time when Spartan warriors transitioned from youth to full citizenship.

Embaterion March - a quick-paced march of the Spartan army, often accompanied by the singing of the paian.

Enomotarch - a platoon (**enomotai**) leader of 32 hoplites.

Enyalios - a variation of Ares, the god of War.

Epaikla - an after-meal dessert, usually a sweet cake.

Ephebos - in Athens and other poleis, a youth aged eighteen who has entered state-sponsored military training that usually ended after two years.

Ephor - one of the five magistrates of Sparta, elected annually each autumn; every ten days they inspected the boys in the Agoge, they selected the three captains of the Hippeis or Knights, controlled the Krypteia, and received all captured booty for distribution in the city..

Ephorion - the civic building in Sparta where ephors met and ate (substituting for their established phidition) during their tenure of office.

Epistoleos - originally secretary to the Spartan navarch; this office evolved into the navarch's second in command.

Exomis - a loose-fitting tunic, often worn with the right shoulder free.

Gerontes - a Spartan elder, aged 60 or older, elected to the council or Gerousia.

Gerousia - the Spartan council of elders, who along with the ephors, prepared and presented matters to the citizen body for a vote.

Gymnopaidia - the festival of the "Naked Youths," one of the three major summer festivals in Sparta. It was one of the times where foreign visitors were encouraged to visit.

Hebontes - name of the age grade given to Spartan males 18-20 years old.

Hellas - Greece.

Helot - essentially a Spartan serf tied to the land. He was owned by the State and could neither be bought nor sold, and was required to turn over a specific portion of his yield to a Spartan master.

Himation - a long cloak.

Hoplite - a heavy infantryman equipped with a bronze helmet, bronze-covered wooden shield, bronze or linen composite body armor, greaves, a sword, and his primary weapon, the eight-foot spear; the forerunner of the modern infantryman.

Hyakinthia - the first of the three Spartan summer festivals that celebrated the end of spring and the coming of summer. The festival centered on the myth of the boy Hyakinthos, who was accidentally slain by Apollo.

Hypaspites - an armor bearer.

Iatros - a physician.

Kaddichos - a bowl used to serve food at a Spartan mess-tent; admission votes were cast into this bowl consisting of rolled pieces of bread; a single deformed piece meant rejection of the candidate.

Karneios - the third summer festival of Sparta (and other Dorian communities) devoted to Apollo.

Kleros - a farm; in Sparta, the farm supplied by the State to each Spartan as a condition of citizenship, meant to supply his mess dues in the phidition; this was separate from any family-owned land, and reverted back to State control upon his death.

Kopis - A thick tipped chopping sword favored by cavalrymen.

Kothon - a large tankard, made famous by its use in the Spartan army; it was designed to hold a large amount of water and its curved lip would both hide and partially filter out any sediments.

Krepides - open-toed boots worn by soldiers.

Krypteia - the Spartan secret police, comprised of youths 18-20 years old (equivalent in age and some duties to epheboi of other poleis); besides patrolling the Spartan frontier, it was their task to eliminate any unruly Helots.

Kylix - a shallow cup, often fashioned with a stem, for drinking wine.

Linothorax - body armor comprised of multiple layers of stiffened linen, with two large shoulder flaps, often fitted with strips of linen or leather just below the waist.

Lochus - in the Athenian army a unit of soldiers of approximately one hundred; in the Spartan army, a regiment of 512 hoplites.

Motos - a compress used to treat wounds.

Navarch - an admiral or naval commander.

Obal - a coin deriving its name form the obolos, or iron spit, which was originally used as currency before the introduction of coinage; equivalent to 1/6 an Attic drachma.

Paides - in Sparta, the age grade in the Agoge comprised by boys 7-14; athletic training was stressed, although dance and particularly singing was included in the curriculum.

Paidonomos - a Spartan assigned with the oversight of the Agoge and other youth-related activities.

Pedagoge - in Athens, a slave assigned to an affluent youth to assist in his education and ensure that he attended all sessions of instruction and kept to the curfew.

Penteconter - an older-style, 50-oared warship.

Pentekostys - Spartan company consisting of 128 hoplites and 8 officers.

Phidition - the name for a Spartan mess; also known as a syssition; acceptance into a phidition was a condition of full citizenship; dues of grain and wine were required each month and failure to provide these could mean expulsion, and consequently the loss of civic rights.

Phouaxir - the final test of a Spartan youth upon completion of the Agoge; the "Fox Time" was a survival test, where the young boy was left to live off the land for almost a year, in hiding and with no assistance.

Plantanistas - the Plane Tree Ground, a competition field outside of Sparta.

Polemachia - the study of weapons use in battle.

Polemarch - literally "Warleader"; in Sparta, a commander of a regiment.

Polis - a self-governing nation or city-state.

Pynx - the hill facing the Acropolis in Athens where public assemblies were held.

Rhobidas - name given to youths in the Spartan Agoge aged 13.

Salphinx - a musical instrument made of bronze, similar in use to a bugle, used for signaling commands before and during battle.

Skias - literally a tent or canopy; it was also the name of the civic building in Sparta where the Apella or assembly met.

Skytale - a stick; in Sparta a skytale could refer to either the messaging system employed by the army where leather strips were wound around a stick, a message written. Only a stick of exact size could decode the message. A skytale could also refer to the wooden identification token worn by Spartan warriors.

Sphaeromachia - battle-ball; a game similar to rugby or American football played by Eirenes.

Stade - a distance of approximately 185 meters.

Stlengis - a curved bronze implement used to scrape oil and dirt from the skin.

Stoa - a long building with a series of exterior columns on one side and a wall on the other.

Strategos - a general; in Athens, one of the ten generals elected annually from each of the ten tribes.

Symposion - a drinking party, usually hosted by the well-to-do.

Triboun - a Spartan military cloak, dyed crimson.

Trireme - a square-sail warship propelled by oarsmen positioned in three banks per side; the crew consisted of 170 oarsmen, 20 marines, and several officers.

Xiphidion - a short sword or dagger.

Xuele - a field knife with a curved blade issued to Spartan youth.

Zomos - broth; in Sparta it was called black broth and consisted of pig's blood and vinegar.

Printed in the United States
30352LVS00002B/28